THE HOUSEGUEST

THE
HOUSEGUEST

A NOVEL

KIM BROOKS

COUNTERPOINT
BERKELEY

The Portions of the book appeared in different forms in *Glimmer Train*.

Library of Congress Cataloging-in-Publication Data is Available

Cover design by Michael Fusco
Interior design by Megan Jones Design

ISBN 978-1-61902-605-6

COUNTERPOINT
2560 Ninth Street, Suite 318
Berkeley, CA 94710
www.counterpointpress.com

Printed in the United States of America
Distributed by Publishers Group West

10 9 8 7 6 5 4 3 2 1

For Pete

You who live safe
In your heated houses,
You who come home at night to find
Hot food and friendly faces . . .

—PRIMO LEVI, *IF THIS IS A MAN*

prologue

THE FIRE

S TEPHEN FIELD WAS sitting at his desk well after midnight, reading letters from strangers pleading to be saved. His apartment was quiet but for the ticking of the dining room clock. Occasionally, he would hear the soft whirr of the elevator ascending, the old doorman Mr. O'Brien greeting one of the building's other residents, wishing a pleasant evening, but these noises and interruptions sounded faintly. This was how he spent his nights. Now, and for the three years before.

Every night he read letters written by the Jews of Germany, Austria, the Western Caucasus, and Poland, Jews who knew with growing certitude that if they did not get out of Europe, they were going to die. He read and read and read; for every letter he finished, five more appeared the following day, all of the petitioners phantoms to him, all writing under the tragic misconception that he, as a Jew, a Jew in America, an American Jew whose name was strong enough to carry across the ocean and through border control and to their desperate pleading hands, could help.

At the moment he held a letter from a fourteen-year-old girl in Vienna. Her father was from Lodz but had been living in Austria for twenty years until the Nazis occupied it, at which point they deported him to Sachsenhausen. The girl was hungry and half-frozen. The letters all came wrapped in their personal forms of darkness and the main chore, he had decided, was to scour them for traces of light. There was a man in the Austrian consulate whom Field knew. It had been a while since any favors had been asked. So he placed the letter in the thin pile to the right of a larger one. If it worked, whatever bureaucratic magic he might conjure, the girl would be dropped on Rector Street or in Nova Scotia or in Murfreesboro, Tennessee. If it didn't her life was likely finished at this, a relatively early point. At a luncheon the week before, a luncheon he himself convened in his role as a director of the Zionist Organization of America, he confided to Louis Brandeis that he no longer believed there was much that could be done for the persecuted Jews of Europe. Three, four years ago—maybe. Now, with the Germans grinding across the continent and the British squeezing off the Mandate of Palestine for fear of hastening war with the Arabs, it was all but hopeless. Certainly some of those in danger could still be saved. The youth, the ones who were strong and resilient. But the old and the weak would perish. They were, as he himself had declared at the emergency convention in Evian, economic and moral dust in a cruel world, *She'erith Hapleitah*. That Stephen Field, son of a man who peddled groceries to laborers on Dean Street, should now act, inasmuch as anyone could, as the line between the living and the dead, made little sense to him. Whatever atrocities were happening over there, one thing was clear: it was the greatest crisis his people had faced in his lifetime. One had come to accept that *history* and *crisis* were essentially synonymous for Jews—Genesis to Gdansk—but what was happening now, what they were experiencing since the National Socialists had taken Germany and Europe after it, was wholly different and horrifying and inexplicable and completely undeniable. The immediacy he felt, the disaster that was literally being delivered with the mail each day, had an energy that was cyclonic. The letters and memos and newspaper clippings from the Yiddish press rained down on his office, poured in from every Jewish agency. He'd read one of these letters, or an eyewitness account from the paper, and he'd feel a pang of helplessness and terror, a sensation of falling through space, accelerating toward some unknown, unknowable catastrophe. But then he'd close the paper or put the letter in a drawer and the feeling would pass. He'd make himself a cup of coffee. He'd go for a walk. And the panic dissipated, faded like a dream upon waking, and then he got on with his day. As a Jew in America in 1941, one could get on with the day. That was the difference between him and the poor souls writing these letters: an impossible, uncrossable distance. Then one evening in June, far past midnight, the phone rang, the voice insisting he come to the synagogue at once, as fast as he could.

THE SYNAGOGUE SEEMED taller, grander in a sickening way. There were screaming bright new levels, it reached higher above the park than it had before. Field, dazed, temporarily staggering through iterations of reality, wondered about the strange new heights of his temple. As it burned, it grew; these fire floors making it almost as big as some of the apartment buildings it shared 68th Street with. A bolt of black smoke rose up through the dome of the sanctuary. It mingled with the dark of the sky. It was morning but not yet dawn. There was a blanketing scream of breaking glass as the dome crashed inward. It dropped down on to the sanctuary and the influx of oxygen made for a burst of flame through the hole. The crowd—good God, yes, there were spectators—yelped at this and stepped away.

Field, having yet to identify himself, to approach the authorities or announce his role at the temple, was just another one of the spectators. An old man roused by the sirens and the smoke, drawn to watch from a safe distance. The urge to look on. The men and the women and even children. Watching was one of the purest expressions of human existence. It affirmed the presence of these people and the reality of the world they inhabited.

Smoke stung Field's throat and nostrils, and he lifted a handkerchief to his face. There was steam in the air from all the spent hydrant
water. He pushed his way through the crowd, the heat growing denser,
the bodies he passed oblivious to his own, aware only of their place.
At last he maneuvered his way to the line of firefighters. There were
dozens of them. Three engines, two more ladder trucks. They moved
around the building in a surprisingly orderly and efficient way, but
one that also seemed almost irrelevant in the face of the flames. Field
went down the perimeter until a large wet hand took his shoulder and
brought him to a halt. His badge, right about at Field's eye level, identified him as a fire marshal. He was an oak of a man with pink cheeks
and pale hair matted and wet from water and sweat. "You can't go any
closer," he said to Field.

"I'm the rabbi here."

"You're the head of this church?" he asked.

"This temple, yes. What happened?"

"It's too soon to tell anything for sure. Don't worry, there will
be an investigation. The best way to help now is to let us work." He
pointed up and down the street. "Right now we're trying to keep the
whole damned block from burning down. You see that building next
door? That's a residential building—forty, fifty units. Sleeping kids.
You get it?"

Field nodded but didn't move.

"So, I'll tell you again, step back."

He watched the smoke billowing out. He knew he should be thinking only about the people in those neighboring brownstones, or about
the people, his congregants, who were losing their place of worship, or
of his own place in the world—was he going to build a new temple,
start again at eighty-four?—but instead he stood there thinking about
what would be lost inside: the bimah from which he'd spoken on the
Days of Awe for thirty years, the brass pipe organ, the Ark and the
parochet concealing it, the five-hundred-year-old menorah inside the

ark, the chair for Elijah donated by the chief rabbi of Palestine, even the Torah scroll itself.

The men in their heavy padded gear, axes wielded, hoses balanced across the bridge of their broad shoulders, knew none of this as they surged forward, toward the structure of rising smoke and shifting, blackening matter, a wall of heat. If they were speaking to each other, or following directions shouted by some other voice, Field couldn't hear it. Nothing was audible in the crowd but the crackling of water into flame, the buckling of wood, the smashing of glass as the windows popped like lightbulbs crushed underfoot. Field imagined what it would take to surge forward into such a scene, the mentality of such men. Surely there would need to be a separation, momentary at least, between action and self, a suspension of the natural laws of self-preservation. They were only a few feet from the building when something stopped them. A rumble, then a boom, then its echo like distant thunder. A support beam collapsed. And then the center fell. The synagogue was now a moat, a ring of a building with a ball of nothing at its center. The men retreated, huddled in a heap around the captain and revised the plan of attack. They would enter on each side now, not through the front. They would enter on faith that whatever supports remained would hold out while they battled from within, swept any protected pockets of the place for people trapped. Field hoped to God there would be none, no one inside so late at night. The conviction occurred to him, and just as quickly dissolved, an awful knowledge taking its place. A sound escaped his lips, something between a gasp and a moan. Mrs. Sobichek, the Polish woman who cleaned the synagogue in the evenings. She was supposed to finish her duties and leave the building by eight o'clock. That was what she'd been told. But she was old and poor. She lived on 89th Street alone. She had arthritis in her hips. She drank. She'd been found sleeping in the synagogue's basement more than once.

He pushed through other onlookers, toward one of the firemen. "A woman," he called out. "Inside." But no one heard him. No one listened. They had already entered the building, disappeared into the smoke. There was a momentary hush, a collective breath-holding all around. And then, from the synagogue's side entrance, the part of the building farthest from the flames, two firefighters were running forward, shouting at something unseen. A third man ahead of them had axed through the door. The marshal was moving toward them now. Field called out, but his words disappeared into the clamor.

The marshal rushed toward the other fighters without looking back. Field angled and shoved against the crowd to get a better view. The side door had collapsed. A thick smoke, gray and dense as dirty water, poured out and up. And then, in full gear, a firefighter emerged, a limp bundle slung over his shoulder. Field crossed the barrier, ignored the protests and shouts of those behind him. The bundle was still smoking, covered in ash. A limp arm slipped from under the blanket, charred and lifeless.

For the first time that night, he felt his age. His legs grew weak, his head light. He looked around for someone he knew, a congregant or friend, some source of support, but found no one. He should have told them earlier. He should have remembered. A terrible loneliness pressed down on his frail bones. He could feel his ribs straining beneath it. He couldn't move. He could barely swallow. He couldn't remember what it was that had once made him believe in God, or in himself, or in anything at all.

A veil of smoke rose up in the distance, spread out until it was thin as breath, then vanished into the blush of dawn above Central Park. All of creation was too lovely and too pitiful to behold. The fire burned on. How badly he wanted to help, to be of assistance to someone, to anyone, to be a part of it rather than outside it, but he couldn't do a thing besides stand there and watch the younger, stronger men scramble to subdue the flames.

I.

THE ARRIVAL

1.

ABE AUER SHOULD have been paying attention to work, not to the picture he'd seen that morning in the *Yiddish Daily Forward*, a picture of a body lying lifeless in the street. Work was work. Work was real. A picture, on the other hand, was only ink. And yet it was the picture he saw while he stood in the middle of his junkyard. It was the picture that lurked in his brain and gave him a queasy, lopsided feeling in his stomach, a pinching sensation behind his breastbone, a sharp pebble in the pinpoint center of his throat, and a nervous, frightened contraction in his temples.

All day, every day, he did his best not to think about these pictures. He opened his morning *Forward* and read about Jews ordered to register in the Netherlands, drafted for forced labor in Rumania, sealed into ghettos in Lublin and Warsaw. Then he closed the paper and went about his business, unloading inventory, processing shipments, making small talk with whoever came by, lowballing potential buyers, factory managers, scrap metal dealers, and construction company owners. He wrote receipts and appraised old appliance frames. He worried about his daughter and was glad for the time away from his wife and kept an eye on his assistant, and if he had the chance, he moaned about the cold or the humidity, or the price of steel, or the dormant ulcer in his gut that occasionally turned non-dormant and erupted a geyser of lava through the tender tube of membrane over his heart. These were normal worries, regular concerns, the accepted method of passing days. This was the way every Jew he knew seemed to be operating lately. There were moans and sighs and pounding of fists at the dinner table and prayers beseeching the wise and benevolent President Roosevelt to find a way to oppose the Nazis and protect the Jews. Then they closed their papers and washed their dishes. Even this morning with news of a synagogue fire not in Hamburg but in Manhattan, they read and worried, lamented aloud and clenched their teeth, and then they closed the papers and washed their dishes. How else could it go?

Abe knew that this was what he was supposed to do. People he loved, his daughter, his wife, were depending on him to continue on with life as usual, just like everyone else. And so he tried. Day after day, he tried. He poured milk into his coffee as he read reports of the Luftwaffe dropping bombs on Warsaw. He buttered his toast, then skimmed an article on the confiscation of the telephones of all German Jews. Just today he'd read about thousands of Jews from the town of Jassy, Rumania—men, women, and children—shot in front of a ditch. Then, he'd carry these details around with him all day, sealed off from the rest of him. It was like a bag of gravel he lugged on his back, grinding him lower, slowing him down. It was important to be informed, everyone agreed, but what one was to do with the information—that was another question.

The best answer Abe could settle on was a mixture of stoicism and resignation. Mostly, it worked. He could keep going. He got by. Only occasionally would he falter, read an article in the *Forward* about an expulsion in Cisenau and then remember something from his childhood in Grodno, his brother Shayke who disappeared one night and never returned, not even when the police came to the house. There were things in his past that he did not discuss. The people who knew and loved him accepted this. Only now, the Yiddish papers were full of news that no one wanted to discuss. The Jewish community was catching up with him; he was good at keeping secrets.

Now he stood in his junkyard, staring at the sky and thinking of the shipments due that week while his assistant kept things running. He stood there, his hands black with oil and his eyes tired from lack of sleep, watching the June sky pass above a hollowed-out Oldsmobile. The car was hooked by a crane and making a slow circle as it inched toward the expanse of rusted rubble, corrugated metal frames, and heaps of burnt rubber covering the ground. It dangled and twisted on its chains as Abe's assistant lowered it, then all at once it crashed down, sending up a burst of gray dust. Then the engine went quiet and Tadeusz Kazimierz called out to Abe. "Hey, shouldn't you be in the office? You're meeting with a buyer at 3:15."

It was the third time that day Abe had forgotten. It shouldn't have been such a hard thing to remember, to meet with a man interested in buying his business.

The man coming to see him was not the first to be interested in Abe's junkyard. Every week they came. Businessmen from Albany, entrepreneurs from Chicago, a few factory owners and manufacturers from New York. Men with money, some from well-off families. Some self-made. They came to meet with Abe and put in an offer on the yard, and they told him, in varying degrees of directness, what kind of an idiot he'd have to be to turn it down. Then he turned them down.

He'd done it so many times in the past year it had almost become a habit. He knew what they'd say before they said it. What the hell was he going to do with a junk heap worth eight times what he'd paid for it a decade earlier? Was he going to melt down all the metal and turn it into artillery to be sent to Europe himself? Did he know how to manufacture machine guns and ammunition? Or was he just allergic to success?

They asked him the questions everyone in town was asking, the question his own wife had been asking for years—was he stupid or just stubborn? How could he not recognize the fortuity of the hand he'd been dealt? He'd bought the yard for nothing in '26 from an Italian family gone broke, bought it with the savings he'd scraped up selling hardware on the East End. He'd bought it without any clue that fifteen years later, with Europe once again grinding toward war, iron would be selling for forty cents an ounce. Steel and aluminum twice that, and factories all across the country would be scouring for cheap sources of exportable metal wherever they could get it.

Three offers a month he got, many of them generous. Scrap metal was not a glamorous business in times of peace. War was another story. Remington. General Electric. The one today was with Chicago Pneumatic. He watched the man pull up in a brand new Buick. He was well-dressed and grinning in the bright light. He walked across the dusty gravel, looked more like he was on his way to a gala than a junk-yard, a perfect picture of the prosperous Jew. Too prosperous, thought Abe. Too lucky. Jews shouldn't have so much luck—they should all start out as Abe had when he'd first come to America twenty-eight years ago, picking rags under the Second Avenue elevated. When a man started out this way, everything that followed felt like a huge success.

"*Takeh a shmelke.*" I'm a huge success, Abe muttered to himself, patting his front shirt-pocket for a pack of cigarettes that wasn't there before finding a single smoke behind his ear, then turning to find the buyer standing in his doorway.

THE MAN'S NAME was Nate Suskind. The offer was a sound one, and he drove home its soundness again and again. They talked across the small round table in Abe's office, an empty table, the wood waxy from the days it spent in the rain before Abe had dragged it indoors. The man's hands were the color of the wood. Everything about him connoted layers of concealment, a fine veneer of gloss lain over weath-ered pulp.

"Now listen," he said, leaning against the table with his elbows. "I wouldn't be making an offer if I wasn't impressed with what you've done here."

Abe resisted the urge to smile. Then he stopped resisting. "If it's so impressive, why in the hell would I sell it to you?"

"Did I say sell? A partnership. Not a sale. You understand the difference?"

"I understand," he said. "It's not so complicated."

There were only two junkyards in the city of Utica. Abe's American Junk Co. and a smaller one on the east side owned by the Campo family. The Campos were in trouble. They could be bought cheap. Suskind wanted to invest in Abe's yard, and he wanted that investment used to buy out the Campos. The two of them would be partners. They'd own all the scrap metal east of the Adirondacks. Together, they could be kings of junk. This was a good position to be in now—exports were rising by the month, production was up—but if America got into the war, it would be more than good.

Abe listened but didn't speak. He sat there staring at the man, then squinted out the window to where Kazimierz was unloading a truck. He hoisted out a large lip of whiteness that eventually revealed itself to be part of, most of, a claw-foot bathtub. He lugged the thing across the yard and then went back to the truck. And came out with another partial tub. This one wasn't as cleanly broken. It was jagged and toothy where the ceramic had been cracked. Someone had done something violent to this tub. Kazimierz stood at the edge of the truck, trying to think of the safest way to get it down. He decided to kick. He dragged it through the yard, then went back for another destroyed bathtub. After a few minutes, Suskind began tapping his foot on the floor, then his fingers on the table, then the palm of one hand against his knee. The stillness was killing him. Abe supposed this man was not used to people mulling over his propositions for very long.

"Do you see this?" he asked.

"What's that?" said Suskind.

"Who breaks bathtubs? Who gathers them? Why do I have them?"

Suskind rolled his eyes. "They're junk, junkman."

Finally, Abe shook his head. "Thank you, but no. Not interested."

Suskind sat still, seemed to be waiting for more, some follow-up, some explanation. When ten seconds passed and still nothing, his smile faded. He leaned back in the chair as though putting space between them would clarify what remained unclear. "Really?" he said.

"Really."

"Take some time. Consider it?"

"I did. Just now."

"Humor me, in that case. Tell me your reasoning."

"I wouldn't call it reasoning. More a feeling. A hunch."

"I don't understand this language. Are you a businessman or a fortune teller? I'm asking you to make a deal, not read my palm."

"I can't do either. Now, if you don't mind . . ."

The man made an elaborate show of packing up his briefcase, putting each paper and binder back in its place. He clipped one latch, then the other. Even the latches on his briefcase were polished, the brass catching the glare of the bulb overhead. Abe could already see him thinking about whatever came next. A man like this would cash in on war, one way or another. The currency of the world was suffering and misfortune. Only idiots like himself sat on the sidelines, watching the weather.

"Suit yourself," the man said, then he knocked the briefcase once against the table and gave Abe Auer the broadest smile while holding out his hand. "*Narishe kop.*" You're a fool, he added, then tipped his hat and strode across the yard.

Abe made his way to his Buick. Inside, the seats were hidden beneath the week's newspapers he hadn't thrown out. The car smelled damp, musky with the day's warm rain. He gathered up the papers in his arms, carried them back to the trash can beside the office. He returned to the car, cranked the engine, wondered what Irene made for dinner, hoped it wasn't chicken. He'd made the right decision with Suskind. Too risky to sell. Why rock a boat that had carried him this far? "*Narishe kop.*"

You're a fool, a voice repeated. He looked out the passenger window, expecting Suskind, seeing his brother Shayke instead, gangly and dark, sharp elbows and knees, a flickering presence, the memory of the ghost of the man, vanished almost before it appeared.

WHEN ABE GOT home that evening, Irene was in the kitchen, cooking. Judith was in the hallway, leaning against the wall and talking on the telephone to her intended, saying something that required her to turn her back when Abe stepped into sight. He took off his hat and stomped the dirt off his shoes, sank down onto the sofa, and stared at the wall for a few minutes until his feet stopped throbbing. Then he stood up again and went into the kitchen. He came up behind Irene, pressed his face into the back of her neck. She was still the woman he'd married, thicker through the middle, perhaps, worn down in her posture, still gorgeous—her gorgeousness wasted on him. She turned to face him. "Hello, husband."

He pulled her closer.

"You want to cuddle or you want dinner?" She held out a wooden spoon. "Taste," she said. He put his hands on her hips as he did. The sauce was too salty, but he didn't say so, just made an appreciative noise and nodded. Then, he continued to watch her when she turned back to the stove.

"I missed you today," he said.

"Oh?"

He pulled a stray apron string tied above her behind. The apron slipped but she didn't bother to fix it. The ceiling above them shook. Judith running to her room. "I thought tonight was Bezique night with Max Hoffman," she said.

"We moved it to Tuesday so he doesn't have to cheat so close to Shabbos."

She pointed her spoon at him. "That man's always so glum. You should let him cheat if it cheers him. You should encourage it."

"I think he finds losing more enjoyable. Some men are like that."

"Go change your shirt before dinner."

He went upstairs, took a white undershirt out of the dresser, dropped his soiled one onto the floor, then thought better of it and tipped it into the hamper. All this without turning on the light. What was there to see? This room, this house, the furniture and walls. It was more familiar to him than the contours of his own face. He emptied his pocket change onto the dresser, emptied the ashtray beside it into the trash. The morning paper was folded up beside the ashtray. He started to read, then stopped, tossed it onto the trash.

Downstairs, he watched Irene sprinkle salt and pepper over a bowl of green beans, and while he watched, he imagined what she'd say if she knew he'd turned down another offer. "You wonder why you're so low all the time," she'd say. "You're low because you have the time to be low, sitting all day at the yard, clipping your nails. I'd go crazy, too. Anyone would. You need a regular job. A get-up-and-put-on-a-suit-and-talk-to-people-throughout-the-day sort of job."

She was wrong, of course. They were different. She needed the things he wanted least: small talk, acquaintances, the everyday meaningless give-and-take. She didn't understand inaction for inaction's sake. The grease sizzled over the pan into the sink, pooling like lava in the water. Everything smelled rich, fragrant, overflowing. The top of her blouse was damp and clinging slightly, see-through like wet tissue. He liked to watch his wife. Also, he wished she would be quiet. He wished he could watch her in pure, perfect silence, like a film. Words ruined everything, even her elegance, but what did it matter? Her elegance was out of place here.

THE EVENING CAME together around him as it always did. A well-set table. A decent meal. An attractive woman to serve it to him. A moody but basically well-behaved girl, loving, sharp-witted, and darkly beautiful. Not a fancy house but good enough to keep the cold out. Not a fancy dinner but filling. What was so bad about all this? What was insufficient? He interrogated himself at times. So Jews were being murdered in Rumania. What was that to him? He tried to push it away but something always drew it back. A feeling he couldn't shake, a feeling that he wasn't really outside it, wasn't exempt. He'd been seeing Shayke more and more. This apparition that came when he failed to sleep.

Irene and Judith sat on either side of him now. Judith was wearing a yellow dress with a black bow along the collar, a watch with false pearls on the band. Her lashes were thick and sticky black. Her hair long with a dark wedge of bangs. Not to his taste but pretty, so pretty these days. She could be on a magazine cover if she would ever smile.

"Stop staring at me," she said.

"Staring? I was chewing."

"Do I have something on my face?"

"I was thinking how beautiful you are, if you must know. Next time I'll keep my compliments to myself."

"Don't sulk. I'm only joking."

"I like to look at my daughter's pretty face. *Es tut dir vey?* Am I hurting you? Is that a crime?" He was asking his wife.

"Do it without discussing it," said Irene. "No one likes to be gawked at. Besides, she has to lose five pounds before the wedding. Too many compliments will sap her willpower."

"My willpower's fine, thank you."

"Did you follow up with Max Hoffman about the ketubah?" Irene said.

"Since you asked me ten minutes ago, no."

Abe stopped listening. He'd stopped following the details of Judith's engagement. It only took a few seconds for his eyes to glaze. Irene and Judith yammered as they passed the dishes. Meat drippings and margarine and soft-boiled vegetables were pushed to the edges of the plates. Water was sipped. Salt and pepper shaken. The windows were faintly fogged from all the cooking. Bread was buttered. Glasses refilled. Meat stabbed. Sauce sopped. The neighbor was mowing the lawn. He could smell it through the window. The sweetness of the grass took his appetite away.

He watched Irene eat. She was the neatest eater he'd ever seen. *Pinktlekh*. Precise. Never a stray crumb or a drop of sauce in need of wiping. *He* was the messiest aspect of her life. As he watched her, an idea occurred to him that if the junkyard, his largest single investment, had appreciated beyond his wildest expectations, Irene's investment in him, as a husband, had followed a path of steady decline from the moment they took their vows.

Her parents, his late in-laws, had tried to warn her. He could still remember so clearly the pitch of his mother-in-law's voice, its shrapnel-whistling rise and fall. She could carry on an entire conversation, a full and lengthy conversation, without ever acknowledging his physical presence in the room. She talked not to him but about him. To her, he was the milkman or the butcher or the boy she'd hired to rake leaves. What else had he expected? She came from good people. Refined people. Assimilated German Jews to whom Abe's parents, well-off as they'd been in Grodno, could never measure up. Abe's father had owned a small factory. He worked with heavy machinery and the men who manned it. Irene's father was a pharmacist from Gloversville. He worked with beakers and powders and pestles, worked the muscles in his fingers and brain and not his back. Abe's mother had spent her life before a stove and sewing machine. Irene's mother chaired committees of her local Hadassah and planned progressive dinners. Abe's brother had been a communist. Irene's brothers were Coolidge Republicans. Eighty years ago in Germany, Irene's family had servants. They'd owned a stationery business, a house and country cabin. They had fifty Eastern workers in their employ, little more than slaves. America had required a slight recalibration in this stature. Still, Irene could have married anyone, any of her many reasonable suitors, and instead she'd chosen Abe because at nineteen they shared a close moment passing in a stairwell and ever after, Irene later confessed, she knew it to be love. A few weeks after he started coming to court her in the evenings, taking her on strolls through the park, he ushered her behind a tree and kissed her deeply, touching her face with one hand while the other lifted her skirt and slid inside her panties and made something happen that she told him she hadn't thought possible.

When she announced the engagement, she'd promised her parents that he would work his way up, build something solid, better himself.

Her father hadn't looked up from his paper. Her mother had twisted up her face and said, "Will he begin by learning to use a knife and fork? Or by learning English?"

"He speaks English fine, Mother."

"The English of a man selling fruit out of a cart. Not the English of an educated person."

"He might not be educated but he's the smartest, kindest man I've ever met. He'll learn. He'd do anything for me."

"He'll ruin your life," her mother predicted. "He'll drain your beauty and youth and leave you with nothing but grief and back pain. These Eastern Jews are all dumb peasants at heart."

She was a nasty piece of work, his mother-in-law, a *yekke*, a true German Jew who looked down on anyone born east of Vienna.

Now he watched Irene spoon green beans onto her plate, her shoulders slumped, hair dyed regularly, yet still graying a little around the edges, but everything around her the same as it had been twenty-one years ago. Same rusted faucet. Same water-stained drywall and drafty windows. The linoleum beneath her feet was turning as yellow as her teeth. And yet he loved her. The knowing smile still warmed him, the delicate slope of her shoulders, the softness of her hands. She was a good woman. It was a good house. A good family. He'd bought the place in moderate disrepair and built it up, kept it going, sanded and hammered and insulated and reinforced the dwelling into something that would last. At certain moments, more than a few, he took pride in it. Tonight, for instance.

After dinner, he took out the garbage while Irene and Judith washed the dishes, stood in the yard and took it all in from the outside, his life. Another Yiddish newspaper tossed onto the front porch, never unrolled. Why bother now? He tossed it into the garbage can, dug into his pocket for a cigarette and smoked it slowly in the yard, savoring it. He'd rather smoke and look up at the stars than read about more news he could do nothing about. *And who says you can do nothing?* a voice inquired, a voice he hardly recognized as his brother's after all these years. He turned away from it, closed his ears to this voice without body, this empty echo. He turned his attention to the north of town where the mountains faded to the deepest shade of blue. Beneath, the crickets hummed a high, soft static. And high above, a thin film of moonlit cloud obscured the view. That was how it always was in summer. Utica's stars were tentative and abundant.

2.

THE FIRST THING Shmuel Spiro noticed when he pushed open the door to the offices of the Committee for a Jewish Army was that the secretary was talking on her phone. Her name was Rachel and she was born in Liverpool; and now, hearing her speak, a thing that had not happened with much frequency since her hiring some weeks back, Spiro was reminded of her origins. The little undulations of her accent emerged. She was talking excitedly. Whoever phoned was hardly letting her breathe.

"I have no idea, sir . . . if you'll only let me . . . no, sir, that isn't . . . I understand, you must believe me I understand . . . I don't know, sir, I really and truly do not know . . . "

Other people in the office were talking, too. Phones were in use. Bodies moved, bumped, and moved on. Hands were waved. Pens were chewed. For the first time the place was alive with activity.

It was all very strange to Spiro.

"Field's Free Synagogue burned down last night," said Dave Metzger, his arms piled with envelopes. "Phones were ringing when we walked in, and they haven't stopped."

A tiny look of excitement passed over Metzger's face. It was a handsome face and indeed, once upon a time, Metzger had been in pictures out in Hollywood. But then he grew tired of playing the sniveling fop or pompous undergraduate whom heroes were constantly wooing women from, so he started writing movies instead. Then the governor of California asked if he'd like to write some speeches for him. Then, at a B'nai B'rith fundraiser on Wilshire Boulevard, he'd been cornered by a small, angular man who asked if he wanted to help arm Jews, the same small angular man he was presently grinning at. He was older than Spiro, but there was something boyish about him: floppy hair, rumpled clothes.

"This," Metzger said, pausing to let Spiro acknowledge the ambient energy that had been entirely absent from the office up until that morning, "this is something."

Spiro nodded. "Shame the same can't be said for Field's temple."

As soon as he made the joke he regretted it. He didn't hate Stephen Field. Field was his rival, his enemy even, ideologically, politically, but he didn't hate the old man. Though he would tell anyone willing to listen that Field was gutless and a traitor to his own people, he found him vaguely charming and more than a little sad. The synagogue he'd built up himself and turned into a pillar of New York's Jewish community gone in a night. The *alter kaker* didn't deserve that. Of course, the countless poor bastards whom Hitler was turning to dust all across Europe didn't deserve that either. But it was Field and his ilk, the American Jewish Committee, the Zionist Organization of America— not Hitler or Himmler, the General Government in Poland, or Pétain in France—with whom Spiro was at war. The Fields of the world were against raising immigration quotas, against arming resistance movements in Europe, some were even opposed to American intervention against the Nazis.

Field, as Spiro saw it, was not a Jew in America but an American Jew. These were two distinct, discrete things. Take first the American. The great swallowing spirit of democracy. The irrevocable, enveloping force. When you came to America, you had to disavow yourself of Minsk or Chelmno or Odessa, or Australia or Abyssinia for that matter. You had to renounce it and could not argue. Field didn't. He didn't argue. Yes, he held on to something Jewish, something mystical, something historical, something binding, but he took a knee before the Constitution, before FDR, who had invited him to tea on not one but two occasions, a fact everyone knew gave him as much pride as the temple he'd founded. This was how it worked for those who were American and a Jew. America ate you and made you one of its children, like a third-rate Greek god.

In practical terms, this meant that any group or organization with Field or someone like him at the helm was—had to be—extremely *circumspect* about what the world was doing. Specifically the parts of the world that included Jews who were not Americans. Of course they were aware that bad things were happening, they being Field and the American Jewish Committee, as well as the Zionist Organization of America, B'nai B'rith, the folks who got invited to eat at the big table— they were aware of how rapidly the situation was deteriorating in Europe. Arrests, expulsions, camps people did not return from, trains filled with living corpses, things called *Totenkopf*, Death's Head—or let's just call them German soldiers. But the way to deal with all this, as men like Field saw it, was not to arm the Aliyah Bet in Palestine, the only ones smuggling Jews out of Europe, not to nudge the British to let a few more into Palestine legally or heaven forbid into America itself. They could not or would not fight for this because they were Americans. They had been through the chutes and were, at a deep but not too deep level, ashamed of the *shtetl* folk, even if they were evidently being slaughtered. These were not Americans. Just as they understood the plight of their (distant) kin they understood (distantly) the rantings of Father Coughlin or Reynolds or Holmans or Elmers or any of the other orthodox bigots populating Congress, men who would sooner see America slide into sea and shining sea than let these dirty and rootless characters settle in their towns. Field got that message loud and clear, and it was because of that that he and his American flock operated the way they did.

But Spiro was not an American. He was born in Russia. He grew up in Palestine. His life had been defined by flight. And he was lucky—some of his flight was by choice rather than the whim of a czar or sultan or whatever potentate you happened to be squirming beneath. Jews moved. They bounced. Sometimes by choice, sometimes not. They could settle. They could make roots, of course. Look at Warsaw or Berlin or Trieste or even Cairo or Istanbul. All cities inhabited by centuries' worth of Jews who knew no other home. That was fine, said Spiro. But that was not the end of the proposition. The end was Palestine. The end had always been Palestine. Your centuries of history aren't a lie, they're just temporary. *Shema Yisrael.* The absolute beginning of the Torah, for Pete's sake. Lord, send us to Israel. Lord, now that a very big *Wehrmacht* is bearing down on us very quickly with its awful fangs and horrific guns, could you send us any quicker? No? Fine. We'll do it ourselves.

Field and his ilk found this balls-grabbing an embarrassment, and it was this embarrassment that was incomprehensible to Spiro. He fought Field for attention in the press, for money, for influence in Washington. Mainly, Jews died and Field won, but as the news brought more and more stories of ships filled with refugees with nowhere to go, ships sent across the Mediterranean in unseaworthy condition, marooned off the Port of Haifa, off the coasts of South America, ships turned back, their Jewish passengers returned to the desperate situations they'd fled, Spiro refused to be embarrassed. It was in his nature to move and make noise and turn order into chaos when chaos was what was called for, and from this chaos sprang his Friends of a Jewish Palestine that he'd now changed, was changing, to the less inflammatory Committee for a Jewish Army, an organization dedicated to creating an army of stateless and Palestinian Jews to battle against the Nazis, to defend their own homes and people. It was an idea as unimpeachable as it was audacious. And yet it barely registered in the public consciousness over here. What voice was heard was the harmless, droning sound of Field, reassuring Americans that they weren't doing anything wrong by turning away steamers full of displaced persons.

Spiro had scant resources to counter such deluded thinking. In fact, he didn't have much that he couldn't see in front of him: a staff of a half-dozen and a dozen more volunteers, mostly unemployed or unemployable Broadway types; the dim, dusty office rooms on Madison Avenue that had been previously occupied by a sect or some sort of free-love movement. But now, for the first time in its history, the office was buzzing. A fire could do that.

"Any idea who did it?"

"Doesn't have to be arson," said Metzger. "Could just as easily be electrical."

The phone rang and rang.

Spiro returned to his desk. On the way, he saw Ron Kellman, a former comrade from Irgun, yelling into the phone, and Dick Shoemaker, the bright accounting director Spiro had poached from the Zionist Organization of America, trying to hear over him while also writing urgently on a notepad.

"How much?" Spiro asked. "How much in pledges?"

"A lot," Shoemaker said, without bothering to put down the receiver. "You know what this means, don't you?"

"No time for rhetorical questions, Richard."

"It means a hell of a lot more ads."

The latest sketch was rolled out on Spiro's desk. A man in bed with his eyes closed, and above him a panorama of men, women, and children with downcast eyes and emaciated bodies marching along a dirt road with tanks at their backs. Above it all in large, block letters: ACTION, NOT PITY, CAN SAVE THE JEWS OF EUROPE. He picked up the drawing, carried it over to where the artist sat.

"Can you do this again?" Spiro said. "Put a fire in the background. A burning synagogue behind the tanks."

"I can," he said. "You don't think it'll be too much?"

"I think it'll be perfect."

Yes, God's wrath could be perfect. Wrath, or a drunk trying to get warm, or a faulty fuse, or who knew what. The well-known place had burned to the ground in front of the neighborhood and people were scared. Smoldering synagogues in Germany or Austria or Rumania were one thing. But an assault like this on the Jews of Manhattan, destruction a person could see and smell and feel in the air, wondering if their own synagogue would be next. Spiro—a student of violence as much as anything else—understood the power of proximity.

Long before this fire, long before the other fires and explosions and artillery-driven assaults he had witnessed around the world, Spiro had believed in fear. He believed in its driving, penetrating force; he believed in it as an angry spirit hanging over the heads of men; he believed in it ultimately as a truth, a germ of certitude buried deep inside every news report and rumor and scrawled letter from across the sea, hardened and blackened and impossible to banish or destroy. The Irgun reprisals that began in '37 with the bombing of the Arab cafe was the first time he felt it, this change. Two persons killed. Five wounded. Hardy a massacre. But then Black Sunday. Attacks in Jerusalem and Haifa at once. Fifteen wounded. Seven casualties, three of them women. It was the first time they'd allowed themselves to do more than defend, to dispense with restraint. And it worked. He could feel there was a palpable change in the behavior of the British, an empirical and real change, as though they were suddenly given new clocks with a thirteenth hour on them. They were afraid of Irgun Bet. They knew the dead officers, the wives, the children; they saw the shards, smelled the cordite that hung in the air, displacing those tangy mineral odors from the hillside that normally coated the city and never sat right in Spiro's nose.

Now it was the Jews of Manhattan's turn to see the fear god in the fire that took away the Free Synagogue and called on Spiro, as one of its prophets, to make sense of the horror. Who did it? Hitler? Is Hitler here? Are they coming? Are they coming for us? Do we stay away? Do we hide? We have services to attend. Shul. Sabbath. The Temple of Our Lord, the blessed and almighty, the sanctuary defiled, swept away on a tide of fire. Was this foretold? Is this the beginning? What is this? The phones rang on and Spiro answered them. The panicked Jews of Manhattan wanted answers.

"My grandson's Bar Mitzvah's next weekend," one fellow in Brooklyn told him. "Should we stay home from temple? My daughter's scared to go. I tell her that's crazy, but is it? I can't sleep at night."

Spiro didn't answer right away. His desk was in what had once been a storage closet. To the outside world it gave the impression of modesty, but in truth Spiro had deposited himself there for the intimacy it afforded him with his own thoughts. He picked up a pen, wrote on the paper before him, How Are You Sleeping? Five Million Jews Remain in Hitler's Path. "Sir," he said, "There's no reason to think that the fire is part of any systematic plan of persecution. And remember, unlike in Europe, when synagogues in America catch fire, we put them out."

The man sighed. "I took the train in to see it this morning. You can smell the smoke eight blocks away. I feel like I should do something."

"You can," Spiro said, "You can make a contribution to our committee."

The old man took a moment to mull this over. "Yes," he said without conviction. "And what is it your committee does?"

"We are a political committee, sir. We are actively lobbying Congress to work with the British in forming a Jewish armed force to fight the Nazis alongside the Allies." Spiro waited for a follow-up question that never came. The line went dead, but within a minute, it was ringing again.

When Spiro had a second between comforting the worried and the appalled, he called his contacts at the papers. Nobody had any idea who set the fire, or if they did, they were keeping it to themselves.

At 5:30, Dick Shoemaker, looking as though he'd just walked to the office from the Sinai, told Spiro that they had raised $3,000 in pledges. Spiro put down the phone and banged his fist against the wall.

"Ladies and gentlemen," he said. "Recognizing that our natural state is one of impoverishment and that our families and loved ones are still in the jaws of a hideous beast, I'd like to take a moment to point out that in the past seven hours we've raised more money than in the previous seven months. It's been a long day. If there's ever been a day that should end at the Cafe Royal, I'd say this is it."

SPIRO ORDERED A bottle of cognac that cost nearly as much as his rent and smoked a stranger's Turkish cigarettes. He listened to an Austrian cabaret singer in a white turban sing the blues, drank until the room went soft, and then whispered compliments into the ear of a woman (he was fairly certain she was a woman) who raved about his accent and insisted on calling him Nigel.

At one point in the evening, he found Metzger at a dark table in the back of the cafe. There was a girl to his right, a girl to his left, one across from him. They were chorus girls but they looked like lazy cats, smoking languorously and whispering into each other's ears. They made quite a picture, but it wasn't the girls that struck him. It was the fact that, tucked away in this dark corner with them, Metzger seemed to hardly notice they were there. He wasn't lighting their cigarettes or ordering their drinks or playing footsie with all three under the table. He was doodling Committee advertisement copy on a cocktail napkin, turning the napkin this way, then that way, then flipping it over, then scraping his pen against the table to draw the ink. It was both touching and pathetic, and Spiro understood completely. This was the essential problem of his existence over the past three years: the way the work invaded, the impossibility of tuning it out. When Metzger finally glanced up, Spiro raised his mostly empty glass of cognac to him, then swallowed it down.

A few hours after midnight, he left to go home. When he stepped into his apartment, there were only a few hours remaining before dawn. He collapsed on the bed in the small, cold room. For a long time, he lay on top of the rumpled sheets in his undershirt, watching the slow rotation of the ceiling fan. He thought about the girl and he thought about the fire and he thought about his wife and children, how a few weeks earlier, after two and a half years of living on separate continents, his wife had sent him not a letter but a three-sentence telegram: Have met someone else—STOP—Moving with children to Haifa—STOP—Forgive me as I've forgiven you—STOP—. He read it in the doorway to his apartment with his cup of coffee. He read it again and again, kept thinking something was missing, that there must be more. He could not really believe that he had lost them, that in the face of his postponements and evasions, she had made the decision for them both. Now, lying alone, he felt her presence. When he closed his eyes, he could see her in the small bedroom of their cottage halfway around the world, her body curled around their daughter as she nursed the child to sleep. He could hear the soft thud of the lemons that fell into their yard all year long, rotting sweetly, seeping into the earth. He saw his wife and children and he saw the American girls' delicate shoulders, the rounded bones pressing out against their skin as they sipped their martinis and puffed their cigarettes and smiled and danced. He saw smoke rising from the sanctuary's domed roof and the news from cables coming out of Europe: Jewish corpses discarded on the street. That was his night. Incessant scatterings, bloody pages tossed into the air, there for him to peruse in the slowly failing dark.

When he woke, he wasn't sure he'd slept. He reached for the place on the nightstand where he normally placed his glasses and found them under the covers by his hip instead. Light was flooding the windows and someone was knocking loudly on the door.

3.

EARLY JUNE, BIRDS singing, the sky wide and blue, the air dense with the scent of new poplars and cologne and tobacco smoke and peanuts and somewhere on the periphery, far enough to be ignored while still being acknowledged, the tang of horseshit. A perfect summer day and everyone in Saratoga seemed glad to be where they were except the horses, and maybe Max Hoffman—a man just clear of forty who somehow felt, sitting in the grandstand, as though he'd lived several lives already. It was on days like these away from the temple it came to him—the peculiarity of the arc of his life. No one was going to call him unhappy, least of all Max himself. It was a restlessness bearing a pathology. Durkheim called it anomie, his sister called it *shpilkes*, and Max . . . Max wasn't blessed with a gift for nomenclature. Max called it living.

"Now this race is all about Peach Tree," said the man sitting next to him. He had been giving a running commentary since the first race without realizing that Max, or anyone around him, was paying him any attention. But now, to ease the anomie or *shpilkes* or just to enhance the lovely day, Max decided to listen.

"Peach Tree's gonna take it."

"What makes you say that?"

The man turned to Max, startled enough to make Max think the man actually was aware that he had been talking to himself.

"Did you see him run last week? Against Market Wise? If he hadn't been put up next to a worldbeater he'd of run away with the whole shebang."

He wiped at his neck with a kerchief. He gave Max a mischievous look that under different circumstances might have been interpreted differently.

"Fella I know knows the vets, fella said keep an eye on Peach Tree," he said conspiratorially. He pointed at his own eye, then Max's. There was a stubby pressure that made Max recoil. He squinted down at the lanes and tried to find the horse the man was touting. It was no use. From such a distance, the thoroughbreds seemed as small as dogs and the jockeys looked like ants. Max let his eyes wander from the track to the lake inside it, to the canoe anchored at the center, painted blue in honor of the year's winner at Travers Stakes. The lake appeared smooth, silver, and still in the morning light, the boat skimming a slow circle across its surface. A cool fog hung high above the track, but the sun seared off more haze with every passing minute. Sitting there, it seemed to Max as though he were watching summer unfold around him, and for the first time in almost three months, his spirits rose. He was glad he'd gotten out of Utica for the day.

It was unease that had kept him moving, that morning when he'd gotten in his car, but also all his life. Chicago. Heidelberg. Paris. Lyon. New York, the Jewish Theological Seminary, then disgrace, then Utica, his home now for four years. At first it felt like circumstance or the wiles of a society he was not comfortable in, but at a certain point, perhaps on a rainy afternoon in February at the place where the Rhône and the Saone diverge, he began to think that this was a natural condition, a fate, for lack of a better word. Do not weep; do not wax indignant, Spinoza had said, so he didn't: a rabbi in a town so flung away it hardly seemed to exist. Now he was in Saratoga for the day, enjoying the feel of the sun on his face and the open air, watching people as he always did, trying to understand them. There were at least a thousand souls around this track, men and women of different ages, different inclinations and stations, and yet what they all cared about right now were horses sprinting laps, stakes and bets and odds, the lure of a little quick cash.

"If you stay here until the seventh," said the man beside him, "make sure to keep an eye on Jumpy Puppy."

"Very aggressive-sounding," said Max.

He pointed to the paper on his lap. "Says here she's a maniac, bred on nothing but cabbages and beets."

"A Jewish racehorse. How could you go wrong?"

The man laughed. "You drive in from Albany?"

"Utica."

"That's a trek, isn't it?"

"Everywhere's a trek from Utica."

The fellow laughed again. It came easy to him. He wasn't a watcher but a *tummler*, a man meant to make noise.

"Those who've seen her run, Jumpy Puppy I mean, they are inspired."

Max grinned.

"You're fooling yourself. It's all dumb luck. One horse runs faster than the others and the rest lose—there's no reason to it."

The man stared off at the track; he gave a bland smile but didn't respond. The way Max's unease could spill into the day, into the jolly lives of others, was uncanny. It was a talent, really. A bell rang out across the bleachers, calling the jockeys to the paddock. "Nice chatting with you," he said to the stranger.

HE ARRIVED BACK in Utica late that afternoon to discover that a thunderstorm had struck in his absence, landing an armchair-sized hunk of elm tree in the middle of his porch. And in case that wasn't enough, there was also a letter from Max's sister waiting for him beneath the mail slot: "Dear Max," it read, "Yoo-hoo? Yoo-hoo? It's been months. I call every day. If you don't start answering your phone, I'm contacting the police. Where are you, baby brother?" While trying to weigh the urgency of each problem against his need for a shower, the floorboards above his head began to shake.

Max lived on the middle floor of a three-flat on Oneida Street. Above him lived a young widow named Mrs. Epstein. Her husband had been killed in an automobile accident a few years back, and she lived on the insurance money and the paychecks she earned working at the public library. *A quiet woman*, he'd thought at first as he watched her coming and going on her way to or from the library. She was pleasant and petite with a quick, nervous walk. He'd watch her hurrying down the sidewalk, hear her showering above his head, smell the fried eggs she prepared for herself most nights for dinner, and he'd feel a mild relief wash over him that he shared a roof with this quiet, inward woman—a partner in solitude. She was a good neighbor, almost invisible right up until a month ago, when she began bringing a man—a Canadian naval officer she'd met while visiting her sister in Buffalo—up to her apartment. Max had heard from the synagogue gossip that he was shipping overseas at summer's end, that in a few months' time he'd be braving German U-boats. Maybe it was because of his impending departure that there had been no courtship. The man hadn't started coming around to the house with flowers in hand, holding the car door open for the widow Epstein, and driving her off for an evening of dinner and dancing. No, he'd come to the house and lead her upstairs to her bedroom, and there they would stay, sometimes for a couple hours and sometimes for a couple days; then he'd leave, an unshaven walking heap, only to return a few days later and do it again. They were up there now—moaning, grunting, straining the integrity of the mattress springs and floorboards. He imagined the soft friction of their naked bodies, the bare skin against cool sheets, the flushed flesh, the entangled limbs, the tense torsos moving together like a single entity, a single pulse. The box spring pounded the bed frame. The grunting grew louder.

Max moved out of the living room to get away from it, trying to put distance between himself and the noise, but his location in the apartment hardly mattered. It was a small apartment. One bedroom, one office, a kitchen that was really just a hallway and a stove. More than enough for a bachelor, though. He had his books spread throughout, organized by language. German in the living room. English in the bedroom. Yiddish and Hebrew in his office. Often, he stacked them vertically, un-alphabetically. He liked not knowing where a particular volume was right away, the process of looking, letting his mind wander while he looked. He'd had a thought to reach for Hegel. Hegel seemed right on a sunny day. But who could deal with *Phänomenologie des Geistes* when two people were fucking right over your head? He let the book drop.

Sometimes wandering, he'd come across some forgotten memento— a picture of himself and his sister in their swimming outfits at 31st Street Beach; a pipe from his time in Hyde Park when he'd wanted so much to look like one of his distinguished professors and had tried (without success) to develop an affinity for tobacco; or a handkerchief once bequeathed to him by a prostitute in Berlin. He'd met her at a subterranean cafe. She had bobbed hair the color of corn husk and bright red lips. She knew he wasn't going to take her home but sat with him anyway, telling him about the family she'd left in a small town in Bavaria. What was it about him that made people feel free to confide, confess, unburden? He'd had this quality much of his life and still didn't understand. It was not a bad quality, he thought, and yet often it left him feeling wistful and lonely, even in good company. He sat in his office, tried to focus on his calendar, his list of calls to make that week.

Just as it began to quiet down upstairs, the phone began ringing, and, thinking it might be his sister, he hurried into the kitchen to answer it.

"Max Hoffman," said the voice on the other end. "You've fled to the deepest part of the interior. Tracking you down was probably slightly easier than finding Colonel Kurtz."

Max tried to place the voice. "I'm sorry. Who is this?"

"This is Radio Free Promised Land, Mr. Hoffman. This is the voice of sacred earth."

Silence on the line. Max still couldn't quite identify the speaker but felt the need to steel himself against something nonetheless.

"It's Shmuel Spiro, Max."

"Shmuel? I'm sorry I didn't recognize you."

"You are forgiven, Max. Memory does almost as much damage to voices as it does to faces, don't you think?"

"It's been since, what," Max wondered aloud, "Heidelberg?"

"Probably," said Shmuel. "Probably, old friend."

It was odd how someone like Shmuel could evolve in memory, how someone who was a decent enough friend at the time now seemed like an intimate, a person of great importance, allowed to slip away. You couldn't trip on a cobblestone in Heidelberg without tumbling into the arms of a leftist or agitator or revolutionary of some stripe—stripes that often changed color by the season or by the week. They met at a cafe swollen with Trotskyites and the next time they saw each other it was in the same setting but the Trotskyites had reincorporated as Mensheviks; later they became adherents of a Dadaist offshoot and espoused public nudity. For Max, these constantly mutating organizations and their central role in one's identity were disorienting, but Shmuel seemed to have no trouble shapeshifting in stride. Max could recall seeing Shmuel charm packs of unrehabilitated Boers and devout anarchists on the same evening. It was like watching a lion tamer who could also train elephants.

Their time in Heidelberg had only overlapped for a brief period. Just on the edge of tipping into something greater, both were lured away from the university, Max by Paris, his determination to write a novel no matter how badly it might turn out, his unexpected friendship with a few artistic types he'd discovered during a week in Biarritz, some British communists and Rhodesians and a stray German named

Hans who'd invited him into their enclave. This luring, he now knew, was a symptom of his habitual tendency to flight, but at the time it felt very much like its own singular event with specific tensions and unearned seriousness. In Paris, he'd set his mind to write a novel and he'd done it. He'd written a very bad novel, shamefully bad. He did not even need the scorn of an editor to tell him how bad it was. He accepted that he was not a writer but a scholar. But by then it was too late to return to Heidelberg.

What snagged Shmuel away from those classrooms in Heidelberg, Max later found out, was Ze'ev Jabotinsky's radical revisionist Zionism. The journalist turned revolutionary had come to give a talk one evening to a group of Zionist youth. People who knew him told Max the transformation was nearly instantaneous, Shmuel moving from gadfly to a man inhabited by purpose. No one could recall what Jabotinsky talked about that night. If anyone remembered the evening, it was for what it did to Shmuel Spiro. A few weeks later he returned to Palestine. A few months after that he was a pleasant, inarticulate shape in Hoffman's memory. After that, a name only evoked by the title of a book or the name of a philosopher.

"Heidelberg," Spiro said. "Surely that was a former life, no?"

"It feels that way. Where are you calling from?"

"New York, as a matter of fact."

"City?"

Max cringed at the stupidity of the question immediately, but Shmuel somehow intimidated him, made him nervous. Shmuel let it go by without mention or even a change in tone.

"That's right. Been pulling together some good men here, trying to organize from solid ground. We're working to pressure the Americans about the crisis."

He paused for a moment. Hoffman thought was going to say more about what it was exactly he was organizing for, but instead he said, "I can't tell you how relieved I am to have found you, Max. When I heard you'd left the city, I thought, this man has set off for something grand. Perhaps you'd gone to the woods to become the Jewish Thoreau. Maybe the mighty and mysterious minds of the US government had found a purpose for you. Never did I think of Utica, New York. What is there, Max? I can only conceive of two reasons: one is a very fertile woman of extraordinary wealth, the other is that you've founded some sort of radical theological institute where no one can bother you."

"I took a position at a synagogue in town. Nothing fancy."

"A position? What sort of position?"

"Well, I'm a rabbi, Shmuel. I have a congregation."

There was a long pause. "This is fascinating news." The silence that followed humbled Max. It seemed to encapsulate everything he had not done since he had known Shmuel in Germany.

"Have you looked at the *Times* this morning?" Spiro asked.

"No, haven't had a chance. I just got back from Saratoga."

"Saratoga?"

"The horse races."

"Horse racing? Truly? Please be careful, Max. You aren't a man who'd do well with gambling debts."

"It was really just a lark, an excuse to go somewhere."

"Well, before you go somewhere else, take a look at page A7 in the *Times*. And then I need to ask you a favor. I'll call you back in ten minutes."

He began to ask what he should be looking for but Spiro had already hung up. He walked outside and found the soaked-through newspaper in his front yard, brought it back to his office and opened to A7. There were no news stories. The entire page was an advertisement.

Jᴇᴡs Fɪɢʜᴛ ғᴏʀ ᴛʜᴇ Rɪɢʜᴛ ᴛᴏ Fɪɢʜᴛ

Tʜᴇ Jᴇᴡs ᴏғ Pᴀʟᴇsᴛɪɴᴇ ᴀɴᴅ ᴛʜᴇ sᴛᴀᴛᴇʟᴇss Jᴇᴡs ᴏғ ᴛʜᴇ ᴡᴏʀʟᴅ ᴅᴏ ɴᴏᴛ ᴏɴʟʏ ᴡᴀɴᴛ ᴛᴏ ᴘʀᴀʏ—

THEY WANT TO FIGHT!!!!

And beneath it, a quotation from Churchill: "Any nation, any man, who fights against Nazism will have our aid."

And beneath that, the claim that twenty thousand Jews had offered their military service in the war against Hitler.

And beneath that, an essay expounding on the terms of this offer and the way it had been shunned by the British.

And beneath that, hundreds of signatures.

He'd never seen anything like it: Spiro advertising his cause the same way Chevrolet advertised its motorcars or Camel its cigarettes. It was so striking it was difficult for Max to know what he thought of it. It bore the undeniable stench of propaganda, eschewing all complexity or nuance or even just the realities of the world. Were the Jews of Grand Concourse and Hoboken going to see this and want to ship out? It had more shove than logic. But then that was the goal. This was Spiro's new way of putting himself into the conversation. Except now he wasn't sidling up to a group of students and making himself sound clever. He was screaming at an entire nation.

He sat down and waited for Spiro to call back. The ten-minute mark came and went. Then an hour. He made himself a sandwich, wrote a few letters for the congregation, fixed the hinge on the cupboard door. He went onto the front porch to drain the potted begonias and pick up the broken branches and to assess the felled section of tree trunk on his porch. He was testing its weight when the door behind him swung open and the Canadian stepped out. He gave the rabbi a nod, shuffled down the steps, and made it halfway to his car when Mrs. Epstein stepped onto the porch and called out his name. The emotion in her voice foretold a scene Max had no desire to witness. He wondered if he might hide behind the tree trunk, but it was too late. She'd turned and spotted him there, and then looked back at her lover with even more sorrowful eyes. Her hair was disheveled and her feet were bare; the top button of her blouse was open, and she reached for it, fastening it with one hand. She held the hot-sweet smell of all the things that intermingle when bodies do: sweat and tobacco and sex and cologne. She seemed thinner than she had a few days before, weak with hunger, unsteady on her feet.

She started down the steps, but the officer stopped her, holding up his hand. "Nora," he said. "I'll be fine." She didn't answer, just crossed her arms over her chest as though she'd grown cold, then leaned against the front door, watching as he got into his car and drove away.

Max was about to go back inside when she stepped forward and sat down on the porch steps beside the tree. "I'm sorry I wasn't here to get this tree hauled away sooner," he said, just to say something, to acknowledge her.

She looked up at him. Her eyes were gray, her cheeks still flushed. Why was it when he was out in public, at the temple, at events around town, he felt so afraid of women, cornered by them in every conversation, hopeless and nervous. But at moments like this one, alone with them, in the presence of some kind of sadness, he felt instantly at ease, and there was a certain relaxation in his demeanor, a natural—was intimacy too strong a word? It was. Call it closeness, then. They sensed it, too. They talked to him in a way they didn't even talk to their husbands or brothers or sons. They let him into their private worries and concerns, just as his sister had always done. He could be close to them because of his isolation. Because he couldn't get himself enmeshed, he could be empathic. They sensed this. They used him for it.

"I sort of like it, actually. I think the porch will seem empty after it's gone."

"We'll keep it, then."

"You're so accommodating, Mr. Hoffman. Do you have a light, by any chance?"

"In the kitchen."

"Could I bother you?"

He walked inside, found some matches beside the stove, returned to the porch. Mrs. Epstein was weeping. She put a cigarette between her lips and turned her head toward him. He sat down beside her, struck the match, held it out.

"Please excuse me," she said. "I'm so embarrassed."

"Don't be. They're only tears. Of all the things to be embarrassed of."

"Damn it," she said, pressing her fingers to her eyes.

"Is there anything I can do to help?"

"Could you keep a U-boat from sinking his ship? That would be nice. All the men I love end up dead." The tears fell as the smoke rose. She spoke through them. "It's only, I'd gotten rather good at being alone. It takes effort, you know, practice, endurance. And now it's all blown to hell and I'll have to start over again. That's the hard part." Max reached over and placed a hand on her shoulder as she wept, left it there until the tears stopped. It was a small gesture, but it felt like the only useful thing he'd done in weeks.

He lit another match for no reason, let it burn down to his fingertips, then shook it out. Inside, the phone was ringing. He rushed back to his office to answer.

4.

ABE ARRIVED AT the train station late in the afternoon, straining to remember the name. Ana Beidler. She was thirty-six. Polish. A refugee. No family. No home. Aboard the 12:17 from Grand Central. These were the things he knew about her—the facts. He repeated the name to himself, clung to the words as he left the yard early, took the No. 7 bus across town and climbed the stairs to the train station.

The train was late, and so he waited outside for the better part of an hour while the sky churned above him, threatening and then delivering rain. He took shelter under the awning of a newsstand as the rain sputtered down, dug out a nickel and picked up the *Forward*. Then for another fifteen minutes he stood, trying to make himself small beneath the shelter, not reading but watching the afternoon go gray as rain dampened the platform.

This, thought Abe, is how the world thanks you for doing good, for doing a friend a favor. By making you cold and wet and at the mercy of the railroads. Here's your appreciation. The compensation for goodness is as likely to be soggy shoes and a wasted afternoon as gratitude or sunshine. If you got away with soggy shoes and a wasted afternoon, you were lucky. His eyes needed only to go in the general direction of his newspaper to have that notion affirmed.

But here he was anyway. No sign of the train. No indication of when it might arrive. But he was here and he was trying to do good, just as he'd been trying to do a few days before when Max Hoffman showed up at the junkyard unannounced, stepped into Abe's office with a lost look on his face, a look like he'd stepped out of an elevator on the wrong floor.

The rabbi's presence at the yard wasn't entirely inexplicable. From time to time, when the temple needed a chair or an elderly congregant needed a new table to eat at, Hoffman might drop by to see what Abe could offer. These were moneyless transactions, Abe insisted. Hoffman tried to offer something, ostensibly out of decorum but also, Abe suspected, because he felt the peripheral presence of shady dealings and wanted to steer as far from that as he could. Abe still refused. "I won't hear the end of it if Irene learns I've chiseled the rabbi out of a few bits for a broken chair," he said during one of their first dealings, with a deep, enfolding laugh he'd learned to deploy in the face of skepticism. The rabbi went along but didn't seem convinced, so Abe let him in on something that was formally verboten, however harmless. A weekly Bezique game, played in the office at night, with a rotating cast of grocers, haulers, salesmen, random nudniks from the city. He wanted to show the rabbi, here is what you think you're afraid of and it's not so terrible anyways, and what you and I do is completely on the up-and-up. Hoffman turned out to be a particularly shrewd, almost cunning player; nearly everyone, Abe included, was in arrears to him. Predictably, he never said anything about collecting.

Abe couldn't decide if he legitimately liked Hoffman or if his affection was born out of feeling sorry for the guy, at how painfully misplaced he was in a burg like Utica, a city of brewers and tanners that did not need—did not *deserve*—a powerful brain like Hoffman's. His services were thoughtful and poetic and wrenched those who heard them into contemplation, more, really, than all these *machers* wanted. They didn't hate Hoffman, he was just far over their heads. Abe tried to keep up, and when he couldn't, more than ashamed he felt a lump of sadness for this guy who worked so hard to compose such heavy stuff. He didn't belong in Utica. And yet he still tried so hard. It was an effort Abe admired.

So when he pulled up and said nothing about surplus or gambling debts, looking tense and bewildered and roiled all at once, Abe was genuinely unsure of what he was about to hear. He brought Hoffman into the office, sat him down, gave him all the time he needed before he began.

"I got a phone call the other day from a friend, a very old friend, someone I knew in Europe, in Germany, when I was a student but then lost sight of for many years, until this phone call, in fact, it was the first time I'd spoken to him in half a lifetime and as it turns out he's right here now, not exactly here but in Manhattan but when you've known someone on a different continent the city and Utica can be merged together as here, don't you think?"

He was hunched forward, elbows on knees, eyes in constant motion, totally stripped of the composure and presence he brought to the bimah.

"Max, take a breath. I have no idea what you just said," said Abe.

Hoffman looked up at him with such a strange energy flashing across his face.

"It took you some time to get here, didn't it?"

"Utica?"

"No, to America."

Abe reached for the hairs on the back of his neck.

"It wasn't an express journey, no."

Max nodded, a little too quickly for Abe's comfort. The energy was still there in his face but was starting to coalesce into something.

"That's why I'm here," he said, and then suddenly slapped Abe's desk. "I knew you were the man I needed to see. You understand, Abe."

Abe tried to remember if it was a forbidden thing to contradict a rabbi. He didn't understand at all.

He heard, in the yard, his assistant haggling with a hauler. The day was moving past Abe.

"Abe, I won't ask you to go back to the time when you had to pass through fire and ice to get to America. I trust those memories will remain with you for far longer than they're welcome. What I'll simply ask is that you think of someone else making a similar journey, now, at a time when things are no better than they were for you."

His gaze hardened on Max.

"My friend, the one in New York, asked if we might take in a refugee from Poland. She's a Jew, Abe. My friend works for an organization that has the means to get her out. They need a place for her to stay. They could find her a room on the Lower East or I could even find the space in my own apartment. But what I thought was, a nice home, filled with nice people, loving people, a place like that could be so much more . . . "

"Comfortable?" Abe suggested.

Max smiled. "Sure, Abe, comfortable. So much more comfortable than any of the accommodations my friend's group usually has access to."

Max sat back, looked briefly at his feet. "Look, I know a phone booth at the corner of Orchard and Delancey is going to be an improvement on Poland. It's an imposition, Abe. But I'm asking."

"You've got to talk to Irene," Abe said. "She goes to those NCJW meetings about the German kids."

"No, this isn't a kid. She's an adult DP. She needs families, people to claim a relation, to sponsor her. And, of course, lending a hand once they arrive. By the time they get here, these people often have nothing left. No money, no family, no ties." He paused. "You're the first person I've asked."

"It won't be too discouraging then if I say no," Abe said.

"You don't have to answer right now," Max said. "And if it's too much, I'll figure something out. I know it's a lot to ask."

A few years ago, Abe would have nodded, been grateful for an easy dodge. He would have asked Max if they were still on for cards the following week and been done with the whole affair. The problem Abe sensed now was not with Max but with Irene, the way he knew she'd react. She'd been finding more and more fault lately, not with Abe himself but with his attitude to the world, which was not generally a positive one. What would she say when she heard about his refusal to help with this, as she surely would?

Yes, he was sure of it. Irene would be angry if he refused Max now. He'd been listening to her point of view so long it now had its own special satellite location inside his brain. She would accuse him of being cold, selfish, misanthropic. And what was so bad about misanthropy, he'd counter, with people being what they were, occupying varying degrees of awfulness? Then he'd add to himself that sometimes he thought those who wanted to help humanity were the ones who needed help most of all. *Then why'd you marry such a person?* she'd ask. And the answer, clear and unspoken, would shame him. Because he loved her. Because she was a good person and a wonderful wife. Because he admired in her the things he demeaned in others: her charitable nature, her depth of feeling. He'd say no to Max Hoffman, then he and Irene would argue about it. The arguing would cool off to resentment and bad humor. They'd marinate in it for a couple days. Then he'd go to her and announce his change of heart, say of course it was the right thing to do, the decent thing, to help some poor refugee with nowhere else to go. But he'd feel worn down and lousy about the bitterness built up along the way. What if for once they could skip to the end?

"How long?" he asked Max. "How long would she stay?"

"I can't imagine more than a few months."

He ran through other details, nationality, age, day of arrival, and yet not the thing Abe really wanted to know. Would he regret it? That was all anyone ever wanted to know, wasn't it? Will this thing I'm about to do lead me to a million bucks or my face down in the gutter or something in between? Will this action or the other add to or detract from the sum of misery and disquiet inside my head, my home, the world at large? Was there ever any other question?

"THEY WRITE ABOUT the fire in the Yiddish news?" the vendor asked him now as he stood before the platform, waiting for the train's arrival. He pointed to the *Forward* tucked under Abe's arm. In Yiddish, he said, "You bought it, but you don't read it?"

Abe shrugged. "I promised my wife I'd stop. Too much bad news. I get—" He had no word for it, the moods that came over him, the darkness that was not just darkness but also like fog inside his head, slowing down his thoughts. "Down," he said. "Gloomy."

The vendor nodded. "Murder is gloomy. War is gloomy. Persecution too. She wants you to do a jig?" The man made a *tsk*-ing sound with his tongue, a sound Abe's own mother had made, thirty years and a thousand miles from where they now stood. "Terrible," the vendor said. "Shameful, what's happening."

"Try the American papers. No bad news there."

"Americans don't care what happens to us in Europe. Christians don't care what happens to Jews. That's the beginning and the end."

Abe nodded, observed how stiffly the man stood. His eyes were large and gray; his skin hung slack from the bones of his face like a sheet draped over a post; and his mouth, no more than a knot above his chin, clamped tightly over his near-toothless gums when he wasn't speaking. Occasionally, a spritz of rain would dampen the man's face, and he wouldn't bother to wipe it away, just kept staring and watching the passerby like an old horse unbothered by the gnats around its mane.

"You have people trapped?" Abe asked. "Family?"

The vendor looked down at his magazine display. "My brother. His wife. Four children. Ukraine. A small town near Kiev. Four months now, we hear no news."

Dead, thought Abe. He'd read the reports about the German units sweeping through, killing every Jew along the way, only the occasional partisan managing to flee and report what had happened to the Red Cross or a government in exile. "Don't assume the worst. The post doesn't work during war. It barely works during peace. You'll get a letter soon."

The moment he said it, he wished he hadn't. What could be crueler than hope? The vendor seemed to agree.

"*Zey zaynen shoyn geshtorbn*," he replied. They are already dead. "I will never see them again. And do you know what the worst part is? The worst part is that at the very moment they were murdered by those beasts, whenever it was, a week ago, a month ago, three months, who knows? At the very moment they were facing it, I was standing right here, selling a tin of mints to some *schmegege* on his way downstate, or smoking my first cigarette of the morning, or eating a piece of bread and jam or taking a dump. That's what this world does to us, turns brothers into strangers. We're all alone in the end."

Abe took a deep breath and nodded, then walked forward to wait in the rain.

HER ARRIVAL BEGAN as a vibration in the platform. Then, down the track, a silver mass took shape against the mist. When he leaned forward, he could just make out the headlamp. It slowed as it approached, the conductor visible as a dark silhouette behind the glass. Abe shrugged his shoulders, tried to shake off any impatience that had settled in his posture in the course of the hour. The worst thing would be to seem put out by the train's lateness, to appear conscious of the fact that it was now five past six and Irene would have dinner on the table soon.

The vibrations grew to a rumbling. He found himself standing up straight, wondering what to do with his hands, where exactly he should direct his eyes. The train groaned to a halt, sweating and steaming in the drizzle, while beyond it, the Adirondack Mountains hovered over the city. Passengers disembarked then hurried along the platform in a swarm of gray. They rushed toward shelter as Abe moved away from it. How would he find her? Should he have made a sign? What would he have written on it, besides? Jewish refugee, this way?

The last of the train's passengers pushed out. He was trying to see around them, and that was when he noticed the woman who wasn't moving at all, a straggler in the thinning crowd, a fixed stone in the current. She was tall and thin, her face obscured by a mass of black hair, her dark eyes framed by sharply drawn brows. He approached her. She didn't smile or nod. She placed her suitcase down then looked at him directly, without shyness, without fear. Not young. Not old. A face equal parts weariness and hope.

"*Gutn ovnt*," he said. "Are you Ana Beidler? Max Hoffman from the synagogue sent me."

She didn't move at first, didn't look away. A tack-sized dimple appeared in her cheek—the sort of dimple that precedes a smile. "He sent you, did he?"

Abe held out his hand, and she placed hers on top in what seemed a continental gesture. Did she expect him to press his lips against it? To bow? Something in her gaze made him stammer. Was she beautiful? Not exactly. There was nothing remarkable about her face except her eyes, from which he found it impossible to look away. They were not brown, not green, neither gray nor hazel, but some combination of each. They were large but not round, narrow eyes beneath narrow brows; they emanated expectation.

"I'm glad to meet you," he told her, shouting slightly to be heard over the din of travelers. "My name's Abe Auer. You'll be staying with us." When she didn't respond, he added, "How was your trip?"

"My trip," she said. "It was miserable, of course. But I wasn't expecting more."

There was a slight slant to her mouth when she smiled. She had straight teeth, a large nose, a pinprick mole between her cheek and upper lip, a way of looking up at him from downcast lids. By now, they were the only two people on the track. The fog began to lift and the sun burned a gash in the clouds. A few fat raindrops fell then ceased, as though sodden rags were being wrung dry above them. Abe realized that they'd been standing still on the platform, that he'd been waiting, hovering, when the normal thing to do would have been to start walking, showing her the way.

"Can I take your bag?" he asked.

She didn't answer right away. Had she not understood, or was this air of hesitation a tic in her manner? A beat was lost between question and answer, but what she was doing with it, where her mind went in that moment, he didn't know. "A gentleman," she said as he reached for the suitcase, and then added, "I do appreciate it. I haven't much, but even a few possessions grow heavy when dragged across the sea."

"You speak such good English. I wasn't expecting that. Where are you coming from exactly?"

She told him that she'd lived in London for a time. Germany, also, many years ago. Rumania as well. But now, now she was coming from Warsaw. Her ship had arrived two weeks before, and she'd spent the time sleeping in a cot in a hallway of the Joint Distribution Committee. She told him all this as they began to walk. The crowd had fled. Only the vendor remained. He tipped his hat to them as they passed. *What did he think?* Abe wondered, watching them leave together, his own prosaic figure next to hers.

"I was told there'd be a house here, warm water. A little food."

"Yes," he said. "My wife is cooking, so more than a little."

Her suitcase was light in his hand. The energy of the moment swept him along, making him feel as though he could carry three bags and a trunk on his back. He led her away from the tracks toward the main staircase of the station. When he glanced over his shoulder, she was lingering behind, looking up at the sky. He wondered if maybe a few screws had been shaken loose by whatever trauma she'd endured. He stopped and waited for her. When she'd caught up, he said, "It's not far to the house. Nothing's too far from anything in Utica. We have the mountains nearby. Parks. Even a racetrack. When the horses get too old in Saratoga, they send them here. Really, they plod more than race, but we all enjoy it."

She didn't answer. She didn't move.

"You have no idea what I'm talking about, do you?" he said.

She shrugged. "I feel a bit . . . I don't know the word in English."

"Say it in Yiddish."

"I can't think of it in Yiddish, either."

"*Tsemisht*? Confused? Exhausted? Uncertain?"

She gave a weary smile then nodded. Then she did something he was not expecting, something for which he couldn't have prepared himself. She reached for his hands, took his short, wide fingers with her long, slender ones. They felt smooth, cold, and bloodless, just the opposite of the air around them, which was warm and damp. They reminded him of the metal of the train on which she'd ridden, the steel railing surrounding the deck of the ship that had carried him across the sea more than two decades ago, his own body when he'd first arrived in New York, always cold, always hungry. Were all things that came from that other world cooled to the temperature of the contraptions that carried them? The journey drained youth and hope, the very things it was meant to restore. Why not warmth?

"You're very kind," she said. "I can tell already. A kind man. Imagine it. I didn't know there were any of you left."

"I do my best," he said.

"I'm grateful," she answered. "The world has not been kind to Ana Beidler."

He paused for a moment, absorbing the fact that she was talking about herself. Then he nodded and led her down the steps to the street below.

WHEN THEY ARRIVED at the Auers' house, Ana Beidler's hat was taken and hand shaken by each member of his family almost before she'd walked through the front door. Abe mumbled introductions that were rendered superfluous by his wife and daughter's boisterous greeting, by Max Hoffman, whose unending smile revealed his unease as much as the sweat on his forehead. Her suitcase was taken upstairs. She was shown to her room to wash up and settle in while everyone else moved toward the dining room to wait.

For dinner, Irene had prepared a leg of lamb, and alongside the lamb, she'd prepared a roast. For side dishes, she'd prepared carrot tzimmes and cabbage stuffed with rice. She'd prepared a kugel as thick as a brick, and a salad made of beets, and for dessert she baked a rhubarb pie and a chocolate cake. Abe and Irene and Judith and Rabbi Hoffman stood nervously in the parlor as the food sat cooling on the dining-room table. Their guest had gone to bathe. "I must bathe," was how she put it, following Irene to the spare room. Abe had assumed she meant a twist of the handle and a toss on the face of whatever come from the spigot, but Ana's definition was more continental, more languorous.

They sat around the living room waiting, and while they waited, Abe forgot about himself, made his actions mechanical. He smoked a cigarette, poured himself a second glass of cream sherry. Finally, they heard the water drain upstairs. Judith was slumped over, her head resting on the table. She pushed herself up as though it required great effort, then set to finishing another drink.

"I'm cold," she said. "I'm freezing!" This was an unbearable habit she'd developed, announcing her own minor physical discomforts as though they were events of great importance.

"So put on a sweater," Irene said.

"It's an icebox in here. Am I the only one who's freezing?"

"You're the only one," Abe said. "We're not running the heat in June."

"Maybe I'm not really cold. Maybe I'm just so hungry that it's beginning to affect my circulation."

"Hush," Irene said. "Who says such a thing with a refugee at the table, a person who probably hasn't had a meal in months?"

"Technically, she's not *at* the table. She's been bathing for an hour."

"And who knows how long it's been since the woman's had a real bath?" said Abe.

"Real bath, real cold dinner."

"I'm sure she'll be down soon," said Max. "Any minute now."

Abe leaned back in his chair and sighed. This, he thought, was the problem with good intentions. People expected things for their generosity: a future favor, a pat on the back, a grateful refugee who knows how to take a quick shower. He was about to get up and pour himself a scotch when footsteps sounded overhead, slow at first, and then faster as the sound moved down the stairs.

The woman who stood before them then only mildly resembled the one he'd met at the station. Her mess of hair had been washed, combed out, and dried, then tied on top of her head in elaborate plaits secured with gold pins. Gone, of course, was the damp overcoat, but also the plain, dark dress, in place of it now, an impeccably tailored blouse, Adriatic green satin silk, gathered just so to show off her collarbone. An egg-sized brooch rested against her throat. Her lips were painted red, her fingernails lacquered, her fingers banded in gemstones and gold.

"So sorry to keep you waiting," she said with that accent, the one that sounded nothing like the country speech of Abe's youth, nothing like the guttural Yiddish of his parents.

"Shall we eat?" he asked.

Ana Beidler took her seat at the table between his daughter and his wife. The dishes were passed. The wine was poured. She smiled and pushed forward her glass, drank half of what he gave her in a single draw.

"What a lovely brooch you're wearing," said Irene. "Is that mother-of-pearl?"

Ana raised her fingers to her neck. "This? A man gave it to me. A director of the Bucharest production of *A Wounded Star*."

"You're an actress?" Judith asked.

"Was an actress. The theaters in Europe have been shut down for years now. The Jewish theaters."

"Are you . . . were you . . . "

"Was I famous? Is that what you'd like to know?" She smiled then, and though Abe could not read the precise meaning behind it, he saw in her expression something that stopped him, that made him put down his fork and sit back in his chair. That ever-present fog in his head cleared for a moment. A rush of joy, almost like pain. His skin tingled. The blood pulsed against his veins as he realized . . . there was something familiar about her. *Oh*, he felt a part of himself saying, *I remember*. And yet he didn't. It was something else, a sense she exuded that was unique to that other world, that other place. Everyone at the table was watching her, but she was looking only at Judith. "My dear," she said. "I'd like you, sometime, to sneak away from here, back to the station where your father fetched me, and go back the way I came, just the last part, back to New York, and once you're there, board the Third Avenue elevated. Head in the direction of 14th Street, a southerly direction, I believe. Look for the theaters. The playhouses. Ask the gentlemen there if they have not heard of Jacob Adler. Of Israel Rosenberg. Of Schiller in London. After they nod, and assuming they haven't thrown you out for an idiot, ask if they know of Ana Beidler of Bucharest, of Odessa, of London."

Abe watched her speak, wondering what it was that made it impossible for him to stop watching. Was it the slightly gray complexion of her teeth? The gaunt contour of her cheeks? Or was it the vanity in her eyes—that sickly ghetto fantasy of being not just accepted and embraced by the outside world but also somehow, impossibly, revered? She drank down the remainder of her wine and held Judith's gaze before speaking. "Ask after Ana Beidler, one of the founding members of the Vilna Troupe, friend of both Jacobs—Adler and Gordin—and watch their faces. Ask about . . . " She paused for a moment, and when she opened her mouth again to speak, her painted lips parted widely, sharply, like the wings of an exotic insect, into what struck Abe as an unnatural, almost deranged smile, one that retreated as quickly as it had appeared. Instead of continuing with her monologue, she looked at Abe calmly, demurely, and asked if she might have another glass of wine.

He reached for the bottle and found it empty. "I'll see if we have another," he said.

"I'll join you," said Irene. "To check on dessert."

He rose, gave a small nod to those remaining seated, then followed his wife down the hall. There was no door between the kitchen and the hallway, and so they spoke in hushed voices.

"Well," Irene said, "this should be interesting."

He sighed. "It's only for a month or two. How was I to know Max was going to stick us with some meshuganah actress?"

"A beautiful, glamorous actress. I forgot to get berries for the cheesecake."

"Who needs berries? It's sweet enough as is."

"You think my cheesecake's too sweet? I've been making it for twenty years, but you wait until now to tell me?"

"I didn't say 'too sweet,'" he said.

"You're watching your figure now? If I'd known, I would have made a fruit salad. Surely Miss Beidler's not going to have any; a woman in show business has to watch her figure. It'll end up in the garbage."

"That, I doubt."

"We'll see," she said, as they passed each other in the doorway. "We'll see."

But they never did get to see what Ana Beidler thought of Irene's dessert because by the time they returned to the dining room, the place where she'd been sitting was occupied only by a crumpled, lipstick-smudged napkin.

"Where'd she go?" Irene asked.

"Unclear," said Judith. "She gave a very loud yawn and then walked upstairs."

"The restroom?" Abe suggested. But a few minutes later they heard her come out of the upstairs bathroom and go directly to the guest room, closing the door behind her.

THAT NIGHT, WHILE Irene showered, Abe undressed, took off his shirt, and studied himself in the mirror beside his dresser. His middle was domed but still muscular. The hair on his chest and stomach was graying but not gray. He smiled at his reflection. He still had all his teeth, a decent face, a respectable hairline.

"What are you doing?" Irene said, coming back from the bathroom with a towel around her head. "Admiring yourself? You need to put your best foot forward now that we have a beautiful actress sleeping down the hall?"

"That's just what I was thinking," he told her.

She dried her hair with a rough motion, hung her towel from a hook on the door, opened a drawer, slipped into her nightgown, then walked toward him, stood very close so that their torsos touched. He loved it when they stood like this. He loved the feel of her body beneath the thin silk of her gown. When they fought, when they bickered, when they disagreed or bristled at each other, this was the place they returned to, the posture that reset them. There was a magnetism about it, more mechanical than erotic. When the world impinged or distorted, they came back to each other, to this position, the way a spring recoils from distortion. She leaned forward slightly. He put his hands on her face, lowered his head as they let their lips come together. Her lips tasted of sweet wine. Her hands reached for him, and as his body reacted, the familiar heaviness returned. She kissed him. He let her kiss him, but he couldn't do more. She looked away, walked to the other side of the bed, and slid beneath the covers. When he did the same, she turned her back to him. Her back was covered by a gown with small yellow nubs on it—flowers or bows, he couldn't tell which. The windows were open, but the night was quiet, the breeze too light to stir the trees. The only noise came from the guest room down the hall, dresser drawers being opened and closed, footsteps, small sounds.

"What's wrong?" she asked. "You're not yourself tonight. You're acting even stranger than our houseguest."

"Am I?"

"You didn't read the Yiddish paper again, did you? More about that awful fire?"

"No. Even worse. I spoke to the news vendor at the station. He stopped getting letters from his family."

"That doesn't mean anything, necessarily."

"Sure it does. It means what it means, what we all know."

Irene turned to face him. Her cheeks were still splotchy from the washing away of her makeup. Her hair fanned out over the pillow. Even the scent of her cold cream was calming, comforting. "No," she said flatly. "Maybe you could volunteer with me sometime at the soup kitchen on Lafayette, or work a little harder so we had more money for the orphans coming out of Germany. But lying here thinking about it, keeping yourself awake—how does that alter anything? Who benefits?"

He smiled. After all these years he still found her sincerity charming. "You're right," he said. "As always. Forget I said anything. Let's go to sleep."

She reached to the nightstand and turned off the lamp. A few minutes later she was unconscious. Lucky woman. He needed sleep so badly, but he was too tired to sleep.

He thought of the woman, Ana, and the thought of her surprised him. Who was she? What did she want and what had she lost? This was all he wanted to know of anyone. Had Max known what he was getting them into? How long would she stay? Where would she go when she left? Irene, he could tell, was disappointed with their refugee. He didn't need her to say so to know it was true. She'd probably been hoping for an old woman poor in English and opinions, a yen for gossip, someone from an irrelevant Galician backwater to whom she could be charitable but also superior. She was a native-born American, after all. A protégé, a project—that, he supposed, was what she had been hoping for when she agreed to go along, and now he could tell she felt tricked, and probably assumed Abe was responsible.

He placed his hand on her back, and when she didn't respond, he pushed off the covers, got out of bed, trod softly down the hallway, down the stairs. In the living room, he lifted a book off the shelf beside the fireplace, sat down in his favorite armchair, and began to read. The words felt heavy in his head. When he wanted to sleep he read in English; Charles Dickens was best. He saw industrial London, smokestacks and chimney sweeps, emaciated orphans and gold chains draped across the bellies of sweatshop owners. Everywhere one looked, east, west, future, past, human suffering stretched on without end. For what purpose? For what cause? His eyelids grew heavier. His breath moved slowly. His eyes had adjusted to the darkness, and now he saw there was actually a great deal of light—moonlight and streetlight. Utica. Quiet Utica. A sleeping city. Peace. He'd been right to come here. Here, they were safe. The curtains were white, half-translucent. The curtains in his childhood home had been thick, velvet ripples of fabric, too heavy to be moved by the breeze, designed to keep out cold as well as light. These were thin as tissue paper. They reminded Abe of a hotel near the Black Sea where he'd once spent the night. Sometimes he still heard the streets of Grodno in his mind. He still heard the sounds of the forest from their summer trips. Abe pulled himself out of the memory. It was a long-perfected trick, a balancing act. He focused on the softness of the armchair's upholstery, the shadows of the ceiling fan. He listened to the ticking of the grandfather clock in the dining room, stared at the red darkness behind his closed lids, a red like the coals inside a kiln.

He was about to doze off. Then, a noise. It was coming from upstairs. Laughter. Hysterical laughter. He sat up straight, waited for it to stop, which it did for a moment. Then it resumed. He rose, climbed the stairs. It was coming from the guest room. The laughter grew louder as he approached. He knocked softly. The laughter stopped but there was no reply. He knocked again, waited, then pushed the door open a few inches. There, on the floor beside the bed, sat Ana Beidler. She had not been laughing but sobbing, weeping. She lay there hunched over, gasping for breath, her face wet and red and swollen with tears. Her whole body heaved as she wept. She was hardly dressed, just a black slip. Her hair hung in her face and was matted with tears. He came in the room slowly and waited for her to look up at him, which she did after what seemed a long time.

"Miss Beidler," he said. "Can I get you something? Some water, maybe?"

When she looked at him directly, he could hardly bear the openness and urgency of her gaze. Her face seemed changed once more. Her lips were twisted, pained, her eyes panicked.

"Yes," she said, nodding.

He hurried back to the kitchen, took a glass from the cabinet and filled it to the brim. His hands were shaking as he carried it, tried to prevent it from sloshing over the edges on his way back up. When he pushed through the door again, she was lying on the bed, her head resting on the pillow, her face obscured. She sat up stiffly as he crossed the room and set the glass on the nightstand.

"Here," he said. "Please, how can I help you?"

"Help me?" she said, no longer weeping but smiling. The words were hardly more than a whisper. "Forgive," she said. "Can you forgive me?"

He sat on the edge of her bed. "But there's nothing to forgive." The words seemed to soothe her. And so he repeated this phrase the way he used to repeat to his daughter the chorus to a lullaby when he didn't know the other words. "Nothing to forgive. Nothing to forgive."

Her skin was darker on the sides of her forehead where her tears had washed away the paint. She looked up at him, calmer, blinking slowly. A long time passed before she spoke, and when she finally did, he was expecting her to thank him, or to say she felt better, or to offer some explanation or excuse. Though they'd only just met, he somehow expected she'd confide everything in him, her deepest secrets and regrets. She seemed to him, right from the beginning, a woman incapable of keeping secrets, a woman who needed to be heard and seen the way others needed the nourishment of food or the oxygen in air. No, he wouldn't have been surprised if she'd told him everything that first night. But when she spoke again, there was a hardness to the words he hadn't expected.

"Leave me," she said.

II.

THE LAKE

5.

IT WAS THE finest morning they'd had that year, the streets and the houses and the cars and the trees washed in sunlight, the town's inhabitants dazed with it, every person Max passed on the street a little drunk on this new softness in the air, the sky's wide-open brightness, the ground that gave off the scent, finally, not of rain and sludge and grass seed but of fresh dogwood blossoms and peeling birch. It was a hard morning to be anything but hopeful, he thought, walking up the Auers' driveway. And so he tried to feel hopeful. He hoped that in the two days that had passed since Ana Beidler's arrival, the family he liked most in Utica and the woman he'd brought into that family's home were tolerating each other's company well enough. He tried to be hopeful that he hadn't somehow made a mistake. The Auer family, as fond as he was of them, always seemed to have a coating, a protective layer around it, a distinct barrier between themselves and the rest of the world. This began in the largeness of Abe's person and continued into Irene, who was lovely but also, if one knew her, quietly shrewd. Even their home itself felt like a kind of keep. Max hoped, with increasing worry, that he hadn't picked the wrong place for the refugee and that they wouldn't reject her. But hope, for Max, had always been hard. It took an active and conscious expenditure of mental resources, a suspension of those feelings that came most naturally to him.

It wasn't a particularly grand house and it wasn't a particularly new or expensive house, but it was a definitively, almost insistently, American house, an example, Max thought nearly every time he passed by it or came to dinner, of how much a man could make for himself in this country, if only he worked hard and had a bit of luck and also, maybe most importantly, threw his lot in with a good woman. He studied the Auers' house now as he lurched up the drive, not stalling exactly, with this visit he sensed he should have made the day before and would have had he not been called away by a plumbing crisis at the synagogue.

It was a typical, two-story frame house, the kind of colonial one saw all across the Corn Hill section of Utica, a small white house with a green roof, green shutters, a green door, a wide front porch with a swing and a couple of white rocking chairs and a view onto the street, the goings-on of the neighborhood. When Max imagined, as he occasionally did, what it might be like to have a family of his own, he saw them in such a house, on such a porch, in such a swing. Leading up to it was a walkway of gray paved stones lined by hedges. The hedges were expertly trimmed, never overgrown, curving gently into the front yard in which Irene and Abe had long ago planted a peach tree that now towered almost to the second-story windows and dropped its soft fruit onto the porch every July. The fruit never rotted there or went to waste. Irene swept it up into her apron, ushered it into her kitchen with its white countertops scoured daily, covered in matching canister sets, its drawers full of egg whiskers and potato mashers, a cozy breakfast nook in the corner and coffee percolating beside the stove. It was a house with everything a man could want or ask for, a house with not just the basics a person needed to survive—heat, plumbing, a roof to block out the elements—but all the small comforts that made it a place that drew a person in, invited him back. Max looked up at the Auers' home, at the sun hammering at the windows, the peach tree swaying lightly in the breeze, the white nubs of a dogwood overhanging the porch like little bells. And on the porch, the person who brought it all into being, a beautiful brunette planting flowers in a window box. Abe Auer had come to this country with nothing; now he had all this. Yet still he worried. Max stood a moment, dizzy in the drinkable summer air, trying to make the disjointed ends meet, and then he remembered why he'd come, that it wasn't his job to solve all the human mysteries of the world. He stepped forward, waved hello to Irene Auer.

"How goes it there, Irene? Lovely flowers."

"Yes, aren't they? Like little gems. At least that's how they seem after our winter. By the time June comes around I've forgotten anything can grow. I found these at the market hidden under a bushel of onions. All the others got swept up the moment they were put out. What do you think? I'm trying to draw the eye away from the state of our shutters. This wood here seems to be allergic to paint. It doesn't even look like wood anymore. You think the red ones in front or the yellow?"

He'd known her for as long as he'd known her husband, and every time he saw her he was gripped by the same question that had formed in his mind the first time they met: Why? Why had a woman like this joined with a man like Abe? Why had Abe pursued her and why had she succumbed to his pursuit? She was as smartly dressed as he was slovenly, as meticulous in her words and home and overall demeanor as he was careless. It surely must have been some sort of mutual self-punishment that had brought the two together, which Max supposed wasn't so hard to fathom. Yet each time he saw her, now, for instance, wearing a neat blue dress, her hair tied back with a wisp of a scarf, her lips pulled tight while she arranged the potted flowers in the window boxes with the care of a curator in a gallery, it struck him anew.

The sun formed drops across the petals and over her arms. "I'm partial to yellow, myself," he said, taking off his hat to wipe the sweat from his brow. She nodded as though he'd said something terribly astute. "Well, don't just stand there. Come up."

He climbed the steps and briefly took her hands in his. Her hands were soft, her smile knowing. Ten years ago she was probably still a great beauty. Even now. But the grunt work and worry of domesticity were wearing her down, not to mention her hours volunteering for the National Council of Jewish Women, the local chapter of Hadassah. She was keeping herself afloat, barely. Soon she'd wither. Still, a woman like Irene Auer would wither gracefully. Abe was the one who took every change hard.

"A nice surprise, Max. It's not Tuesday, is it? I thought Bezique was Tuesday. It keeps changing."

"It is Tuesday. I was hoping to have a word with Miss Beidler."

"Ah, our elusive guest."

"Is she so elusive?"

Irene came farther onto the porch, glanced up at what he took to be the guest room's window. "Miss Beidler," she said softly, "is sleeping. Miss Beidler is often sleeping."

"At noon?"

"Yes, I know. A bit peculiar. It seems she sleeps all day. Never at night. I put a tray of food beside her door, and she must open it at some point because an hour later it's empty. But other than that, I haven't seen her. Yesterday she woke around that time, came out of her room, went into town for a few hours to visit the library. Then she joined us for dinner and regaled us with more of her stories of the stage, which I must admit are enchanting. She laughed at comments no one else found funny, pecked at her food, guzzled her wine, and then after dinner she left abruptly and stayed out the remainder of the night."

"A night owl," Max said.

"Is that what they call it?"

"It's quite likely she's thrown off by her ordeal. Insomnia's not so uncommon, really. I've had a bit myself."

She was smiling, not at him but at the flowers in their pots, lifting them out of the soil, dark and damp as coffee grounds, untangling the roots.

"And what do you do, Max, when you have your insomnia?"

"Oh, I don't know. Read, mostly. I read a lot at night. Sometimes I listen to the radio. Sometimes I get up and make myself a sandwich."

"Do you ever leave your house and walk around town all night in your pajamas?"

He looked up at the guest room window, opaque in the afternoon light. "I suppose I don't."

"I'm sure she has her reasons." Irene began to say something else, then stopped.

"We all do," Max offered.

Irene tilted her head to the side slightly. She pressed her lips together in what might have been a smile but could have also been something else, something far more disconcerting.

"How long do you think Miss Beidler will be staying here? I'd been meaning to ask you. Not that I mind having her, of course. But it occurred to me that we never really discussed what happens next, where she'll go, how long she'll be with us. Will she stay in Utica? Move to a city? It seems there must be more work for an actress in the city, more opportunities. And other immigrants. Not to mention the arts. We haven't got much to offer her in that regard. Abe and I went to see that traveling production of *Oklahoma*. The lead actress couldn't carry a tune. I kept wanting to get up and offer her a glass of water. It was like listening to an animal die."

"You and Abe go to the theater a lot?" Max asked.

"Every seven years whether we want to or not. You know Abe. He prefers to take his entertainment alone in his armchair. Crowds make him nervous. And people, generally. But he does enjoy your Tuesday Bezique. How about you, Max? Do you get out much these days?"

"I went to Saratoga the other week."

"Oh, that doesn't count. How are you going to meet a nice girl at the horse races?"

Max then remembered an exchange from the night before with the synagogue's secretary. The girl was thirty, a thin brunette who could type at lightning speed and balance budget ledgers in her head. She'd been breezy and pleasant when they'd first met and he'd pegged her as an amiable spinster, the sort with no real desire for a conventional domestic life. But a few weeks into her employment it became clear to him that she was, in fact, the other sort of spinster, the heartbreaking kind. She came into his office, closed the door behind her, then turned, offering up a tense smile. "Do you like the clarinet, Rabbi Hoffman?"

"The clarinet?"

"Artie Shaw is playing at the Colonial Theatre next Thursday. My brother got me some tickets, and I was thinking maybe . . . "

There must have been something painful-looking in his expression.

"But you probably have better things to do . . . "

He gestured to the office. "I'm still behind. I feel a little underwater, that's all."

She nodded slowly. "I just thought I'd ask."

Irene was still looking at Max, waiting for him to answer. "So how long did you say she'll be staying?" she asked. "Honestly, I wouldn't care if it weren't for Judith's wedding. Girls these days make such a to-do. When Abe and I got married all I wanted was a glass of champagne and a one-way ticket out of my mother's home. Judith, on the other hand, wants to be carried across town on a chariot. It's a lot to pull off."

Max glanced up at the window again, saw a brief flickering of color, a curtain drawn. "Not more than a couple months, I'd guess. Long enough to let her get her bearings. I'd expect to hear more from the agency in New York soon. My assumption is she'll head back that way, that a woman of her disposition would be more at home in the big city. And the synagogue's Hadassah is putting together a fund for her."

Irene nodded, not hiding her relief. She brushed the soil from her hands onto her apron, made a last adjustment to the flowers. "Summer," she said. "You know, on a day like this, I have no complaints. How could anyone be unhappy on such a day?"

"It would take some doing."

A breeze rustled the elm trees and the wisps of hair poking out from her scarf. She reached out and took his hands. "It's good to see you, Max. You should come to dinner again soon."

"I will. I promise. In the meantime, would you tell Miss Beidler I came by? I'd love to talk with her and see how I might help her acclimate once she's settled in a little."

"I'll tell her, Max. You're good to come."

HE RETURNED THE next day, and again, Ana Beidler was sleeping. When he called again the day after that, this time it was later in the afternoon, an hour before dinner, a time when no one was asleep, only alcoholics and the truly deranged, and if she was sleeping he would insist on waking her up to see if she fell into either category. She wasn't asleep, though neither was she home. Irene informed him and then a moment later, he was being commanded to sit down at the table and two lamb chops were being placed before him, though he hadn't planned on staying.

"Really, I can't," he tried, but it was useless.

"You want rice or potatoes or a little of both?" Irene said. Then, before he could answer, "Take a little of both. I made enough for our phantom houseguest."

"Maybe she really is a phantom," Judith said, sitting down across from him, placing a bowl of peas on the table, "a Yiddish ghost holed up in our guest room."

"What sort of a joke is that to make?" said Abe. "Girls your age in Europe aren't worrying about their weddings."

"Calm down," Judith said, turning over her shoulder to her mother. "How do you stand being married to a man who takes everything so seriously?"

"Practice. Years of practice."

"You see what I live with?" Abe said to Max. "The attacks on my character. Tell us what you think, Rabbi. What does the Torah say about cracking jokes about ghosts when the paper has an article every week about more Jews murdered?"

Max held up his hands, "I try not to take sides in domestic disagreements."

"He's polite," Abe said. "He knows I'm right."

Irene sat down at last. "I set aside a plate for our ghost," she said, looking at Abe.

They fell into silence as they began to eat. Halfway through the meal Irene paused, blotted at her mouth with a napkin. "We should talk about this seriously. I've gotten at least eight calls in the last few days from people wanting to come by and welcome her to town, invite her to dinner. Sarah called from Hadassah and Edith from the JCC. Several others. We hear you have a Yiddish actress refugee living in your house, they say. Can we meet her? I don't know what to tell them."

"How do they know she's an actress?" Abe asked.

"Is it a secret?" said Irene. "Was I not supposed to mention it?"

"I don't see any harm," said Max. "It's not as though you're spreading gossip."

"What gossip would I have to spread? I've hardly seen the woman. She hides in her room by day and traipses across town by night. We've barely exchanged 'hello' and 'good-bye,' much less had a proper conversation. That's the point. People are calling and I don't know what to tell them."

Abe looked from Max to Irene. "Why don't you tell them the woman is a human being, not a carnival attraction. Her misfortune does not exist for their entertainment. They'll meet her when they meet her."

"They'll meet her when they meet her," Irene echoed. "As though you own the key to the city. These are our neighbors, Abe. They don't mean any harm. They know she's here and they want to welcome the woman, to make her feel at home. What's wrong with that?"

"She's not *at* home, that's what. She was chased out of her home at gunpoint, remember? Her home no longer exists. She's a refugee in a strange town, a strange country, speaking a strange language."

"I thought her English was quite good," offered Judith.

"And if I were a stranger here," Irene said, "I'd want to be welcomed. I'd want to meet people, make connections. Wouldn't you, Max?"

Max held up his hands, gave Irene a drowning look.

"But you're not a stranger here," said Abe. "And you never have been. *Nu.*"

"I'm still a person. I can imagine what it's like to feel frightened and alone."

"You can imagine feeling that way as yourself, not as a refugee. People are different."

"No one's claiming they're not. All I'm asking is whether or not at some point in the not-so-far-off future, it's fair to expect the woman to be a little less reclusive, a little less mysterious, a little more . . . "

"American?" Abe offered.

"I was going to say gracious," said Irene. "It would be nice to have an actual conversation with her, to find out what her plans are, where she'd like to settle."

"Lots of things would be nice. A good cigar. A nightly foot rub. But I don't expect them."

"I'm not asking the woman to rub my feet. I'm wondering if she might wave hello to the neighbors, say a word to the people who come to meet her. Doesn't she owe us that small courtesy?"

Abe picked up his fork, opened his mouth, then closed it and put the fork down. "I'm sorry, but I disagree. The woman doesn't owe us anything," he said. "For all we know, she's escaped a living hell, endured suffering none of us have experienced. She's our guest now, but she doesn't owe us or anyone else a window into that world. The view belongs to her alone."

No one spoke after that. They finished the meal in a solemn silence that Max took to mean the discussion was closed. He assumed this would be the pattern, Abe defending the woman, Irene demanding information. It was a surprise to him then that after coffee and dessert, Abe approached him as he was leaving the house, walked beside him in the early darkness until they reached the end of the drive. "Listen," he said. "I need you to tell me the number of weeks she'll be here, and I need the number to be small."

He stopped walking. "Is it that bad, Abe? I thought . . . "

"I try to make the best of situations. But the truth is Irene is right. And we've been bickering as a result. You see how it is. Do I need more evenings like this? And believe me, you haven't heard the worst of it. I haven't told you everything about our guest."

"There's more than the insomnia?"

"Much more," Abe said. There was her slovenliness, muddy-soled shoes abandoned under the coffee table in the parlor; pins and barrettes, which Abe could only guess had liberated themselves from her heavy tresses, appearing in the carpet; her feminine garments washed out in the bathtub and never reclaimed, a cold and somewhat disconcerting surprise for the next person inclined to bathe. There were the entrances (tipsy) and exits (unexpected). She rose mid-course during a meal that had taken up the better part of Irene's day in preparation, and wandered forlornly onto the back porch as though she had unpleasant business that needed attending out there. One evening, she'd had her dinner at the oyster bar by the rail station instead and not returned until the bottom of the morning, announcing her arrival in a thick and clumsy mumbled Yiddish. She treated their house not so much as a home but a cheap hotel she'd mistakenly been booked into, and Abe was beginning to wonder if perhaps there had been a mistake, if she was somehow under the impression that this was not a private residence opened to her out of his family's generosity, but an inn of sorts, a way-station, a temporary bed until proper lodgings could be secured.

"I don't think there's been any mistake," Max said. "I think I just need to talk to the woman."

"I'd appreciate it." Irene and Judith's voices drifted toward them from the kitchen window. They were arguing again, about what, Max couldn't say. The sentiment came off more clearly than the words. "You understand. Irene's heart is big but her kitchen's small."

"I understand," Max said.

THE NEXT MORNING he sat at his desk and wrote Ana Beidler a letter, saying he hoped she was settling into town without difficulty, finding everything here she needed. He'd be more than happy to help her in any way that might be useful. Would she come by and see him some afternoon at the synagogue, or if she found the evenings more convenient, at his home? He penned both addresses at the bottom of the page, slid the note into an envelope, slid the envelope beneath the Auers' door the following morning.

In the days that followed, every time there was a knock on his door, he thought it would be her. He waited, but three days passed and she never came. He spotted her one afternoon, boarding a bus downtown. Two days later he thought he saw her stepping into the Boston Store, but he was never close enough to stop her, never bold enough to chase after her or get her attention. A week and a half after her arrival, they still hadn't spoken, which seemed surely to be a failure on his own part, if only he could figure out what he'd done wrong, what he could have done differently.

July arrived, and with it a number of other matters vying for his attention, the usual slog of Bar Mitzvah scheduling and nuptial counseling and fundraising, the demands of the synagogue addition. He was wading through it so intensely that for a few days he was nearly able to put the matter out of mind, and just when he'd begun to do so, the phone rang and it was Shumel Spiro. "How goes it in the provinces? I've been meaning to talk to you for some time but since Field's temple we've been bringing them over by the dozen, it seems like. Sending them to places that don't make Utica look so ridiculous. One Rumanian should be getting off a train soon in Lincoln, Nebraska. I'm tempted to feel sorry for the man."

"You probably shouldn't."

"The refugee. The woman. How is she adjusting to your little hamlet?"

"Oh, fine, fine. Fine, I assume."

"I gather she's doing fine, then. Wonderful."

"Do you think you'll be sending more our way? I've spoken to a few other families."

"It seems unlikely for the time being. But listen, you've been an enormous help to us, to me personally. I can't thank you enough. And I want you to call if there's any trouble at all."

"Have any of the others encountered any trouble?"

"No. Nothing that I'm aware of. But trouble, Max, it doesn't schedule an appointment. If something comes up, you tell me right away."

"Well, there is one small issue. When I said I assumed she was fine. I haven't exactly been able to verify that. She's always out or sleeping when I come by. I've started to wonder if she's hiding from me."

"Don't be silly, Max. Why would she hide from you?"

"I have no idea."

"Max, I can understand if you feel a certain sense of ownership or responsibility for Ana. No one played a bigger part in bringing her to Utica. My people, our group, we know that, under normal circumstances, she is a good and remarkable woman. Dramatic, maybe, but we all carry bits of our work around in our daily lives. That's what this American capitalism does. It makes your work who you are. Ana's work is being dramatic. She's caught on quick. All I want to check on is that she isn't having any sort of allergy to your town or that the weight of what she went through—and this part I want you to think about carefully—isn't causing her any undue grief."

"If I knew, Shmuel."

"I understand. You want to lay eyes on her yourself, make sure all is in place. Don't fret. Tend to your flock. Don't waste your energies racing after this poor woman. Should you happen to encounter her, you can let me know. How does that sound, Max?"

"Fine, I suppose."

"You and me, we're men of action. There's nothing harder for men like us to tolerate than those moments when nothing's required of us. It's another reason I'm calling you, in fact. I wanted to tell you more about our operation here, the Committee for a Jewish Army. It just so happens, you see, that at this particular moment, I'm in desperate need, we're in desperate need, of a rabbi."

"A rabbi?"

"To take on a project for us." There was a clattering in the background, people arguing. "Listen, Max. I'll be brief. I've asked one great favor of you and now I'm asking another. All I can offer now is to say how much this demonstrates the esteem I hold you in. There's a conference coming up in Chicago convened by the American Jewish Council, a gathering of Jewish leaders, organizers, rabbis from all over the country, all of them coming together to discuss the refugee problem, and I want you to attend as our representative. I had hoped to go myself, but

it seems I'm not welcome, not American enough. I was wondering if
you might go as my proxy, report back to me."

"Spy, you mean?"

"Call it what you will, Max. You'd be doing a *mitzvah*. You have
family in Chicago, no?"

"My sister."

"It's perfect then, don't you think?"

"I'm flattered, Shmuel. I am. But I don't think I'm the man you're
looking for."

"Just do me this kindness and consider it, will you? You'd be doing
us at the Committee a great service, not to mention the millions of Jews
still trapped in Europe. If things continue on it may well be thousands
by the time you go."

"I wish I could do it, Shmuel. But the timing . . . I'm behind on
everything."

"Yes, we're all behind, aren't we? That's why we're in this mess.
Thousands are perishing as we speak because we've fallen so terribly
behind."

Max felt a strange déjà vu, a falling back in time to Heidelberg, that
other life. The man hadn't changed at all in the years since Max heard
him speaking before a group of Zionists, riling them up, rallying them
forward. He did what he needed to do, asked what he needed to ask of
people without a tinge of embarrassment, without an iota of fear that
they'd say no or be offended. He wondered what it must be like to live
that way. "Just like that?" Max said. "You say, 'Go to Chicago,' and
I hop on a train."

"I knew you would understand, Max. I knew you were exactly the
man for the job."

"I'll think about it. That's the best I can do."

"I'll take it."

Max hung up the phone, sat at his desk for the next few minutes,
not doing anything but reflecting on what five million people looked

like. How many baseball stadiums of people? Five million seconds was a lifetime. Five million steps to walk around the earth. The phone was ringing again. He assumed it was Spiro calling back, that he'd forgotten something.

"I'm thinking about it," he said into the receiver.

It was a woman's voice that answered. "Could I speak with Max Hoffman, please? This is Ana Beidler."

He picked up a piece of paper on his desk, folded it in two for no reason.

"Miss Beidler. I'm so glad you called. I've been waiting to hear from you."

"Yes," she said. "I've been waiting, too."

6.

HER NAME WAS Sonia. Sonia the beautiful. Sonia the prostitute Abe met and made love to under the bridge on the banks of the Neman nearly thirty years ago. *Make love?* he interrogated. Does a sixteen-year-old boy *make love* to a whore? To her, he did. He doted on her, dreamt about her, hungered for her affection and approval. He stole things for her, brought her flowers and jewelry and perfume and books. Of course, she wasn't only a whore. She was also an intellectual. A member of *Hitahdut*, the Socialist-Zionist Labor Party. "A revolutionary from the waist down," she called herself if anyone asked. This dark figure from his past was who Ana Beidler brought back to his mind. The memory, long buried, coming up to him not in images at first but in sounds, the timbre of her voice. Her breathing heavily in his ear, the distant train, the traffic over the bridge as they made love in the high grass. Sonia. Her favorite customers were older men—journalists, agitators, anarchists, university professors, not sixteen-year-old schoolboys, the bourgeois son of the owner of a cigarette factory. But somehow, the day she met Abe at the market, convinced him to buy her an apple, then ate it in front of him, relishing it, licking the juice off her soft lips, she took pity on him and asked if he'd like to walk her home. He could still remember the sweetness of the apple on her breath, the stickiness on her fingers. They never made it farther than the bridge. He muddied his clothes and bruised his knees on the rocks.

Then he emptied his pockets without the slightest regret. This was how it went. Sometimes he paid her and sometimes he didn't. It depended on her mood, how things went between them on any day.

"I like you, Abe," she used to tell him. "You're a funny boy. Tell me a funny joke and then you can have it for free."

Other times she'd be strict. "Fifteen rubles? You must be joking. That was worth fifty, at least."

"Come on. You know I haven't got that much."

"Meet me tomorrow then and bring some of your mother's jewelry. Your parents are rich, aren't they? She won't miss it."

He protested, but eventually gave in. Regardless of what they did together under the bridge, he thought she was the most beautiful girl he'd ever seen, and not beautiful in the way the girls at school tried to be. Her face was covered with freckles. Her eyelashes and eyebrows were white-blonde. She painted her lips dark red, but he suspected that without this paint, they'd be as pale as her lashes. Her dresses were wrinkled and threadbare but somehow more lovely to him for this quality. She had wide hips and small breasts and a mole on the lower part of her neck, which he liked to kiss. It was not only the way she looked but also the way she smelled and the way she laughed and the way she sat under the bridge while they talked, legs apart, back rounded. She sat like a man, without shyness or modesty. He loved the dirty way she talked, too, the bit of gravel in her voice, and the way she wasn't shy or prickly or stuck up like the other girls he knew. It seemed to him his feelings were, at least a little bit, reciprocated.

"I like you," she told him often. "I do. Even if you are a strange kid."

"What makes me so strange?" he asked.

She thought about it for a moment, then said in a more serious tone of voice than he'd heard her use before, "Most people want to lift themselves up. If they're dirty, they want to make themselves clean. If they're poor, they dream of being rich. If they're ignorant, they want to go to school. But you, you're good and clean and clever and rich enough, and you want to be filthy and low."

He smiled. He had the feeling that no one, not his parents, not his brother, had ever bothered to look at him as closely as she.

"Now," she said, "Tell me some of the fancy things you've learned at school this week."

He began reciting Pushkin's *The Gypsies*, but she interrupted him after a few verses. "That's enough," she said. "Now, want me to teach you something new, something that will serve you well the rest of your life?"

The next day, he brought her a single strand of his mother's pearls.

"They're seeded," he told her while she held them to the light.

"What does that mean?"

"That they're valuable."

She laughed then, at his earnestness, his generosity. When she laughed, he didn't care if he was caught or not. He didn't care about anyone but her. And yet the night he came down from his bedroom unable to sleep, it was not Sonia's ghost he saw in his living room but his brother's, Shayke's, sitting on Irene's ivory sofa, leaning forward and rolling tobacco between his fingers like it was gold leaf. He was exquisitely careful rolling the tobacco and yet he'd never been careful when it came to living his life. He was still wearing his worker's cap, still wearing his muddy boots. If he'd been real, Irene would have had a conniption for the mess it would make, but Abe knew he was not real because he could not perceive him with his other senses. He had no scent and his movements, his shifting on the sofa, leaning forward, sitting back, made no sound. He sat suspended in silence, and Abe knew that this silence was death. He smiled, raised his eyebrows at Abe, who now, at forty-seven, was more than twenty-five years his senior. Of course, it was not Shayke. The arrangement of skin and bone and blood and brain and uncompromising spirit that had been Shayke no longer existed. Abe knew that. He was neither religious, superstitious, nor delusional, and yet there Shayke sat. Leaning back on the sofa, crossing one leg over the other, he lit his cigarette without a lighter or a match. The paper ignited quicker than a lock of hair, an orange spark that flared then shrunk to nothing. He brought the cigarette to his lips, inhaled, then exhaled until the exhalation became a sigh.

"What are you doing here?" Abe said.

Shayke put the cigarette into his mouth and put his hands behind his head, leaning back on the sofa. "I could ask you the same thing."

"I live here," Abe said.

Shayke laughed softly. When the cigarette was gone, he stood up and began looking around, picking up picture frames with photos of Irene and Judith, running his fingers over Irene's crystal ashtrays and porcelain figurines. He walked across the parlor to the piano by the fireplace, pushed a key near the middle, then near the top. It made no sound, or none that Abe could hear.

"Have you ever had this thing tuned?" Shayke asked.

"Why bother? No one ever plays it. Irene wanted Judith to take lessons when she was a kid but the girl would never practice. No patience."

Shayke played another soundless chord. "Do you remember that girl back home, beautiful Sonia? She knew how to play . . . the piano and other things. You used to follow her around."

"Until you took her from me."

"You never forget anything, do you?"

Abe closed his eyes, willing the vision away. But when he opened them his brother remained. "Why are you here, Shayke?"

"I am here and not here—nowhere and everywhere."

"*Drek.*"

"Is this any way to greet your brother? Why are you here? Why have you come?"

"Go back to Grodno then. The living can't get entrance visas; why should the dead?"

Shayke stood slowly. He walked to the china cabinet across the room, picked up a kiddush cup, one of the few objects from their childhood home that Abe still possessed.

"Careful," Abe said.

He tossed the kiddush cup into the air, caught it with the other hand. "You have anything to put in this? I'm dying of thirst. Vodka is what I'd really like. Cold, cold vodka. There was a guard at the camp who slept with a bottle under his bed. He used to call prisoners in and give them little thimblefuls to use as antiseptic in exchange for sex. Now, who's this lovely lady?" He was pointing to a portrait of Judith on the mantle above the fireplace.

"My daughter."

Shayke picked up the picture and held it closer. "So it is, so it is. Look, she has my eyes."

It was true, his dark eyes and his high forehead marked by creases where his stubbornness seemed to reside. Abe had noted the likeness before, and each time, the observation strained something inside him, twisted his guts up until they felt like gnarled roots. He noticed the resemblance and then he had to bury the knowledge of it, cover it over with the more pressing, less painful details of his life.

Shayke returned the portrait to the mantle, looked at Abe and smiled. But there was something amiss with the smile, too much space between his gums and his teeth, between his lips and his chin. His eyes were dark, hollow orbs; they were not for seeing.

"They starved us, the camp guards," he said to Abe, in way of explanation. "But at least they let us smoke. Did you know that smoke is a heavy thing inside an empty body? Even air has weight. Cold air is lighter than warm air. It squeaked inside my chest, made a harp out of my ribs."

"Please, Shayke. Don't tell."

"But you knew already. You knew."

Abe glanced down at his hands, and when he looked up, Shayke had vanished.

"What did you know, Mr. Auer?" Ana said.

It was not Shayke who was sitting on the ivory sofa but Abe himself, and Ana was speaking to him from the doorway. "You were talking in your sleep," she said.

"Was I?"

"I didn't mean to disturb you. I'm only coming in from a walk."

She moved closer, sat down beside him on the sofa, all that dark beauty set against the pale fabric. "What were you dreaming about? Your eyes were closed but you were smiling."

He rubbed his eyes, his forehead. "*Antshuldikt mir.*" Forgive me.

"No need for forgiveness, Mr. Auer. You haven't done anything wrong." She paused. "Do you mind if I join you? It's very late yet somehow I'm still not tired. In fact, there are few things I find more enjoyable than watching another person dream. Or even sleep for that matter. There's satisfaction in watching other people benefit from what I can't do myself."

"You can't sleep?"

"Not at night, no. At least not with any regularity. It's terrible. A curse." She tucked her legs up beneath her the way a child would, removed a cigarette from a black leather case on the coffee table, then snapped closed the small brass latch. "Then again, I have time to read, to think, to walk under the stars." Her fingernails were smooth and red against the white paper. Her hands showed her age more than the rest of her.

"I'm sorry I disturbed you," he answered. "I thought you were upstairs."

"No, I returned from a walk a few minutes ago."

"So late?"

"Yes," she said. "I like to walk at night. You may have noticed. I went to see Max Hoffman today. He was so kind and helpful, and we talked for a long time about my situation. But sometimes after such a talk it's good to be alone, let words settle. The evening got away from me." She was looking at him more closely than she had before. "Would you like to sit with me a while?"

He nodded. "Can I get you something first?"

"A bit of company is all. Maybe a few drops of whatever you're drinking."

He looked at the coffee table before him, noticed the half-empty glass. He'd poured himself some vodka when he'd first come downstairs, which explained the bitterness on his tongue. He started to rise, but she stopped him with a motion of her hand, stood and walked to the liquor cabinet. Her feet made no sound against the floorboards. He listened to the clink of ice on glass, the liquor pouring.

When she returned, he said, "I've been meaning to ask you if you're finding everything you need here? Settling in."

"Settling?" And there was something strange about the way she said the word. She said it the way Irene or Judith said it, so smoothly, swallowing the "l." Was she mocking them? Or was he imagining? "Yes. I suppose I am. Your wife is so lovely, so gracious. She made me an omelet yesterday with little bits of onion in it and yellow cheese. She showed me how to use the iron. She's the sort of wife every man I've ever known has yearned for."

"You should tell her so. She doesn't get the compliments she deserves from me."

She turned her head and smiled, not at him, but at some private thought. "You've been married a long time, haven't you? Sweet words are for the young . . . or the stage."

"Twenty-one years we've been married."

"That is very long. Did you meet in Utica?"

"When I arrived, I lived on the Lower East Side. I got off the boat, moved in with my uncle who owned a butcher shop on 9th Street. I was supposed to work for him there, but I couldn't stand the sight of all that blood, so I found something else to do, something equally glamorous. I started picking rags under the elevated, selling them to sweatshops."

She shrugged. "You survived. That's nothing to be ashamed of."

"After a year or so, I moved up in the world, found work assisting one of the tailors. His store was on the bottom floor of a six-flat. Irene lived with her parents on the second floor. She was born in the Bronx. A real American. For months, we didn't do more than nod at each other in the vestibule. I was too embarrassed of my accent to say 'hello.' But one day, I noticed as she was hurrying past that she had a button hanging loose from her coat. I chased her up the stairs with a thread and needle. We married a few months later, but we were both so fed up with the city by then. She had family in Gloversville. We moved there, then here."

He'd told this story a dozen times, or heard Irene tell it, yet never in the telling had a listener seemed to savor every word, every sentence. As he spoke, her eyes opened wide, her mouth resisted, then succumbed to a smile, her expression shifting gradually as the memory progressed, her whole body leaning forward as though to say, yes, yes, go on.

"That's quite a love story," she said when he was through. "An American love story. And I must admit I'm a little jealous. No one has ever chased after me with a needle and thread."

"It was more fumbling than chasing." He began to say more but stopped. There was still an inch of vodka in his glass. He swirled it, then drank, then, for a moment, he let himself do nothing but watch her. Irene and Judith were right. Something didn't fit, though he couldn't say what or why. Europe and all of its misery hung on her loosely like old clothes. She had the grayness beneath her eyes, the exhausted, crumpled posture, but not the sallowness or frailty, not the dead gaze or broken teeth. When she smiled, her face seemed to contain all the light of the universe concentrated, condensed. Such smiles weren't possible in European soil, not for a Jew. But then, before his eyes, the smile faded and there was that familiar blankness and anguish he remembered, though he'd tried to forget. Now, she was neither smiling nor frowning but occupying an in-between place.

She shivered slightly, then let out a long, soft sigh, blinking slowly, bringing the cigarette to her lips in a careful movement, returning his gaze as she exhaled. He didn't look away as he normally did or hurry on to more small talk. The room was quiet, dark, only a sliver of moonlight from the window. The cover of darkness set him at ease, emboldened him. It shifted something in the air between them, allowed for this unabashed looking. She must have felt it, too, because she leaned forward and said, "I feel so comfortable with you, Abe. I can't tell you what a relief it is, to be here with you and not an American."

He snorted. "I'm not an American?"

"Of course you're not. You've been here quite some time, I know. And you have an American wife, an American daughter, an American home, but this country, it's not in your blood and never will be. I can see it so clearly. I could see it the moment you greeted me at the train. Is it not clear to you?"

He hesitated. "No . . . I don't know. I don't talk about my life before I came here."

"Of course you don't. That's exactly what I mean. You're like me. You left a part of yourself when you came here."

He waved it away.

"You think I'm wrong?"

"I think you overestimate me. I'm not as complicated as that. *Ikh bin stam a yid*. I'm a simple man."

Her eyes pressed into him, penetrating. "Very well," she said. "I'll take you at your word."

Neither spoke for a moment. Abe sipped his vodka, thinking that in a moment, she'd yawn, announce that she'd grown tired and stand to take her leave. Instead, she waited until he set his glass down on the table, then said, "May I tell you a secret? May I tell you why I go for my walks so late at night? Would you like to know?"

"I'm glad to listen, but only if you—"

"Please. No more politesse. It's too late for manners. It's an easy question, really. You want to know or you don't. Yes or no?"

He waited a moment. "Yes."

"There are two reasons, and one has nothing to do with the other. The first reason is superstition. I believe that if the police come for me, it will be at night. I have no facts or reasons other than my intuition. But intuition can exert a great force."

"But who would come for you here? There's no Gestapo in Utica. You're safe with us."

She didn't respond to this at first, just stared at him, weighing his words, tapping her feet against the carpet. "Yes," she said at last. "My mind knows this, or a part of my mind does, but there's another part."

He began to speak, but she stopped him. "I know what you're going to say, that I'm here, in this world and not in the other, and I know that means that I'm safe. But sometimes, I get confused. I forget things. The worlds blur together. I hear a loud noise in the night, and for a moment, I'm back in our flat in Warsaw, terrified, preparing to flee. So I do the only thing I can do. I leave my bed and I leave your lovely home and I go for long, aimless walks through town."

"I understand," he said.

"But there's another reason, and this one is harder to explain. You see, I'm visited by my husband at night. We walk side-by-side, the two of us. We go downtown to city hall, to the train station and the park. If I lose my way in the dark, he tells me whether to turn left or right, just like in our life together in Warsaw."

"Will he be joining you here one day?"

"No," she said. "I don't think so. I'm afraid I won't ever see him again, or any of those I left. I haven't heard word in almost a year. He worked with the Resistance. He's probably dead by now. I try to think sometimes what I must have been doing at the moment a bullet pierced him." She drank. "It's strange, the things I think about. My mind wanders, won't hold still."

Abe slid his empty glass across the table. The wet rings rolled across the wood, and he wiped them with his sleeve. There was a calmness to the quiet between them. He was afraid to disturb or disrupt it. After a few minutes passed, he responded as simply as he could. "I'm sorry," he said. "I'm sorry for your misfortune."

"But I don't want your condolences. I want to know what you think of my reasons for wandering the streets of Utica at night. And before you answer, let me be clear. When I say I walk with my husband, I do not mean that I feel his presence as I walk, or that I feel close to him or my memories of him. I mean he is there beside me, talking to me, conversing. I perceive him with all of my senses as clearly as I perceive you right at this moment. Now, tell me, am I crazy?"

"Many people see those who are gone, who are missed. Husbands, brothers. Some might feel it's a comfort." He shrugged. "You've been through a horrible ordeal. I suppose it's possible that—"

"Many things are possible. But what is true?"

He raised his hand to his mouth, covered the stubble of his chin for a moment while he looked at her. "Let me ask you this: Do you like seeing your husband on these walks? Do you enjoy his company?"

"Of course I do. He was the love of my life."

"In that case, I don't think it matters whether you're crazy or not. I'll take comfort over sanity any day. In fact, now that I think of it, a person would have to be a little crazy to stay sane in this world. To hell with sanity, I say."

She didn't react at first. She held her face in perfect stillness, perfect composure, so coolly and without a trace of any humor or warmth that he thought perhaps he'd offended her. But just as he was about to say more, her mouth widened into an enormous smile, the butterfly smile he'd seen that first evening. Then it retreated as quickly as it appeared. Her eyes softened. A tinge of color rose to her cheeks. "Thank you, Mr. Auer. That's very kind of you. I think perhaps you're one of the few people in the world who understands."

She looked as though she was going to stand up, but instead she leaned forward and said, "Will you do something else for me, Abe? Will you tell me a story? A pleasant one. I don't feel quite ready to sleep yet. This is another problem we creatures of the theater contend with. It's a nocturnal existence that's not so easy to reverse. But here we are with our vodka. It's a summer night. Your family is sleeping. We have our health and good company and the moon in the window. Instead of the usual pleasantries, why don't you tell me your fondest memory of your life back there? After all, you're not so different from me. We're both strangers here."

He waved it away.

"I'd love to hear it. I would."

"I can't remember anything from before last week. Probably, I breathe in too many fumes at the junkyard."

"So many excuses. I can't accept them."

He closed his eyes. He knew he had them. But what was the point of recalling pleasant things forever passed? "It's been too long," he said. "I left when I was seventeen and I've spent the last twenty-six years not thinking about it."

"And yet you do remember some things. I can see it. My father used to say to me when I couldn't sleep at night, 'Imagine summer. Imagine the sea.' What do you imagine about that old life that wasn't dreadful?"

She leaned closer, and he became conscious not just of her body but of its proximity to his own, the narrow space between their knees, their arms.

"All right," he said. "There's one thing. I was twelve. It was one of the nights the Cossacks visited our village. I don't know why, but that was what we called it when they came. Visits. A bomb had been set off in the neighboring town during a welcome parade for the czar, and so they came searching for anarchists or any Jew they thought might be making trouble. They didn't make any distinction between the two.

My older brother Shayke was gone, attending one of his socialist youth meetings. My sister, Lorka, she was only twelve; she'd had a friend playing at our house. I can't remember the girl's name, but she was very small and had bright red hair. I liked her. She was a smart, sweet kid. Sometimes I'd help her with her Russian, and when she came to see my sister, she'd bring me these wonderful Turkish apricots—I never learned where she got them. Maybe she had a relative in Palestine. Each year a few more Jews from our town would leave. Palestine or America. . . . That was the big divide. She'd walk up to me so shyly and ask me to hold out my hands, and when I held them out to her, she'd place a couple apricots wrapped in tissue paper in them and then run away, giggling."

"It sounds like she was in love with you."

"No. She was just a girl. So small. Small for her age. And a bit sickly. She had tuberculosis at one point and she was still frail. She was at my family's house on this night the Cossacks came. Her father was sick—everyone was sick with something, it seemed, and she pleaded to go home after dinner, but of course it was out of the question. Too dangerous for her to go alone, too dangerous for anyone to go with her."

"So she spent the night with you?"

"No. My parents thought she would have to, but I had an idea. We lived on the top floor of a house with three families in it, and often, when I wanted to be alone, I'd sit on the roof. From there I could look at the stars, see the lights of the town. The houses were all very close together, so I walked her all the way home along the rooftops, hopping from one building to the next. It was a summer night—so still. We could see the Cossacks going from house to house below, but to them we were invisible."

He leaned back on the sofa. That was over thirty years ago, yet he still remembered the elation of the night, his taking the lead and not Shayke, the confidence he'd had as he'd ushered this child to safety above the purple hue of the streetlights, below the clouds that seemed in the moonlight to glow from within, the excitement of protecting something precious, and of his impending adulthood, which at the time he mistook for freedom. Most of all, he remembered how unafraid he'd been.

"That's a lovely story," she said. "A story with a hero is the best kind. There aren't enough of them these days."

"I'm glad you liked it."

She placed another cigarette between her lips. At first her lighter only spat a few sparks into the air. Then it ignited, and she drew in deeply. "Will you tell me another story?" she asked.

"I can't. That's the only one I have."

"How can that be?"

"It's the truth. And besides, it's your turn now to tell me a story. Isn't that the way it works?"

She leaned forward, balanced her cigarette on the ashtray. "The way what works?"

He pointed to her and then to himself. "This. What we're doing. Conversation. I tell you something. You tell me something. Back and forth. It's more interesting that way."

"And what is it you'd like me to tell you?"

Who are you? he thought, but said instead, "What will you do now? With your life? You won't stay in Utica. There's nothing here for a woman like you."

She leaned back, her eyes gleaming. "Let's not think about the future now. The truth is, it's the future that frightens me more than the past, more than these ghosts. Let's agree to meet here tomorrow and talk again of everything but the future. Midnight. We'll meet downstairs after everyone is sleeping, and you'll come with me on one of my walks, and together we'll reenact that wonderful story of the rooftop escape, the two of us. It will be the moonlit tour of Utica I haven't had. A tour with a story behind it. The Cossacks are all around. We don't know if this city will be here tomorrow, or if we will. But I am an alluring young maiden, sweet and vulnerable and all those things men find so irresistible, and you are determined to see me home, safe across the city, rooftop by rooftop."

He snorted.

"You think I'm joking? I'm serious."

"It's a truly interesting proposal, but no."

"Why not?" she asked.

"It would feel disrespectful, for one. People were dragged off to prison that day."

"It will be in their honor. They'll be our audience. Their spirits will spur us forward. Don't you think the dead want to be entertained as much as anyone? What's your next excuse?"

"Irene and Judith. There are a few other people living in this house, if you haven't noticed. We'll wake them."

"They'll turn over and fall back asleep."

"If they don't, and see us both gone, what would they think? Besides, you already have a companion for your nighttime strolls, don't you? If I come along, won't I scare off your husband?"

Her face, which had been so happy only a moment ago, hardened. "Didn't I tell you?" she said. "We had a terrible argument the other evening. I have no wish to see him right now."

"I didn't know ghosts could argue," Abe said.

"Why should it be different in death than it was in life?" She rose, carried her empty glass toward the kitchen.

"Ana," he called out to her, though he had nothing to add, nothing to ask. He'd simply wanted to speak her name.

From the doorway, she looked at him over her shoulder. "Tomorrow," she said.

7.

SOMEWHERE IN PENNSYLVANIA, the train carrying Max Hoffman from Utica to Chicago killed a man. One minute they were barreling along, chasing the low-slung sun southwest across the dairy farms and prairie grass, past splintered, wind-burnt barns and slow-going trucks hauling hay or displaced migrants below the summer sky; the next minute, the train was breaking sharply, metal grinding metal, until it stopped without a station or city in sight.

The passengers seemed more wearied than disturbed by the incident. Across from Max sat a wide-waisted man in a brown coat—a retailer or factory foreman or grocer; he could easily have been one of Max's congregants. Next to the man sat a thin woman with a pinched nose and nervous eyes, and across the aisle from the pair sat a few more men in suits and a well-heeled family who looked as though they'd been squeezed out of first class. They all sat in silence. Eventually a gaunt conductor walked through the carriage, asking for patience, adding under his breath, "You'd think these folks in Pennsylvania might learn how to put a pistol in their mouths." Half an hour later they were moving again, the unseen suicide sinking into the farmland behind them while through the wide panes of glass the sunlight turned brass and the factories outside Philadelphia rose up like medieval cities unto themselves.

Max shook himself free from his own thoughts, noticed that the passenger across the aisle, a heavy man with the thin wife, seemed bothered by the return to silence. "A shame," he said. "Doesn't happen as much as it used to. I've been riding this route twice a year since '32. Used to be as many jumpers as stops. What do you think it feels like, to step in front of a train?"

"Carl," the woman said. "You're being morbid."

"It's a long trip. Longer when we have to stop to scrape someone off the tracks."

"So read the paper like everyone else. Smoke a cigarette. Take a nap."

"I beg your pardon, but I prefer to talk now and then, not sit in holy silence like some monk. It passes the time." He turned to Max. "You don't mind, do you?"

Max gave something between a shrug and a shake of the head.

"See, he doesn't mind."

"Or he's too polite to say so."

"Eh," the man said, waving the suggestion away. "Is it so perverse to wonder what compels a man to step in front of a speeding train? I mean, I've seen some miserable human beings in my time, but they still stayed clear of the tracks. What does a fellow have to be feeling to actually jump?"

Max had the strange sensation of restarting a conversation that had been going on sporadically for years. What was it like, Max wondered, to take this wish for nothingness and make it real, to take the step, to make one's last act on earth a negation? He pondered the question often, usually in a moment of personal darkness, turned over possible answers, whittled them into abstractions and waited for the updraft that would cause his mood to rise.

Plenty of people, he thought, at one point or another, stared the question down—desperation or rage or a feeling that, somehow, the world would be a better place with one less person in it, that it was at least as meaningful to die as to live. They experienced, essentially, exactly what he did. But how did some of them miss or avoid or fend off the upward movement, remain in the depths for so long that action became possible? Max refused to be theological in his thinking. These were questions strictly for the earth.

"People just feel sorry for themselves," the wife said. "I'm sorry, but that's all it is."

"You're a cold woman, Helen."

"Clear-sighted," she corrected. "People shouldn't be coddled. All over the world men and women are dying, sick as can be, killed in wars, in accidents, in tragedies. And then some folks have a perfectly good life and throw it away. For what?"

The husband had no answer. He turned back to the other passengers. "I'll tell you the other thing that's strange," he said. "If we were walking down the street and someone stepped in front of a bus, every one of us, everyone who saw or heard what had happened, would be shaking, cursing, wailing, puking, hugging each other. Maybe some would say Kaddish or cross themselves or give a look to the sky. But because we're on a train, and there are three inches of steel between us and the poor schmuck out there on the tracks, we all sit around drinking coffee or napping or reading *Look* while they clean up the bits and pieces. We act like nothing happened."

"You want to say Kaddish, say Kaddish," said the woman.

The man lit a cigarette instead.

"What can we do? Will fussing and weeping bring the poor soul back to life?"

No one answered.

"And even if it did," she continued, "who's to say he wouldn't try again? Some people don't know how to live."

Max sat across the aisle, listening to his fellow passengers' musings and trying to understand, not just accept but really understand, human beings' general lack of compassion for one another. These people beside him, these regular just-riding-on-a-train people, the way they talked astounded him, like it was nothing, like a suicide was a thing to be joked about and bantered over, like they were discussing a picture they'd seen or the outcome of a baseball game. His sister and father had always called him *sensitive*. Sensitive beyond reason was the implication. Emotional. Soft. And maybe they were right. But was this a weakness? Since he'd begun working as a rabbi, he'd seen the consequences day after day of people's lack of feeling to each other, the consequences of selfishness and cynicism and a dearth of understanding. Parents chastised and humiliated their children. Children scorned and disrespected their parents. Men slept with other men's wives. Women despised their husbands. And in all of these instances when he'd tried to help his congregants untangle the messes they'd made over the years, the thing he learned that he wanted to say but never could bring himself to actually convey, whether through weakness or mislaid politeness or a belief far into his core that said it was futile, was that all of this breast-clutching and hand-wringing and investment into one's own woe added up to absolutely nothing. An utter nullity. A turning of the back on the world. "For My thoughts are not your thoughts, neither are your ways My ways," as Isaiah had the Lord putting it, but that wasn't an invitation to act like garbage, or to cry blindness as a defense. Here he wasn't above thinking rabbinically. This was the business of souls. You had to pull away from yourself and into the world. It was only when you set aside the slings and arrows of your own experience that emptiness began to recede and that something else might be allowed in.

They're a mystery to me. That was how Ana Beidler had said it to Max, in a quiet park in Utica, the moment when Max realized he would have to board this train. That was the refugee's view of the world he lived in. A mystery.

The day he'd met with her, he'd arrived early at the restaurant on the top floor of the Boston Store, found a seat at a small round table. He sat alone, drinking weak coffee, cup after cup. The diners around him all seemed to know each other, or to be a part of a single cast. Their chatter reminded him of seagulls, a littered beach, the bleachers of a ball game. They crowded into the other small round tables, ordered their coffee and egg salad sandwiches and pie, ate, paid at the till, and still he sat and waited, alone. He wondered if she'd really come. There was a large ceiling fan directly above the place he sat, inlaid in a domed, plaster roof. It spun slowly, stirred the air without cooling it. A waitress with a large bosom kept writing different types of pie on the chalkboard above the entrance to the kitchen, standing on tiptoes to erase. Blueberry became lemon meringue; lemon meringue became peach. Her fingers were yellow from the chalk. The waitress's hair was two-toned, platinum with an inch of brown. She was flirting with the cook, whose face he couldn't see. There were two young mothers at the table beside him. One chided a boy and pushed a buggy with one hand, back and forth. The other blotted lipstick from the corners of her mouth. The boy was making funny faces at Max. He folded his napkin into a paper plane and launched it toward his table. The mother looked up from her buggy then back at her friend. This was what he'd wanted when he left New York. All around him life was pleasant, easy and full. And it made no difference, it made him no less out of place. There was an exceptionality to his loneliness. It followed him wherever he went. It was a raft tailored to his exact proportions that both guided and contained him.

He drank the dregs of his coffee, picked a bit of grounds from his tongue, and when he looked up, a woman stood before him, a woman he almost didn't recognize as the displaced person he'd met that night at the Auers'. Gone were the elaborate plaits in her hair, gone was the heavy makeup and costume jewels. It was almost as if she'd gone back to Europe and fled yet again. In place of the velvet dress she'd worn that evening, the woman before him wore a simple gray skirt and blouse. She stood very still, arms at her side, as though her main concern was that she not take up too much space. She didn't smile exactly when she saw him. It was more like a loosening of her frown. She walked toward him slowly, as though she were afraid. It was so strange—she was now the refugee he'd been expecting that first evening, the one who had never shown up.

"Miss Beidler," he said, standing as she approached the table. "I'm so glad you came. Will you have a seat? Order something to eat. The tomato soup is delicious."

"Tomato soup?"

"Or . . . anything you like. Have you eaten lunch?"

She sat down, unfolded her napkin delicately, opened the menu with care. When the girl came to see what they wanted, Ana began what seemed more a monologue than a lunch order. She'd like to try this here, she said, pointing, this tuna melt. She didn't know what it was but she'd like to try it. It sounded wonderful. She hadn't realized one could melt a fish. And could she also have a bowl of soup? A Coca-Cola. Also, the French-fried potatoes. And after that, a hot-fudge sundae.

"Hungry?" Hoffman said, smiling. "The Auers have been feeding you, haven't they?"

"Oh, of course, of course. Mrs. Auer is a wonderful cook. But this American food—I don't understand how or why, but the more I eat of it, the more I want to eat. It's not like food in Poland," she said, then added, "what we could get of it."

"I'm sure it's not," he said, remembering now that it was Poland she'd fled, not Germany. Her accent seemed to fall someplace in between. He couldn't quite pin it down. At some point, in the great redrawing of borders and flushing of bodies that constantly took place in what once was Austro-Hungary, she had probably lived in many different countries without ever even moving.

"How is everything going there?" he asked.

She nodded and smiled.

"I feel awfully bad that it's taken us so long to meet. You're not the easiest woman to track down, Miss Beidler."

"I know. I am sorry," she said. "I try to keep myself busy, even in a new place. Too much idle time and my mind gets away from me. You understand, don't you?"

"Of course."

"I sense it is the same with you."

"I've never thought of it that way, exactly. But I suppose it's true."

He knew the food was arriving by her smile. The girl placed the dishes between them. The sundae was farthest from Ana but she reached for it first, dipping her spoon tentatively into the pile of whipped cream, pushing aside the cherry the way a child might, then tasting slowly, savoring, her face melting with the sweetness. "Wonderful, wonderful, wonderful," she said.

He laughed. There was a childishness to her that had been absent that first night, an innocence and timid curiosity.

"You're looking at me strangely," she said. "Am I doing something wrong?"

He hesitated, then smiled. "It seems we've come a long way since that first night off the train."

She looked down at her food. "I wasn't myself that evening. I'm sorry. I find myself thinking about this again and again. To be here . . . I feel like once every third or fourth day I am reborn. I wake up and I am new. I apologize but I do not mean this in a way that's in every sense good. Of course, you know what must happen first in order to be reborn."

Max gave her a solemn nod he had practiced many times.

She tapped her fork lightly on the table. "To be here," she said again. "Wherever I went, people shared daydreams about this precise sort of moment. Of proud, big-bellied America and being in it. But none of us knew . . . none of us understood any longer what it means to belong to a place. Do you understand? Once we were evicted, we were no longer German or Polish or Austrian. Our country was an unreal place. I heard stories of exit visas being stamped with *Traumland* as the destination."

"Dream land," said Max.

"It most likely never happened, it is simply a joke that people on a ship could laugh at. But now I am not on a ship and find it makes much more sense than I would like it to."

"And yet it's entirely logical," said Max. "You have probably seen things that defy our ideas of what should make sense. Everything is distorted. Nothing looks right."

She tapped the fork again, looking at the table. "I would . . . " She paused and her face grew taut. She gave a small shake of the head and took a bite of sundae, no longer bothering to go on.

"I don't mean to probe," said Max. "I can only imagine what you've been through, what it must have been like, and now, having to start over. That's why I wanted to see you, to let you know that the synagogue, and, well, me in particular, that I'm here to help. I want to help you in any way I might."

She moved from the sundae to the sandwich, the sandwich to the soup, back and forth without any logical progression. Then all at once, she put down her fork and spoon and looked at Hoffman intently.

"Of course you do, Max," she said. It was the first time she'd used his name. The sound of it caught him.

"Why of course?"

"Because that's what you do, isn't it? You try to help. You're not like the others, are you?"

"What others?"

She raised her hands, gestured toward the diners in the cafe, the crowds of shoppers moving past and around it. "These others," she said. "All these people living their small and pleasant and meaningless lives. Eating their tomato soup and their ice cream and thinking that because they have food in their stomachs and fancy clothes and enough money to go to the movies, that all is well with the world, not feeling the need to do anything bigger. I watch them sometimes, and I can't understand it. They're a mystery to me. They frighten me." She seemed to grow pale. She pushed away her food, raised her hand to her face.

"Miss Beidler, are you feeling ill?"

"The noise," she said. "The lights. Sometimes it's too much for me." He looked around and for a moment he could see and hear it as she must have: a shrill and swirling force, cyclonic, unrelenting, a storm of voices and lights.

"Come with me," he said. He put money down onto the table without waiting for a check, helped her to her feet. She leaned into him as they made their way toward the exit, past the glass cases of silver trinkets and silk scarves, past the counters of cosmetics, fat men buying gifts for their wives and the shop girls lording over their bottles of perfume.

They found a patch of grass near a bench on the edge of the park, a shaded spot next to a small pond where lily pads, green and wide and oily, floated on top of the dark water. There were ducks drifting toward them, the sound of children playing in the distance, a willow tree with a couple beneath it, stealing moments. See, he wanted to say, there are good things about this place. Good and tranquil things. You can find safety here. He didn't say any of this out loud but he could sense that she was relaxing.

"This is better, isn't it?" she said.

"Much. I never cared for crowded restaurants, either, to tell you the truth."

"They used to be my livelihood, large crowds. I depended on them as an actress. They never used to bother me when I was on stage, when everyone was watching, waiting for a misstep, when it would have made sense to be bothered. No, then, I loved them, the sea of faces. In fact I sometimes feel as though they were what was keeping me afloat, lifting me up into the role, carrying me through the show."

She looked off in the direction of the playing children.

"Of late I have come to feel that whenever I am around more than just a few people, four or five, that I am an intruder or an imposter. And this is something people can see. They know what I am."

"This is a decent place, Ana. It's not without its faults but I can assure you that most people here are happy that we've helped someone in a situation like yours."

"Are they? Just before I arrived I read about a synagogue in New York, burned to cinders. There is a place, Washington Heights, they knocked out the windows, painted unspeakable things on the walls. Jewish children beaten up on the streets. Jewish children beaten in Munich, Jewish children beaten in Lodz, Jewish children beaten in Manhattan."

"These are terrible acts, but they are isolated. And they are far from Utica. And what you have to remember is that when synagogues catch fire in this country, we put them out."

"For now you do. In Warsaw, Jews speak of the Americans coming to save them, all two million of them, as though it were inevitable. It is the *Traumland*. But they are not going to be saved, Max. There is no help for them, for us. The Jews of this country are so lucky, so protected. Nothing happening in Europe is real to them. I see that, even with the Auers. The ones who knew violence before they came here. The ones who saw the putsches and pogroms. America has washed the memory from them. Things they learned with their blood and bones are not real to them any longer. Europe is your *Alptraumland*, Max."

He tried reading her face to see if she had meant it as an insult, for that was how Max took it. There was no way she could know, no way she could know that Max, sensitive as a burn, would take having Europe called "Nightmare Land" as an affront. It implied he did not understand enough to be anguished. It presumed that he did not scour the JTA, the American papers, even the BBC by shortwave radio, for every tiny scrap of information that could escape that place, which *was* a nightmare but not one he ignored or wrote off or could even sleep through. She was simply making her own observations. Life with the Auers probably could suggest a certain historical amnesia had set in. But that wasn't him. He hadn't fled the Pale as Abe had, he couldn't claim that, and lacking that common currency that Abe and Ana shared, he couldn't contradict her, not in that moment.

He stood, brushed the dirt and twigs from his pants, took a deep breath of the grassy air.

"Did you have a copy of Halmoli's *Solution of Dreams?*" he said.

"I am sorry, what?"

"The dream book?" He looked down at her. She held her knees to her chest and watched the pond.

"I know it was once quite popular, almost a household item for my classmates' parents in Heidelberg. In Yiddish, of course. Your family didn't keep a copy?"

"No."

"I'm sorry. I thought it might have been familiar. It held all of the Talmudic interpretations of dreams, if I may reuse a phrase from one of our more psychoanalytically oriented coreligionists. If you had dreams of a tree outside your house with dead cats hanging from the branches, for instance, it might tell you that the Berakot of the third century suggests that there are wild dogs loose in your neighborhood and you would be well-served to be rid of them."

"My family were not superstitious people," she said after a moment. Something about the question had upset her.

"I don't mean to stir up difficult memories. The only reason I mention it is that you keep talking about dreams and nightmares and, forgive the example, these things don't exist as specters alone. There are ways of making life out of them."

He extended a hand down to her.

"You yourself," he went on, "you got to *Traumland.*"

He felt her hand in his, her grip surprisingly strong.

They walked through the park at a distance where they might have been mistaken for a bickering husband and wife. The daylight was failing, larks were taking to the sky in curling formations.

"There are people," Max said to her back, "there are people who want to act."

"Who? Tell me," she said without turning around.

"Well, Shmuel Spiro, for one."

She stopped. Her shoulders slumped.

"Shmuel Spiro. I cannot speak ill of a man who is responsible for my safety but if he believes he can do for all Jews what he did for me . . . "

"He seems to be trying. He seems to think if he can get people's attention, wake them . . . "

He thought she was crying at first, but when he looked, she was laughing, an almost girlish giggle. "Wake them? From their coma? One little Palestinian Jew and his dozen followers, half of them washed-up Hollywood actors or crooked politicians or charlatans or thugs." The laughter took hold of her. She stopped walking, put her hand to her face to stem the sound. "I'm sorry. It's funny."

"I'm glad my optimism is so amusing."

She shook her head as though to say, no, he shouldn't take offense. But she was still smiling, a weary, patient smile.

"It's touching," she said. "It makes me like you even more than I did a few minutes ago. But Max, my dear Max. The people here, the Jews in charge here, the *machers* in their fancy suits and fancy cars, they hate Shmuel Spiro almost as much as they hate Hitler. Don't you know that? They find him crass, uncivilized, shrill, a political outcast, coming from where he does. They think he's a fascist, a Jewish terrorist. They won't listen to him, Max. They certainly won't help him. And without help, without a foot inside that world of money and influence, what is he—one crazy Palestinian Jew with a funny mustache, shouting from the rooftops, 'The world is on fire, the world is on fire!' Who will believe what one man from across the sea has to say?"

"I believe him." He didn't know it until he said it. It was in speaking that the feeling was made real.

She noticed the change in him, a sudden charge in the air that hadn't been there a moment before. She leaned closer. Her smile softened. And then she did something he wasn't expecting, something that so surprised him that for a brief moment he lost his bearings, forgot exactly how or why he'd come to walk beside this pond with a refugee actress. He spoke the words, and a moment later, she reached out and took his hand in her own, kindly, almost sisterly. "Of course you do," she said. "Of course you believe in him. You believe in him because you're not like the others, are you, Max? The other Americans in charge. You're different. You've always been different. It's the most important thing about you. We've only just met, but I can see it so clearly. I see how you're better."

He shook his head, felt a warmth rising in his neck. It had been so long since someone had spoken to him with such intensity and certainty and depth of feeling, spoken as though she knew who and what he was at his essence, beneath all the bells and ribbons and good intentions. What made her think she could get away with it, speaking as though she already knew him? *You're different, Max. You've always been different. It's the most important thing about you.* It was nonsense talk, the talk of an unmoored woman, a woman untethered, floating between worlds. He tried to shake free of it, to keep his head clear, his feet grounded, but found he could not. Her words cast a spell on him. That was how he'd think of it later. She cast a spell with her voice, a voice both foreign and familiar, a voice that stayed with him all that day, into the next morning. It was still with him when he called Spiro back and told him that yes, he would do what needed to be done for him, for his Committee for a Jewish Army. He would go to this rescue conference in Chicago.

8.

FOR AN HOUR Abe feigned sleep, lying beside his wife, who really was asleep, out like a light, as they say. Her body had a soft and indeterminate presence, like someone had left a pile of blankets on the bed. He eased himself away from her in tiny movements. When he wasn't inching toward the edge of the bed he held himself stiff, trying to imagine the way a sleeping body was supposed to look. But his eyes were open. They took in strange bits of light through the window, the unfamiliar shadows that occupied the room when he wasn't usually looking. At 11:45, Abe pulled himself up and stood trembling in front of his dresser. He pulled his trousers on and buttoned his shirt in the dark. The buttons had a strange and heavy texture. In his fingers they were like bolts. He could hear Irene breathing across the room. If she woke, what would he tell her?

"Abe?" she said. "*Vos tustu?* What are you doing?"

"Nothing. Go back to sleep."

"Everything all right?"

"Fine, fine." He stood very still, hoping she wouldn't sit up and see him in his clothes. "A little hungry."

She mumbled something, turned onto her side.

He waited until her breath slowed again, then he walked softly out of the room, closing the door behind him. Down the stairs. Stopping at the bottom. Like an idiot, searching for something in his own house.

Seeing only the furniture's bleary outlines, the moonlight on the walls, then, in the far corner, two long slashes of white, crossed at the ankles, a curl of smoke.

"You came," she said. She spoke like she was acknowledging the inevitable, without surprise, without doubt.

He opened his mouth to speak but stopped, then moved himself across the room in small, boyish steps that made him feel ridiculous, away from the stairs, and even when he reached her, could make out the entirety of her shape, could only speak in a something just beyond a whisper.

"It sounded nice to me, an evening walk." She did something with her eyes he couldn't decipher in the dark. "Fresh air," he went on. "Summer won't last forever."

"It's true," she said, a small smile on her lips. "We can't waste any time."

He followed her to the front door, out onto the lawn. The grass was wet with dew. It squished beneath his shoes as he and Ana crossed over to the sidewalk. Over the mountains to the north the moon waited, not quite half full. The neighborhood was silent. Even the crickets had gone to sleep. Every noise they made, their steps, her humming, the rhythm-less jangle of his keys in his pocket, it all sounded discordant in the silence. It was hard for him to imagine they wouldn't wake someone with their footsteps, their hushed voices, and yet when she began to walk and called back to him, she spoke as though it were noon.

"Hurry up, don't be a *shleper*."

"You didn't tell me it was a race," he said, speaking as loudly as she had. "And do we have a destination?"

"Don't ask me. I'm the stranger in this town, remember?"

Remember, he repeated to himself. She slid the word out cleanly, not making the same glottal indentations with the Rs as he still did.

"I can show you where I work," he said. "It's a bit of a walk, but it will take us through town. I can give you a tour of the junkyard."

"I've never been to a junkyard. Is it dangerous at night?"

"Very."

He led her along Summit Street into the center of town, past the park and cemetery, past the stoplight at the intersection at Oneida that broke at least once a month, past the steep hill where he'd taken Judith sledding every winter, up onto the marble steps of the library. Their shadows overlapped against the sidewalk, black on gray. Occasionally, she leapt across the cracks of the pavement as though skipping rooftops. Along the riverbank they stood, listening to the water's lapping without seeing it. Sometimes they talked and sometimes they walked in silence, but always slowly, easily, as though they were not really walking but being carried by some gentle, unseen current.

The unlit city demanded nothing. Its inarticulate landscape felt more like the endless fields no more than a few minutes run from his house as a boy than a place of commerce, of human action. The asphalt was sleek with reflected light. The shuttered shops and the dead cars seemed to withdraw everything they insisted on during the day, turning inward. Even the few signs of life—the lit window, the passing Buick, the Negro coming up the sidewalk, doffing his hat to Ana—had nothing in common with what transpired in the same place during the day. These were weightless events. Their only impression was mystery, the question of what they were doing out at that hour. Ana fit seamlessly into it all. A graceful wraith in a robe. Abe could only wonder what kind of figure he cut, what kinds of questions trailed him for the eyes he couldn't see.

"Here we are," he said as they approached the entrance to the yard. "My heaven of garbage."

He'd been there many evenings after dark, but never so late, and now, the quality of the darkness, its totality, seemed different, made the whole place new and strange. During daylight, what struck the eye were the largest heaps, the gutted cars and grand pianos, the mountains of metal scrap, the contents of an entire house crushed and smashed and spat out like broken teeth into a single pile. But now, in the dark, these larger objects were the least visible, as though their gravity swallowed what little light there was to see. They appeared more shadow than substance, more like bodies of water one could sense without being able to make out their location. Ana held her arms out in front of her as she walked forward. Abe knew his way by heart and placed a hand on her shoulder to guide her and catch her if she stumbled. More visible than the car frames, the towers of gouged mattresses and scattered sofas, were the smaller bits and pieces everywhere that coated the ground and captured traces of light. It was a carpeting of junk, the jagged texture of this peculiar place he'd built for himself.

They descended deeper into the yard, away from the office.

"I feel as though I'm on a beach," she said to him, "walking toward the water. I can't say why it seems that way to me but it does. Perhaps I'm dreaming. This would be a very good setting for a dream."

Abe reached into his pocket for a cigarette, stood there smoking, following the woman's voice. For so many years this place, this world of his work and his family, had seemed solid and real to him, while that other world of Russia, the world he had left, the world of his parents and his brother and sister and their small home, had seemed unreal, far away. But now, standing beside Ana Beidler, it was the objects around them, the present and visible world, that seemed distant and dream-like, while the life he had left behind thirty years before felt so close, so present. He felt if he closed his eyes and reached out his arms, he might touch it.

There was a radio on the ground. She walked to it, turned the brass knobs. "Shall we dance, Mr. Auer?"

"Definitely not," he said. "I have two left feet, and you, in case you haven't noticed, are still wearing your night robe. If someone sees us, they'll call the asylum."

"But who would see us?" She slipped out of the robe. She was wearing something silk beneath it, a gown, a negligee, something through which he could see the lines of her torso, the curve of her breasts. She rounded her shoulders and lifted her arms, encircling a partner who wasn't there, tilting her head as she began to sway and twirl across the gravel. *She's mad*, he thought. And yet her madness seemed natural and right, his own sanity a handicap. The moon slid behind a cloud. His life felt light, his heart unburdened. He moved toward her in the darkness.

"You're going to join me?" she asked. "This song I've saved for my dear one, my great love. But the night is young and there are many more songs."

"I prefer to watch," he called out.

And yet even watching, he could imagine what her arms would feel like, their warmth, their softness, their graceful curves. Watching her, he could feel her, the same way he could sometimes feel his brother. So maybe Judith was right. Maybe she *was* a ghost. Her skin shone palely in the moonlight while the rubble around them glinted, a harsh patchwork of surface and shadow. They danced across this broken landscape to music no one else could hear.

By the time they returned to the house, only a few hours remained before dawn. They climbed the steps of the front porch, and she leaned against the railing.

"Careful," he said, reaching out to steady her.

"That," she said, "would make a very nice scene on stage. I could practically feel the steeple slopes beneath my feet." She paused, then pushed up onto her toes like a ballet dancer, then fell flatfooted against the planks. He realized for the first time that she'd never put on shoes; her feet were bare.

"You could have hurt yourself, shredded your toes. It's a miracle you didn't."

"You must believe me, Abe, when I tell you I sometimes feel as though nothing can hurt me anymore."

"A piece of glass in the ball of your foot would do the job."

"You're so practical. A practical, American man."

"I'm not American. I'm *fun der alter heym,* from the other world, like you."

"Maybe so. But you hide it well. You act as though you've been here a million years."

"I'm good at pretending."

He unlatched the front door, holding it open for her. Not a light on upstairs. Not a sound. No one had awoken. No one had noticed.

"Is there time to finish our vodka?" she asked.

"There's always time for that."

He had only just sat down on the sofa when he felt an unexpected courage rise up in him. "May I ask you something?"

"Anything," she said, sitting beside him.

"Tell me who you really are."

Her smile didn't fade. It seemed to go on against her will.

"Your accent," he continued. "It's lovely. It's like a poem. But I grew up in that part of the world. You sound like you come from . . . "

"From where, Abe?"

"I can't say exactly. Someplace else."

She didn't answer. There was a single cube of ice in her glass. She spilled it into her palm, held it between her fingers, letting it melt through them onto the table. He listened for what seemed a long time to the ticking of the clock, to her quiet breath. "Perhaps that's for the best," she said. "Because the truth is, I don't come from anyplace anymore. The place and people I'm from will be gone soon. Vanished. Dissolved. It will slip away just like this ice between my fingers."

"You shouldn't say that."

"Why not? It's the truth. Why shouldn't we say what is true? Do we think that if we keep quiet, that if we don't say it, not even to ourselves, we can stop it from happening?" She laughed. "We're like small children who think we can make a person disappear by closing our eyes."

"Maybe we can. Maybe it's better not to know, to sleep through it."

"Hold out your hand," she said.

He did as she said, held it there as she dropped the sliver of ice against his palm. "I know you don't believe that," she said softly. "It's only that you've been numb for so long, you've forgotten how useful pain can be." She was about to say more when a clattering sounded from the neighbor's yard.

"What's that?" she said, shaken. "Who's there?" She leaned across him, peering out the darkened window with wide eyes. Abe looked through the glass, over her shoulder. She was trembling slightly, breathing quickly. He shushed her, leaned toward the window for a closer look. The neighbor's light was on, its electric beam illuminating the movements of a family of raccoons gorging themselves on garbage. "Raccoons," he said. "Our neighbor forgets to chain the trash can. That's all."

"Raccoons," she repeated.

"Here, in Utica, in our house, it will never be more than that. I can promise you. You're safe here. No one can hurt you."

"I want to believe it," she said, two large tears gathering in her lashes. "You're so kind." She thanked him once more, nonchalantly, as though he'd handed her a handkerchief or passed her the salt. Then she cried quietly and smiled at him through her tears while he sat beside her, not speaking, not moving, one hand lain firmly on her shoulder.

"All is as it should be," he promised her. And yet how strange it seemed to him that in a few hours, his wife would be cracking eggs into a frying pan, his Irene and Judith arguing over who would shower first. How odd it was that the neighbor's dog would be barking at the milkman, the men of Corn Hill tying their shoelaces and hurrying down porch steps to begin the day's work. All common things seemed strange and unlikely. At the same time, the feelings he had for this woman, this houseguest, seemed natural and familiar. He couldn't account for it. He couldn't do anything but sit beside her.

So they sat there for a long time. He sighed and she smiled and neither stood to leave. In a few hours, it would be dawn and regular life would proceed. But not now. For now, they were together in the dark, quite still, fingers touching. Instead of speaking, they sat and listened to the raccoons' rampage of his neighbor's yard: claws on metal, flesh in debris, the inhuman pitch of animals rifling, a frenzied, disordered noise amid the quiet.

9.

MAX ARRIVED MIDDAY to find Union Station exactly as he'd left it, a temple where people came to worship not God, not goodness, not even the wonder of the machines that moved them but movement itself, the ability of people to hurry, to push past and stand aside and forge ahead and get the hell out of each other's way. He'd hardly planted both feet on the platform when bodies shoved him from behind, elbowing and angling their way toward the main concourse, the wide staircase, the relief of open space. His knees and neck loosened as he walked toward the arrival hall, shaking off the stiffness of eighteen hours in a seat. What a blessing it was just to stretch the knees and straighten the elbows. His joints crunched and creaked as he pushed forward, let himself be pulled along by the current of bodies, the steam and noise and heat, all the while trying to master the idea that he was really here, home, back again to the pinpoint center from which he'd fled fifteen years before.

In the arrival hall, he crossed the marble floor with a slow gait, a feeling of heaviness, a sense of his life's own gravity. The rail lines radiated out from a central hall. The hall was more air and light and dust than steel. The great steel girding was nothing more than a shell. The pigeons perched above, balancing on rafters; they plucked and skittered and didn't seem to realize they were trapped. Dust rose beneath them, suspended in drifting light. Outside, it might be raining or snowing or arid as the Sahara. The station was a world contained; it made its own weather.

Max moved through it, through the crowds of fellow-passengers hurrying in a hundred directions: left, right, cross-wise in loops and diagonal arcs. They moved with the randomness of marbles dropped on glass. For just a moment, Max saw himself as the pigeons would have seen him, one of these marbles sliding far below with no logical direction or destination. But then the clock at the hall's center came into view. A half-dozen figures surrounded, waiting, checking watches, setting suitcases at feet. In the middle, a woman more poised than all the others. It didn't matter that her back was turned; he would have known her by the part in her hair or the way she clutched her purse. He slowed as he approached, felt himself flooded with fondness and relief. As though sensing his approach, she turned around before he spoke her name, held out her arms.

"Well hello there, stranger. You've done it. You're truly here."

"But I'm a stranger now?"

"Two years, Max. Two long years."

Their embrace was warm and unrestrained. She smelled the way she always smelled, a mix of violet and Wrigley's spearmint and talcum. "Two years," he repeated. "Really? That long?"

"Don't pull that on me. You know exactly how long it's been."

"It's good to see you."

He leaned in and kissed her on the cheek, laughing a little.

Max's sister hadn't changed much in the years since he'd seen her—in truth, she never changed much: there was something generous and good at her core that made its way out to the surface and defied decay. She was, she had always been, a decent girl: agreeable and without pretension, intelligent without the hollow dressing he'd seen so much of back east, pretty in a practical, unfussy way with brown hair that fell in brambly brown strands and warm brown eyes and a smattering of freckles on her nose that had faded in adulthood but never disappeared entirely.

Their mother died from flu when he was six and she was ten, and while materially provided for (indulged, many would say), they were emotionally orphaned by their father, a successful but stubborn businessman who'd opened a small department store forty years earlier that was now the fourth largest in the city. That was how Max came to be cared for by a series of tidy, efficient spinsters in an airy house on Goethe Street, near the lake, who could keep house and speak unaccented English. But Elsie was the one who had loved and protected him. He lived in near constant fear of roving hoodlums, Slovaks, Ukrainians, other empire throwaways who seemed to hone in on him, instantly aware of some weakness in himself he could not even name. When he was eight, a classmate was cornered coming home from school by a group of Irish boys who called him a "Christ-killing bastard" and bloodied his nose and tore off his shirt and painted a cross on his chest that had to be scrubbed off with turpentine. While Max had never faced any attack that dramatic, he lived in steady fear of it and faced down quieter taunting on a near daily basis. Elsie said, "When you can, ignore them. But if someone's really going to pick a fight, and they won't have it any other way, look them right in the eye, then do something crazy. Slam your fist into a wall. Stick your tongue out to your chin and scream. Kick something. Curse like you're possessed. Or just hit them, as hard and as fast as you can."

Elsie was also his companion, his partner in petty crime. Together, they had experienced the city as few children do, with freedom from parental meddling but without poverty. They dressed well enough to gain access to the nicest doorman buildings—the Standard Club (on whose board their father sat), but also the Knickerbocker, the Palmer House, the Edgewater Beach Hotel, places where they could pretend to be the children of socialites or foreign diplomats and order steaks with béarnaise sauce and French-fried potatoes, where they could play games of hide and seek inside the stairwells and smoke stolen cigarettes on the rooftops with the whole city twinkling around them.

Growing up, his worst fear had been that she would someday leave him, because then he would have no one. It was worse than his fear of falling from an elevated train or drowning in the lake. "I'll never leave you," she must have told him a hundred times. And she never did. It was he who left, tentatively, first, only a few miles south for the University of Chicago, then for New York and rabbinical school, then Germany, then back to New York, then finally, inexplicably, Utica. And through all of this leaving she kept her word and stayed put, built her career as a high-school English teacher and her marriage to John Harris, a chemistry teacher and amateur musician around the city of their birth, so that she was always there, waiting, consistent as a compass's fixed foot.

More than ever it was a pleasure and relief to see her and hug her amid the tumult of Union Station.

"Come on," she said, "it's a cauldron in here. Outside at least there's a little breeze coming in off the lake. Well, more like a draft than a breeze. Should we go swimming while you're here like the old days? John is teaching himself to swim great distances. He can go all the way from Montrose Harbor to Navy Pier and he has it in his head that he's going to cross the English Channel when the war is over, if the British win, of course."

"If they don't win, he'll have bigger things to worry about than his breast stroke."

"I keep telling him. I also keep telling him that Lake Michigan is not the English Channel. Channels have currents and sharks and riptides and God knows what else. But you know how he is. An odd man I married."

Outside, the crowd swelled around them. They pushed their way down the platform, up the stairs and out of the grand hall of Union Station and onto Madison Street. "How was the train ride?" she asked along the way. "It must be a beautiful ride. I don't care what anyone says about Indiana—America's breadbasket and the heart and soul of Klan country. What's not to love? If you hadn't become such an Easterner snob, you'd know as much."

"Upstate is not the East Coast. It's a region unto itself."

Now that they had cleared the station's crowd, the breeze of which she'd spoken delighted his skin and cooled his head when he lifted his hat. It smelled of summer, of the greasy meat sold by street vendors and the perfume of passing women and car exhaust and sewer steam. He'd forgotten the pleasure of feeling the lake air rubbing up against the mammoth towers of commerce; he'd forgotten summer in Chicago, which came between the last week of June and the third week of July and revived the city's inhabitants like an unexpected pardon. He'd forgotten the stark contrast of light and shadow amidst the skyscrapers, the hum of a million human lives crowding in, how it made a man feel small and big at once.

They boarded a northbound Ravenswood car toward his sister's home, a place he could picture well from her letters but had never seen. It was a rambling Uptown three-flat, a north side enclave of old money and young bohemians, another world from the Gold Coast they'd known as children, their father's world. They'd both left that behind, but each in their own way. Max's flight was physical, intellectual, demarcated by distance and great passages of time. When he left Hyde Park, he did so with the intention of never returning. He'd imagined the whole city going black behind him as his train rolled out, imagined that if he pushed the memories down deeply, they'd eventually shrivel and fade. Elsie, on the other hand, required neither time nor distance to make herself anew. A few months after her marriage to John (the marriage took place before a magistrate at City Hall), the new couple had purchased the drafty Victorian with plenty of space for letting at low rent to former students, local artists, writers, agitators, aimless types who they hoped would contribute to the character of the place or to their own amusement. This was the quality he admired most in his sister; she did as she pleased and never questioned her right to do it; she was fearless and open to the world.

IT WAS MID-AFTERNOON by the time they arrived at her house. The door to the flat was open, the living room flooded with light. It was the type of house she and Max imagined for themselves when they played make-believe as children—a grand piano in the corner, stacks of sheet music and towers of books. All the windows thrown open. And beside one window a birdhouse with a blue canary perched on a swing. Closer to the kitchen, the smell of lemons and clover. Beyond the windows and the lines of poplars, the throb of the city's north side, close enough to feel but out of sight. As he followed Elsie up the stairs he couldn't help but wonder how his life might be different if he lived in a house like this, a neighborhood like this. Would he crave less meaning? Would he want different things? The guest room was as welcoming as the rest of the house, a small square room with a tidy bed draped in yellow linen, a bureau, and lamp and daisies on the nightstand.

"Take your time and unpack," his sister said. "I suppose I should throw something together for supper."

Upstairs, he emptied his suitcase and washed his hands and face, then sat before the window and watched two boys pass on bikes below. In the yard across the street, a woman was gardening. The mailman was hurrying up the stoop.

"Are you coming, Max?" his sister called. "John's home early. I'm making a pitcher of Tom Collins and no one can stop me. What do you say to that? Come down and drink with us and tell us all about your life."

He did as instructed, came downstairs, shook his brother-in-law's hand, accepted a drink. They sat on the porch, sipped their cocktails, and made small talk until Elsie announced her stomach was growling. Then they returned to the dining room where the table was set.

"How's Utica treating you?" John said. "They have a good amateur orchestra?"

"Couldn't say. I suppose they might."

"A small town needs three things to make it bearable. A good amateur orchestra. A good diner. And a bookstore. Everything else you can do without."

"Easy for us to say," said Elsie.

"You're very lucky," Max said. "I've always loved this part of the city."

"You going to stay and visit a few weeks?" John asked.

"Wish I could, but no. I'm only here for a conference. A friend of mine asked me to go, and I couldn't get around it."

"Yes, tell us about this conference. Is it only for rabbis?" Elsie asked. She was coming back from the kitchen with a plate of chicken. John put his arm around her waist, held her there until she swatted him on the back.

"It's not for rabbis, in particular. It's a rescue conference. A conference for the leaders of different organizations, a chance to put heads together, figure out how we can help with the crisis in Europe."

"That doesn't sound like much fun at all, Max," his sister said. "That sounds terribly depressing. Will it be helpful, though? Is there anything to be done?"

"Sure. There's always something to be done. The question is whether or not we do it. It's a matter of will, not ability."

"I don't know," John said, passing Max the plate of meat. "I have to think if there were any reasonable thing to be done, FDR would be doing it."

"John adores our president," Elsie said. "He writes the man love letters."

"Make fun. Fine. I'm not ashamed. I happen to think that when a man saves a country from economic collapse, he deserves a bit of respect."

"He has a shrine erected near the radio for his evening talks. It's John's temple, over there."

"The man's sensible, that's all. A sensible, intelligent human being in the Oval Office. He's been there eight years, and I still can't quite believe it. He explains. He doesn't condescend. He presents things as they are and then says what needs to be done in a calm, well-reasoned fashion. How does such a man rise to the highest office in a country full of crazies, of idiots and bigots and loons? You read the papers. You've heard what's going on in Boston with the Coughlinites. And New York, too. Washington Heights. Synagogues vandalized. Jewish kids beaten up for no reason. Of course, the anti-Semites, they always give a reason. When it comes to picking on Jews, the gentiles have a million reasons: Those Jews, they keep to themselves too much or not enough; they're too frugal or they spend too much money; they're overly cultured or hopelessly crass. So they break windows and beat up kids. All this happening while we've got a man like Gerald L.K. Smith well on his way to becoming the next US Senator from Michigan. Anti-Semitic, anti-Roosevelt, anti-refugee, anti-Europe, anti–New Deal, anti-everything. And the Christians, they love him. They eat the stuff up."

"It's intoxicating to them," Elsie said.

"It's like a sport," added John. "We could have a person like Smith in charge. Can you imagine? Instead, we have Roosevelt, a rational, educated man who wants to do some real good for the country, and for the Jews, too."

Max laughed. It was not an expression of any real mirth, but a brief and sudden eruption of something darker: bitterness, disdain. His sister gave him a look, not quite chiding.

"I get worked up," John said. "But I'm right, aren't I?"

"Not for me to say," said Max.

"Come on. We're family. You disagree with me? Tell me so. I enjoy a lively debate, particularly with a learned man like yourself."

"I'm not so learned, believe me."

"Please, do me the honors."

Max opened his hands before him like a flower in bloom, an oratorical gesture, but he didn't follow it with any oration. Instead, he glanced toward the table. "I find it a little amusing is all, the devotion of people like yourself toward the president."

"People like myself? Oh, now he's gonna let me have it. Mild-mannered Max. You listening, Else?"

"I don't mean anything personal by it."

"Well, what do you mean?"

"Exactly what I said. I find it strange is all. I find it peculiar the way so many people like yourself—intelligent, thoughtful Jews—hold unwavering allegiance to a man who does not deign to lift a finger for our brethren across the sea."

"That seems unfair, now. I can't believe he's not doing everything he can do without sabotaging the British?"

"Not a finger, John. Not a finger. I can assure you of it. It's one of the few things I know about."

"You're saying he should raise the quotas?"

For a moment, Max assumed that John was joking. But John didn't smile. He didn't change his expression at all. Max saw then that his sister's husband had been completely serious with this question, and he remembered with painful clarity the thing that he so often forgot, the thing he willed himself to forget—how little, how astonishingly little, regular Americans, even intelligent, well-educated, well-intentioned Americans, understood about what was happening in Europe. *Raise the quotas?* he asked. The truth was that since 1938, the country hadn't even come close to meeting the quotas that were already in existence. The quotas were a formality. They were beside the point. The bitter, impossible-to-swallow truth was that even when these people could get out, they almost never could get in. Max had seen it firsthand during his time working for the refugee aid agency in

New York, the job he'd taken when he returned from Europe, the job that had eventually driven him to Utica.

That job had been a bureaucrat's nightmare. The towers of applications on every aid worker's desk, the walls of papers waiting to be processed. And while the walls stiffened and the towers grew, the opposition to the people and families and lives behind these papers hardened. Senator Holman blocked important legislation because it aroused his suspicion that it relaxed the immigration laws, even though he admitted later he knew nothing about the bill. One of his colleagues implored the Senate to channel refugees toward all shores other than our own. And not long before Max left New York, the VFW and the One Hundred Percent Americanists coordinated measures to block a bill that would have allowed a onetime exception for ten thousand refugee children to enter the country. These were kids, German Jewish kids, most of them under the age of ten, children American families had agreed to take in and provide for, children whose parents would give them up just to know they were safe. But none of it mattered to these people. The wife of one of these legislative ogres had summed it up so nicely in an interview reprinted in the *Times*: "The problem with these cute little Jewish children is that they all grow up to be ugly adults." He'd read this sentence sitting at his desk and he thought he was going to be sick. But vomiting across his typewriter wouldn't change anything. Outrage only fermented into apathy and cynicism. He could already feel it happening.

You think he should raise the quotas? his sister's husband asked, as though it were a thing done so easily, a measure no one had attempted. It was like asking a blind man if he'd ever considered opening his eyes.

"Raise them?" Max said, trying to keep his voice steady. "How about meeting them? With the bureaucratic hoops we make these people jump through to get a visa, the quotas go unfilled. The quotas are a fiction."

"You can hardly hold Roosevelt responsible for that. He didn't create the problem of Hitler's madness."

"Madness has to be confronted."

"Confronting sounds a lot like war to me. You want us in the war? God forbid. And I mean that. If Roosevelt brings us into the war, I don't have to tell you what the Christians across this country will be saying. They'll say, 'See, that Jew-loving son of a bitch got us into another war.' They're already saying it and we're not even fighting. Impeach Roosevelt and his Jew Deal and his Jewish war; that's what they'll say. I saw a flyer on a street pole the other day. I tore it down and stuffed it into my pocket. Do you want to know what it said? 'From the shores of Coney Island / Looking out into the sea / Stands a kosher air-raid warden / Wearing V for victory.' This is what we're dealing with, Max. Now, I don't pretend to be an expert. I'm not going to any conferences, but I just don't see what you can expect him to do."

"Help them."

"With what money? With what ships?"

Max leaned back in his chair, looked down at his lap, then up at his sister. She wasn't smiling anymore. She was hardly looking at him. The kind, civil thing to do would have been to end it. *I'm sure you're right. We're all allowed our own opinions.* That was all it would take. And yet he couldn't. He felt vitalized by what stood before him in the coming days, this strange opportunity to see these esteemed Jews of power trying and failing to make history, the opportunity to pretend to be one of them, to spy. "Yes," he said. "Of course, of course. That's the State Department line, isn't it? Sorry, but we just don't have the ships. Funny, isn't it, how there are never any ships around when there are persecuted Jews that need transporting? Non-Jewish Poles need to be moved to a haven in East Africa? Slavs and Greeks need moving to the Middle East? What do you know, a ship at the ready. When non-Jews are fleeing, there are Portuguese ships and Spanish ships and Turkish ships and League of Nations ships. The British

Navy's been transporting thousands of Yugoslav refugees across the Adriatic to save them from the Nazis, but when it's Jews, all the ships just disappear. Jews must repel them somehow? Are they unknowing torpedo targets? Because when a thousand Jews are crowding a port, Southampton or Eindhoven, fleeing unconscionable persecution, not a single seaworthy vessel can be found. All the captains of the world go deaf. Funny thing is, at this point, I'd venture a lot of these Jews would be more than happy to swim. After they've seen their friends and family dragged from their homes, arrested, shot. Do you know what they do in Rumania, John? Do you know what they do to Jews? How they deal with them? Bombs or fire or even fists? Nothing as human as any of that. They load them into locked boxcars, drag them out to the countryside, and leave them all to suffocate. It's kind of genius, really. Good for you, Rumania. Using the most natural resource of all, *air*, to kill old men and small children. The Enlightenment certainly didn't pass them by, wouldn't you say? After all that, I'd venture the icy waters of the Atlantic don't seem so ominous. A ship? I think most of them would take a raft about now, or a life vest. But I understand, those cost money, too, and take time to procure. And why should Roosevelt bother when there's nothing to gain, when his loyal Jewish base stares at him with stars in their eyes? That's all I meant when I said I find it all amusing. But what do I know? I'm sure I'm wrong. Here . . . " He raised his glass toward the center of the table. "To my beautiful sister and my shrewd brother-in-law. And also, to FDR. A great president and a great man and a great friend to the Jews. America's Jews, that is. The ones that matter."

"Max," said Elsie, raising her voice. He hadn't seen her look at him like that in years.

He sank into his chair. "Please," he muttered. "Forgive me. I get carried away."

Elsie and John looked at each other. After a moment, she stood, tried to smile. "Let's see what we have for dessert," she said. "You're tired from your train ride. I know . . . There's some leftover cobbler in the refrigerator. How do you feel about blackberry cobbler with whipped cream? The blackberries are beautiful this time of year. Big as plums."

"Let me help you," Max said.

"Don't be silly. Sit."

After she'd gone, John, the man who'd been so warm and full of goodwill earlier, now sipped his Tom Collins, smiled blandly, looked at the clock across the room, the loose thread on his napkin, the hair on his hands. Anywhere but at Max.

"Well," he said at last, "Elsie makes an amazing cobbler."

AT DUSK, HE sat on the porch, listening to them argue while his sister washed dishes. He couldn't hear what they were saying, exactly, but he could read the tone. Three blocks east, Max could feel but not see the energy of Broadway, the vibrant pulse of music halls and jazz, automobiles idling roadside while young people stepped out, flirted and gossiped. But here, just west of Uptown, it was quiet. The apartment buildings held their ground against the encroaching nightlife. They had a nightlife of their own—the people who lived in them coming out now in the darkness to sit on the second and third story balconies, the porches and perches. Max couldn't see them clearly but could sense their silhouettes, hear the edges of their voices without understanding their words. It was a shadow world and somehow Max felt more comfortable in it.

He'd been outside a few minutes when Elsie stepped out, sat in the rocking chair beside him. "This seat taken?"

She dropped herself with a suddenness he didn't know.

"I should apologize," he said.

"Well. . . . It was quite a stem-winder, Max."

"I get carried away lately. I have no excuse other than to say I don't mean anything by it. I'm in a strange mood lately."

"What's that from?"

"Moods need origins?"

"No, but yes," she looked at him, side-eyed. "People don't go feeling strange on account of nothing. There's a job or a girl or a man he owes money to or a voice he hears coming out of the plumbing. These are the things that make people feel strange."

He laughed again. Laughter felt unfamiliar and good.

"I promise you, it's none of that."

She didn't answer. When he looked up at her, her face was taut with worry.

"If it's none of those," she said, "I hate to think what it might really be."

It occurred to him how little he associated family with truth. Liturgically, in his work, these things were practically synonymous, although it only took the Torah a couple chapters to introduce familial deception to the world. Always, always, he counseled and sermonized to Utica that if there were one remaining bastion of truth, it was family. He told the adulterers, the indebted, the misguided: *that* is the place where all must be seen. It was ingrained, it was held solemn. And folks believed it, which only increased its value. But Max—sitting on his own sister's porch, contemplating truths, a truth, however many small, discrete truths he stuffed into his pockets at every moment—all of it felt inaccessible. Because that was how it had always been.

"Everything's fine, I promise. I mean, Hitler has made a solemn declaration to rid the earth of Jews. But besides that, everything's perfectly pleasant and boring. The synagogue just finished a new addition for the Sunday school."

"So much insincerity. It's not like you, Max. It makes you sound like our father."

"Unless he's formally joined the Axis there are few people I'd less wish to sound like."

He rocked back and forth on his chair. Elsie was doing the same, rocking, looking out at the street, down at her feet. "I'm sorry," he said. "I'll stop now."

"Max, what's wrong? You arrive here out of the blue when you can't even be bothered to show up for my own wedding, which I admit was not a grand affair but you could have come. Utica is not Attica, last I checked."

"I should have come. I know. And I shouldn't have raised my voice like that. I didn't mean to offend. Can we leave it at that? I like John. I knew I would. I think he's a good man. He loves you, and I'm happy for you."

"Daddy thinks he's a pansy. He thinks only a pansy would teach ninth graders for a living."

"Our father's a bully and a fool."

"A bully, yes. A fool, no. That's what makes him so impossible to tolerate. We had lunch at his club the other day. We had a lovely lunch, a truly pleasant and grown-up conversation about this chemistry professor he had drinks with in Hyde Park. Then, at the very end of the conversation he turned deadly serious and said, 'Sweetheart, now don't take offense to this. Really, don't. But is John doing what a husband should for his wife? Because if he's not, there are steps that can be taken. You have recourse.'" She began to laugh. "I wish he could just be a human being, that he could be decent to John. And to you. The three of you are the only people I have. I wish he could appreciate what wonderful men you both are."

"He's not capable of appreciation. He looks at people and sees them only in terms of how they're useful."

"But why? What makes a man so narrow and selfish?"

He waved it away. "Selfishness is too common to wonder where it comes from or why it exists. Better to ask why people do good, why they ever act charitably."

"Well, why do they?"

It was a good question. It was a question to which he wasn't sure there was an answer. But he didn't tell her so. Instead, he said, "They're good *because* they're selfish. Because they get selfish pleasure out of selfless actions."

The worry that had been slowly fading from her face returned. She leaned closer, as though it was the physical distance or the darkness of the night that kept her from seeing into his state of mind as she'd done before. It was not with fear or hostility but with true uncertainty that she asked him then if that was why he had come here. "Are you trying to do good again?"

She said it so earnestly, without a trace of irony or guile. Naïveté became her. It was impossible to take offense.

He shook his head, reached across the arm of his chair for her hand, just as he had thirty years earlier, walking across the cemetery toward their mother's grave. He told her the truth: "I don't know why I'm here."

10.

GOD PROVIDES, HER mother had said, leaning against their doorframe. Looking at young Ana without seeing her, looking out at the narrow, soot-smeared streets beyond their window. *God provides to those who are willing to accept.* Sometimes upright, sometimes clutching at the edge of the door for support. *If you are not willing to accept, God looks for the next soul in need.* Ana, at the table by the stove for all of these recitations, all these impromptu rehearsals when her mother would forget breakfast, forget bathing and dressing, forget even the tea kettle on the stove until it howled across the apartment, forget everything other than the part, the role, the new person she'd decided to become for a new director whose charm and fame Ana measured by the trill in her mother's voice when she spoke the name. Ana watched her weep and sigh and speak of God and death and love, the God and death and love of Yiddish melodrama, watched her seized by forces unfamiliar and bleak. *If you do accept, you must take what you are given without question.* A supplication like this made so little sense with an actress for a mother. It was always, as the Americans put it, feast or famine. Ricocheting between food, good food, food good enough for a czar, caviar and sturgeon and chocolate and tea, and the gnawing, withering pain of without. Why throw yourself at the feet of a power so inconstant? An actress for a mother. A God with no center who took more than it gave. *If you question what you are given, God*

135

takes what you already had. Why not find a steady god, a god who wasn't as interested in laughter and light as in good credit and keeping her children clean of lice? Her mother's god toyed with her and her mother let him. *If you can accept without question, you will never be out of the Lord's sight.* What useless *drek.*

And yet it was this same Lord, this unreliable, nearsighted, forgetful, wrathful, monomaniacal piece of shit to whom Ana was halfpraying that a telegraph promised from Shmuel Spiro might have finally arrived.

She had already made a few, uneasy trips into the Western Union on Genesee Street to see if anything in her name had come, but when the eyes of the boy behind the counter grew a little too narrow, she decided it would have to wait. If it was coming at all. He had promised her he would send word—word of her future, her fate, some rough summation of what would come next. Word was an awful thing to wait for—from God or Shmuel Spiro or anyone else.

The Auers clearly had a more useful god than hers. It was far too efficient to ever draw Ana's adherence, efficient and tidy and regular. These were all traits Ana understood but was repelled from, as if by instinct. Watching Abe and his family, sated, undoubting people, she did not begrudge them their comfort. That was too spiteful. To hell with what they once said in Alexanderplatz but material joys were just fine. What threw her about Abe was how little wonder seemed to infect his life. He was not like the others, but he'd pretended to be like them, to be small and practical and sated, and now he'd lost track of where this pretense ended and reality began. And yet there were things about his life worth having. Regular, American things that Ana didn't remember from her own childhood. The Auers had a pantry. She hardly knew the word when she first heard it. It was an entire room devoted to food, each shelf lined with jars of jam and boxes of shredded wheat and bags of beans and tins of fish. So much food. Not a closet. Not a cabinet. A pantry. An altar to plenty. Sometimes she stood inside it and ate sardines when no one was home, licking the oil from her fingers, then moving on to a handful of chocolates. A child in this house would not learn to steal food off a cart, would not know the pain that came with a blow to the back, gravel against knees, dirt under nails. There'd be no need for theft, for hoarding, for always wanting more, what was deserved but withheld, always out of reach.

She couldn't say where it came from, this sense she'd always had that what wasn't hers was not forbidden, that nothing was as out of reach as it might seem. She only knew she'd never been without it. Even as a small child, a girl of twelve, a woman of twenty, when she saw plenty, she wanted to make it less. Abundance called out to her for correction. Bins full of sweets at a corner candy shop needed depleting, and she remembered the joy of depleting them, the satisfying feel of the smooth shells as she stuck in her fists and filled her pockets. Later, she discovered that people could be picked up and taken away. Girls from proud homes lured into sins of the flesh. Aging actresses displaced. Faithful husbands unmoored. Audiences craved to be relieved of their worries, their disbelief, their money. This was how it seemed to Ana, not that she plundered others' good fortune, but only that these fortunes begged annihilation. The Auers' home seemed no different from those bins brimming with candy, those aging divas, all the handsome, hopeful men, men like Szymon, who had so much and wanted her to make them less.

The Auers were not rich, but they had so much they took for granted, things they'd long stopped seeing. They had a shiny black Buick with seats soft as bread. Inside the house, two radios, three ottomans, a piano no one played. Judith had a closet crammed with sweaters in every shade of beige. Trinkets, stockings, galoshes, bedspreads, knickknacks, framed photographs, candy dishes, porcelain figurines. But no music. No poetry. No drunken arguments or noises of love drifting down the hallway in the middle of the night. No laughter. It was the opposite of what she'd known as a girl, a childhood among her mother's people.

Here, it was different. *Tainted*, her father would have said. *The taint of bourgeois tastes, mindless consumption.* She told Abe about her father one night. Her father was a socialist, drawn to the cause after being conscripted. The only objects he had use for were the ones he needed to lure beautiful women, women like Ana's mother.

He never lured me anywhere I wasn't already going, her mother said to her one morning. She still heard her, more since she'd arrived in this place.

She heard her now, in the Auers' home, their spare bed, her neck stiff and her feet cold. The bedspread was thin but pretty, pale blue, lined along the edges with fleurs-de-lis; the mattress was lumpy. She'd forgotten to close the curtains the night before and now her whole body was swimming in light, shadow and light swaying over her with the rhythm of the trees beyond her window. Yes, her mother was all around her here, inside her, guiding her through what needed doing.

She dressed slowly, to take in what she needed to see in the mirror above the bureau. The cheeks. The breasts. The gaze. America was dulling her, efficiently.

Halfway down the stairs she saw the wife. She was sitting at the dining room table, humming softly, hands inside a shoebox. Ana watched her from the bottom step, watched the careful, focused motion of her arms until she understood what she was doing, polishing the cutlery and serving spoons, picking up each piece, rubbing it inside a felt rag until it lost its tarnish, until it shone to her particular specifications, then setting it out on the cloth. And all the time humming, humming, so happy to be polishing forks and ladles and salt shakers shaped like clovers, so happy to be polishing the silver like an old kitchen maid, to be doing nothing, to be nothing, a wife, a mate, a helpmate. It was an enigma to Ana, as much a mystery to her as the pantry or the logic of dreams or of falling in love. And yet, Irene Auer was not without a certain country charm. A healthy milkmaid of a woman, was how Jacob would have put it, a simple beauty with a blush in her cheeks and an auburn tint to her hair, a high German Jewess who'd never known Vienna or Berlin, who'd only known small towns like this one, kitchens like this one, lives like her own.

"Good morning," she called to Ana without turning her head. She must have seen her reflection in the silver. "You're up early today."

How long had she seen her standing there, staring? "Yes, I forgot to draw the blinds. The light woke me."

"It's lovely this time of year, isn't it? I love the early light. It's really the darkness of the winters here that bothers me more than the cold. Come sit with me, will you? Have a cup of coffee."

The pot was already on the table, a cup and saucer, a dish of sugar cubes. Ana approached, took one cube, crunched it between her teeth, let it melt on her tongue, sat down and poured herself a cup. She sat there sipping for a few minutes when it occurred to her she was being rude. "Let me help you with this. Do you have another rag?"

"Don't be silly. You're our guest. Guests don't polish silver. Besides, I like to do it, believe it or not. I find it relaxing."

Ana picked up a spoon, turned it over in her fingers. "You have lovely things," she said.

"That's nice of you to say. They all need cleaning, though. That's the problem, isn't it? But I'm so glad you like it here, that you feel at home."

"How could anyone feel otherwise? A beautiful house. I'm not sure if I've told you so, but it is. I'm grateful for your generosity, your company, too." She paused, placed the spoon back into the shoebox. "People assume the hardest part of coming here must be the loss, but the loneliness is far worse. It's the loneliness that keeps me awake at night."

The dense scent of the silver polish filled the room, made Ana think of something indistinctly mechanical: a shed behind a railway platform; an unwound watch on a nightstand.

"This is a horrible place to be lonesome," said Irene. "I don't just mean Utica."

"You?" said Ana. "You feel lonely?"

Irene smiled in a way that Ana did not expect. Then it dropped. "No, not so much. I do miss Abe during the days. The junkyard can be a demanding mistress. But I do know. There's a difference."

"Between missing someone and loneliness," said Ana.

"That's right."

"The lonely man has no one to miss."

"Is that it?" said Irene, scrutinizing a spot on the grip of a fork. "I don't know if I agree with you. That feels wrong. Disagreeing with a houseguest. One . . . like yourself, no less. But I don't know if what you said is right. Loneliness isn't not having anyone to care about, or not having anyone care about you."

She continued to work the fork. For the first time she took the time to consider her words.

"It's more like looking up and seeing a planet where there is no room for you, looking out and seeing a great wall of people, like the one in China, surrounding the earth. And then, somewhere out on the hills, away from the wall, there's you."

She put the fork down on the table. When she had stared at it for too long Ana took it and put it in the pile of clean utensils.

"You're very eloquent, Irene. I have known a number of people who thought of themselves that way and few are as well-spoken as you."

Irene rolled her eyes.

"All practice," she said.

Ana did not understand the remark.

"Well, Abe's a good listener. It was one of the things that made me fall in love with him, believe it or not. The other boys I knew growing up, no matter how handsome or well-to-do or intelligent, whenever I spoke, me or any girl, I could see a kind of light going off in their eyes, like they already knew what I was going to say and knew it wouldn't be anything too interesting and now had to wait patiently until I finished saying it. It was like they were already thinking more about what they wanted to say next than about the words coming out of my mouth. It was so common, I thought it must just be the way men were. My father and brothers were the same. Abe was the first man I ever met who was different. I could be telling him about what kind of toast I had for breakfast, and he'd be hanging on every word as though I were reciting a poem. And whatever I told him, he wanted to know more, more, always more. Why did I think what I thought about this or that? How'd I arrived there? If I made some grand statement or pronouncement, he'd ask for an example. He knew when I was contradicting myself or exaggerating even before I did. It made me lose my head, to be listened to like that. Everyone told me to run the other way, said I could find a man with smoother edges. But I saw it different. I thought, handsome men get old and ugly. They go bald and grow hair out their ears and nose. Rich men can go broke. The smartest men can sometimes be the cruelest. But a man who listens. How could that be wrong? Who could ever take that from me?"

"No one," Ana admitted.

Irene gathered up the silver to be brought back to the cabinet. "Enough of all this," she said. Then, "Listen, some friends of ours invited us up to Old Forge next weekend. Won't you come with us? There will be swimming, boating. It's so beautiful. We'll all go."

"I can barely swim," Ana said. "I don't even own a bathing suit."

Irene scowled. Ana knew then she was doomed for the lake.

"We'll jump off that bridge when we get there."

Ana smirked, then frowned.

"Sorry, sorry. I forget everyone everywhere doesn't use the same expressions I do."

"Do not ever apologize, Irene," said Ana. "Never. For nothing. I, however, need to go into town, and for that I am sorry because I have truly enjoyed sitting with you."

"Not to worry," she said. "I was just on my way to the Boston Store to pick up a few things for myself. The silver's as polished as it's ever going to get. Now where are you off to?"

"The druggist," said Ana.

"Lutzenkirchen's?" said Irene. "I need to be down the street from his shop in half an hour. Let me drive you. Please."

As disarming as talking had been, the idea of getting into a car with Irene suggested an intimacy Ana was not prepared for. But Irene was already at the door, her coat on, Ana's in her hand.

And so Ana found herself rolling through Utica in the Auers' Oldsmobile. Irene drove slowly and tentatively, aware of the car's massiveness, its potential for easy destruction. Cars going in the opposite direction veered to the side of the road when they passed, even though Irene stayed well within her side. The car was like an expression not of wealth or tumescence but of one's unending uncertainty of existence. Irene piloted cautiously, cautiously, saying little. As they approached the drugstore, with her eyes fixed on the road, she said, "You've had trouble sleeping? I did hear you leaving the other night. Abe went with you, didn't he?"

Ana didn't hesitate. She was nodding even before she answered. "He's so kind, isn't he? He saw me going and worried about me losing my way in the dark. We had a nice stroll. You don't mind, do you, me stealing him for an hour here or there?"

She laughed without opening her mouth. "What's to mind?"

"That's generous of you. I enjoyed the company."

Irene put the car in park and turned to face Ana. "May I take you to lunch? Once you're finished with Lutzenkirchen's? I'm enjoying this a great deal, talking to you."

Behind the open, inviting grace of Irene's face Ana thought she detected something sharper, but did not take the time to decide if it was truly there or not. She accepted. They would meet outside Woolworth's in fifteen minutes.

She walked to the druggist's door, waited until Irene's Oldsmobile had fully vanished around the corner, then started the other way, into a surprisingly cool wind. She kept her head down and walked quickly.

When she gave her name at Western Union the narrow-eyed boy held his gaze, as though she had still been coming each day, before reaching into a large wooden box behind him. He handed her an envelope addressed to "A. Beidler of Utica."

PERMANENT RESETTLEMENT STILL UNCLEAR—STOP— HOMELAND NOT AN OPTION—STOP—LIKELY TILL DOOMS- DAY—STOP—WILL ADVISE—STOP—WARMLY SPIRO

She read quickly, one time only, then tore the paper to shreds as she stepped onto the street, dropping them into the nearest waste bin, cursing the man beneath her breath. For that bit of non-news she'd endured the car ride with Irene, and now lunch. But she wasn't surprised. It was exactly the sort of theatrical flourish she'd come to expect from him, that balanced proportion of earnestness and mocking that made it impossible for her to measure where she stood. *Keep holding breath*, he might just as easily have said. Now she'd go back to waiting, counting the days.

Ana was surprised to find a group of women waiting for her outside the Woolworth's, Irene's women, four of them pretending to be talking and enjoying the chatter, but really just waiting for Ana to appear. What struck her most forcefully as she approached the group was their sameness, the surprising, almost martial similarity in their dress, demeanor, posture. They were like different drafts of the same basic premise: provincial, Jewish, American women. Only as she came closer did small discrepancies emerge. Irene was the prettiest, the softest of the bunch with her full bosom and rounded hips, sharpness only in her eyes and chin. The woman to her left had a similar figure but a grimace on her lips, a look of perpetually frustrated expectation. Her hair was thick, coarse curls straining against pins. It fell in her face as she looked down into her handbag, looking for what—spare change, Pall Malls, a file for her nails. Beside her stood another brunette, darker, narrower, more petite than the others in an elegant shirt dress and single strand of pearls. Extremely feminine and yet somehow sexless. Her name, Ana thought, would be Betty or Bea. She was the kind of woman men liked to pick up and carry in their arms across thresholds, across puddles, into bedrooms—though what they did with them there was harder to imagine. And the fourth woman, who appeared to be the leader of the crew, blended qualities of the other three, but all Ana could see when she looked at her was her bright coral lipstick, her elaborately coiffed hair, and her arms reaching out to welcome Ana with a manic, vaguely threatening vigor.

They didn't so much greet her as engulf her in goodwill. *Here she is so nice to meet you we've all been looking forward to welcoming you and now you're here wonderful wonderful wonderful.* Ana reminded herself to breathe, to offer up a smile. She'd been hoping they would pull her into the Woolworth's, that lunch would consist of a club sandwich eaten at a counter, a ten- or fifteen-minute affair. Instead she found herself down the street at Magnolia's, a restaurant with heavy chairs and heavy tablecloths and a menu engraved on heavy paper.

"Now Ana," said the small one. "We hope you know we've been asking to meet you for weeks. Almost since the moment you arrived. Irene has been hiding you away, though. But you must know we're all here to help with anything you need."

"Help?" Ana repeated, as though even this one word were difficult to recall.

"Anything, anything at all," said the curly-haired woman. "It can't be very comforting, spending your days cooped up with Irene. Have you gotten into town much? Met any people? My husband and I are hosting a dinner for some friends next weekend. You are welcome to join. Also, we have a weekly bridge group. A progressive dinner through Hadassah. A summer potluck for the synagogue."

The synagogue to which they alluded was the center of their social if not religious life. Ana sat and listened for the better part of an hour as they described this congregation that seemed to have no more to do with the rituals of Jewish worship than a social club or athletic league. At this synagogue, there were no yarmulkes or tefillin, or interest in Hebrew as a modern language. The Hebrew uttered in ceremonies was the old Ashkenazi Hebrew of Paris and Berlin and Vienna. There was no talk of a Jewish homeland in Palestine. If the children in religious school wrote papers about their Jewish homeland, they were papers about America. And yet, it filled them. It made them happy, was enough. Ana sat there listening to their pleasantries and gossip, wondering how long she could maintain the timid smile, the soft voice and attentive gaze. Each passing minute seemed to slow the next. And in the middle of this chatter, a strange, unsettled feeling came to Ana, a feeling she couldn't have predicted. In the middle of them, she found herself missing Abe Auer. She hardly knew him, but she missed him, wished he were there, his hard, unsentimental gaze. Sitting there, she felt something for him the same way she always felt for men in the beginning—a commingling of interests, a camaraderie against the world. *And then, somewhere out on the hills, away from the wall, there's you.*

"Ana," Irene announced, "is coming to Old Forge with us next weekend. We only have to find her a bathing suit and teach her how to swim."

"Don't you listen," said the one with the coral lipstick. "The water's freezing anyhow. Better to stay on the beach."

"A nice bathing suit is imperative, however," said the small one. "I've got it. Let us take you now to the Boston Store. We'll all chip in. We'll have a little fashion show."

"Oh, no, please. I . . . "

"Come now. It'll be fun," Irene said. "Don't be shy."

And so she followed them, these lovely, kind-hearted, horrible women. She did what needed to be done, followed through, just as her mother always did. Fainting onstage had been among her many talents. "It's easy," she insisted, chiding Ana for being so easily impressed. Much easier than love scenes where sweat and fetid breath are so often involved. For fainting, all you do is hold your breath until you feel your head go light. A good audience can tell when you're faking. Just keep smiling, she told herself. And yet she wondered, what did these women see when they saw her? *Keep holding breath*, Spiro should have said. Like her mother's God, he was an unreliable, wrathful, monomaniacal piece of shit.

Ana's thoughts were interrupted by Irene's voice. "Far nicer for us all to walk together on a beautiful summer afternoon than out on the streets in the middle of the night. Don't you agree?"

11.

THE CITY THAT passed beneath the elevated train was a roaring one. Max remembered it as having a clumsy, lurching momentum, heaving, pulling, torquing. Call it the influence of hearing too many stories from the dead-eyed, trunk-armed grunters who worked the stockyards. His memories had a hacking rhythm. But the Chicago he saw now, barreling downtown, was smooth and brutal. It was too broad to replicate Manhattan's friction dynamo. There was space here for the expressions and yearnings of the people below to be seen. He saw cars zoom through wide streets, saw barrel-chested children walk out and stare down these cars, saw their giantess mothers haul them back into their dark, gaping homes. It was like he had come to the inside of a capacious machine.

At Belmont the man sitting opposite him got off and left his *Tribune*. Max reached across the aisle, nearly swiping the backside of a woman who'd just boarded. She was redheaded and busty and looked at Max aghast before settling halfway across the car. Max wanted to put the paper over his head but instead started to read it. Soon, his eyes could not focus on the words.

REFUGEES MAKE WAR BOOMTOWN OF MARSEILLE:

FRENCH PORT TOWN FABULOUSLY RICH—AND HUNGRY!

Marseille a year after France's armistice is France's most amazing and incredible city. To believe such a place exists you must see it. It is overcrowded with refugees who cannot find any place to which to escape. It is a Mediterranean melting pot squirming with defective vitality. It is a contrast of poverty and opulence, the largest and the highest-priced city in unoccupied France where, however, all classes seem to be hungry.

Every train seems to loose another flood of arrivals and the struggle for hotel rooms begins at the station. Hotel clerks say the desperate newcomers offer them money, sugar, ration tickets, a leg of mutton, a couple of chickens, sausages or smoked ham as bribes for a room. Many refugees seek only a comfortable room until the storm blows over or until they can get to America. The latter, incidentally, is becoming more difficult. No visas have been granted from the local American consulate for many days.

The fear of hunger haunts nearly all guests. Wardrobes are stocked with hoarded food and this has led to an epidemic of mice. One refugee in a swank hotel kept three ducks in his bathroom.

There was life. *To believe such a place exists you must see it.*

He sat on the train and read the paper and watched the windows and brick facades speed past and was furious that the next stop was not on La Canabière or someplace else that must be seen. His heart shuddered. The redhead across the car, smirking at another man now, glanced at him and threw him a wink. He wanted to punch the nearest window and dive out of the train and back into the world.

HE EMERGED FROM the station into light, pushed his way through the morning crowd of men in suits. At the corner of Michigan and

Monroe, he tossed his paper in the trash, stepped inside the club's lobby, took off his hat and immediately looked up, as he guessed Sullivan and Adler had wanted him to do. Above his head was not a ceiling but a wide, domed roof with a skylight in the middle, sunlight flooding in and illuminating a hunting mural that swirled out from the glass, broad strokes of paint in rich, Renaissance color. Strange to be trotting down Michigan Avenue one minute where everything was cheerful and bright and standing the next beneath a scene of broken-necked quail and disemboweled fawns, hunting dogs with shiny pelts and glossy fangs and the blood of the hunt dripping from their jaws with such life-likeness it seemed the drops would plunk onto his face.

"Makes you want to kill something, doesn't it?"

He looked down and saw a thin man in suspenders watching him from beside a water fountain. He was half-leaning on it, one hand in his pocket, the other holding a cigarette. He drew from it, exhaled up toward the high ceiling.

"The goyim and their guns," he said. "Nothing says beauty to them like a sweet little deer with its innards spilling out. Where's the sport in that? Now, if the critters had guns, that might be interesting."

"If the critters had guns, they'd be the ones painting us," said Max.

The man nodded, looked down at his watch. He didn't like what he saw there because he cursed softly, inhaled again with greater force. There was something familiar about him, Max thought. He knew this person, had known him, had known someone who looked like him or had the same quality, the look of a clever, watchful, irreverent wiseass with good intentions.

"You lost?" he asked, and Max realized he was still standing there, waiting.

"I'm not sure. I'm looking for a meeting. The American Jewish Council."

"Fourth floor. Elevator's that way. Better hurry. I think we're late."

"You're headed there, too?"

"Right now, no. Right now I'm headed no place. My solitary goal for the next few minutes is to stand here, finish a cigarette, and try to clear my mind of nonsense. Right now what I'm doing is standing still. Sometimes it's the best thing a man can do."

Max touched his hat, began walking down the long hallway. "Take the elevator on he left, not the right. The one on the right tends to stop a foot too low. I almost fell on my face this morning, would have if a little old lady hadn't caught me."

"Thanks for the tip," Max said, walking away, sensing the man watching him even as he turned his back.

When he stepped into the ballroom, the meeting had already begun. There were a few familiar faces from the Refugee Service, a few men he recognized from the Joint Distribution Committee, but mostly, they were strangers. The people working on the crisis in '36 and '37 had been fired or had quit. The aid workers sitting around the ballroom seemed both hopeful and perplexed. Max took a seat near the back, took out a notepad and pretended to take notes. The speaker, who looked like he'd eaten his way to Chicago from Washington, mumbled and fidgeted, said words about Senate Select Committees and East Africa. A few minutes later, the door swung open again and the man from the lobby walked in. The speaker, sputtering, noticed him and said, "Come on in, David. I won't waste time with lengthy introductions. For those of you who don't already know, David Hirschler is going to be taking over for Felix as head of the New York office. In addition to his work at the JDC, he's done amazing things at the IGCR and the National Refugee Service. He's worked in the field as well, so he knows what's actually happening over there better than any of us. I'll turn the floor over."

Hirschler walked onto the stage, took his time getting comfortable before the podium. He tapped the microphone that had been adjusted for him, cast his glance widely. He thanked the obese man who had introduced him, thanked everyone in attendance, promised to keep his presentation as brief as possible because he knew there were many others waiting to contribute, others with far more experience and knowledge than himself.

"Ladies and gentlemen," he said. "We're gathered here today to propose solutions and emergency measures regarding the Jewish refugee crisis in Europe. You've come from near and far for this purpose. You've come at your own inconvenience and expense. So believe me when I say it's with more than a little embarrassment that I have to begin by confessing to you that I have no solutions or emergency measures to propose. I have no suggestions, no easy answers, no miracles at my disposal. I came with such things to a similar conference convened in Washington three years ago, a few months before the German invasion of Poland. I saw some of you there, and I gave a little speech about the graveness of the situation, the need to pressure Congress on immigration quotas, to impress the urgency of the situation. But the tenor of my message was deemed hysterical, the message itself, inconvenient. So it should be a relief to many of you that now, three years later, I come with no such agenda. Now I come only with news." He paused. There was a glass and a pitcher of water on a table beside the podium. He poured some, drank it slowly. Then he said, "Ladies and gentleman: I come here to tell you that we've failed."

A murmur moved through the room. Near the back, a man stood. "This isn't the time for theatrics, Hirschler. This isn't some fucking play. We are working days and nights in rooms the size of broom closets to do whatever the hell we can. For two goddamn years I've done this, day and night, and I will not let you shit on those efforts, and the efforts of many of the others here like me, in order for you to put on a performance."

Others in the audience seemed to agree. Max watched Hirschler, waiting for his next word.

He reached below the podium and pulled out a pile of newspaper clippings. "These are from the past month," he said. "Reports from every Jewish paper and even a few American ones. What we're dealing with here is no longer a problem. It's a crisis. It needs to be responded to as such."

The man in the back, a beak-nosed type in rimless glasses, stayed standing. "Everyone here understands that. And we're doing the best we can with a small staff and a smaller budget and a State Department and a Congress that never misses an opportunity to miss an opportunity. We're working on it from every angle."

"You may be working on it, but the Germans are working faster." Hirschler flipped through the papers again, pulled out an issue of the *National Jewish Monthly.* "Every person in this room at some point in the past five years has been accused of exaggeration. We've been accused of it by the State Department, by immigration services, by Representatives Rankin and Dies. You yourself, John, got yourself called what, 'a zealot telling monster stories' by Senator Reynolds. Maybe we've even been accused of exaggerating by members of our own ranks, by our friends and loved ones, our fellow Jews."

He paused then held up two fingers. "Two," he said. "Two pieces of information are printed in this material before me, two pieces of information which should make painfully clear the scope and urgency of the situation abroad. One," he said, holding up a single finger and looking around the room. "The Germans are systematically moving Jews out of the city centers of occupied Western Europe. Berlin. Vienna. Prague. Bucharest. The Jewish populations of these cities are gone. Vanished. And if the information we're getting from Resistance leaders is to believed, they're being shipped east, which makes no sense whatsoever. It's completely counterintuitive to everything we know about the German war machine. The Nazis are in bad need of labor in Germany on both the Eastern and Western fronts. That's where they need their workers. So why take hundreds of thousands of able-bodied prisoners and ship them away from that need, away from the factories, away from industry? It makes no sense."

He paused, then held up another finger. "Two," he said. "Soviet guerrilla forces in Eastern Poland and the Ukraine report no Jews in all of White Russia. They're sweeping through these areas every day and are telling us there's not a Jew in sight. One recounts a *shtetl* abandoned as though the plague had swept through, cows groaning in pain with no one to milk them, laundry left flapping on lines. But no people, not a one. So Jews are being shipped to the East, systematically, thousands every day, but according to the Russians, the East is free of Jews. So where are they, friends? Where are the Jews of Europe? This is the question we must ask our dear friends in Congress and in the White House and in the press when they accuse of us hysteria and exaggerations."

Hirschler stood in silence, looking out at the crowd. Then he raised his hand and spoke: "Ladies and gentlemen, I say to you again: We have failed."

Without waiting for further comment, Hirschler turned and walked off the stage. A few more speakers followed, all of them seeming flaccid and punchless coming after Hirschler. None of them knew what he did. None of them could convey it in the way that he did. It stirred something deeply in Max. The information and the delivery. The terror and the charm. It was like he'd remembered something he'd been told long ago and since forgotten, something important, something meaningful. He hardly heard what the subsequent speakers said. The room grew restless too. Max fidgeted, took meaningless notes for Spiro, failed to focus on anything in the room for more than a few seconds. What he felt was different from the boredom or letdown that the rest of the audience was experiencing. What Max felt was clawing and rising. He felt it on the back of his neck. In the bottom of his gut. In his breath.

The fat man who had introduced Hirschler returned to the podium to adjourn for lunch. People began to rise then. The orderliness and accord of the meeting unraveled, broke apart into competing strands

of discord. Max gathered himself. He could not be of any use to Spiro
in a state like this. He looked around for someone, some group to
attach himself to, people he could milk for information of any sort.
But he couldn't penetrate any of the circles of bodies that had already
formed. Factions huddled. Friends leaned into each other conspiratorially. He saw no openings. He slanted himself into conversations only
to be shouldered away. Open faces closed. He was not a snitch, not
a kibbitzer, had no gift for eavesdropping or teasing out news. Spiro
probably would have had enough material to start several world wars
by now. All Max had was a page of incomprehensible notes and the
echo of a roiling sensation.

He decided to look for a place to get a cup of coffee. He wandered
back onto the street. Such an odd mixture of exhilaration and dejec-
tion. He stood looking at windows, stood dumb, stuck, when he heard
Hirschler.

"You see," he said, "If I'd wanted to be merciful this morning, I
would have misdirected you, told you the conference was being held
across town at the Palmer House. What a missed opportunity to spare
a man an awful morning."

He was leaning against the building, smoking again, and this time
Max came up beside him.

"It's a mess, isn't it?"

"A mess? My bathroom is a mess. What John Ford did to *The
Grapes of Wrath* is a mess. That conference in there? That is a disaster.
It's a hippo trying to fuck a rattlesnake. But you know what I've just
now realized?" He took a final drag on the cigarette and dropped it to
the pavement. "It's not for me to fix. That's the thing to remember.
You do what you can do, but there has to be a limit. Otherwise you go
off the edge." He paused, then shrugged. "Still, I would have been a
mensch to spare you a useless morning."

"I took the train here from Utica. I'd feel like an ass coming all that
way to Chicago to wander around the wrong hotel."

"Utica? That *is* a schlep. Who're you with? I don't think I've seen you before."

"Because you haven't."

"So on whose behalf have you materialized?"

Max hesitated. He hung back.

"Well?"

"I'm mostly here to listen."

"Are you a spook?" said Hirschler. "A spy?"

"Sent by John Edgar Hoover himself."

Hirschler didn't smile and he instantly wished he could take it back. He felt himself being moved by forces beyond his control, beyond his own consciousness. He was expecting Hirschler to push for more, but instead he lit another cigarette.

"Want to take a break from spying and get a late lunch? Failure stimulates my appetite. Where do people eat around here?"

He held out the package of Luckys. Max hadn't had a smoke in years and accepted one immediately.

EIGHT STEPS DOWN. Lit with dim-wattage bulbs and occasional, unwanted flashes of daylight. The waiters all ancient Slovaks. Built halfway into the underneath of Chicago, at some point in the strata between the sewage and the subway. It was a place for teamsters who needed to be in the loop, men with long delays between trains, lawyers who didn't want to be seen. Max didn't know if Hirschler had known about this place or had just wandered them into it. But he ordered them sweet German lagers and tongue sandwiches as though they were mother's milk.

"First time in Chicago?" Hirschler asked.

"No, born and raised. But it's my first time back in years."

He must have read a subtle change in Max's face. "It can be tough. Coming back to a place, it can throw you off balance. The places change; we change. Hard to tell one thing from the other. I can't go back to Brooklyn without feeling seasick almost. You go home and no matter how much you've grown, your younger self, whoever you were before you left, is there waiting to haunt you like some stupid unemployed ghost."

They ordered another round, then another. There were certain things about Hirschler Max couldn't help notice. He chalked it up to the poor light, the way it made him lean more closely than he normally would have. The smallness of his hands, the creases on either side of his lips, the murky green of his eyes. His voice. The same one that had come scything through the ballroom earlier, softer, eased, but still of a very strong caliber.

For nearly two hours they ate and drank. Hirschler did most of the speaking. He seemed more comfortable that way. He talked about his contacts in various Resistance movements throughout Europe; at a certain point, after a certain number of beers, the details began to collide for Max, and he could not remember if it was the French who had dynamited the grounded Stuka or the Ukrainians who had left the door unlocked on the cattle car bound for a transit camp or the other way around. It didn't matter. It didn't, because Hirschler said so. More than once he threw up his hands, those surprisingly tiny hands. Spitting into the wind, he said.

Max's head was heavy with beer and excitement. Hirschler excited him, he could at least acknowledge that to himself. He knew things. He was in possession of truths. What he could carry into the air, facts and numbers and stories that were hidden to Max and nearly everyone else in this blinkered nation, seized Max tightly.

"Lord," Hirschler said suddenly, leaning back from the table. "I haven't let you get a word in."

"I don't mind. Remember, I'm a rabbi. This is what I do."

Hirschler smiled and, for the first time, seemed to size Max up.

"Bushwah," he said. "There is a story in you dying to get out. Tell me. Let it out before it bursts through your guts."

Max leaned back as well.

"I could tell you, I could give you the details, I could get you from there to here, but . . . " A jolt of sobriety hit him. His words needed to be right. "Compared to many of the people you've dealt with I don't amount to much, and I'd feel pretty silly talking about myself after them."

Max looked up from the table to see Hirschler smirking.

"Do you always have such a high opinion of yourself?"

Max smiled. He gestured to the table, the plates, the emptied steins. "I'm sorry," he said. "This I'm not used to."

"Getting tight before 3 PM?"

"Well, yes, that. What I meant though was having someone ask me about myself."

They had reached a point where they could retreat back into congenial, casual amiability, irrespective of the topic that brought them together in the first place, or they would have to continue forward into a deeper, more binding closeness. They apprehended each other for a moment in the poor light, trying to tease out of the other's face whatever each man wanted to see.

"Listen," Hirschler said, taking a mug from the table and draining the last few drops. "We're both far too drunk to be helpful to Europe's Jews. So why don't we get drunker and you answer the stupid question."

And so Max told him. He started with the day he left Chicago, which he liked to imagine was the beginning of his consciously lived life, and pulled this stranger along beside him, recounting his years at JTS, his studies in Heidelberg, the few months in France when he'd thought he'd convinced himself he'd go to fight in Spain, the failure and shame he'd felt returning to the States, then his years working with the refugee agency in New York, the exhaustion and frustration and loneliness and uselessness that he felt, that took him over until he walked out of the city and into the hinterlands, an act of cowardice and self-preservation and one he was ashamed to say he never doubted. There was good to be done in Utica. It was modest and small. He thought that if he couldn't save Jewish lives, maybe he could change them, help make sense of them despite the indecipherable heap of his own. He could be sturdy there. He could be constant. Unlike New York, where he felt like a molecule flitting through infinite space.

When he was finished, Hirschler said, "Sounds like you've chosen the more difficult path."

"How's that?"

"If you go to a congressman in Washington or a rabbi in Philadelphia, you can say, look at what's happening. This is an emergency. A crisis. A pogrom of unprecedented proportions. Temples are burning all over Europe and now, even in Manhattan. When people are faced with an emergency, they act. Or they try to act. Or they convince themselves that they will act. And what you've done has borne something out. But when it's a man's own life that's rotten and crumbling from the inside out, month-by-month, day-by-day, how do you convince him he's imperiled? This is a Jewish problem, maybe. We don't believe in sin. We haven't got a redeemer. We believe in God and ourselves and when God's not there as an earthquake or an army of Philistines or a cancer of the liver, that leaves just one. And you, Max in Utica, you've got to coax those *machers* through it. How do you do it? We're all so fucking on our own in the end."

"Be prepared," said Max.

Hirschler screwed up his face.

"It's what God said to Moses. Well in advance. But still. Sound advice."

"What do you mean, really?"

"I mean, you have to acknowledge that pain is inevitable and aloneness is the condition we're born and die in. Once you've got those in hand, walking a fellow through his darkest isn't quite as daunting as it sounds."

Hirschler cocked his head from side to side at Max, the green eyes flashing when the light hit them. Then he pulled a wad of crumpled bills from his pocket and dropped them on the table. He put on his hat and stuck a cigarette in his mouth.

"Come on," he said. "I need to get you out of here."

THE PLATFORM RUMBLED as a train approached. The car they entered was nearly empty. They sat side by side on the cool metal seats.

"An elevated train," Hirschler said. "This is the only way to travel. Who is it who decided it better to dig into the ground and make people ride with the rats?"

"They would have here, but the ground was no good. It's a city built on quicksand."

He couldn't remember where he'd heard this, if it was true or imagined. But Hirschler didn't probe. He was humming something faintly, his face obscured in light and shadow. The light poured into the car from every angle, through every window. It seemed not to come from the sky but from some secret, interior source. The warmth was liquid, honeyed, all-encompassing. The humming had stopped. For minutes, Max sat there with the weight of the silence, the non-knowing, the painful anticipation. And then, just as he felt he might be crushed beneath it, just as the train turned a sharp corner at Addison and the metal frame rumbled and barreled forward with what felt like reckless speed, Max felt something, a pressure, and when he looked down Hirschler's hand was touching his, the side of his hand only, resting on his own knee but touching Max's palm and wrist. He didn't move. His stillness seemed to take up all the space inside his body, inside the car, the city. The rooftops slid by beyond the glass. The mortar and brick pulled along like a ribbon. Max closed them out, released his breath, opened his eyes.

"Let's get off here," Hirschler said.

After that, it was he who did the leading, urging Max forward, off the train and along the platform, down the stairs and down the

sidewalk, across the street and up three blocks, a narrow alley entry-
way into a lobby, into an elevator, down a thickly-carpeted hallway
and through the door to a room and onto a bed there. He let himself
let go, be drawn forward. Another's body: pressure and breath and
being stilled and moved and stilled again and yes, this was life, what
he'd sworn he would do without. He'd sworn it and he'd meant it and
now here it was.

WALKING HOME THAT evening, the city streets seemed darker, more
menacing. A car sped past him, the driver cursing out the window. A
brunette in teetering heels and a low-cut blouse sat on the curb smear-
ing lipstick. A bum leaned over a trashcan, picking out bottles and
relieving them of their last drops. The smell of piss and smoke and
cooking rose from the gutter. A man stinking of shit and sweat stopped
him just north of Lawrence to tell him that next Tuesday would bring
the end of the world.

Elsie was sitting on the porch again when he reached her house.

"Max. So late. Is everything all right? Did it go as you expected?"

"Worse," he said.

"Well, then. Stay outside with me for a while. Sit and talk."

She went inside and came out with a pitcher of lemonade she spiked
with gin and a bowl of cashews. "Now tell me," she said, once they
were settled.

He didn't speak right away. He couldn't answer.

"Max?"

"I shouldn't be here. I shouldn't have come."

"Why in the world not? You have as much right to be at that conference as anyone, with all you've done."

"I don't. I don't belong there. These men, these old Jews. They're
exactly like our father. They have their ideas about how things are done
and nothing will ever change them. Certainly not me. The man who
sent me here . . . he's called Shmuel Spiro, he does things differently

from them, less conventionally, and so they call him a Jewish fascist and an imposter and try to have him deported. That's how they view the world. You're either one of them or you're nobody."

She looked off in the distance. He could sense her sizing up this speech—was this just self-pity or something else? She was waiting for the image to resolve, measuring her words.

"I'm sorry," he said at last. "It was a difficult day."

"But it sounds just like all the others, Max. That's the thing I don't understand. You can't sit here and act as though it's news to you what creations people can be, how small-minded and selfish. You've known it since you worked with them in New York."

"Well, maybe I'm tired of knowing it. I'm tired, Elsie." The truth of the statement descended on him. Exhaustion. Hirschler had told him about a ship full of refugees that capsized off the coast of Turkey. Someone on the rescue vessel had described how the passengers who'd drowned were the lucky ones. Less fortunate were the ones who found some scrap of debris and floated along the surface of the Mediterranean for a day or two, the life leaking out of them slowly, drop by drop. *They die of thirst. They die of sun. They die of sharks. Sometimes, they die simply of exhaustion.* "A man can only take what he can take," said Hirschler. Max had had enough of such reports. The world's vast stores of human misery had exhausted him, drained him dry. He didn't want to know any more. He wanted to stay in that room with the light coming through the curtains, playing across David's chest. The smell of his cologne. The pile of clothes on the floor. The feeling of knowing another person, of being known.

He turned his face away from his sister.

"Max?" she said. But it was too late. He wept openly, without restraint.

12.

THE CAR WAS packed with enough provisions for a cross-country migration, a crossing of the Rockies or the great, dusty plains. This level of preparation for a simple day at Old Forge was beyond him. What did they actually need? If it were up to Abe, just a sandwich and a bucket of Utica Club beer. But no, it was only, according to them, his lack of sophistication that made things seem simple. In truth, the outing required sun hats, swim costumes, dresses to cover up these costumes, baby oil, two picnic baskets, magazines, enough books to fill a small library, towels, bathing caps, swim goggles, and blankets. Also, four umbrellas in case it rained.

"In case it rains," he repeated. "I don't understand. If it rains, we'll come home."

He said so standing by the front door while Irene and Judith piled equipment around him to be carried to the car. They didn't respond, but looked at him as though he'd asked why the lake was filled with water.

"I thought you were loading," Irene said.

"I am loading."

"You're standing."

He picked up another bag, carried it out. Picked up the picnic baskets, carried them out. The trunk was packed nearly to capacity, the car already smelling of coconuts. "That's it," he said, coming back into the house. "All finished." But it was not just Irene and Judith standing there to hear his pronouncement. Ana Beidler was leaning against the banister near the bottom of the stairs.

"I believe I am ready," she said. "Is it time to depart?"

He wasn't sure if it was the swimsuit she was wearing or the proximity of her and Irene's partially bare bodies paired so close together, but the site of them standing there made him lighter on his feet. Irene, her hair loose over her shoulders, arms freckled, a swimsuit that had once been black and sleek, now rough with small knits and faded to something less than black, navy or rainstorm gray. He could recall seeing her crawl out of the Jones Beach surf in the same suit, laughing, sopping. It was days with some friends or another who had long since passed into afterthought; Abe had been laid out by an unimpressive malady—sinusitis? infected toe?—that kept him from getting in the water, but Irene had not given a second thought to bolting into the water while he sat in the sand. The day was scorching; one of the people they accompanied was convinced the seawater had aphrodisiac properties. Something about saline coming up to the tender organs. Saline, saltwater, and the initial life fluids (this forgotten friend explained) were close relations. Reimmersing ourselves in it was experiencing birth backwards, culminating with the moment of conception. All of them laughed at this hogwash but Abe, sand-bound and hot, seeing his new wife emerge from the water, the seminal bath, was filled with desire for her. She had fallen asleep on the train home, her head on his shoulder, his arms around her body, urging the train deeper into the city until he could have that body to himself. Seeing his wife in this burnished light took no effort of memory.

Ana's costume was elaborate and new. It was all white, a bright, satiny fabric around her thighs and breasts. A white, translucent scarf holding back her hair. Sunglasses white around the rim and as dark and opaque in the middle as the glacier lake to which they were driving. She stood in the foyer, watching him as he hoisted the remaining bags.

"I think it's time," he said.

"HAVE YOU EVER been to Old Forge?" Judith said as they set out onto Route 5, the city growing small behind them.

It was a Saturday morning and so not much traffic. They rolled down the windows to let in the breeze. It was a cool breeze, yet still, four human bodies inside a cube of black steel-generated heat. Abe could feel the sweat collection on his collar, his elbows, the inside of his shoes. "It's one of my favorite summer places," Judith continued. "Not as lively as Lake George but a lot prettier, more peaceful."

Abe let his eyes alternate between the road before him, the wife beside him, the sliver of Ana Beidler behind his head, the only part of her he could see in his rearview mirror. Judith was nothing but a disembodied voice, chattering away at Ana and her mother and sometimes at no one in particular. His daughter had a running monologue that she altered and expanded according to the occasion, but never really abandoned entirely. It had been this way since she'd learned to talk. People had two ways of responding to this style of conversation. Either they allowed themselves to be swept up in it, became equally effusive, mirroring her enthusiasm, or they shut down completely, grew limp against the force of her thoughts. Ana seemed to be choosing the second tack. She was still and silent as Judith talked about her friends, her soon-to-be husband, her wardrobe, her wedding. Abe wondered if Ana was listening at all or if the look of concentration on her face, the firm set of her mouth, was masking some inner dialogue. As Judith talked on, Ana's body emitted stillness. Her eyes remained hidden behind her sunglasses, just two dark lenses flashing back the sun. Her lips, richly painted, didn't budge or tremble. She didn't shift as the car maneuvered around a corner or over a bump. She looked like a woman being carried off to serve a sentence.

"Judith," Irene interrupted at one point. "When would Ana have gone to Old Forge? Did you forget where she comes from? You have to pardon her, Ana."

"No pardon necessary. To answer your question, I have not been to this lake, my dear, but I have been to many lakes in years past, mostly around Northern Italy in the Lombardy region. A few in Switzerland. I knew a man once, a Hungarian cellist, who suffered a spell of bad luck and decided to drink himself to death on the shores of Lake Garda. He invited me to come along. It was a glorious summer of dancing and romance."

"And suicide," said Irene. "What set him so low?"

"He was in love with me. Though typically he preferred young boys. He saw me in a production of *The Lost Daughter in Odessa* and something about my performance captured his imagination. He convinced himself that I would be the woman to save him. He was a stubborn man, as great musicians often are. It was very hard to un-convince him of what he thought he knew."

"Did he really kill himself?" asked Judith.

"Of course not, dear. For about a week, he sat at a little table on a stone beach on the shore of Lake Garda, drinking cognac until his eyes turned orange. Then one day a waiter took pity on him and offered to accompany him to a spa in the Tyrols—a kind of luxurious sanato-rium. They returned a few days later and he was a new man."

"That sounds like quite a summer," said Irene. "I could use a few days at a sanatorium in the Tyrols, myself."

"You and everyone I know," said Abe.

"How old were you that summer?" Judith asked.

"Oh, not much older than yourself. But I left home when I was twelve, ran away with a troupe of actors and never returned. So by the time I was twenty I felt like an old soul."

"It must have been exciting, to be free like that. To be on your own and have all kinds of adventures."

"Yes," she said, her sunglasses flashing in the mirror. "I suppose it was. But then, everything is exciting in the beginning."

A streak of black whizzed past his face. "Abe!" Irene screamed. He jerked the wheel hard to the right, than back to the left, the horn blast tapering off behind them. "Sorry," he said, setting his eyes back to the road.

"Well, it was a nice life," Irene said. "I truly enjoyed it."

"I said I was sorry."

Irene looked away from him, leaned her face against the window, pressed her hand to her forehead. Abe kept his eyes focused on the road after that. The highway narrowed as it rose in elevation. They merged onto Route 28, followed the winding road up into the Adirondacks where it became a river in a vast sea of pine and spruce. The sun had felt abundant when they'd left Utica but now, not yet risen above the treetops, they drove through deep shadow, a lush, low-lit summer day.

"How long until we're there?" Judith asked. "I have to pee."

"Judith, are you seven years old?" Irene said. "You couldn't go before we left?"

"I drank three cups of coffee this morning. I'm sorry, I didn't realize we were in a hurry."

"I'm honestly not sure how you're going to make it down the aisle without a rest stop."

"Thank you for your compassion, mother. I really appreciate it."

"Could the two of you hush and enjoy the scenery?" said Abe.

"It's hard to enjoy anything when your bladder's about to burst."

"God almighty."

"Look, a gas station. Pull off, Papa."

Irene, it turned out, needed a break as well. The two of them stepped out of the car, still bickering, went into the small shop beside the station to relieve themselves and maybe buy some cigarettes and candy. Beside the car, a Negro in a navy cap approached with the pump. A Packard convertible pulled up on the other side of the station, a yacht of a car with a handsome couple at the helm. The woman's hair was tied back and covered with a cherry-patterned scarf. The man was tall, lean, the picture of vitality and health. Abe cleared his throat and for the first time since swerving, let his eyes return to the rearview mirror.

He didn't know how Ana did it, but her lipstick was still fresh, her hair un-mussed. And she still held the same look of resignation, of a woman who's detached herself from her surroundings and sits slightly above them, gazing down. *Say something*, he thought. But nothing came to mind. His silence seemed to amuse her. Even wearing her sunglasses, he sensed she was laughing at him with her eyes.

"Comfortable back there?" he said. "Sorry for that bump in the road."

"Please, Abe, I've been within an eyelash's length of death so many times, I'm no longer fazed by close encounters. When it happens, it happens. That's how I view my own mortality. Valuing one's own life so greatly seems a bit absurd, doesn't it?"

"What else are you supposed to value if not your life?"

"Surely it's better to prize art or love or some lofty ideal above a skeleton with some flesh slung across it."

He grunted. "A skeleton's a beautiful thing when it's your own."

"Oh, of course it is. Ignore me, Abe. Ignore everything I say. I feel myself slipping into a state."

"Carsick?"

"No, a state of despair. It happens sometimes when I'm confined in close quarters with others. I'm reminded of my ordeal."

"Let's get out then. Take a walk. There's no reason for you to be uncomfortable."

He reached to open the door but she stopped him. "Please, no. I'll feel better when we get there. When I can take in the open air, feel the water on my skin."

"I thought you didn't swim."

"I don't, but I still like to wade."

The passenger doors opened. Irene and Judith stepped in.

"Much better," Judith said as they pulled back onto the road.

They drove for the next half-hour in silence. Only as they passed through the town of Old Forge with its festive atmosphere, its vendors and cheerful throng of leisure-goers, did the mood in the car seem to lift.

"This lake," Judith said as they drove through the thickening traffic. "Is it similar to Lake Como?"

Ana said, "More like Biarritz."

"It's lovely," Irene said. "A nice family spot. The water's cold but clean."

"I'd sink to the bottom like a bag of rocks. But I'll enjoy myself all the same."

"We could teach you to swim," Abe suggested. "You kick your legs and move your arms. Nothing to it. We threw Judith in when she was three and now she could cross the English Channel."

"Thank you, but no."

"Maybe you'll change your mind when you get there."

"Don't pressure the woman," said Irene. Then, turning around, "Ana, no one's going to force you to do anything you don't want to do."

"Except," said Judith, "listen to Myrtle Greenberg go on about her chiropodist son, what an eligible bachelor he is. That conversation is mandatory for all. It's an annual tradition."

"You have a hard life, Judith," Irene said. "I don't know how you stand it."

"It's a miracle, mother. A miracle."

IT WAS NOT yet noon when they arrived at Old Forge, but already the beach and the piers extending into the lake were crowded with bodies—old bodies and young bodies, shapely and bulging and broiling in the sun. Irene led the way to a cluster of blue chairs on the less-crowded, southern side of the lake. Abe dumped their bags into the sand, then stepped away, as though to say, I have no idea what to do with this. Irene and Judith immediately began setting up camp: towels unfurled, chairs brushed clean, baby oil applied to limbs, magazines opened, snacks unpacked, their own little island of leisure, while Abe and Ana looked on from opposite sides. Within three minutes of setting up camp, a woman was calling Irene's name. And a minute after that, a half-dozen other women were hurrying over. *You made it, wonderful, so glad you're here, gorgeous weather, what a day.* Irene seemed to forget about her family for a moment, then looked back at them, held her hand out toward Ana. "Come meet some of my other friends, Ana."

"Ana was about to go for a walk," Abe said. "She was feeling a little carsick."

She looked at him with a gratitude close to love. "Yes, a walk, to . . . what is the saying in English? Stretch my legs?" She placed her own belongings down beside Abe and then hurried off in the less populated direction. Abe sat down, dug his heels into the sand, watched Irene and Judith settle in. Two beauties, one fair, one dark, surrounded by other Jewish women, a circle of well-groomed legs, polished toes, swimsuits in every color. All of them gabbing, dozing, drunk on sun. They'd lived upstate so long the rays had this effect on them, knocking them out as abruptly as ether. He watched as it skimmed the surface of the water, shimmered like tinfoil behind the dark green needles of high, swaying evergreens and pines. It even tried to penetrate the mass of Ana's black hair as she grew smaller, walking away into the distance, tried and failed, flickering purple in a spot or two then moving on to lighter matter. Abe sank into the sand and watched the bathers and swimmers. He liked to watch them, even if he felt outside of them. The sand was cool beneath his fingers.

"I'm going for a swim," he said, patting his chest. Irene and Judith neither acknowledged nor protested. The water was the color of liquid mercury, a bracing, brittle cold as he waded out. It stung his legs, waist, chest. When the water reached above his shoulders, he took a big breath and pushed himself down. The coldness was bright and clear against his open eyes. He wanted to see how long he could stand on the bottom without coming up for air, so he let himself sink, shot up, took a breath, tried again. On his third try down, something felt different. His head was light. His spirits calmed. This was surely how life was meant to be lived: immersed, submerged. He held his eyes open, hoped to see fish, an old tire, anything interesting. Instead, he saw a dark form, a human form. He swam toward it and saw it was his brother Shayke floating a few feet away, his body youthful, undulating in the unseen current, strong and whole as it had been before. Shayke had arms and legs and lungs that worked, that expelled bubbles small as pearls, up from his mouth and nose to the light at the surface above. Abe pushed his feet hard against the rocks below and shot to the surface, gasping at the top.

He treaded water, looked back toward the beach. His wife and daughter were barely visible—he could sense them more than see them. He should swim back, dry off, but he didn't want to. There was a bend in the lake around which he could swim, and he knew from experience that far on the other side there was a small dam on which he could walk, an anchored raft next to it. It was a good swim, a half-mile at least. At the height of his fitness it had left him exhausted and panting, but he would try it just the same. He remembered Ana's voice, low and sultry in his ear: *valuing one's own life so greatly seems a bit absurd.* Shayke had known this, too. Danger nourished the soul.

OLD FORGE—ANOTHER one of those American names that made no sense; what could be built in this tub of silt?—had the sole redeeming quality of being broad enough that one could locate zones of tranquility around it. Ana, more than the sunlight, the warmth, the heat on her body, wanted to seize this peacefulness. It was a rarity, a commodity, something to be gathered and hoarded. Didn't these sun-drunk Americans realize that? Of course they didn't. All they knew was space, even the tenement mules could ride the train to Coney Island, and space was peace.

If one of these supposed pioneers could have seen Lake Balaton as Ana recalled, they would have gone raging back into their locked homes and never ventured into the sun again. When Ana and Szymon and their friends visited Balaton it was impossible to tiptoe from shale to surf without tripping over a couple fucking or drunken revolutionary face down in his own sick. On their first visits she wanted to seem composed for Szymon, unimpressed, unmoved by hips thrusting in the water, though she could tell by the way he looked at her he knew she was discomfited. It wasn't the lack of modesty that threw her but the volume of the debauchery. Under pine trees and in row boats, in parked cars, at the dusty roadside, in the lake well past dark: moral uprightness was kneecapped by anyone who could.

Eventually the scene around her became less stirring, more serene. This was Poland before the storm, a year after she arrived there from— she couldn't even remember what came before. *What's wrong? Don't you swim?* Szymon had asked her. She'd been standing on a pier, watching a kite rise in the distance. It somehow seemed a certainty that it would falter. "Of course I swim," she answered. "What do you take me for?"

"Exactly what you are."

He'd grabbed her above the hips. She indulged him for a moment then slapped his hands away, shooed him back. Then she'd stepped to the very end of the pier, curling her toes over the edge. She'd straightened her back, lifted her arms above her head, raised her gaze to the still-rising balloon, and then leapt, a swan dive into the shimmering blue drink.

"Please, Ana. Don't. Don't jump."

Abe yelled after she'd already leapt. She didn't understand what he was saying at first, had already forgotten what she'd told them in the car, the little lie she'd hoped would help her detach herself from the Auers. When she came up for air, he had stopped shouting and was swimming toward her with great speed. The water frothed around him as he slapped and kicked the surface, swimming as though his own life, not hers, depended on it. "Hold on, hold on," he said as he made contact. At first she fought, straining against his grasp, against the hands running under her back, along her sides. It was an unnatural sensation, to let your body go limp, to be dragged through water, but eventually she relaxed, let herself be carried.

She was carried by a voice that said her name. That said her name over and over.

On shore they both sat panting. The earth beneath was slick and muddy. She fell to the ground, pulled him down with her.

"Ana. Ana. No. Ana."

Abe tried to hold her still, but the firmer he held her the harder she thrashed. Free from his grasp she fell into the mud. Her white suit blackened with it, her arms and legs coated with mud. Her hair dripped onto her shoulders. She pushed the hair out of her face and got mud onto her forehead. And then her panting turned to laughing.

"Why are you laughing, Ana? You could have killed us both."

She laughed even harder. "It would have been romantic to drown together," she said. "Don't you think so?"

"No," he said, but then added, "I don't know. I don't know, Ana."

He moved toward her, lowered himself onto his knees. One of her bathing suit straps had slipped from her shoulder. He pushed the strap down farther. Her nipple was dark and firm, the color of bark.

She spoke his name. "I'm sorry, Abe. Can you forgive me?" He hardly heard her. Instead of answering, he put his finger to her lips. He told her that everything would be well, that he would keep her safe from herself.

"It's what I've always wanted most," she told him.

He nodded, then kissed her, holding her shoulders, her face, her chin. He swallowed her breath as it moved in and out of her. She was something brutal and delicious, something both cruel and unavoidable, the angel putting out Isaac's hip, the guards pummeling Shayke with their clubs, the nightmare stories he read in the papers. She was all that he feared, all that he denied, everything that had to happen. He pulled her closer, brought his mouth to hers.

Everything would collapse and be covered in mud. He held her body in it as he kissed her. He did not stop because he could not. He only paused for the time it took to breathe, to notice she had opened her eyes and they were filled with an emotion he could not quite name. It was less than joy and more than pleasure. In her eyes, he saw his own abandon, his own not caring. And so he kissed her again.

III.

THE HOTEL UTICA

13.

H E WANTED A metaphor for Hirschler's body. It wasn't like other bodies he had known. He wanted a proper metaphor to define it.

Each day, when the conference ended, or rather when the shouting and cursing and poorly thrown punches all began to collapse into a slurry of incomprehensible cant and petty name calling, Max searched the ballroom until he found Hirschler, usually surrounded by five or seven different men, all of them arguing their own individual cases while Hirschler fended them off one by one. He couldn't tell what they wanted from Hirschler, but Max enjoyed watching him deflect and deflate. He knew the freckles on the elbows he used to keep a pocket of air between himself and his furies. He knew the coarse stubble on the knees he shifted his weight on. These men knew him as a rhetorical object, an instrument in a coming war, but Max knew his body, his hands, his voice.

Once Hirschler freed himself he would give a sign, indirect, barely perceptible, that meant it was time for Max to follow him to the apartment on Belle Plaine. A movement of the lips toward the exit. A quiet thought that ended with a glance in Max's general direction. Then he was gone.

Max was not allowed to travel with him.

His body was a boundary, a series of demarcations and fortifications and disputed territories.

The day after their first night together, Max approached him, found himself caught in the throng of appellants. The subject was ships. Boats full of Jews that had sailed from Europe and were now looking for safe harbor. Nobody was allowing them to dock. Cárdenas in Mexico, Vargas in Brazil, especially Brú in Cuba, whom everyone was certain was going to exit office via a coup but probably too late to hope for a useful successor. They managed the Atlantic without being torpedoed and were stuck in international waters. "Screw America," a man with a goatee and rust-rimmed pince-nez said. "We need to be lobbying the Dominicans, the Colombians, the Cubans. Anyone facing the Atlantic who isn't part of the Commonwealth or the French Republic. That's our best bet, David. That's our only bet."

"You don't think we haven't cashed in our life insurance policies to send men to Santo Domingo, to Bogotá? They're all scared shitless of Franco and are afraid they'll have battalions of Falangists at their doorstep if they piss off Hitler."

His body was an encyclopedia of messianic literature.

"They know liberation movements," said pince-nez. "They understand. The Haitians, David. The Mexicans."

Hirschler looked down at him and spoke very slowly. "They understand that they don't need thousands of penniless, stateless foreigners they can't afford to feed or house stumbling in, muttering thanks in Yiddish."

"So where do they go, David?" said pince-nez. "Do we send them to Palestine? Let them fight off the Turks for a patch of desert?"

"They come here. We camp them all right in this fucking ballroom."

He saw Max staring from the middle of the pack. "What?" he said to him, sneering, and turned and marched off.

It wasn't until Max wandered outside, stunned, bereft, that he saw, halfway up the block, Hirschler leaning against a wall with a cigarette. He nodded at Max. Before Max could approach, Hirschler got into a cab and Max was left to retrace their drunken El ride. The train knifed through the city at dusk and Max could only wonder what he would find, if he could find the place at all.

The answer was Hirschler, sitting on the apartment's dirty sofa, a glass of bourbon in his hand, his pants unbuttoned.

His body was the moment dusk turned to night.

"The Jews in this country have nothing to fear and all of them are afraid," said Hirschler, naked on top of the sheets. "They're afraid of offending their Christian neighbors. They're afraid of offending the British. The French. They want to be so goddamn innocuous, they'd rather pretend there isn't a slaughter of their families going on in Europe than risk making some people uncomfortable."

"When I saw 15,000 brownshirts march at Madison Square Garden, I was afraid," said Max.

Hirschler scoffed. "That's a kid plugging his ears in a thunderstorm."

He went on and Max, wearied, battered in a way that was lovely, drifted into half-sleep before Hirschler brought him back into the world of the living by stroking him, still bemoaning frightened Jews.

His body was the Minotaur's. The Satyr's.

The conference staggered along. Max willed all his attention onto it even though he knew nothing would come out of it. The debate about ships raged pointlessly. A fistfight broke out between men from the Zionist Organization and the AJC about whether or not it was worth it to make a public enemy of the Grand Mufti of Jerusalem, a useless old man who'd allied himself with Hitler. Real Jews were dying real deaths in Europe while they ate lunch. He wired Spiro to say he should have saved the money for his train ticket and Spiro wired back: *Keep listening.*

"Did you hear, DiMaggio got another hit today," said Hirschler. "What is that, forty games in a row now?"

On the El in the mornings, he felt a rising pressure as downtown grew closer. It started at the bottom of his spine and traveled upward until it felt as though a hand was wrapped tightly around his torso, his chest, his neck. It's these stupid train seats, he thought. It's from sleeping in an unfamiliar bed. It's from Hirschler. He shifted and stretched and tried to find comfort in the small space he had, and all he did was earn bitter looks from the men seated beside him.

Why was he even here? What had he come to Chicago for? He was there at Spiro's behest, the head of an army that nobody wanted to arm, nobody even wanted to exist. He dropped the name of the army in conversation one afternoon and heard a chorus of derision, of scorn that roiled into disgust and mockery. They called Spiro a fascist, agitator, yid. "Those nuts can take their fifth column and fuck themselves in the ass with it." He might as well have suggested Mussolini as a viable savior. But who was he? What right did he have to question when he was there as a cipher, a wandering ear? The angel asked Jacob what his name was before renaming him Israel. From now on I will be known as Max Hoffman. That is all I will ever be known as.

Hirschler's body was the angel's wrestling Jacob.

In the men's room he overheard someone say that deep inside Poland the Nazis had built camps with no worksites attached. No IG Farben. No Krupp. Just places that rail cars rolled into. And stopped.

This he wired to Spiro and got no reply.

The city in July was hot, not a heat like he remembered in Manhattan, where heat was dense and bodily. In Chicago the heat was something unraveled, an accumulation of forces in the atmosphere that were unscrolled and laid across the city in sheets. He felt it rise and undulate, he saw the wind ruffle it, he saw it descend in the afternoons when he left the conference just for the sake of leaving.

They had to stretch as far apart from each other as they could on the bed. Max always wanted beds to be places of inherent closeness, no matter how vast or wide, if another body was there you found it and made it close. These heated nights the presence of another body nearby was too oppressive to sleep. Hirschler let Max have the side closest to the window. It made no difference.

"This city," Max said, "is so quiet at night."

"The parties go until dawn in Buffalo?"

"Utica," said Max. "I live in Utica. But really I was just thinking back to New York. If you left the windows open and the curtains drawn all the time you wouldn't know midnight from noon. But here, night is obeyed. Same as in Utica. Buffalo too, probably."

Hirschler turned to face him.

"This is all very hard for you, isn't it?"

The question hit him fast and hard.

"You mean, what, you and I?"

Hirschler saw his panic and smiled. "No, no." He put a hand on Max's shoulder, then removed it. "Well, no and yes. You and I but also the conference. The noise. The confusion. The . . . " He briefly shook Max's body with two hands to communicate whatever idea he hadn't the words for. "You're rattled. It's fine. You're surrounded by people yelling at death and it doesn't sit right on you. It isn't a defect in your character. Not many can tolerate people standing around yelling at annihilation for days on end."

He kissed Max, a conciliatory gesture.

"You belong in Utica more than you think."

His body was the conference. Yelling at annihilation for days on end.

May God strike us down before we're old enough to see how this all looks to history, he told his sister from a phone booth, while a little boy threw rocks at a dog outside.

There was more talk of boats. Boats that tried to dock in Florida. In Brazil. No one knew what to do. No one had any contacts in the Navy or the Coast Guard. The lawyers present pretended not to be violently ignorant of maritime law. Boats. Surely the oldest form of flight for the wretched and abused. The sea was refuge. It carried you to safety or swallowed you whole but it didn't send you back. This wasn't supposed to happen. Virgil knew this. No one crossed a sea to be sent home.

It was the last day of the conference. The time for joint demands that would be made to the highest powers they could collectively reach. By one in the morning they had a ninety-three-word letter addressed to all ninety-six members of the Senate.

Max did not follow Hirschler back to the apartment. He walked along the lake. Gusts leapt off it and jostled him. He moved among drunks and lovers. He understood nothing. He thought if he looked out at the strong black expanse of water he would see the unwanted boats, all of them, jammed with bodies, edging up against the city. As if, by some deep, excavated instinct, he began to chant the Mourner's Kaddish. He said the words over and over.

> Yit'gadal v'yit'kadash sh'mei raba
> b'al'ma di v'ra khir'utei
> in the world that He created as He willed

A cop told him to shut up or he'd arrest him, and Max took a cab back to the apartment.

Hirschler was still awake. He greeted Max with a mixture of relief and resignation. They made love one last time, slowly, in half-time; Max couldn't tell if this was through lethargy or the heat or a desire to absorb as much of each other as they could.

His body was his body.

"All of this is just playground stuff until we get close to Roosevelt. We need to get through to Morgenthau. Once he's listening, once he's heard us and told FDR, then things will begin to happen. And even then we'll be up to our eyeballs in the Jews-control-Washington bullshit but at least—"

"Enough," said Max.

Hirschler's stare was empty.

"Please, just for one night, can we not . . . "

In the morning they packed in silence. Hirschler showered and emerged from the bathroom clean-shaven, beginning to transform himself back into the gleaming machine he was during the day.

"Got time for breakfast before your train?"

Max shook his head.

"You look hungry. Let me buy you a plate of eggs."

"I've got one more meeting," said Max. "It isn't one I can dodge."

The closest thing to humility he could muster crossed Hirschler's face.

"I'm sorry to hear that."

HE LUGGED HIS suitcase through downtown. The day was chokingly humid. A thunderstorm was almost certainly coming. The sidewalks were clogged with men with their heads down, their strides slowed.

In his nervousness, Max forgot the address of the restaurant. He spent thirty minutes circling identical-looking streets. Each intersection seemed like it would be the one to open up on to the place he was looking for, or rather it felt that way, that the grid of the city somehow owed him the favor of momentarily reordering itself so Max could cease being lost. The buildings looked the same. The faces began to duplicate. He had no idea what time it was. The lunch could be finished by now. His train could be pulling out of the station. He leaned against a lamppost and posited two possible outcomes: asking for help or spending eternity lost beneath the elevated tracks.

He raised his arm for a cab. One pulled up immediately. Max hauled in his suitcase and sat down heavily, letting out a deep sigh.

"Where to?" said the hack.

Max gave him the address. The hack rolled his eyes and pointed to the opposite side of the street.

"Where you're looking for is right there."

A wave of shame hit him. And he hadn't even seen his father yet. Max gave the driver a dollar for his troubles and got out of the cab.

"Both ways you gotta look before crossing," the hack called, pretending to smile.

He entered the restaurant with his head down. He had known he would be defeated by his father but hadn't imagined the capitulation taking place before they had even greeted one another. What had happened in the days preceding left him open, raw.

He gave the hat-check girl his things and moved through the deep crimson and gold dining room. His father, by himself at a table in the corner, armed with several newspapers, looked as though Max's presence were wholly optional. He could have wheeled around, taken his things, begged Hirschler for eggs, and the old man might have noticed in a few weeks.

Instead Max trudged to the edge of the table.

"How are the stateless persons?" his father asked. This was how he began, his first face-to-face words with the son he hadn't seen in years. Not hello, how are you my boy, my flesh, my only son at last returned? None of that conversational shuffling. Max's father had no patience for small talk. Even greetings came across as interrogation.

Max sat down. The table was already laden with food. He wondered if his father was expecting anyone else. The collision of scents made him feel ill.

"You know you have people you are related to by blood who are being killed. If you think it's good, jokey, lunchtime talk, I'd be happy to share with you the various ways in which they're apparently being dispatched."

"Apparently," his father repeated. "Apparently, Max. We have the accounts of a few frenzied refugees and some knock-kneed Brits. This does not constitute Armageddon. Besides, I'm only using the lingua franca of our trusted news sources."

He waved a hand at the pile of newspapers beside him. Max could have pored over every item and would have found only passing references to *stateless persons, displaced persons, refugees.* Not once would Jews be mentioned.

"Stop carrying the weight of the world around your neck and have a drink. Do you need to ruin our one lunch of the Roosevelt administration before you've even started the meal?"

No matter how many times he studied the old man's face, he could never find in it the faintest resemblance to his own. It was an oval face with oval eyes the color of algae. He'd been bald for as long as Max remembered, bespectacled and slightly fat, but strong-seeming in the back and neck and forearms. With an average-sized nose and average-sized ears, it was his lips that betrayed him, thick and fleshy and more vertical than expected, the shape and color of wild tubers, but still manly somehow—they claimed their stake on his face even before words escaped them.

"I think a lot was accomplished this week," he said to his father. "I think we made a lot of progress toward bringing together a lot of very differing groups into a common cause."

His father swallowed his food and nodded.

"And what about bringing a unified front to our family? Any progress there?"

"Utica is home now," he said, looking at a plate of scalloped potatoes, speaking a little more slowly than he would have liked to.

"This is a beautiful city," his father said.

"I know it is."

"This is a beautiful city that made you, that's watched you run halfway across the planet to devote your brilliant life to the scruffiest errata and that will still take you back. It's a generosity no woman—or barely even a parent—would extend. But here it does."

"You speak more poetically than you want to, Papa."

He meant it affectionately, he felt, after his father's imprecation, the smallest spark of affection, but his father's expression had devolved to full-fledged scowl, even with a mouthful of food.

"There are people in Utica who need me and I won't leave them. I hope you recognize a commitment."

"What I recognize is someone who makes a life out of running from one place to the next. I'd honestly rather have had you rob banks if that were going to be your way of being."

Max didn't answer. He held his chin in his left hand and looked away from his father. Gray light pooled at the window. He was aware of the clenched noise, the muffled action that took place in restaurants like these. It brought back the ache of the El seats, the pain seizing his body. He tried conjuring the memory of Hirschler as a palliative but he'd already faded into a frazzled murk with the conference.

"I remember," said his father, "that stinking, dim cheder my uncle dragged me into each week and those foul old men whose existence was spelled out in a gibberish alphabet and the meaning of acrostics. You were meant to be so much more than that."

He had forgotten that beyond the blunt instrument of his father's face there was grossly deformed love, wretched, misbegotten, with its mangled arms always open. This love that only expressed itself with scorn. It was too much for Max. Had always been but now went past the limit of what could be carried.

"I am going to eat," he said. "I have a train to catch soon and I don't know when my next decent meal might be. So I'm going to eat now."

He was certain his father wouldn't remember—why would he?—but this was precisely what his father had instructed him to do some thirty years earlier on a punishingly cold day at Rosehill Cemetery, as they'd stood over the open grave of Max's mother and Max had allowed the first sobs to escape. As wretchedly sad as he was at the loss of his mother, he feared crying in front of his father almost as much as he grieved for her. It would be an unforgivable lapse, as far as his father thought, a further concession by the living to the lazy menace of death. The morning and the graveside service had been a series of sighs and clenched lips and tightly squeezed eyes but finally, with the cold bearing down and the simple wooden casket laid with awful delicacy into the ground, a whole world of absence opened up before Max, a feeling of loss as an energy, a swirling force, what he would later recognize in Heidegger's *das Nichts*, nothing as a real and true and living thing, and this empty power ripped the sobs from his chest. He hugged himself and trembled, unable to stop the tears, aware that his father could not let this go unnoticed. All he said was, "You need to eat now." It was a deeply confusing response, inapt and illogical (where was he going to find food in a graveyard?), enough so that Max gathered himself, and then a train roaring past allowed him to look away from his father while the wind burned his raw cheeks.

He looked up at his father for signs of recognition and saw only the familiar, patient disdain.

"Your next decent meal would be in about five hours if you'd put your head back where it belonged and just came home."

Max ate. He ate a far bigger meal than he needed, one he would pay for on the train, but one he felt he had to in his father's presence. He stuffed himself with meats and potatoes and vegetables drenched in creams; foods of density and volume. He had wine and brandy and ice cream. He made noises and stains. As long as he did not need to look at his father, he ate.

When he decided he was finished he stood up and said thank you.

"You won't be missed," said his father. "You were once but we've learned. We've adapted. I'm sorry to say. Life here progresses fine without you, Max."

14.

WELL, IT WAS true; she was getting the thing she'd always wanted—a wedding to a man she loved, an apartment she could make her own, and a one-way ticket out of her parents' home and the Siberian backwater that was Utica, New York. Judith knew her life was full of blessings and good fortune and all the rest, and yet still, at this moment, she wanted to scream. The cause was simple: staring into the drab abyss of her bedroom closet, she realized that, with an important evening before her, maybe the most important evening of her life, she had nothing, absolutely nothing, to wear.

True, she'd uttered the words to herself at least a thousand times before, but they had never seemed as urgent and unbearable as they did now as she stood before her bureau mirror in her newly hemmed skirt, her darkest red lipstick, her tightest sweater. Plain, she thought. Bland. A schoolteacher dressed for a night on the town. There was no getting around it: all her shoes were too flat and too scuffed; her jewelry consisted of a few small pendants she'd received as birthday gifts from her parents, a single strand of pearls her mother had lent her for a dance and never asked her to return, the silver-plated trinkets she bought from the department store. There was not a single dress left to pull out of her closet. No other vibrant belts or sashes. No sleights of hand to fall back on. This seemed to her at that moment the great struggle of her life: to fool people into thinking she was something other than what she was—an immigrant's daughter, a junkman's daughter, a dull as dishwater Jewish girl from too far upstate. Oh, it was awful, so awful that in a moment of not caring, she let out a sharp, shrill scream. It was not a bloodcurdling scream and not a scared-for-her-life scream, but it was a scream nonetheless, loud enough for her mother, who was cleaning downstairs, to call up, "Was that you, Judith?"

"No, mother. It wasn't me."

There was a pause, and then the sound of the sink running again. Judith picked up a pillow from her bed and screamed again, this time muffling it. Then she threw the pillow at the wall and walked to the windowsill where she kept her cigarettes in a small ivory box her father had given her on her thirteenth birthday, a box he'd bought from the rummage shop where he worked before he bought the yard. She lit the cigarette while staring down at the empty street, waiting for Sam to arrive.

In less than thirty minutes, he was going to pull into the Auers' driveway in his new Buick to take Judith to the finest French restaurant in Utica—the only French restaurant in Utica—and then they were going to the Hotel Utica and make love. They'd decided it would be best this way, one month before the wedding. Judith had decided. It was the first time for her but not for him. She didn't want to lose her virginity on her wedding night—it seemed too old-fashioned. They were engaged, after all, and they loved each other, so why not? Do you hear me, mother, she said to herself. Why the hell not? Her mother would of course pretend to be appalled if she knew. She would spend a day giving her the silent treatment, acting scandalized. Irene had a talent for thinking one thing and behaving as though she thought another. She supposed it came from growing up in such a stuffy household—her grandmother was lodged in Judith's memory as a powdered old matriarch who could issue commands without opening her mouth, her grandfather a clenched, silent, haughty old German. To escape their judgment, to become American, her mother had become as much a performer as the flamboyant diva currently living in their home. As Ana Beidler passed across her thoughts, Judith's mood, which had been weighed down by her dreary wardrobe, suddenly lifted. Of course, she thought. She would borrow a dress from Ana Beidler. After two months of eating their food and using up all the hot water and gazing at Judith's father across the dinner table, it was the least the woman could do.

THE MOMENT THEIR houseguest descended the stairs that first night, Judith had felt a deep uneasiness, an almost instinctual suspicion of this woman who defied her every expectation about what a Jewish refugee would be. And yet, despite the dinner monologues and nocturnal walks, there was a part of Judith that thought, if I have to grow old (or at least, older) and I have to one day become what I know I must—a middle-aged Jewish woman—let me be like this one. Let other people look at me the way they look at her, as though my face contains a mystery. No one ever looked at Judith's mother that way, or her aunts or her cousins or her mother's friends. Sometimes Sam looked at Judith with that same intensity for a moment here or there, but then it faded and she'd go back to being just her usual self, dear to him, yes, but dear in a familiar way—dear as in dependable, sweet, and common. Still, she was his and he was hers, and the simply symmetry of this pairing had made her feel for the first time in her life as though all was well with the world.

He was finishing law school at Hamilton and would graduate that spring, a few months after the wedding. The ceremony would take place at the synagogue, and then a wedding luncheon at the Auers' home. A lovely winter wedding. Not too big or too small. Her dress would blend with the snow. She also had an idea about a white fur stole, something she'd seen in a magazine. She had another idea about taking the dining room door off its hinges so that she could make an appearance, walk down the long hallway from the back door to the parlor, and so a few days earlier, she'd stood and watched as her father unscrewed the hinges from the frame, trying, as he always did, to appease her while letting her know through his slightly pained expression just how ludicrous these whims in fact were.

"Perhaps," he said, getting down on his knees beside his toolbox, "we could suspend you by wires from the ceiling. And then you could fly down the aisle."

"You're hilarious, Papa. A riot."

"It was only an idea." He paused.

"What's wrong now?"

"I'm wondering if the door will be easier to get off than it will be to get back on. You're sure about this?"

"Let's wait and see how it looks. Come on, it's not so hard."

He sighed deeply, opened the box, and examined his tools. Perhaps it was the droop of his head or the curve in his back. Perhaps it was the way the late light through the window hit him, casting half his face in shadow, but for some reason, at that moment, he seemed old to Judith, worn down, defeated. How sad it was, but at the same time, infuriating, because he wasn't old or sick or feeble. He was the same old Papa who'd carried her around on his shoulders well past the age when it was appropriate, only for weeks now he hadn't been sleeping. From her bedroom she could hear him, rising in the middle of the night, turning on the sink, skulking up and down the stairwell, talking to himself. Worrying, probably, about nothing and everything. And so on her wedding day, he'd appear like a tired old man instead of the man she knew him to be. She imagined it, and for a brief moment her cheeks flushed with anger.

"Papa," she said, as he tried one size screwdriver, then another. "I have a question for you. Will Ana Beidler be here for the wedding?"

He continued trying to force in the screw.

"Papa?"

"Can you hand me the other screwdriver? The smaller one."

She passed it to him. "Well?"

"I have no part in any of this. Your mother is sovereign over the wedding. I'm a humble laborer is all."

"I'm only wondering if you think she'll still be here."

"Judith, do I work for the refugee agency? How am I to know these things?"

"You're not, I suppose. I thought though that maybe she would have shared her plans with you."

He turned to glare at her.

"Why is that something she would do?"

"I don't know, Papa." She held up her hands in a gesture of surrender. "I saw the two of you speaking on the porch. You seemed very close, like people who confided in one another. That's why I didn't think it so far-fetched to ask if you knew her plans."

He tossed the screwdriver back into his toolbox, reached for a hammer, put it down beside him, and inched on his back along the floor to find a better angle. "The porch," he said, "when am I on the porch?" He said it as though she'd claimed to have spotted them on the surface of the moon. "Oh," he said. "I remember. We were talking about a theater troupe she was in for a short time that came through Grodno. We were discussing the town hall where I used to go with my family."

There was a time when this mention of his past would have made her lean forward, ask for more detail, more stories. What had the town looked like? What were his parents, her grandparents like? His brother, Shayke, who she knew had died young? Was it a loving family, a warm home? She knew his life had been difficult, but had there been any happiness or joy? And what had he, her father, been like as a small boy, a teenager, a young man? As a child, she'd felt an insatiable curiosity to know about the life her father had left in Russia. But month after month, year after year, she'd faced only reticence and coldness, a blank discomfort spreading across his face with each question. Gradually, his reluctance to talk about life before America had worn down her curiosity until nothing was left of it. When she imagined her father's childhood now, she saw a gray sky, a barren field, punishing snow, and a pot of thin soup.

He had only begun to speak when she interrupted him.

"We'll need to know one way or the other if she'll be at the wedding. No surprise guests. And Papa, what if I said I didn't want her there? Would you think I'm a terrible person? I can picture it. She'll wear that heavy black gown and drink too much wine and make a speech about some actor she bedded."

"You've made your point. I'm sorry you don't like her, but she's our guest."

"It's not that I don't like her. She can be very charming and all; that's the problem. I can never tell what's real, what's put on. Her accent changes, I think. She'll talk about her life on the stage and it sounds so lovely, so exotic, but it's hard to know if any of it's true. I mean, the great Jacob Adler, my elbow. Sometimes I think she was more likely a barmaid. A chiseling little clerk in a customs office. A secretary."

"Keep your voice down, Judith."

"Why? She's sleeping . . . or doing whatever she does in the guest room all day. Does she have supernatural hearing in addition to all her other talents? Besides, even if she were listening, it wouldn't matter. The woman never hears a word anyone says. She listens only to her own monologues."

"So we should gossip at will?"

"Oh, Papa. You're such a bore when you moralize."

"Who was moralizing? I asked a question. Tell me, what if she was a barmaid or a clerk? You'd hold it against her?" The screwdriver slipped from his hand, the rust from the frame cutting his finger.

"Don't get ruffled. I'm not out to get her. Of course I don't care what she was in Europe. I don't care in the least. What I can't tolerate is people putting on airs. If she was a barmaid, let her say she was a barmaid. When someone asks me, I tell them plainly who I am. The day that Sam came into the store, I didn't prance around pretending to be Judy Garland. A diva of the Yiddish stage. It's too much. And I'm not the only one who thinks so. Mama said the same."

"Not to me, she didn't."

"Of course not to you. In case you haven't noticed these past twenty years, my mother is allergic to conflict. Swatting a fly sends the woman to bed."

He gave up on the hinge, pushed himself up to sitting, then tapped the door with his knuckles. "Judith, dear, if you want to make an entrance down the hallway at the wedding, you're going to have to walk through the wall."

She looked at him as though this were a challenge. "You're really admitting defeat so easy?"

"The door frame's about to buckle. It's an old house."

"Maybe Ana Beidler put a curse on it."

Slowly, he opened his mouth to speak.

"Whatever you're about to say, Papa: Don't. I'm not trying to be mean. I don't hate Ana Beidler and I'm well aware we don't know what the woman's been through, the particulars of it. I'm only telling you that you shouldn't take everything she says as fact. We can't let ourselves be taken advantage of." She paused for a moment then added, "I see the way she looks at you."

Abe laughed a little louder than was called for. "And how is that?" he asked. "How does the diva of the Yiddish stage look at Abe Auer, the local junkman, her humble host?"

The smile was gone now, her expression determined. "Knowingly," she said. "Like she's trying to sell you something."

IT WAS ALMOST five now, and Sam would be arriving any moment. Judith pulled off the sweater she was wearing, dropped it onto her bed. The least she could do, she repeated to herself. When she entered

Ana's room, it was not the mess she'd expected it to be. There were no silk slips strewn across the floor, no garden of perfume droppers and atomizers on the tabletops or bureau. The room was tidy—the bed made. On top of the bedspread was a book lain facedown to mark the page—a book by someone with a name she couldn't pronounce. The desk was covered with newspapers, stationery, small notebooks, novels, all so boring. Where were the love letters and diaries and scripts and journals, Judith wondered. After a moment of looking, she gave up, crossed to the closet, opened it quietly. Inside hung dresses of every shade and style—silk shifts and graceful A-lines, full-length gowns with plunging necklines and tailored black suits, beaded blouses and translucent scarves with Japanese prints. The one she took out was blue-gray, the color of storm clouds or tarnished silver. It was knee-length and full around the skirt, but it seemed to weigh nothing. The fabric was lined in silk and intricately pleated. It felt softer than her own skin. At the waist there was a navy sash lighter in color than the rest of the dress, gray but more like mist than metal, with dark beads sewn into it, a design embroidered in black thread. She returned the dress to the closet, couldn't quite work up the nerve. But then, on her way back to her room, she noticed a cigarette case on the nightstand. She walked over, opened it, and took out a slim, mentholated cigarette. There was a lighter on the nightstand. She picked it up and sparked the flame and only then did she realize it was her father's, his large, silver lighter, smudged with thumbprints and tarnished a little on the bottom corner. She turned it over in her hand, held it up so it reflected the rounded, blurry edge of her forehead, put it down on the nightstand, then picked it up again, then put it in her pocket. She imagined her father standing where she was now, the lighter in his hand. She imagined him sitting on the edge of the bed, leaning forward, elbows resting on knees, the way she'd seen him sit countless times before. A shadow moved across the floor. It was the door opening, Ana Beidler standing in the doorway.

Judith tried to think of a lie, spoke the first words that came to mind. "I came in to see if you needed anything. More linens?"

Ana smiled and walked closer. "No, my dear. No, thank you. You brought me some yesterday, don't you remember?"

"Oh, yes. I do now. Well, good. Perfect. I'll be off then. I won't see you at dinner tonight."

"No? Do you have exciting plans?"

"Just going out with Sam."

"I see," she said. "That is exciting." She paused. It was in her pauses, her moments of stillness, when Judith thought maybe she really was who she claimed to be. She didn't fidget or shuffle her feet or slouch. She knew how to wait, how to listen. "Are you and this boy of yours very much in love?" she asked.

The question took Judith aback. She'd been asked by friends if she really liked Sam, if she adored him, if she trusted him, if they'd "done it yet," as her best friend Lynne put it. But she'd never been asked if she loved him. Until now. "Of course," she said. "He's wonderful."

Ana Beidler nodded. "For a wonderful man you need a wonderful dress. Why don't you pick one out of my closet to borrow? We're about the same size, aren't we? Surprise him with something unfamiliar."

"Oh, I couldn't."

"Of course you can. It's easy. Just go and pick one. Any one you like. Do you not like my dresses?"

"I love them, but . . . "

"A woman has to believe that she deserves the things she wants. It's one of the most important lessons I've learned in life. Wherever you go, my dear, whatever you do, there will be people to tell you your desires are silly or foolish or impossible or even depraved. But you mustn't believe them. The world runs smoother when women don't want much—but smoothness isn't everything, is it?"

"No," she said. "I suppose not."

"So go to the closet and choose a dress."

Judith walked to the closet, slipped the silver dress off the hanger.

Ana nodded. "It's just what I would pick for such an occasion. Now try it on. Don't be shy. Remember, I've spent most of my years around shrieking, half-naked chorus girls."

Judith angled her body toward the closet, then unbuttoned. She slipped out of her blouse, handed it over to Ana who folded it and placed it on the dresser. Then she did the same with her skirt and bra.

"Here, let me help you," Ana said, holding the dress as Judith stepped in. "Now, sit over here and let me fix your hair. You can tell me your worries about this evening, about this boy. I can see the worry in your face. And you know, I can listen from time to time, as well as talk."

Judith sat down in front of the mirror, watched her reflection as Ana gathered up her hair. "It's nothing serious," she said. "Probably just wedding jitters." But through all the stammering and half-truths, Ana Beidler looked at her as though she were waiting patiently for the real story to follow. And so Judith tried to tell her. "I love him," she said. "I do. It's only that when I was younger, I always had this feeling that—it's so hard to describe—but I had this sense that I would do something wonderful one day, live someplace beautiful and be surrounded by beautiful people and have great adventures and have a different sort of life than my parents, different from the one they expected for me. When I was little, I used to go around saying I wanted to be a princess when I grew up. Then one day, I said it to my father, and he leaned close and squeezed my chin and said, 'Listen to me, little girl. I come from a place where there were princesses, and those princesses weren't so nice.'" She laughed out loud at the memory. Then in the middle of the laughing, her eyes welled up. "It must sound childish, I know."

Ana, smiled slightly, eyes shining. "It doesn't sound childish at all. I was that girl you're describing, my dear. And not only was I that girl myself, I've played her many times. It's a familiar script. The cherished but overprotected daughter of a kind but fearful patriarch. A forbidden attraction to the romance offered by the wider world. The young maiden escapes her provincial family for a more fanciful life. You're living inside a Yiddish melodrama. The only thing missing is an alluring stranger on horseback."

"You make it all sound so common and childish."

"Not at all. I played many parts over the years, and I can tell you that as far as Yiddish dramas go, there are worse ones you could be living. A few weeks ago, I received a letter from a Polish friend who was able to escape to Switzerland, an actor I worked with in Warsaw. He described a scene that took place a few weeks before he was smuggled out of the ghetto. A man and woman were walking side-by-side toward a ration line, a young couple holding hands. The woman was pregnant. Even strolling through hell, they appeared to be in love. A German officer noticed this and found it repulsive. He called them out to the front of the line and asked them if each loved the other. They didn't answer. They stood there frozen, too terrified to move or speak. He told them that as Jews they had no right to hold hands in public, or to participate in any other display of affection. He told them to turn their back on one another and to walk in opposite directions and to never approach each other again. He told them that he patrolled the quarter every afternoon, and that if he ever saw them near one another, he would shoot them both without hesitation."

"That's a terrible story."

"Only it's not a story. Though I understand what you mean. I, too, read this account and began seeing it onstage. I thought, this is how love stories will go from now on. No more nineteenth-century melodramas. No more lovelorn maidens. Now the great love stories will be played against machine gun fire and barbed wire, against the rumbling of tanks." She said all this as though in a trance, then looked up, quite suddenly, at Judith's reflection. "Look at you. What a vision you are. Be careful with the dress, though, won't you? My husband gave it to me during our honeymoon in Argentina. Every time I wear it, I'm dancing with him again on the steps of the Plaza Dorrego."

"I'll be careful," Judith said. Ana smiled, placed her hands on Judith's shoulders, and at that moment, Judith felt an unexpected warmth for the woman. She felt bad for all the unkind things she'd said about her over the weeks, the warning she'd issued to her father. At that moment, she wanted to be wrong, wanted Ana Beidler to be a good person. She wanted her magic to be real. She was how the past should be: elegant and faded and beautiful and sad. She turned away from Ana, gave herself one last glance in the full-length mirror beside the door.

"How do I look?" she asked.

"Like the world will bend at the knee for you."

Outside, the sound of an engine, Sam's car pulling into the driveway, idling for a moment before it cut off.

THEIR DINNER WAS everything she'd hoped: they ate snails in butter. They ate bread with their snails and then moved to oysters and then to boeuf bourguignon, which had to be eaten with a good Burgundy wine. They drank two bottles of it. The waiter refilled her glass before it was empty. They ate crème brûlée for dessert, which tasted to Judith like something she'd loved as a child but couldn't quite remember now— salted caramels, taffy? Somewhere between the crème brûlée and the coffee she agreed it was time for the room at the Hotel Utica.

In the lobby, she hovered behind while he checked them in. The elevator man was at least ninety, seemed to see nothing but the buttons before him, maybe not even those. They rode the elevator up to their room without talking. The hallway was all burgundy carpet, brass doorknobs, dusty wall sconces. Sam fumbled with the key while Judith leaned against the wall, watching him. Inside, she took off her sweater, stepped out of her shoes. She went to turn on the lights but before she could he was behind her, holding her. She turned to face him. The lights were low and she could hardly see.

"My Judith," he said. "You're mine, aren't you?" He ran his hands along her arms, the seams of Ana Beidler's silver dress. "You've never worn this before."

"Do you like it?"

"I don't know. . . . You don't look like yourself."

"No? Who do I look like?" She turned in a slow circle, put her hands on her hips.

"A czarina. A princess."

"A princess," she repeated.

There was a pale blue glow to the room, an airless pallor. She thought of her father on the porch with Ana Beidler, how closely and intensely they'd been speaking, his lighter on her dresser. She saw so clearly at that moment what had eluded her before.

"What is it?" he asked. "You seem nervous. Did you change your mind?"

She shook her head.

"Because it's fine if you did."

"I didn't," she said.

He walked closer, ran his hands down the length of her arms, laced his fingers through hers. "Something's wrong," he said. "You can tell me."

"Nothing's wrong," she said. "Now kiss me."

He did as he was told. She kissed him back, and instead of simply letting the kiss linger the way she usually did, she drew his hands under the fabric of the dress, over her hips, her stomach. He reached behind her to unzip the dress, but she stopped him. "Not like that," she said. "Just tear it."

He acted like he hadn't heard, kept unzipping, kept kissing, kept whispering things into her ear. But she said it again and again.

"It's too nice."

"I don't care how nice it is. Tear it." He stepped back from her, looked her in the eyes once more, as though to see if it was really okay.

Then he took the front of the dress, one hand on each front panel of the silver-blue fabric, and pulled in opposite directions until the dress ripped open at the seam with a sound that caused a pleasant cramping in her legs, a lightness in her head, a flush all along her neck and chest, and a thrumming magnetic warmth between her thighs. She saw then how easy it was to let herself be carried away by urges she hardly understood; she saw then that she was weak like her father.

15.

THE SLIP APPEARED one morning in the branches of the elm tree that stood on the eastern edge of Abe's lawn. He noticed it as he was returning from the junkyard: a patch of whiteness in the otherwise unbroken expanse of green that the tree became in summer. When he saw it, halfway between the Oldsmobile and the front door, he stopped to watch it. Initially he couldn't tell what it was; it flapped in the breeze and just looked like something cloth and whitish and angular, turning and slapping like a wind sock or prayer flag. There were a million things that it might have been. As he got closer he made out the lace patterns, the pallor of the silk. His immediate reaction was to look away.

It certainly wasn't Irene's. He knew by the size and the sheer nature of the thing—it was a slip that was meant, at some point, to be seen, whereas his wife, whose legs were nothing to be ashamed of, only chose underthings whose primary characteristic was invisibility. They were not supposed to exist anywhere but in the closet and the laundry.

He doubted it was Judith's. It took a painful, almost mournful thought-inspection to make the determination, but when viewed closely, when placed with his eyes closed on the body of his girl, the size was all wrong, and the shape. It simply didn't feel right.

That just left Ana.

He tried imagining what kind of event might culminate with him now standing a few feet beneath this strip of silk that hung like obscene fruit and then whipped out violently when the wind started. It was possible that there was nothing indecent about it. The past few days had been full of wind and rain. A loose article, dropped from a basket of wash or left to dry on a windowsill (is that fully decent? no matter), gets yanked away by the breeze and catches in a branch. By that logic it might not have even belonged to someone in his house.

Otherwise. Otherwise.

He had left earlier than usual that morning, even before the summer light had broken in the east. He had gone to the yard to accept a shipment of scrap iron that had come from Massachusetts and before that the Maritimes and before that he didn't dare ponder. He knew that fragments of the war in Europe had been known to wash up on far Canadian shores. Or maybe it wasn't. Scrap at giveaway prices was scrap at giveaway prices. You got no greater discount for acknowledging your conscience. He paid the driver, a lanky Quebecois who kept smiling mischievously.

"If your country gets into the war," he said finally, "your army gonna come and take all this."

Abe felt an enormous hatred swelling for the smile. It looked like it had been applied to his face with a hacksaw.

"Then I'll be a very rich man."

"You might."

After he had finished unloading and what passed for surveying the inventory, he drove back home. He would have breakfast, see Judith and Irene before their wedding preparations carried them off. He would have the proper beginning to his day that the early delivery had delayed. It was conceivable that he would see Ana. He did not dwell on the possibility long. It was impossible to know when she would appear and when she wouldn't. Planning for either eventuality made him uneasy in ways that had no business in his head.

And he hadn't encountered either, Ana or the absence of Ana. There was a token of her body, a few feet over his head.

He was used to incongruities from the yard. The physical misplacement of things. A cash register filled with forks. A decapitated mannequin resting in a three-legged crib. He worked in a place beyond the meaning of objects. It was the end, or an end; nothing was required to play by the rules it was bound by in the world.

The slip in the tree, though, did not fit this system of discarded meanings. For one, it was on his lawn, not his junkyard. And also the thing in the wrong place still had an owner, a place where it was meant to be, a place Abe could not stand to think about steps from his house.

He went inside. Irene and Judith were gone. He did not call to see if Ana was home. He found a broom and went back out to the elm. Holding it by the bristles he jumped up and down, trying both to dislodge the slip from the branches but also to snare it on the broomstick—the sight of Abe leaping with a broom at a lady's undergarment in a tree was troubling enough. He did not want anyone to see him chasing after it as the wind carried it up the street.

The jumps clattered his back and knees. Bristles broke off into his palm. The tree did not want to give up the slip. The twigs had found their way into the stitching, the lace; leaves held the hem. Finally he was able to batter it free. Half a branch fell with it. It now looked the way he had hoped never to see it: like it had been tossed away deliberately. He picked it up, took the whole of it into his hand, breathing deeply, attuned to the softness, to the memory of the body it held. He clutched it tightly and as he moved toward his house, turning and squeezing with doing his best to hold all of it inside his fist, not to hide it but to devour it.

And then he walked inside. The house was dark, cool in spite of the heat. It was unusual to feel such stillness in his home where Judith or Irene or now Ana was usually creating some sort of low-grade havoc. He stopped at the foot of the stairs, his breath still heaving. The slip fell from his hand while he looked up, and he walked quickly back outside to his car.

It was only halfway up the block that he looked into his rearview mirror and saw the broomstick and branch, dead together on the lawn.

HE FOUND MAX Hoffman in his office at the temple. His desk was covered with an array of newspapers in a number of different languages. Abe saw English, Yiddish, Polish, something in Cyrillic that wasn't Russian. Open books, loose pieces of paper. A Greyhound schedule. Max seemed to govern over it all in a very haphazard way; if there was anything systematic about his mess it wasn't readily apparent to Abe, who knew all about the proper governance of messes.

It had been noted by quite a few members of the congregation that Max had seemed tired or distracted since his return from Chicago. Abe had only seen him once and nothing struck him as unusual. Men get weary, thought Abe. It is a right. The murmurings took on a harsher note seeing Max now. He was immersed in what appeared to be a conversation between two of the newspapers. He went back and forth between them, making little dots and lines with a pencil. He had greeted Abe but done nothing more than that before going back to the papers.

"How are things, Max," said Abe.

"Things are things," Max said.

"All recovered from Chicago? It's a devil of a place from what I understand."

"You understand well."

"Irene said you missed the Hadassah meeting Friday."

"Yes. I went to the movies."

"Oh. What did you see?"

"I don't know. I left after the short."

He looked up for the first time, not at Abe but in his direction.

"Do you know who we should send to fight the Germans?"

"Who's that?" said Abe.

"Bugs Bunny. He's indestructible and has no moral center. He'd finish the *Wehrmacht* before his second carrot."

He went back to his papers.

"Max, listen, I apologize to trouble you about this but I'd like to ask about Miss Beidler."

"What about her?"

"Considering what she has been through, and what the Torah has to say about guests in the home, this is a little not easy."

"Are you planning to turn her out to the Sodomites like Lot did to the angels? I would advise against that, Abe. Your wife would make a miserable pillar of salt. Especially with the wedding coming up."

He had never seen Max this way. There was nothing present about him. His present was the paper wreckage on his desk. Abe felt like he was a transmission from someplace far off that Max could only hear in bits and pieces.

"You mention the wedding, Max. This is the thing. Irene, Judith as well, that is where their attentions are. This is no small undertaking. And Miss Beidler. She, I don't think, it doesn't seem as though she is comfortable with all that is going on."

Abe paused for Max but Max did not say anything.

"I came to see if we might move her out of the house and into a hotel. A hotel fitting for her. Where she might have her own space and feel less a sense of intrusion."

Max made a small movement of his neck and shoulders whose meaning evaded Abe.

"I was thinking the Hotel Utica," Abe went on. "I'd pay for it, naturally. I wanted to ask, first of all because the refugee agency may have rules or regulations about where its people are put up. But also to inquire at the place where you operate, if I may be violating something by asking her to leave my home. Even if I'm giving her someplace else to stay."

"It's fine, Max. Send her wherever you want."

"Like I said, I think the Hotel Utica for her. Nothing less."

"Have you thought about the Salvation Army instead?"

"Pardon?"

Max looked up again, this time directly at Abe. His eyes were alert in a needless way. They drove into something that wasn't in this room.

"Do you realize, Abe, if we get into the war your entire livelihood could be endangered. Scrap materials of all sorts would be requisitioned by the government."

"I haven't given it a lot of thought," Abe said. "You're the second person who's mentioned that today."

"I wonder if the other fellow was at the conference too. There was a whole afternoon dedicated to the issue. At the conference on Jewish refugees."

"I doubt he was there."

"Well," said Max, lifting his arms to stretch. His shirt was untucked and lifted over his stomach, revealing a line of soft brown hairs. "It may all be moot anyway if we keep to ourselves in this quiet little corner of the earth."

He exhaled and let his body droop. He took a quick glance at his desk, and something familiar, a sad seriousness that Abe always recognized in Max, returned to him.

"You've got a beautiful daughter whose day of joy needs your attention. Get back to it. Once Miss Beidler is checked in let me know the room number. You've done more than enough already." Max shook his head slightly. "Honestly, if you didn't make the first move these things might linger on forever."

IT WAS RAINING when Abe left the temple. He ran to the Buick and wiped the damp hair from his forehead. He sensed at once, enormous relief and also hollowing disappointment. This was simply the way life was, he reasoned. Nothing without its opposite. Forces and forces against forces. Wants and obligations. Nothing easy and nothing damning. You bore the brunt standing upright and that was how you managed decently. He drove toward the Hotel Utica as the rain continued to lash the city and the people within it.

16.

"**T**HINK ABOUT IT," said Irene, "and I speak to you here"—she cast an overly long stare at her husband—"as one woman to another. Think of the privacy. Of the space. All your own."

"All at the synagogue's expense," Abe added.

"And of course you can come back here whenever you like. Whenever you need a home-cooked meal. But when you want your space, you have your space."

Abe nodded as though for emphasis and lit a cigarette. He wouldn't look at Ana directly. He looked above her, beside her, at the table before her and the linoleum beneath her feet. But not at her face. Not in the eye. Which was fine. Fine, she told him without a word. She held her mouth in a clenched half-smile, slowly rose to her feet.

"I understand," she said.

"If it weren't for the wedding," said Irene.

"You don't have to explain. You've both done so much."

"But it's not as though we're going away. We're still here whenever you need us."

Ana sat at the table, hands crossed in her lap, listening to these assurances. She listened and nodded and clenched her lips into the slightest of smiles, and all the time she was thinking about this thing she'd always known but occasionally forgot, this unacknowledged fact that places—cities, towns, entire countries—were not as impartial as people assumed them to be. A place could turn against a person. This was a thing Ana had realized long ago, the daughter of a mother who was always moving, always looking for what came next.

It was not only other groups of people or governments or public sentiment or ideology that grew hostile. She believed this, that a place was more than the ground you walked on and the buildings you entered and the sky above your head. Places, she thought, were the dispensers of curses and good fortune. It was a thing she'd learned to recognize as a child dragged around the world at her mother's side—when a new place was lucky and when it wasn't. Sometimes places seduced you at first, drew you in—suitors appeared, good food and parties, all kinds of luxuries and entertainments—and then, when your back was turned, something shifted. A place could tire of you as easily as a lover. A place could decide to teach you a lesson. Wasn't that what Germany was doing to its Jews now? Places could decide to punish you. They could pretend you didn't exist, close themselves off. Ana had learned to sense such changes, to feel them in her joints the way others read the weather. Once a place turned on you, it didn't matter what form the turning had taken, whether it appeared in the form of a jealous wife, an unpaid hotel bill, a streak of bad reviews, or a pogrom. When a place turned against you, whatever the reason, you left.

She had always known this and she had tried to explain it to Szymon back when there was still time to get out of Poland, when the situation was less desperate. Of course he wouldn't listen. He had his theater, his friends, his other women. And so they stayed until the situation grew desperate, until the city had turned against all its Jews. Only then did he let her try to save them.

She'd begged for favors, written letters. She was composing one when she heard a low, violent moaning rise from the floorboards, an awful sound like a sea animal being dragged ashore. The sound was Mrs. Dolinsky downstairs, mourning her husband who'd hanged himself in the shower. Mrs. Dolinsky moaned and wept and Ana wrote, stood, paced the length of her living room, then sat down and wrote some more. She was writing letters, not only to old lovers but to every Yiddish actor in America she could think of, asking them to help her family flee. The writing calmed her, kept the terror at bay as the Germans closed in on the city. She wrote to Pinsky and Peretz, to Latainer and Goldberg. She wrote to all the Second Avenue figures, old and young. She wrote to them as though they were on intimate terms. Certainly they remembered her, little Ana, daughter of the great diva. She'd been living and working in Europe for years, but surely they remembered, or had heard of her work—Ana Beidler of Odessa, of Bucharest, of Paris and Warsaw. She might be living in Poland but she was a citizen of the world. That was how she posed it. On and on she went, singing her own praises and her husband's as well, begging for papers since it was her fault they were trapped.

She'd wanted to leave for America years before, the day after the universities began their boycott. "New York. Buenos Aires, wherever you like." But they had their theater, their circle of actor friends and artists around Warsaw. They had their art and their life. Her husband was a playwright, the founder of the Sambatyon Theater. Ana met him her first night in Warsaw and married him a month later. She described their family of the stage in letter after letter. Her husband was a Polish national. She, an American by birth, living abroad for many years. They wanted to come home to New York, she wrote. It was no longer safe for Jews in Poland. The two of them would begin again in America and would not be strangers in such a place, would find work in a theater, would contribute to the culture of the Yiddish stage. But first they needed affidavits, promises of support, an entrance visa. Ana signed the forms, sealed the letters. The widowed woman's moaning softened, then petered out. Now there was only the sound of the living room clock, the radiator clicking, distant sirens, the soft scratching of her pen.

She sent in the applications and the letters, then waited. She waited for months. When the reply arrived, she knew before she opened it that it was too thin. As an American, she should return without delay. For the Polish husband, there was nothing they could do. Two, three years before, maybe. Now that the war had started, no.

Szymon read the letter over her shoulder. She'd called him to her so they could discuss the matter. "There's nothing to discuss," he said, deciding it for them, taking the paper out of her hands, pressing his fingers onto her shoulders, then onto her cheeks. She was six months pregnant. She would go because one would be two, and also because abroad, she could be of use.

"And what use will I be if you're arrested?"

"I won't be arrested, because you'll arrange my papers. From America, you can arrange it. And you can have the baby someplace safe." He said this all so calmly, as though they were in the theater again, she rehearsing lines on the stage, he sitting in the dark, suggesting, adjusting.

She began to cry. He came close, leaned into her, held her chin in his hand. "My little squirrel," he said. "You have to be strong."

"I can't leave the theater," she said. "You . . . maybe." She laughed through the tears, and the laughter gave him the chance to push forward.

"Listen to me," he said. "Close your eyes and listen."

She closed them, felt his hands on her face, his lips close.

"Do you remember our first tour together in Bucharest, how terrified you were, opening night of *Love's Melody*?"

"I wasn't terrified."

"You threw up three times during our last rehearsal. Just before the curtain opened, you tried to run away."

"It was an awful script. My Rumanian was laughable." She remembered. The theater was rundown, a creaking stage, bad lighting, the faint smell of manure from the surrounding pastures. It sat on the edge of the town center, across the street from an old stone church. The church bells rang through rehearsals. She and Szymon were still new to each other. One morning, before rehearsal, they made love in a field of poppies behind the church. They were exposed but hidden, somehow, by the ringing of the bells.

"It was a miserable script," he agreed. "It was a cast of amateurs. And there was a band of troublemakers in the neighboring town who warned us there was no place for Yiddish theater in Rumania. They came to the show with barrels of onions. Do you remember? You were terrified. You said you couldn't go on. But what happened? Tell me."

She opened her eyes, laid her head against his chest, let herself be comforted by the familiarity of his scent. "They wept and fainted and threw flowers at my feet."

"Of course they did."

She wiped away her tears. "If I can't get you across," she said, "I'll kill myself. I won't go on without you."

He dug out his cigarettes, removed one, placed it between her lips, then took one for himself. "I'd expect no less," he said.

Dinner that night was a bony chicken, dimpled potatoes, a glass of warm milk with a spoonful of sugar for dessert. Szymon poured wine, a dusty bottle of Bordeaux he'd been saving for a celebration. It tasted sour but Ana drank it anyway. It was a cool October evening. The windows were open. Every few minutes, the quiet of the apartment would be fractured by the sound of glass breaking, a truck door slamming, the distant percussion of gunfire. Ana and Szymon pretended not to hear it. They tried to eat slowly. Dishes were washed. A bath drawn. She sang while she soaked, combed his hair and clipped her nails. They made love once, quickly on top of the covers, then lay down beside each other and watched shadows shift across the ceiling. She watched him drift off, then she did, herself. They slept curled around each other all night, a pinwheel of bodies. In the morning, the bed awash in light, he stroked her hair and spoke into the back of her neck, so she could feel the words as well as hear them. "You go," he said. "I'll follow." And so she did. She left him.

17.

"**A**S WE ONCE again begin the Sabbath, another late summer Sabbath, not quite late enough that we can actually feel autumn's chill seeping in over the mountains but far enough along that the evening light is gone noticeably earlier than it was just a few weeks ago when we all fled to the Poconos or the Finger Lakes; as we enter a Sabbath notched just a little bit closer to the Days of Awe, to Rosh Hashanah and Yom Kippur, with our thoughts turning to fallen leaves and football and, as much as I hate to say it, school; with so much behind us and yet so much directly before us, our thoughts turn to what is ours, to the things we hold fast, to the things we hope will help carry us through the cold and the dark that we know, that we may not want to admit but that we know, is not so far off. We are aware of what lies ahead. It is not easy. We think of our loved ones. We think of cherished memories. We think of the freedoms we possess, of the liberty that we know is our due. Even in poverty and in sickness or the deepest, most lonesome sadness, there are comforts for us. It is quite easy to become blinded to the privileges that surround us at all times. That we may gather here, in this sanctuary, as Jews, without fear of persecution or intimidation or the threat of violence. That we may choose who governs us, from this city all the way to the peak of the nation. That we may associate with anyone, no matter what their creed or belief. We forget these comforts because they aren't placed directly in front of us. Because we're asked to imagine them, to view them as abstractions, things that can be, things that are but that we cannot immediately see. Moses, after his years of travail, begs God to cross the River Jordan so that he may at last see the Promised Land. What is the Lord's reply? He says no. He not only says no but He tells Moses never to ask again. And as if that isn't enough, He effectively tells Moses he's being fired, and that it will be Joshua who leads the Jews into the Promised Land. This happens after God has told Moses to climb Mount Pisgah and 'behold with thine eyes' all the land that he will never know. It is at once cruel and inspiring. To stand at the threshold of the place he has yearned for, to behold its beauty, to see his people gathered, awaiting permission to cross that river, and to know none of it will ever be his. The crossing or the land or the people inside. It is tempting to be reminded of Tantalus, who as punishment for serving his own boiled son as a meal to the gods on Mount Olympus, was condemned to spend eternity in Hades where fruit to eat and water to drink, while directly before him, always moved aside before he could lay hands on them. Of course Moses committed no such enormity but still he met a similar fate. But what was his response, to God's denying him entry to the Promised Land? He did not complain or curse the Lord or sulk. What he did was remind the Jews to obey the Lord's law, to not alter or spindle it in any way, because this is what would allow them to live upon this land they were being given. It is this part of Deuteronomy, *Va'etchanan*, from which this week's Haftorah is taken. Yet today there are many still who stand on an opposite shore, waiting for clearance to enter a chosen land. We know that God operates on His own timetable; we know that He does not always act in time to do what we, bound here on earth, feel is immediately necessary. But must we remain beholden to an unseen other? Must we wait for an affirmative transmission before we choose to act? Mercy does not defy God. Humane necessity does not defy God. We must behold with our own eyes. We must look from this lofted vantage westward, and northward, and southward, and eastward, just as God told Moses, and what we see. What we behold. With our eyes."

Max looked out at the sanctuary. There were several dozen bodies in the pews, all of them stiff and attentive. None of them had faces. Or they all had faces like the morning sky, blank and smooth. He took a quick gulp of breath and blinked quickly. Nothing changed. A crowd of unfaced beings sat before him, waiting for him to continue. Their featurelessness implored him to go on, to continue, the non-eyes expectant and wondering, the fused mouths expressing confusion or concern. The longer he looked the more blank the faces became, blank beyond muscle, beyond bone, receding toward dim, dusty clouds that must have been their spirits. There were things he wanted to scream. Exhortations to return to their bodies. Demands that they stand with their feet on the earth and march. He wanted to scream but he could not. As long as he stood before them he could not and if he didn't, if he did not scream to bring them back, their faces would be lost forever.

He stepped off the bimah and walked out the side door of the synagogue usually reserved for deliveries.

AN HOUR LATER he was on a Greyhound bus rushing east on Highway 20.

BY DAWN HE was walking down Fifth Avenue, looking for the headquarters of the Committee for a Jewish Army.

THE ARMY'S OFFICES were in the Garment District, on a block of tall, gloomy buildings. The front door was locked. The passage of time had evaded him. It was now Saturday morning. Few people had any business being out and about and those who did were moving with far too much purpose for Max to read. He leaned against the concrete, hugging his knees to his chest. Windows full of blank-faced mannequins above him. The subway rattling beneath.

A sensation, warm, binding, overtook him. He recognized it as relief, maybe a version of relief, a feeling of having reached someplace he felt he ought to be. Even at his closest with Hirschler he hadn't felt this way in Chicago. Everything there had been unmoored sound, an unremitting series of yells and doubts. It had made him feel simultaneously narcissistic and obsolete—the self wanted the entire powwow to coalesce into meaning for him but his irrelevance meant that it would not. Here, now, was a power that could draw and actually hold him, that wanted him. It wasn't relief, not yet, but it made noises like peace and sank a heaviness into his chest.

He fell asleep and dreamt of trains. A train that would carry him from Utica back to Germany. His sister was aboard; so was his father, unseen. Hirschler walked by him in a corridor. Ana Beidler explained how they were all going to be shot when they disembarked.

It was Spiro who woke him.

"Max?"

He helped Max to his feet, dusted him off thoroughly, almost roughly. Then laid an affectionate arm around his shoulder. In those moments, while his mind restored itself to the speed of the living, he realized that Spiro had not been coming into the building but going out.

"I see a body outside my door and think these Jewish Committee people must really want to intimidate me." When Max didn't laugh he added, "They usually start with a brick through the window."

Spiro began to walk and Max followed. They turned onto Sixth Avenue and suddenly there was the sun. The light pierced Max. He stopped to let his eyes adjust and had to run to catch up with Spiro, who was just about to enter a coffee shop.

He spoke to the man at the counter in what Max recognized as broken, colloquial Greek. The counterman answered with nods and smiles until Spiro asked one final question. The Greek shook his head gravely and gave a long, angered reply. Whatever Spiro brought up infuriated him at some fundamental level, elicited some revulsion that Spiro could only quell, or rather slow, by saying in English, "Vassilis, I understand. I understand. We are in the same boat. The same sinking boat."

Vassilis shook his head miserably and had a waitress bring them coffee.

"The Italians are massing at the Albanian border," Spiro said. "It's only a matter of time until they invade. The Greeks want support from the British but are only getting it in verbal form. If you believe Vass over there the Greek army is made up entirely of members of his extended family. He has a right to feel left in the lurch."

Spiro took a long drink. He had an effortlessly dissecting quality about him. Max felt like he'd been read two times over since Spiro'd woken him up. Still, Spiro asked, "Why were you sleeping in my entranceway, Max?"

Rather than answering, Max said, "What happens if the Italians do invade?"

"Then quite a few Greeks will be dead. Perhaps a few Italians will also die in the process. One of the fathers of Western civilization will eat its twin. Mussolini would like to have most of the Mediterranean for his own personal swimming pool and a little bit of the Indian Ocean to dip his toes in at night. There isn't much more than the Greeks in the way at the moment. So."

He took another drink of coffee.

"Would you please now tell me what you were doing a little bit ago?"

Max reached into his pocket and took out a well-folded piece of paper. He smoothed it out in front of Spiro.

For Sale to Humanity
70,000 Jews
Guaranteed Human Beings at $50 a Piece

It was an advertisement, full-page, that Spiro's Committee had run in the *Times* weeks earlier. Spiro smiled, half-heartedly, maybe a little wistfully.

"Good work, isn't it. Some of our best."

Vassilis came by with plates of eggs and potatoes. He muttered something in Greek but Spiro didn't respond. He kept his gaze on Max and while Max felt it was scouring layers of himself away, he knew he wanted Spiro unsure of his motives.

"If you came to purchase one of the Jews, I'm sorry but we've sold out. There was no way they would last at cut-rate prices like that."

"You've gotten a lot of business since the fire at the Free Synagogue, is it?"

"Business is a narrow way of putting it. We're far closer to the fronts of many minds, how's that?"

"Not in Chicago, you weren't."

"No. Sorry you had to experience all that rot. Now you know what I'm up against." His expression shifted. "If it means anything, I appreciated your cables."

"It was a mess. It was hopeless. If that represented the bulk of the effort to save Jews . . . "

"Then we're probably better off trying to build machines to quickly count the dead than we are trying to get the living to someplace safe. I know."

The ease with which Spiro was able to talk, the basic conversation over eggs about the annihilation of a people, as though he were talking about baseball or a new pair of shoes, it staggered Max. But at the same time he understood: the deeper you fell in, the more you incorporated the depths. It was like living in a new climate; for Spiro death was atmospheric. He had no choice but to deal with it this way.

"I met . . . a few decent people. A few who would agree with you."

"Of course," said Spiro, with a mouthful of potatoes. "I could probably name all six of them. It isn't as though the entire movement is made up of cowards and defectives. But we remain firmly entrenched in the shadows."

They stopped talking and ate, the silence broken by the clink of forks against plates, of cups hitting the Formica table, of Vassilis's barked orders in the back. Max had forgotten what it was like being in Spiro's presence, to be confronted directly with the man. Time had done him few favors. And yet. And yet. Though he was short and wiry and looked like he was held together with staples; though his clothes might have been filched from a morgue and the tips of his fingers looked like bits salvaged from an automobile wreck; though his lips were violently chapped and his shoes falling apart, despite all that, he radiated a force that was both magnetic and propulsive. You couldn't avoid his energies. Max figured Spiro could get Vassilis and the few other schlubs in the coffee shop to march to the White House if he had ten minutes to grandstand.

With his plate emptied Spiro took out a cigarette and looked at Max sharply.

"Look, Max, I am grateful for what you did for us in Chicago. I am grateful for the help you've given with Miss Beidler. But that does not change the fact that I found you asleep outside my door this morning, which is a profoundly strange thing. Now I have an office to run and business to conduct, even though it is a Saturday or the Sabbath. So you're going to very succinctly explain this strange thing that I saw and then I need to get back to work."

He lit the cigarette and waited.

Max put a finger on the newspaper ad.

"What?" said Spiro. "What does that mean?"

"I want to join. I want to be a part of the army."

Spiro made a noise of exasperation and stood up.

"Come," he said. They walked out of the restaurant without paying. At the door Spiro yelled something in Greek to Vassilis, who just grunted.

Outside, Spiro's stride was even quicker than it had been before. Max got the distinct sense Spiro was trying to get away from him though he periodically slowed to look back and make sure Max was still following.

The army's office occupied several rooms, what appeared to have once been a doctor's practice or perhaps a very specialized sales operation. The amount of activity for a Saturday morning surprised Max. The place was hardly full but each room had several bodies moving about it. Any number of telephones were in use. Typewriters were hammered at. Everywhere, voices. Footsteps and voices.

"Quit gawking," said Spiro. "Come."

He led Max down a hallway, pausing to stick his head into an office to ask a man who was visibly, badly, sleep-deprived, if the birthday gifts had arrived. It was code for something, that much was obvious. The man nodded, looking warily at Max.

Spiro went into the last room in the suite. He pulled down a string and a feeble burst of light illuminated something that didn't really meet the definition of a room. It was a space. An opening meant for things, not people. It was meant to be a pantry or a supply closet and still carried a bitter, slightly medicinal stench. There was room for a desk, which looked like an object lesson in industrial decay, and a chair. Spiro had to inhale and squeeze himself against the wall to reach his chair. He pointed to a three-legged stool for Max.

"Max," he began. Then he let out a long exhalation of breath and put his face in his hands. He rubbed his eyes with the bottoms of his palms.

"Max, war is very tiring," he said. "It takes up residence inside of your head and makes so, so much noise."

"I'm here to help," said Max. "I am here . . . to fight."

"What about Utica, Max?"

"Don't talk to me about Utica."

"There are people there who need you. Whom you serve."

"Fuck them. Fuck every last one of them."

"Max."

He leaned back and forgot he was on a stool. It was only the room's smallness that kept him from falling to the floor. Instead the back of his head met the wall with a quiet thud. The impact didn't bother him as much as he would have imagined. He repeated it a few times.

"No, I didn't mean that," he said softly.

"Oh," said Spiro. "I might've hoped you did."

"What I mean is that I cannot help them. The way they live, the particular problems their lives churn up, the way they think, I don't know it. They've been bred to think that anyone who calls himself a rabbi is a living answer to every one of their problems. And I know none of it, Shmuel. They are crying on the shoulder of a machine who says things that sound more or less appropriate."

"I think you grossly undersell the strength of your compassion. Your problem isn't that you don't care, it's that you care too much."

Max sparked to life.

"That is precisely it and this"—violently slapping Spiro's desk—"is what I care about. There is one thing and one thing only and that thing is life. There is not love, there is not illness, there is not money or children or the weather or a failed business or an ache in the soul. There is just life, life, life. *Das Leben alles ist.*"

"*Jedem das seine,*" Spiro said, perhaps a little too softly.

It was a very old expression, one Max recalled from Heidelberg that got kicked around in taverns and parks frequented by elderly Germans or those with implacably self-destructive dispositions. You get the life you deserve, basically. It enlivened Max even further.

"What do you mean by that?"

Spiro shrugged and shook his head. It was a defeated gesture, one that suggested that whatever he had meant was something very different than what Max heard.

"I've steered myself straight into Utica, is that what you mean? Exile was my fate not my punishment. Right? No." A punch of the table this time. "I'm not going to dissolve there. I will not melt into that earth. Let me fight, Shmuel. You've said you need all the help you can get. I am here. Use me. Send me to Washington or London or to the godforsaken Mandate. Give me a sandwich board and I'll walk up and down Madison Avenue asking for donations."

None of Max's remonstrance seemed to have had any effect on Spiro at all. In fact he looked entirely elsewhere. His mind was on work, his own work, and here was Max, chewing up his time in a cramped room.

"Causes, Max. Causes, motives, drives, compulsions. All dangerous, dangerous things. Purpose frightens me, do you know that? I'm not scared of the SS man with a Mauser. I'm scared of the child in Dusseldorf cheering him on."

He stopped speaking and started to organize the papers on his desk. He moved slowly, sloppily; things slipped from his fingers and he replaced them haphazardly. He was stalling. Max knew that whatever he said when he looked up was not going to be pleasant.

"You and I," he said at last, "we never talked about the Irgun, did we?"

Max shook his head. "No."

"I too was a volunteer. I'd got myself into Jerusalem and talked my way into their ranks. Granted, I didn't need to put on such a show as this to have them take me on but still, it mattered to me. I cared. And because they knew I cared they put me to work on their most dangerous activities. We wanted to bomb the British out. We wanted to blow them up, two by two or six by six until they had enough and left the desert to us. But first I had to learn. A bomb's a fiercely complicated thing and you don't do much good dropping them in open ground or too loosely packed."

As if spurred by the memory of flame he took out a cigarette. He smoked to calm himself. Max had noticed how he switched from the third to the first person, them to us, as soon as he brought the subject to bombs.

"They sent me to Jaffa. There was a cafe that was popular with the British and their families. The owner was a Syrian, a Copt. I never met him. I had nothing to do with the operation except to observe. I waited across the street. I remember watching a girl walking in. She wore flat sandals, a pleated skirt, and a white blouse. She was holding a book under her arm that looked heavy against her elbow. What else? Her arms were dark against the white blouse. Sometimes, now, I dream about her, the girl with the book, dream of her hands, her fingers turning pages. I could see her through the cafe's window. I saw her raise a hand to her head, slide a barrette from her hair, and slip it between the book's pages to mark her place. I watched her place it, this small gesture, right before she stepped inside the cafe. I remembered it because the gesture was familiar to me. I'd seen another woman use a barrette as a bookmark in this same way . . . my mother or my sister, perhaps.

"And then we blew her to bits. The girl with the barrette and everyone else who happened to be in the cafe. *Kaboom.* An arm skidded across the road and landed just a few feet from me. I wanted a closer look, to see if it was her arm, the girl's arm, but then I saw my comrades running in opposite directions, as they'd been assigned, and knew I had to leave."

Smoke had filled the tiny room. The light from the lone bulb was poor and had a burnt quality. Spiro's face was obscured but Max could still see his gaze fixed on him. What haunted Max most about the anecdote was not the gore, or the revelation of violence. It was that he knew it had no moral. Destruction on that base a level, witnessed so closely, could not come alone, not in Max's conception. There couldn't be horror without meaning. Spiro had lain it out as a sheer matter of history, with nothing wider to be extrapolated. Max knew he was supposed to think about the actness of the act, its singular habit of being, and whether that scared him off or drew him in or left him in knots of doubt was up to him.

Spiro stubbed out the cigarette and said the name of a movie star, asked if Max had ever heard of him.

"He's a yid from Minsk, though there are people in Hollywood who'd kill you if you ever said that. I think he might be queer too but that's not relevant. I'm due at his apartment on 12th and Fifth in half an hour. I'm close to talking him out of quite a few dollars. So if we may."

He followed Spiro outside, into the dry, hot day.

"One final question," Spiro said, squinting. "In Germany, did you ever visit the Ettersburg?"

Max hadn't but he knew of it, a supposedly lovely little mountain near Weimar.

"The Germans have built a camp there. They call it Buchenwald. Jews from all over Europe are being shipped in." Spiro paused. "*Jedem das seine*. Evidently that's what they've written on the gates."

You get the life you deserve. He gave the same defeated shrug he had earlier, then tipped his hat to Max. Spiro walked off, a short, ragged figure, swallowed quickly by the city.

THE THOUGHT OF walking to Penn Station and catching a train back to Utica came to Max but it entered his brain like an alien, foreign presence, scratching against his skull, the backs of his eyes. His reaction to it was so physical, so violent, that he stopped and leaned against a lamppost, giving himself time to expel it.

Instead of going back he wandered Manhattan. He was aware, like shadows at the edge of his vision, of people he knew, people whose addresses he could have conjured up. Friends who would give him a place to clean himself up, get a decent sleep, maybe a change of clothes. He had lived here. He had inhabited a life here. But it no longer felt connected to the person moving sluggishly across the sidewalks now. A skin he had shed long ago, no more meaningful than a shirt he'd given away, a pair of frayed trousers tossed into the garbage can.

By the time the first hints of evening slipped into the western sky he was uptown. He could not deny the weariness or the hunger he felt but neither carried the discomforts they did ordinarily. Instead he told himself, I am tired, I am hungry, and let those declarations stand in for real feeling.

The sidewalks were lively with couples on their way to dinner, families outside, enjoying the late summer night. Max kept as far away as he could. He walked at the edges of the curb or against walls. He wanted to keep his eyes upward, at the cliff faces of the apartment buildings, the glimmering beacons of the skyline, the easy rustling of the few elms and hawthorns that lined the streets.

At a certain point he became aware of an absence in the landscape, an opening in the rows of buildings where one wasn't meant to be. There was too much space in front of the next building to the north, too much of its brick siding was exposed. Something had stood in front of it and was gone.

It was space where the Free Synagogue had been. Now a complete emptiness, blocked off from the sidewalk with orange hoardings. Any sign that this ground had once held something was stripped away. Max leaned over the barriers, searching for what, a scorched prayer book, the leg of a pew, a cup, a spoon, a scrap of paper, anything that suggested that this blankness wrongly pressed into the landscape of the city had ever been anything else, had not come into the earth fully formed as a lot filled with carefully tended dirt.

To be this devoid of remnants was a conscious undertaking. After the official investigation was finished, someone had come and sifted through, collecting whatever the fire had not incinerated. Max could not think of any theological or Talmudic imperative for this. From what he knew of the fire, the destruction had been total; he could not imagine there would be anything worth salvaging for when the synagogue was rebuilt—and of course it would be rebuilt, between insurance and the resources of its congregants they could build the world's first skyscraper synagogue if they wanted. But first they had to announce their decimation as utter, unsparing, complete.

He went east through the park, feeling slightly sick to his stomach. In Yorkville, he found a flophouse where he was able to get a bed for the night with the two dollars he had in his pocket by haggling with the owner in German.

The room he was given had cots for several men but for the moment was Max's alone. For that he was grateful. He took off his shoes and lay down and immediately there was a knock at the door.

Standing in the hallway was a white-haired Negro, almost precisely Max's height, dressed in clothes for much colder weather, a bulky woolen cardigan, heavy wool slacks gone thin at the knees.

"Traveler, have you come far?" he said in German.

"No, not especially," Max said, slightly bewildered.

"You look weary. You have come to a good place." His German was immaculate, the accent sounding of Frankfurt or otherwise Hessian, only traces of American floating in the lumpier compounds.

"Thank you," said Max. "I am quite tired. Your German is excellent," he added. "Where did you learn?"

The Negro smiled pleasantly. "I took part in the Herero uprising in German South-West Africa," he said. "As one of the few survivors I was kept on by the Colonial League as a coolie."

As Max began to do the chronological and logistical arithmetic the claim prompted, the Negro's smile widened.

"Friend, I'm joking," he said, switching to English. "I was Army Military Police, part of a detachment in Fort Douglas, Utah, where we guarded German prisoners following the war. My captives were far more willing to talk to me than my brothers-at-arms. I learned the language from them."

He gestured around the room but seemed to mean the whole of Yorkville. "I find plenty of speakers to converse with but few of them want to talk to an *afrikanisch*. I heard you downstairs speaking to Herr

Rodl and thought you seemed like a good soul with whom I might converse in the *Muttersprache*."

It was odd to Max that he would refer to German as his mother tongue. It clearly was not. As tired as he was—the fatigue he had denied for so long had begun creeping up his body, gradually stiffening him from toes to tongue—and as glad as he had been for the empty room, it didn't feel right sending the Negro away. He seemed both hopeful and lonesome. His appearance at Max's door had an air of desperation to it. It cleaved at something deep inside of Max, a part of him that abhorred the loneliness of others. So Max, giving half of himself over to sleep, began a meaningless conversation in German with the Negro, who introduced himself as Frederick. They talked about the war in Europe, about baseball, about life in New York City. Max found that he did not need to pay any attention to what he said. The words, somehow catching whatever cues Frederick left, simply left his mouth. As far as Max could tell the conversation never veered too close to himself.

The feeling of partial wakefulness was as pleasant as anything he could recall experiencing. The beige walls breathed and contracted; the crucifix beside his bed receded into the wall. From the closed window came a current of cool air that blanketed him. Nothing had felt so physically soothing since those moments with Hirschler in Chicago—and as soon as he flashed through Max's consciousness he was there, in the room, on the bed next to where Frederick sat. They sat in twinned poses, hands on knees, hunched forward slightly; but whereas Frederick nattered away in German, Hirschler just smirked, the tightening of his lips that he got away with calling a smile. Max smiled back and joy surged through him, as if to remind him that it did, in fact, exist in nature.

I die and I continue to die, killed and reborn, re-birthed for the slaughter, yoked to the iniquities of the living so that I may see

the grief of the dead, neither survivor nor victim, neither wit-
ness nor bystander but the chaff of history's thresher, spun and
tossed and hacked and unseen and trodden upon through the
entire unceasing winter.

It seemed that Hirschler was talking without speaking, still smirking, invoking this inexplicable voice that filled the room—none shall
return without learning of the bones—in perfect, sonorous German.

It was Frederick speaking. Max opened his eyes fully, allowing
Hirschler to fade, and saw Frederick hunched far forward, almost
as though he were doubled over to wretch, bobbing while he spoke.
His face was bright and alert, tinged with something that looked like
delight.

"What did you say?" Max asked in English.

"Yesterday I was crucified for killing Jesus. Tomorrow I will be
crucified again. Today I am allowed to rest because it is the Sabbath."

Max stood up and led Frederick from the room. The Negro offered
no resistance. In the hallway he looked back at Max with the same
expression he had had only a little while earlier in this same place.
Now what Max saw was not loneliness but someone in a place where
he was the only inhabitant, catching a short and strange glimpse of an
alien world.

HE RETURNED TO the Committee's office in the morning. The door
was unlocked but the rooms were nearly empty, only a few wan and
shifty presences. He found Spiro in his warren, smoking and typing.

"Good, you're back," he said. "You want a job? I have a job
for you. A situation has arisen. There's a ship, the *St. Louis*, it left
Hamburg for Havana and the Cubans aren't letting the passengers
enter. It's something to do with transit visas, it's not entirely clear yet.
But this boat is just sitting in the ocean filled with people and it can't
do that forever. All the agencies are meeting in Miami. I need you to

go down there, not to be our ears but to be our mouth. Can you do
that? You wanted to help, I'm giving you this chance. But you must go
now. No, first you must change your clothes because you look like you
just walked off a refugee ship. Does anybody know where we have the
petty cash?"

18.

"I THOUGHT YOU WERE at work," Judith said.

A drizzly late August morning, more redolent of autumn than summer. Brisk Canadian winds beginning their march down over the Adirondacks, the opening salvos of a cold that would stay put for months. Now, the rain. The house so empty. So quiet. Irene busy putting her home back in order, the process of removing Ana and the tiny, unexpected messes they were only now discovering: a blanket with small holes cut at the bottom, possibly for toes; the decaying remnants of an apple in a dresser drawer; dozens and dozens of hairpins stuffed into a butter dish thought to be missing. All of it evidence of a boredom or an unhinged mind. Judith busy with herself, fallen into the lovely bottomless pit of her wedding. Only Shayke now to keep Abe company. He sat across the table, watched Abe eat with hostile eyes. He seemed to take on an especially nasty air whenever Abe did anything corporeal—eating, going to the bathroom, making love. *She was your guest*, he answered, when Abe implored.

Abe slammed his coffee onto the table, spilling a few drops. "I had no choice," he said.

"No choice about what?" Irene asked. "You turned down another buyer at the yard?"

He didn't answer and she let it drop. Better that way. He was running late, for one, had overslept, dreaming of a woman, not Ana but

someone with ghastly white skin and an inviting laugh. While Irene
showered, he stood in the room where Ana had slept, nothing there
but the slip he'd retrieved from the tree, white silk washed and ironed,
dangling from a wire hanger in the empty closet. Now he stood staring
at a piece of stationery, stained with coffee around the edges. He raised
his pen. A stomping down the hallway. His daughter barging through.
Judith had forgotten her umbrella. She came into the kitchen twirling
it, then poured herself a splash of coffee, glancing sideways from the
counter.

"You've stopped working when it rains?" Judith said.

"I'll be there when I'll be there," said Abe.

"Has mother told you?"

"Told me what?"

"We're going to Albany next weekend to look at wedding veils."

"They don't sell wedding veils in Utica?"

"They don't sell anything in Utica but mufflers and beer."

"I probably could put together a veil from those things."

"Will you be able to fend for yourself while we're gone? There's
seven pounds of meatloaf left in the refrigerator because mother always
makes too much."

"I'll do my best."

"What are you doing with your hands? You look like you're
praying."

"I'm reading the paper."

"No, you're not. You're writing a letter. Who's it to?"

He put it down. "Judith, all human beings deserve a bit of privacy
now and then."

"Privacy? Now I'm really curious."

"Well, go be curious someplace else." She's going to see it, he
thought. She's going to look down and see. The phone rang. Judith
hurried to answer. It was Sam, her betrothed. By the time the conversation ended, she'd forgotten about spying.

"I won't be home for dinner tonight," she called on her way out. "I'm going to the movies with the girls."

"Tell your mother," he said.

"I'm telling you."

After she left, he looked down at the letter before him. He'd written, *Since you left, I think of no one else.* Once Judith was gone, he tore it to shreds. He didn't want to be the sort of man who wrote what he could not say.

SHMUEL—STOP—IN NEW ACCOMMODATIONS—STOP—THEIR DURATION UNKNOWN I ASSUME—STOP—PLEASE ENLIGHTEN WHEN POSSIBLE—STOP—AB

She did not begrudge the Auers for moving her. The room was more comfortable, the hallways populated by visiting railway executives and steel manufacturers and low-level politicians who, like the Auers, made few attempts to hide their stares but at least these had lust in them, rather than mistrust or impatience or confusion.

THERE IS A WAR GOING ON—STOP—YOUR PATIENCE IS REQUESTED—STOP—YRS IN CHRIST SS

Writing to Spiro was her primary pastime. She wanted to know where she was going next. Utica, New York, was not a terminal place. She was a person of unique and easily identified flaws but she knew she didn't deserve that.

Her life had been defined by constant movement. Her mother had essentially considered her an additional piece of luggage. *Never, dear Ana, let a man lodge you at a cheap hotel,* her mother told her. *Do you hear me, darling? It is the one indignity from which a woman cannot recover.* They were staying at the Hotel Adlon in Berlin at the time, living off a German diplomat, her mother's admirer of the moment. She understood very clearly what it meant to be moved at the whims of unseen others. A show booked. A lover guilted back home. A visa stamped. (That same diplomat had simply paid the bill and closed down their rooms when he was given a sudden assignment someplace in Asia.) But never had she felt so thoroughly *suspended*, as though the current of her existence had been dammed up and was left with nowhere to go except back over itself.

I AM GRATEFUL TO BE HERE—STOP—I WILL BE MORE GRATEFUL TO BE ELSEWHERE AB

For every half-dozen wires she sent he responded to one. She realized she actually missed the leery boy at the Western Union office whom she'd been beholden to while she lived with the Auers. The ramrod solicitousness of the Hotel Utica staff bored her. They were kindness Stakhanovites who did not gossip or fantasize or wonder about the endless notes she was sending. She might have been wiring troop counts to Hitler and this scurrying race of desk people would have just smiled.

EVEN THE RABBI WALKED AWAY FROM THIS PLACE SHMUEL AB

Alive and languishing. She let a podiatrist from Philadelphia and his wife buy her dinner. She entertained them in exchange for a meal. When the wife excused herself to use the restroom, the podiatrist slid his hand under her dress. She let it stay there, let it explore to the point that she could feel his fingers trembling, and stood up and left the moment the wife returned, leaving him maroon-faced and lurching in a very obvious direction. At least the Auers could be counted on for a kind of domestic theatricality, something like Chekhov under excessive anesthesia. This hotel stifled itself. A show that ended before the curtain went up.

At the end of her second week at the Hotel Utica, she received a letter that read simply:

Dear Ana,
You are ridiculousness incarnate.
Warmly,
J

She had become so focused on waiting to hear from Shmuel that she had forgotten she had written Jacob in the first place. She balled up the letter to drop in the trash, then thought better and burned it, held a match to it right there above in ashtray on her nightstand. It flared more than she expected. The letter seemed to fight back against the flame. She had to carry it into the bathroom, drop it in the bath. She tried to call room service to tend to the mess of ash that remained, but room service was indisposed at the moment. Well, she thought, sometimes one must listen to what the universe is shouting. Its message to her was unambiguous and emphatic: she was no one's problem but her own.

19.

THE SENSE OF certitude Max had hoped would materialize on the train down to Miami never appeared. Of course he felt right about what he was there to do, was satisfied that Spiro had brought him on board, believed he was prepared to invest all of himself, rhetorically, physically, intellectually, theologically, into the efforts to save these hundreds of Jewish souls aboard the *St. Louis* bobbing in the ocean under the warm sun. But bundling down along the Atlantic seaboard he waited for his resolve to coalesce into something sturdy and vigorous. He wanted to present himself like Spiro or Hirschler, to project what he knew and what he believed in a way that could not be ignored. Night fell as they entered Virginia, then the Carolinas. What he summoned inside himself stayed hazy, elastic.

With the money Spiro had given him, he bought his train ticket and a new suit, forgoing new socks to have money to phone the temple in Utica, letting them know that an uncle in Cleveland had suffered a stroke and he was needed by the family to offer spiritual assistance. The call was brief. He still had a little money left.

Without knowing why, he gave the operator the number of Mrs. Epstein. The line rang for quite some time and the operator asked if he'd like to disconnect the call. No, Max said, she often takes her time.

When she did pick up her reaction to hearing her landlord was a mixture of relief and sorrow. It was the voice of someone who had become far too accustomed to being abandoned.

"You've been away all weekend," she said, "and they said at your temple, that you just left . . . "

"Everything is fine, Nora," he said. "How are you doing? Any word from your Canadian friend?"

"A letter," she said. "Ten days ago. He's been seconded to help defend Hong Kong."

The name of such a remote place made her choke up. It had a disheartening effect on Max as well. What he was involved in was on a planetary scale. A nice fellow from Ontario was needed to defend an island in the South China Sea. What sorts of forces were required to leave the world so fully skewed, to have such dislodging powers?

He was about to offer reassurance but the words fell like lead in his throat. He hadn't the strength to utter more fictions.

"He's tremendously brave, Nora. It takes extraordinary courage to do that. And no doubt he gathers a lot of that from you."

She sobbed on the other end of the line.

"Nora, I'm sorry to bother you but I need you to do something. Are you listening?"

"Yes," she said miserably.

"I need you to arrange to have the elm tree in front of the house pruned. A few of the lower branches look to have rotted. We wouldn't want another branch to fall on us. I meant to do it myself but never found the time."

"Can't you take care of it when you return?"

"Of course I could, but I would hate for one of those branches to come smashing through the windows if a good rainstorm reaches town before I do. Do you think you can manage that?"

"Mr. Hoffman, Rabbi, I—"

"In the upper-right drawer in my desk there is an envelope with money inside. Five dollars ought to be enough. I'm grateful. And if anyone asks you tell them I'll be back as quickly as I can."

Barreling through the Southern night he could not imagine summoning as much force in Miami as he had on the phone with the widow Epstein. His desires, even when placed right in his hands, always had a way of eluding him.

THE CONFERENCE WAS taking place in the ballroom on the fourteenth floor of a hotel along the water. The whole room was filled up with glaring light. For a hotel so luxurious, the windows were filthy. The dirt—maybe it was salt—on the glass was white in the sunlight and obscured Max's view of the beach and the sea below, a bright, green-blue sea, calm and waveless from this height, where the refugee ship had been floating around for three days.

The looming disaster of the *St. Louis* was now floating off the coast of Florida. The Cubans didn't want it. The US didn't want it. Representatives from the National Refugee Service and other agencies, including, somehow, the Committee for a Jewish Army, had been sent to try to negotiate a deal with Immigration and Naturalization by which the ship could anchor.

It was a large vessel, 937 passengers, most of them Jews. The saddest part about the whole episode was that most of them actually had papers, had somehow obtained a Cuban entrance visa, which Max knew from his work back in New York was no easy feat. What the passengers didn't know was that the Cuban president, a fickle and politically insecure man with the heart of a fascist and a mercurial disposition, would decide (long after the boat had launched and the shipping company officials in Hamburg been paid) to invalidate all previously issued visas. The ship had sat in the Havana harbor for the better part of a week, the captain hoping the president would relent or another country would intervene. On day seven, the president expelled them. For a few hours Washington held its breath, praying the captain would steer south, down through the Caribbean, east along the coast of Brazil. There were so many nice South American countries where a Jew might find a home. Pick one, they were all thinking. No such luck. The *St. Louis* raised its anchor and veered north to Miami, invitation or not. It was so close to Miami the passengers (if reports from the captain were to be believed) could see city lights at night, the lights of the country that would not take them.

The table held about twenty-five men. Max recognized a few. There was Louis Rothstein from the Joint Distribution Committee and Harold Sacks from the Refugee Placement Service. At the far end of the side of the table Max was on was David Hirschler.

After the initial briefing there was silence. Everyone seemed afraid to talk first. Finally a man who Max knew was the president of the American Jewish Council cleared his throat and said, "Well, gentlemen, I just got off the phone with Congressman Dickstein from the House Immigration Committee."

"What'd he say?" Rothstein asked.

"That we should go fuck ourselves."

"He didn't elaborate?" asked Sacks.

"There's an election in November. He elaborated on how much shit the administration and the party would find themselves wading in if Americans open the Sunday paper this weekend to pictures of a thousand Jewish refugees disembarking in Miami."

The same silence reclaimed the room. Twenty-five men, gathered for the rescue of a thousand Jews, were downed at the knees after ten minutes and one phone call.

"Dickstein wants us to come up with something else," the man from the AJC said, "to call London, talk to people in Argentina, figure something out. We need something. This isn't Chicago. We're dealing with a crisis that is nearby. There must be a solution."

How did the city lights look from the boat? They almost certainly lacked definition, especially to the provincials, the *shtetl*-bound. To their eyes, Florida was probably a cluster of mountain villages, some tropical recreation of Carpathia or the Massif: glimmers at elevations that normal topography didn't allow for. In that regard, in that familiar way, there was likely something hopeful about the place. Not just that it was a place of refuge but that it was a place not unlike home. You stood above decks at the end of another sultry day and understood passage was notched just a little bit closer, it had to be, it simply had to be. The world doesn't reflect itself so perfectly only for the mirror to turn its face away. These stifled and unknowing people, Max could not believe, were wholly reliant on this room for their salvation. Dumb and pinched faces, drooping mustaches, constipated spirits, guts and odors and their own disowned or bowdlerized or rewritten pasts. Salvators.

"I have an idea," said Max.

"Who the Christ are you?"

"Rabbi Max Hoffman. Representing the Committee for a Jewish Army of Stateless and Palestinian Jews."

"Shmuel still won't show his face. Pity. What's your idea?"

"Torpedo it."

"That's very funny."

"It's not a joke. Have you read the news coming off the Yiddish wire? If we're not going to let it dock, we should be merciful and blast it out of the water and be done with it. That's what the Russians would do."

Sacks opened his hands. "How is that kind of talk helpful?"

"I'm illustrating a point."

"You don't need to illustrate it to us," Hirschler said. His tone was imploring, either to get Max to save himself or to leave the limelight to someone with more clout.

"Apparently I do because I don't understand what's happening here. If we won't let them in, why on earth would anyone else? They'll bounce around from port to port for a few more weeks and when they get low enough on supplies they'll have to go back to Hamburg. They won't even need to worry about U-boats since the Germans have far more efficient ways of killing them on land. We might as well do it ourselves and save everyone the time and frustration."

"What do you suggest as an alternative?" said Sacks.

"We need to get onto the boat. Bring reporters. Interview the passengers, the captain, take pictures of the children. There are two hundred children on that ship."

The director of the JDC leaned forward. "Nonsense coming from the Jewish Army people is nothing new but are you even hearing the words coming from your mouth? You're talking about taking pictures and writing stories as though that will change the minds of men who often can't tell a Jew from a cocker spaniel. Even if you're trying to be absurd, are you fucking serious? Get reporters to do the job? Your Spiro might get a little kick out of his outlandish newspaper ads, but as someone who has dealings with more than a dozen sane people, I can tell you for a fucking fact that using public opinion to solve this mess is about as feasible as *building* these people a new country. Public opinion moves at a glacial pace and the only time it speeds up is when it's moving away from you. You fucking ideologues and your fucking ideas of human participation." He turned away from Max long enough to give a knifing look to Hirschler. "If we are to move anything we need to turn the gears that are already in place. You, Rabbi Max Hoffman, representing the Committee for Insane Jews and Stateless Lunatics, will have no part in that. Now what about Argentina? Who's going to call London?"

At a certain level, Max felt the hot sear of humiliation pass through him. At a different, rather parallel level, listening to the JDC man was like listening to the roar of the surf. It washed over him, left him drenched, but seemed compelled by powers that Max neither knew nor fully comprehended. His cheeks burned but the noise still rattled in his ears, unintelligible and alien.

20.

FROM THE OUTSIDE, the Hotel Utica was a fortress—a broad, blocky structure taking up the whole corner of Lafayette. Red brick, mostly, with checkered white columns, the top four floors bumping out past the face. It reminded Abe of that more daunting city he'd left behind years before when he'd moved upstate. The hotel was out of place here . . . too big, too elegant, a landmark leftover from the textile tycoons of half a century before. Nothing about it fit the Utica of today, which he supposed made it the right place for Ana Beidler.

The thought of her weakened him as he stood outside, but he took a deep breath, pushed past his hesitation, stepped into the revolving glass. The light changed, the street sounds faded. Inside, he was greeted by a doorman in a starched black cap. "May I help you, sir? Checking in?"

"Just visiting," Abe muttered, stepping further into the lobby. How many rolls of carpet it must have taken to cover such a lobby. How many armchairs and sofas and cocktail tables and footstools to furnish it. This was a habit of Abe's, to see every place in terms of the materials it would one day be reduced to. Two grand pianos not unlike the ones he'd hauled in pieces to the yard sat unmanned and silent—one near the back and one near the bar. The only music was human chatter, heavy footsteps across the marble floor, complaints and questions and laughter floating up, spreading out into the white, domed roof. From the ceiling, at least a dozen chandeliers drooped like teardrops, scattering stars across the faded carpet that felt stiff underfoot; pillars finely carved, a few unlit candelabras that hadn't been dusted since Prohibition, and presiding over it all at the main desk, a dandy of a concierge, a man with dyed black hair and waxed eyebrows. This was the limbo to which he'd consigned her. This blind stab at something elevated and cosmopolitan but not quite getting there—the Hotel Utica.

Abe approached the front desk slowly, placed his hands on the desk.

"I've come to see a guest—a woman named Ana Beidler."

"And is Miss Beidler expecting you?" the clerk answered. It was a good question. He'd promised to check in on her the day she'd left, but men made promises. They made them and broke them. Had Ana assumed she was done with him the day she departed, regardless of what he claimed? Had the assumption brought her pain, relief, comfort?

"She's expecting me, yes," Abe said. Then, before the clerk could challenge, "I'm here from the synagogue. She's a refugee. We've arranged for her room, and the synagogue sent me to check in on her."

"Very well, sir. Very well."

He gave his name, then waited while the clerk called up, announced his presence, nodded curtly. "Yes, of course," he said. Then to Abe, "Miss Beidler asked you to come to her room at quarter past seven."

He looked at his watch and saw that it was five. "Seven?" he said. "Could I talk to her now?" The clerk was already on to other business, answered without looking back. "I'm afraid Miss Beidler was sleeping when I phoned up. She didn't think you'd mind the wait."

"AT LAST," SHE said. "You're here." She blocked the doorway but he could see inside the familiar disarray that she had inflicted on his own house.

"Well?" she said.

"Well."

He had his hands in his pockets. In the right he pressed his fingers against the slip, the return of which was his ostensible reason for coming to see her. He had laundered and ironed it himself. He couldn't hand it to her in the hallway, in plain view of any bellboy or respectable traveler who happened by.

"I wanted to see you, to see how you're doing," he said.

She stared at him directly, refused to retreat, even though physically speaking, he had to admit she was not at her most presentable. Her hair was matted in the back. Soft gray half-moons of yesterday's makeup shaded her eyes. She looked thinner, poorly rested, less like a guest and more like a prisoner.

She didn't respond right away, stared blankly instead.

"And? What is your verdict? Am I doing well here? Am I flourishing? I've been sitting in this room more or less for two weeks. No one to speak to. Nothing to pass the time. Nothing but my own miserable thoughts to keep me company. Does it seem to suit me, this solitary life?"

"Ana. . . . It's not so bad. Please, may I come in?"

She stepped aside and let him enter. He looked around the room, wanting to convince himself as much as her about the room's opulence, but the truth was that it wasn't what he'd hoped. It was spacious but dim, certainly nicer than any accommodations he would allow for himself, but not a place perfectly suited to a woman of a melancholic disposition. The lights were off, the bed unmade, the light fixture above the bed held a cemetery of dead moths. Here is where he'd put her, the glamorous Ana Beidler, only slightly less glamorous in her state of dishevelment.

She was dressed in simple slacks, a blue sweater. The bureau was covered not with perfume or costume jewels but with newspapers in every language, some folded neatly, some opened and torn apart. She crossed to her nightstand, lifted a cigarette from the ashtray, stood there a moment, then walked with it to the window. Smoking, she looked out at the street below, the cars and buildings and people shopping, hurrying to work, small and faceless. "Abe," she said. Something was different about her voice. It sounded less guarded, somehow, more direct. She spoke without turning away from the window. "Where are all the Nazis, Abe?" she asked, laughing softly. "Do you ever wonder where they are in this country? What kind of a country is this without Nazis?"

"A safe one."

Again, she laughed. "You think such a thing exists?"

"Why wouldn't it?"

She continued to stare off. "I had a friend once, a friend who was a director. He cast me in a play when I was hardly twenty. I died at the end of the first act and appeared as an angel all through the second. Originally, the part had belonged to another girl, a younger actress, much prettier than myself. But Jacob wanted her to float across the stage in one of the scenes, to levitate by wires. And at a rehearsal, she kept asking him if it was safe. . . . Was he sure it was safe? Was he certain? Without any warning, he fired her. He called on me at home that evening and said, 'Are you afraid to fly?' I spoke without thinking. I said I wasn't afraid of anything. I've told so many lies in my life but I think that was true."

"Have you lied to me?" he asked.

There was a flask of cognac on the bureau and she pointed toward it without waiting for an answer. "No, not to you. Of course not to you. Pour us a drink, why don't you, since you've come all this way."

Only one glass sat beside the flask. He poured the liquor high, took a sip, then held it out to her.

"How is Irene? Is she glad to be rid of me? She must be relieved to have her home all to herself again. Her husband, too."

"She's fine—away for the weekend. She and Judith went to Albany to look for wedding veils."

"Ah yes," she said, smiling lightly, lifting the curtain over her face. "A blushing bride." Then she dropped the curtain, picked up her cigarette again. There was a nervousness in her face he hadn't noticed before, a restless, pinched agitation. She didn't know what to do with her arms, whether to pace or hold still. Finally she reached them out beside her, tilted back her head and let out a great moan. "*Vey iz mir!*" she said. It sounded more like a climax than a lament. She stood tall then, composed completely. "What?" she said. "Why do you look at me that way?"

"I look at you because I can't not look at you. And because you seem like a woman who likes to be looked at. Sometimes I think you're always performing."

"Maybe I am. It would make sense. What else have I ever been taught to do? What else do I know?"

He came closer. Her face was neither inviting nor accusing. It seemed fragile to him then, birdlike. He remembered their kiss at the lake, touching her face with his fingers, and then with his lips. At the time, the danger of it had both thrilled and frightened him. It had made him sick with fear. Now, he'd only wish he'd taken more. He was ashamed of his boldness, but also his restraint.

She shook herself free from his gaze. "I'm hungry," she announced. She stood and walked to her nightstand, picked up an open box of chocolates. "I stole these," she said. He thought she would explain but she didn't, just sat on the bed, cross-legged like a child, placing the chocolates on her tongue, one by one. He went to her, sat beside her tentatively.

"Ana, what's wrong? You're not yourself. Do you want to come back to our house? Would that be better?"

"I don't feel I can, not without the blessing of the rabbi."

"Ana."

"Do you know where he, what's the word, skedaddled to?"

"No one does. Least of all me."

"I knew several actors who walked off the stage in the middle of shows. It wasn't such a shock, really. There were reasons. Always reasons. The bigger problem was the people who rioted for their money back."

"A rabbi isn't an actor," said Abe, "and services aren't a show."

Ana opened her mouth but caught herself.

"I am your guest, Abe, so I will refrain from commenting further."

With more hostility than he wanted, Abe said, "Good."

Her face held firm. Then it softened and she began to laugh. The laughter grew louder, wilder.

"I've said something funny?"

"Everything you say is funny, Abe. Every word." She didn't explain, only laughed harder.

I've made it happen, he thought. She's come unhinged. But as soon as the idea occurred to him she calmed herself, lit a cigarette, smoked as she began moving around the room, picking up clothes that lay crumpled on the floor, folding the newspapers, tidying the small knick-knacks and hairpins and earrings that lay about. She acted as though he wasn't there, leaned toward the mirror above the dresser, peered at her reflection, combing her hair with her fingers, wiping away the smudges beneath her eyes. Then suddenly, she stopped, stood straight and still as though an idea had occurred to her.

"Abe," she said, her eyes brightening.

"What is it?"

"It just came to me what I'm going to do. I'm going to leave this place. I can't stand it one minute longer. But I can leave. I'm not a prisoner here. I can leave any time I like. You can help me."

"Leave the hotel?" he asked.

"The city. Utica. The whole awful town. I'm going to pack my bags, go to New York, start a new life there. And I want you to go with me."

"Ana."

"It's not as crazy as it sounds. I'll need your help at first, but I have a plan. That friend of mine, the director I mentioned, Jacob Feinman; he can help us. He's putting together a great pageant of Yiddish talent to be performed in Madison Square Garden. I'll go to New York and audition." She said it quickly, evenly, as though it were all decided.

"Ana, nothing is as easy as you make it sound."

"But for me it is. Don't you see, Abe? I have to do something, to be of use, to find my place. Otherwise I'll disappear. I know I will. This could be my comeback. A new beginning."

"A pageant," he said. "A beauty pageant?"

"Don't be a fool. It's a theatrical pageant. A production. A play. Haven't you read the paper?" She tossed it at him and he read.

October 9th. Madison Square Garden. Two hundred rabbis. Two hundred cantors. Four hundred actors and one hundred musicians. Some of the biggest names in show business had signed on. It was organized by a man named Shmuel Spiro, a Jew from Palestine who had come to America to raise a Jewish army, to make people see what was happening to Jews abroad.

When he raised his eyes from the paper, she was looking at him intently, her face close to his own. He tried to object but she shushed him, then lowered her lips to his, softly at first, then again. She kissed his lips, his eyes, his cheeks. She took his hands and kissed his fingers, pressed her face into his neck and kissed him there.

He pulled away sharply, tried to catch his breath.

"What's wrong?"

"What's wrong? You don't know?"

When she didn't respond he said what he'd been holding back all these months: "What's wrong is that I'm in love with you, Ana. I'm sick with love."

"We'll go together to New York. Then after the pageant, we'll go farther. It hardly matters to me anymore, as long as it's someplace new. Someplace vibrant and alive. I've always wanted to return to Argentina. Or maybe Palestine. We'll go together."

"Ana," he said, "There are millions of Jews across Europe who would give their limbs to get into America, and you want to get out. It makes no sense."

"So you won't help me? You won't come with me?"

"Come with you?"

She didn't speak. She lay her hands on his shoulder, drew her face close. "Yes, come with me, Abe. The two of us, we could go to Palestine. A summer sailing after the war. We'll never be cold again. We'll be lost and hungry and poor, but we'll never be cold. Can't you see it, Abe? A room in a plain, sunny building with laundry lines draped from all the windows, a courtyard maybe with a lemon tree. I don't cook so we'll go to the market and buy oranges and almonds and olives and eat them on the floor of our little room."

"I do like oranges," he said.

"Then it's decided."

He walked to the window. Outside, a gray haze hung over the city. A ladybug walked across the sill, then onto his hand. It was going where it was going. He transferred it to the tip of his finger. He wished his own life to be so tidy, so simple.

She stood close but her voice sounded distant. "Did you hear me, Abe?"

He put his fingers against the slip again, as though it might convince him to change his mind.

NEAR MIDNIGHT, THEY walked once again through the city's darkness. As they walked, she spoke of her life as though it were a fairy tale. "Once upon a time," she said, "There was a beautiful Yiddish actress named Celia Epstein."

"A friend of yours?"

"In a sense. She died ten years ago, but I talk to her occasionally, ask her for advice. Forty years ago, she was the most glamorous, the most mysterious figure of the Yiddish stage. But she didn't begin that way. She began with nothing, drew her first breath in a cold cellar in Warsaw, the daughter of half-starved factory workers. Her parents were so poor they had to swaddle her in newspapers and potato sacks to keep her from freezing. One day the landlord who owned the cellar mistook her for a food delivery and sent her to his cook's kitchen to be added to the soup. When she opened the burlap and found a child, she was so horrified that she ran away that day and returned to her native country with the girl in tow. After a few months, her Austrian relatives were able to find her work as a nanny on a wealthy estate outside Vienna. She spent her girlhood there, materially provided for but basically unloved. She grew up in limbo, not quite a servant, not a member of the family. She was forbidden from playing with the other children, but because she couldn't play or speak, she began to sing. She sang to soothe herself, to amuse herself, no one else. Her voice was not what anyone could have expected. The tone . . . the range. No one ever told her to be quiet when she was singing.

"At sixteen, she ran away to London, landed a part in the chorus of an East End production. As legend has it, she spent eleven hours preparing for her first performance. She curled her eyelashes and crimped her hair with stones heated in the fire. She painted her face and lips with a crimson tint. She tried on eight costumes, and happy with none, she tore three different ones apart and sewed together the choicest parts. All the chorus girls laughed at the time and care she took. Didn't she know she was only one of twenty, that her job was not to be noticed but to fade in with all the others? But they were jealous. They saw how beautiful she was. And they weren't laughing when the show was over."

"Let me guess. She landed the lead."

"No, there was no time for that. Even before Celia left the stage, an Indian prince who'd come to see the performance sent his servant backstage to fetch her, then swept her away by carriage, absconding with young Celia across the sea to his palace in Bombay. No one heard news of her for four years. They assumed she'd been sold into white slavery, or had fallen ill and died. But they were wrong.

"One day, a theater on Second Avenue called the Orpheum announced her return to the stage as the star of *I Am Singing*. Opening night, she stepped before an audience of thousands, more radiant, more beautiful, more exotic then before. Her voice, always melodic and sweet, now sounded low and enchanting. It brought to mind the wind of the desert, water lapping on the banks of the Nile, nightingales rustling the fronds of fig trees. Also, her appearance had changed. She'd brought back so many trunkfuls of glittering gowns and exotic saris that people bought tickets to her shows simply to see what she would wear. A year after returning, every Yiddish-speaking Jew in New York had come to see the show. People close to her described how that first year, she never really stepped foot in the city because her fans carried her wherever she needed to go. After the show at the Orpheum ended, all the other theaters fought for her. Directors and producers wooed her with gemstones, private carriages, Italian dressmakers, and French perfume. Gordin dedicated three plays to her. Other playwrights competed for the honor. There was a rumor that Thomashefsky once came to her dressing room, lovelorn beyond reason, and begged her just to let him sit there while she prepared herself for the show. He sat on the floor watching her comb her hair, and when she was finished, she glanced at him in the mirror and said, 'Very well then. Now you can write a play for my hair.'

"A few months later they were married. But one man could never hold her attention for long. She seduced actors, directors, poets, revolutionaries. She toured all the great cities of Europe, her charm and glamour transforming the hotel rooms she occupied into salons for the Yiddish intelligentsia. On one of these trips, she married a Russian journalist who followed her back to New York and made her pregnant. By the time the children were born, she'd left him for another. And then there was another. And still another. But none of them pleased her for very long. None of her men, none of her admirers or friends, not even her children, could fill the space that needed filling, the pain of those years in that mansion in Vienna when she'd been invisible, when no one had seen her or loved her. Their devotion couldn't reach back far enough, and so the more fervently they loved her, the less she felt their affection, the less she was able to let it in. The only time she was truly happy was when she was on stage. The only love that mattered to her was the love of her audience, the love of strangers. But audiences, as any actor will tell you, make the worst lovers. They can swear eternal devotion to a star, but the years pass, the star ages, her shows begin to flop, and suddenly they have nothing to give her. The love dries up. The actor is left with nothing. Only then did Celia turn back empty-handed to those who had tried to love her in earnest, the husbands and friends and children. Only then did she try to rekindle what they'd once felt for her. But by then it was too late. She was a stranger to them . . . to us. So over the years, her name grew fainter on Second Avenue and the stages of Europe. The woman who'd been carried across the Lower East Side in the arms of her fans died alone in her apartment, cold and uncared for, just as she'd been at the beginning in that cellar in Warsaw."

"Did you ever meet her?" he asked. "This Celia Epstein."

She laughed without shyness, without fear of being heard. "Of course," she said. "She was my mother."

THEY WENT TO bed early. The sky in the window a cobalt screen. All those nights, when he'd imagined how it would be, what he'd come upon was a single, ecstatic moment stretched out through the night. But in reality, their hours together were full of interruptions. After their first, brief experience of each other, Ana slept an hour, then woke abruptly, stood, paced. She couldn't settle. She wanted to make love, to smoke, to drink, to plot her departure from Utica. She walked the circumference of the room like a trapped animal, threw herself across the bed, flipped from her back to her chest to her side. He imagined Irene sleeping peacefully in the guest room of her cousin's house, felt a pang of longing and remorse, but then Ana drew him back out of himself with the immediacy and warmth of her body, her voice. Her shoulders and hips were finely curved; her calves were strong like an acrobat's. Once, as he was about to finish, she pushed off of him, stood naked before him and began to dance. In her negligee and stockings, a cigarette hanging from her mouth, she reminded Abe of Sonia.

In the morning, as the sun rose in the window, she finally slept. When he tried to rouse her, she told him to go home and gather what they'd need for their voyage, but would not open her eyes. He dressed quickly and clumsily, hurried through the lobby, down the street.

He still had her slip.

The house, when he stepped inside, was empty and silent. It had never seemed so lonely. He had the feeling of being watched, though no one was home. He kept checking the door, expecting to see Irene. He showered beneath a near-scalding stream, scoured and scrubbed every part of his body. After he'd dressed, he tended to the small chores around the house, the ones he knew Irene would expect of him; he took out the garbage, mowed the lawn, cleaned leaves out of the gutters, doing it all in half the time it would normally take.

Then he returned to his bedroom, removed a small suitcase out of the closet, a suitcase Irene had bought him years before that he'd never used. He stuffed it with a change of clothes, a bottle of cologne, a toothbrush, and nail clippers. He packed his checkbook. He packed the three hundred dollars he kept in a coffee can in the pantry. Then he turned off the lights in every room as though he were going to work on any normal day. He would go to the yard and make the necessary phone calls. He would sell everything he'd worked for to whomever had made the most recent offer. He locked the door behind him and got in his car and decided that for once he would behave as though his life was his own, as though he could do with it as he pleased, without fear or remorse.

21.

H E WENT TO his room, stared out the window for a few minutes at the Atlantic coast, almost as if he stared hard enough he might see the *St. Louis* out there on the water. He then rode the elevator down seventeen floors to a lobby King Louis XIV would not have sniffed at. Smack in the center of it hung a chandelier the size of an automobile. Around this centerpiece sat velvet chairs with bronzed feet, crystal vases bursting with lilies, stiff-spined doormen in tasseled jackets rushing trunks and suitcases onto luggage carts, lounging women in large white hats, men in Bermuda shorts, and honeymooning couples laughing and sipping colorful cocktails out of tall-stemmed glasses. He thought he might sink into one of these chairs for the remainder of the day but now the prospect of sitting here among such people, people in couples, people going about their business while the refugee ship drifted ten miles out at sea, filled him with dread. He was deciding what to do when Hirschler appeared before him and said, "Hey, want to go see the races?"

Max thought he was kidding at first and laughed.

"Hialeah Park. It's supposed to be something. A big new grand-stand. It has a Renaissance Revival Clubhouse."

"I have no idea what that means."

"Neither do I, but who cares? The architect built a goddamned lake on the infield and it's crammed full of flamingoes. Hundreds of them."

"What do flamingoes have to do with horse racing?"

"What the fuck do phony belle époque mob-owned hotels have to do with refugee ships? Come on. I get a kick out of watching people lose money."

"I don't know."

"Come on, Max. It'll be easier to talk there."

"It's hot outside."

The look Hirschler gave him was again imploring; he no longer had the brute, mechanical force that slung Max all over Chicago. If he had wanted to he could have commanded Max to his room, had his way with him and said whatever he needed to say. Max was too pummeled by the morning's meeting to fend that off. The fact that he was asking rather than dictating and wanting to go someplace as odd as a racetrack implied a wariness or even desperation on his part. Max saw him surveying the lobby, gnawing his lip.

A few minutes later a doorman in full livery was helping them into a cab.

THE BLEACHERS AT Hialeah were so high and the crowd so dense and the cheering so loud that Max could hardly make out anything on the track below. From where they sat, the flamingoes on the lake in the middle of the track were not flamingoes but a swath of pink. Everyone around them was well-dressed and sweating—sweating into their Panama hats and sundresses, fanning themselves with newspapers, holding cold glasses against their faces. Hirschler bought two bottles of beer and slouched, his hat tilted so far forward there was no way he could see anything but the brim and his feet.

"That was a hell of a way to make an introduction," Hirschler said, "going down in flames."

"I said what I needed to say."

Hirschler took a swig of beer and grinned under his hat. He wasn't going to let Max get away with anything sanctimonious, even if it was sincere.

"You said all you *could* say. I'm guessing Spiro could have given you a little more ammunition if he'd wanted to."

It seemed like he was on the verge of saying more but he stopped and finished his beer in one long draught.

"What race is this? Guy in the gents' at the hotel told me to keep an eye on a filly called Superia in the fifth."

"Why didn't Spiro tell me anything more?"

In one clean motion, Hirschler lowered his beer bottle to the grandstand floor and put his hand on Max's knee. It wasn't a touch that was meant to be hidden. A fella slaps his pal's knee. Its meaning was unknown, the length and the firmness of the touch visibly innocuous but transmitting a heat deeper than the day's.

"You want to go put every cent we have on Superia? If we win, I don't know, maybe we start talking to the Haitians. The port in Port-au-Prince is part-owned by a bunch of Americans. If they'll cozy up to the jigs maybe they'll be friends with Jews too."

That eyeless smile. Nothing but the umbra of his hat and the slant of his lips.

"This whole conference is just going to be reaching in the dark, isn't it?"

"It's all we've ever done, Max. It's all we ever will do."

The hand inched a little higher up his leg.

"Seeing who doesn't hang up the phone first," said Max. "Who can be bribed the most easily. Who's got the most valuable favor."

"You're a doomed literalist, Max. It's a charming quality. We can't truck in anything that definite. Do you know what had to be exhausted to get Dickstein on the horn? These are one-shot deals and we don't even know where the target is."

Slowly, Hirschler removed his hand and lifted up his hat. He sat up, elbows on knees. He was the same Hirschler who had appeared to him in the flophouse, only now with sagging shoulders and a halo of sweat on his brow. The re-apparition did not startle or unsettle Max.

Everything was beginning to unwind, had already started, was sagging toward an incomprehensible rift Max now knew he had been looking into for as long as he had been running.

As if sensing Max's despondency, Hirschler said, "You're right."

"About what?"

"That everyone on that ship is already dead. No port is taking it."

A bugle sounded and a roar of cheers went up. Hirschler turned to a man in front of him and asked which race this was.

"Fifth."

"Shit," said Hirschler. "So much for Superia saving the Jews."

The man gave Hirschler, and then Max, a confounded, disdainful stare.

"Look around," said Hirschler beneath the noise. "Do you think anyone wants to risk any of this?" The horses and the flamingos and the beer and the women in frilled dresses and the men with their skin searing joyful pink and the lake that God didn't create and the sky and the sky and the sky. "Nobody wants a war. And nothing is happening without a war."

He took advantage of the race-entranced crowd to find a free vendor and buy two more bottles of beer. "Maybe if Hitler hadn't fouled up at Dunkirk and the Brits weren't still alive and kicking, we'd have no choice. Maybe Hitler gets far enough into Russia that Roosevelt decides it's time. But this is months, we're talking. Years. And it has nothing to do with Jews. We'll stand up and muster everything we can and scream till our throats bleed and die still roaring and no one's going to hear it over the clamor here."

Hirschler drank and so did Max. The noise in the crowd undulated as the horses circled, the sound following their brutal motion around the oval, and as they approached the finish it became total again, overtaking everything in the park except Max and Hirschler, who drank their beers and stared at the sweat-blotched shirt backs of the men in front of them.

Superia finished in second by a nose. Hirschler let out a long, mournful laugh when the result was announced. He looked to Max. Laugh along. Laugh.

Everything died down as the park entered the lazy interregnum between races. A confetti of loser bet slips rained down from the upper reaches of the stands. It floated in corkscrews and thermal-driven zig-zags as crude planes and wadded up shells. It landed on heads and hats, meant solely to be stepped on, ground underfoot, a burial rite for dead schemes, never-had-and-lost fortunes, blown nights, blown lives.

"No matter the outcome of the conference," said Hirschler, looking at the mess. "My wife and boys are coming down here when it's done. They want a few days at the beach before school starts up again." He was looking directly at his feet now. "Ten and eight, in case you were going to ask."

Max kept his eyes ahead, gazing out at the racetrack, which now seemed suspended in that moment of stillness, of pure anticipation right before the start, even though the next race wasn't close to start-ing. A hush had come over the crowd, as though a collective moment were needed, to exhale, to look at the time, to wonder, to forget some-thing, to reach over and gently elbow the person sitting next to you, hey buddy how's tricks, to make note of the heat on this day, to rec-ognize where in space you stood; and then the crack of a gun and its instant echo, then a bright burst of dust and animal strength beneath a dizzying sun.

22.

BY THE TIME Ana, exhausted and pregnant, climbed the gangway in Southampton, she'd been traveling by land for six days, sleeping sitting up, an hour here, an hour there. She could smell her own body's sour stench, kept bending forward to stretch her lower back. Hundreds of passengers and onlookers crowded the dock. She made her way up the gangway, bodies pushing in from every side, old bodies barely strong enough to tow a bag, young ones straining against their parents' grips, infants held close. Ana wondered how many were fleeing like herself. She heard German, Yiddish, Polish, Russian, other tongues she couldn't name. A clawing, claustrophobic feeling came over her so she kept her eyes on the distance as she pushed through the crowd. Waves crashed against the rocks below while seagulls swooped from above, painting wide arcs across a hazy sky.

She'd purchased a ticket in a second-class cabin, a room the size of a water closet with two coffin-sized cots. On the cot beside hers lay an old lady in a gray dress, gray stockings, short gray hair. She was clutching a photo album to her chest. Her eyes were closed, and Ana assumed she was sleeping until she spoke without looking up.

"*Sprechen Sie Deutsch?*" she said in a weak, even voice.

"*Ja. Ein bisschen.*" Ana spoke German with a Polish accent.

The woman didn't respond for several moments. Ana sat down on her cot, was about to unlatch her suitcase when the woman said, eyes still closed, album still clutched, "*Noch eine Ostjüdin.*" Another Eastern Jew.

Ana pushed her suitcase under the cot as a low rumbling sounded from the bowels of the ship. Inside her there was movement as well, a subtle rotation, as though the child were trying to discern its new position in the world. She left the room to watch the ship lift anchor.

THE FIRST TWO days at sea passed calmly. The weather was cool but clear. Ana walked back and forth on deck all day, tried to read, to write to Szymon, but couldn't make her mind hold still. The food was stale, served on metal plates with nothing but water, but she had no appetite anyhow. She paced all day, avoided her cabin, tried not to think of the future or the present, instead let her mind drift back to her early years on stage in Odessa. She'd been nineteen, fearless. She'd had a string of love affairs, enough that she couldn't remember the men, only the places they had taken her around the city. There was one who carried her onto a boat along the Kodyma River. There was another who took her to the Gorodsky Gardens and read her Turgenev beneath a lemon tree. She could remember the play of shadow and light on the river, the forsythia along the garden path, but not the faces of the lovers themselves.

She wrote more letters, tried to eat a little, tried to hold her loneliness at bay. She played chess one morning with a pleasant old man, a Frankfurt doctor with a kind face and a neat mustache. "And where are you from, my dear?" he asked her. "I can't place your accent."

"Everywhere and nowhere," she told him, admiring his shy smile. He seemed to possess all the warmth the woman in Ana's cabin lacked, asked how far along she was, brought her tea before their games, then tried to let her win. She was terrible at chess and he couldn't quite manage it. He'd offer her an opening, and she'd pass it by, distracted by the clouds, a banking of the ship. "I'm a little better on land," she told him. "But only a little."

"You're perfect, my dear."

Her third afternoon at sea she was on her way to a game when the weather turned gray and a feeling came over her that something wasn't right. She thought it was seasickness at first, a clawing, dizzy nausea. She paced the deck, gripping the railing, but the air felt dank, clammy. The fog had the strangest smell, like salt and corroded metal, like dead things rotting on the sand. Then she realized it was her own smell, that it was coming from her, something sour. She began to shiver.

By midnight she was bleeding. The doctor from Frankfurt came to her room but said there wasn't much he could do. He held a stethoscope to her belly, placed it here, there, told her to try to stay calm. He might have done more to ease her suffering on land, but here he had no supplies, no nurse, no medication. Even through her agony, she understood; he was a good man, a refugee, a Jewish-German doctor with problems of his own. He stood beside her all night while she bled. The floor looked like a butcher's block by dawn. The pain came in waves, then in pulses. She begged to be clubbed, thrown overboard. At one point, a steward came by to see about the wailing. "It's frightening the other passengers," he told the doctor.

"Would you have me smother her in that case?"

"Don't you have something you can give her?"

"Have something?" he repeated. "I have many things. Medicine, equipment. Nurses. They're in my office in Frankfurt. They belong to a German fellow along with the rest of my belongings. Here, on this ship, I have my hands, a bottle of antiseptic, and a toothbrush."

The steward walked off without reply.

By morning her palms were covered with crescent-shaped cuts where she'd pressed her fingernails into her flesh. Then, all at once, the pain gave way to pressure, a wave rolling through her. The baby was born early the next morning. A child the size of her hand and the color of a cloudy day.

FOR NINE MORE nights, they sailed. She laughed in her sleep and cried all day, dreamt of shipwrecks, watery deaths. When she closed her eyes, she saw torpedoes spinning through the ocean, imagined the jolt that would crack the ship from stern to bow, and then the rush of water rising up like a geyser. She indulged the strangest thoughts; she convinced herself the whole world should be covered by water. The land belonged to the Nazis now. Everything good and pure was better off drowned. But she didn't throw herself overboard, didn't end things at sea, as she might have. She thought only of what she'd been sent forth to achieve. "You'll go," Szymon had commanded, "And from there, you'll help me cross." He'd spoken as though it would be so easy, as though she couldn't possibly fail. She held his voice in her heart, as the ship dropped anchor.

On trembling legs, she walked down the gangway to Ellis Island.

WHEN SHE OPENED her eyes, everyone was talking, and no one understood. Three hundred voices in every tenor, every pitch. Yiddish, German, Polish, Russian. The words were not words but bursts of noise, rising, falling, merging, spreading over the auditorium, a noise like an engine, a din that softened in the evenings when they shut out the lights but never really ceased. It was three hundred different voices asking where they were and what they'd do next, why were they waiting and who could help them and where was the toilet, the person responsible for processing papers, and did anyone know where the pats of butter in tin foil had come from, where you could get more, or the little toothbrushes being handed out. Occasionally, she could hear one question clearly above the rest, the way, if you stare long enough, you see a fish break the surface of a calm sea, but mostly there was only noise, thick, impenetrable, a wall of it on every side, a blanket of sound she pulled up to her chin the few hours she slept, the first thing she noticed when she opened her eyes.

The auditorium was on the third floor of a gray building on 59th Street, and the building was the temporary home of the Joint Distribution Committee's headquarters.

She didn't know this at the time. What she knew was a high, raftered ceiling that trapped and bent and spread the noise down in every direction, and the narrow cot on which she lay, not quite long enough to hold both her head and her feet. She was one of three hundred. The cots had been placed in rows of twelve like cartons of eggs. Ana was in the middle of a carton, neither the youngest nor the oldest, neither the calmest nor the most distraught. Her first day there she did little besides rest, turn from one side to the other, covering her eyes with the thin sheet, drifting in and out of sleep, a fever passing through her. As she recovered, it grew harder to ignore the noise, the damp heat, the flickering windowless light, the proximity of strangers' bodies, strangers' voices, the forced intimacy of watching people change shirts and slurp soup out of small metal cups, and weep for those who weren't with them, sometimes quietly, crumpling into themselves, other times without shyness or shame.

By the end of the first day the bleeding had stopped but her body felt weak, leaden. Her back ached. Her throat was parched. It took her two hours to find the hallway where a nurse behind a makeshift clinic was passing out cups of water and aspirin. The second day she was better able to walk, to lean against the wall, survey the others. They were men and women, old and young, newly arrived and stranded for weeks. Some hardly seemed to know where the restroom was. Others were entrenched, surrounded by stashes of candy bars and cigarettes and nail clippers and dental floss. The man beside her had a black coat, black hat, gray beard, the angular, ageless face of the Orthodox. She'd passed someone like him a thousand times in Warsaw. Hadn't she once described the Orthodox as mice? "They're everywhere," she said to Szymon. A rainy fall day five years before. They were standing under an awning to get out of the weather, huddling close for the first time while the water fell in sheets around them. He was smiling, a smile that connoted both attraction and something else—bemusement, disdain. "You really don't like Jews, do you? You're going to tell me you're a Nazi, now. A Yiddish actress Nazi."

"I don't like sameness. I don't like mindless uniformity. I want everyone and everything in the world to be distinctly itself. That's all."

"That's all." His smile became laughter. The rain kept coming, harder now. She put her hands inside his trench coat. "I'm cold."

He leaned forward and tasted the rain on her cheek.

The Orthodox man lay beside her now, as close as a lover. He prayed quietly, facing the wall, his six-foot frame closed up like a clam shell, rocking gently. On the other side, there was an Austrian woman shaving her legs under a hand towel. She'd draped it over her knees, set a bowl of soapy water by her feet, pointed and flexed her toes as she moved the blade. Beside her, a Polish girl was nursing an infant. And all around them, up and down the hallway, strangers waiting, distinct but the same. She was one of them now, more one of them than herself. It was her old fear coming to pass, the reason she avoided parades, political rallies. She feared losing herself to large numbers the way others feared fire or heights.

Her third day, she ventured out of the auditorium, into the stairwell, onto the floor above where there were offices and secretaries instead of refugees. During the First World War, the Joint Distribution Committee had saved Palestine's Jewish colonies from blockade, then the villages of the Pale from postwar famine. Now, from what she saw, the organization was not battling war or famine but bureaucracy itself. The entire headquarters was awash in papers, affidavits, immigration applications. The windows of the small offices were stacked with unread files. The morning sun streamed in through cracks in the stacks. Officials walked the hallways with pillars of paper in their arms, moving the documents from room to room, cabinet to cabinet.

There was an office with the door ajar, a single office at the end of a long hallway. She walked slowly, alone for the first time in weeks. Someone was humming inside the office. A man's voice. A familiar tune. She peered in, saw only hands typing. A throat cleared. She knocked softly, pushed through. The man hardly looked at her. On either side of him sat stacks of files reaching higher than his head. "Can I help you?" he said. "Ladies' room at the other end of the hall, back the way you came."

She combed her hair with her fingers.

"You speak English?" he repeated. "Bathroom?" he said.

"I speak English," she said, stepping forward. "I speak many languages. English. Yiddish. Polish. Russian. A smattering of French. You choose the language. Then we'll talk."

He'd been glancing up at her while he typed. Now the typing stopped. The glance became an earnest gaze. He pushed back a little from his desk. Then, in his own good time, he made a motion with his head for her to come into the office. So, he would help her. It was hearing the way she spoke that had done it. Not for the first time, her voice, her mother's voice, had lifted her above the fray.

"My name is Spiro," the man said. "Why don't you take a seat?"

SHE WOKE TO the sound of the ringing. In her dream, it was a round of applause so bright it chimed across the air, a chorus of gulls. As she came to her senses, she realized it was only the phone beside her bed, in the empty room at the Hotel Utica.

"Yes," she said, in the voice that wasn't hers.

"It's me," said Spiro.

23.

MAX WAS NOT allowed back into the conference and the captain of the *St. Louis* was forced by Coast Guard boats to steer his ship back into the Atlantic with no clear indication of where it should go. Max sat in the hallway outside the ballroom. The Negro bellboys working the floor eyed him with pitiable fascination. One brought him a glass of water. Max listened. There were few raised voices, little movement, only a low, steady drone of wretchedly amenable chatter. Finally he heard a mass scraping of chairs and the noise moved toward the doors. They swung open and the entire conference, all the sallow men in suits, streamed into the hall. They said little. Their faces were expressionless, taut, unmoved. A few of them looked down at Max and muttered or shook their heads. Hirschler walked by without acknowledging him.

Max could not glean what had happened from the little bits of passing conversation but he knew it was not good. It was Harold Sacks from the Refugee Placement Service who stopped, and in a voice that did not lack kindness, told him the boat's fate.

"And Cuba?" said Max.

"From what we can gather the president has authorized his navy to fire on any foreign ships that come within two thousand yards of his ports."

Sacks was small, taciturn; in the moments Max had observed him he had done nothing to demonstrate that he held Max in anything higher than ambivalence. He was a face, a muted voice, a neutered spirit. But now as he stooped, shared the news with Max and offered a look of condolence, Max could hardly bear to meet his gaze. Sacks extended his hand.

"Thanks for trying," he said.

As the ship full of Jewish refugees sailed (or drifted) into oblivion, as the sun was melting into the horizon with an intensity of color that made Max think of the South of France and the blood of fallen soldiers and the fact that one day the sun would burn itself out and everything—the oceans and continents of land and warring peoples of the earth—would pass, after all that was over, Max called Spiro with the news.

"Lovely," said Spiro. "Just lovely." From his flattened tone Max could tell Spiro already knew.

"Is there anything else . . . ?"

"No, Max, there isn't."

"I was thinking, I thought something public." Max's voice was so small again, squeezed by the phone booth, by the tiny black wires connecting him to New York. "If we could organize rabbis. A hunger strike on the steps of the White House. Let everyone see us die the same slow death as the people on the boat."

"You wouldn't make a good martyr, Max. We'll wire you the money for a ticket back. There's work to be done still."

"What's next for them?"

"Who knows? No one can tell the future. Did you know a giant wave once washed over the entire Florida peninsula where you are? They can tell by the silt on either side. A tidal wave. You can be safe one minute and gone the next. All of us. We do the best we can."

Max suddenly felt very claustrophobic. The dim phone booth cut off from the soaring hotel lobby. The thought of Spiro in that cramped lightless non-room. The day spent in the hallway.

HE DECIDED TO go for a swim.

It was nearly night. Only a few children remained on the beach, digging into the sand on the shoreline. The sky and the sea seemed a single, silver entity. He took off his shoes and placed them on a beach chair. He set his wallet and notepad beside them. He walked out into the water, up to his knees at first, then up to his hips. The ocean's perfection surprised him. It had absorbed the day's heat, eternity's, and diffused it into something soothing, balm-like. When it reached his chest, he slipped out of his clothes. His pants and undershorts fell right off. His shirt floated on the surface of the water, the arms extended in a gesture of mock terror or relaxation. He was naked but he was not ashamed. In Chicago, Hirschler told him that shame was the most destructive emotion in the human repertoire of feeling. Nothing good could come of it because it turned men into cowards, broke down the parts of them that were strong and buoyed the ones that were weak. He'd said this with his normal bemusement, with that thin, impenetrable smile.

He closed his eyes and floated, then swam farther out, then floated again. The sky housed stars and a few purple clouds. He found some aesthetic pleasure in these white, pulsating movements but knew that what he saw was, essentially, nothing. These were not even the real heavens. Only small bright suggestions of the impossible beyondness that encompassed everything. The real thing he knew (or imagined) was glorious and blazing, arrangements of geometric light and time that he hadn't the vocabulary for. The space you got, that the water held you up against, was a token, bits of sluiced infinite lodged in the sticky atmosphere. You admired it with the understanding that the true experience wasn't seen but internal. The closest you got to the unending was in your blood, your marrow, your bones, the inextinguishable elements that spread into you just as they did through the sky beyond the sky. You felt that, and you understood, you could sense the lingering vibrations of creation and annihilation.

He flipped from his back to his stomach, paddled forward. The water grew cool around his feet and legs. A noise rose from his throat— a high, soft sob. He was afraid. He closed his eyes.

When he opened them, the space that had opened between himself and the shoreline was startling. In the opposite distance, he could see a line of light, a change in color, the shallow slope of something solid. The line was the *St. Louis* and every other ship with no place to go but the lands they'd fled. The change in color was the place where the ocean met the sky. The solid thing was his body.

24.

JABOTINSKY LAY PERFECTLY still on the small bed. Once great Ze'ev Jabotinsky, now a terribly old man in a small bed. It pained Spiro to see the man who had made and shaped him and so many of his other comrades, so close to the end. The man who fought with the British to eject the Ottomans from Palestine and then fought with Israelis to eject the British. The man who had worked tirelessly to export the Jews of *Mitteleuropa* before the Germans could liquidate them.

His eyes were closed. Lozenges of sunlight lay across the sheet on his legs. If he was breathing, Spiro couldn't see it. To be an exile is to be experiencing a constant form of death. But to be a dying exile is to know a special degree of aloneness. Something purgatorial, a sentence, a spell. Jabotinsky had been in the United States for eighteen months, and he was going to die here. In a small bed. He had come to America to try to rouse support for a Jewish army, and while doing so was felled by a heart attack that every doctor consulted agreed was a fatal blow. The actual moment of expiration was the only question that remained. Spiro walked to the window to let in some air, and when he turned back to the bed, the old man had opened his eyes.

"Shmuel," he said. "I thought you were still in Warsaw."

"Not me," he said. "I came to see you last week." It still didn't feel right to treat him with anything but deference. Even his mental crevasses had to be catered to. "Too much of a coward, me. I've been here a year. You remember."

The old man winced at something, an itch or an inner pain.

"How are you?" Spiro asked.

"I haven't been killed yet," he said. "Or kidnapped and sent back to that prison cell in Johannesburg. So that's something. As for the heart attack, I have no opinion on this, in particular. It is what it is, neither my friend nor foe, and thus of no interest to me. I'd rather hear about you, your Committee. Did you change the name, as you said you would?"

So he did remember. The barmy ancient might have been an act. A disarming gesture while his mind got up to speed.

"We're calling ourselves the Committee for a Jewish Army of Stateless and Palestinian Jews," he now answered.

"Good," he said. "Clear. Direct."

"I had wanted something a bit more flowery, but the others put up a fight. Someone said if we called ourselves the Girl Scouts people would like us even more."

Jabotinsky nodded in approval.

"What do you need?" Spiro asked. "Tell me what I can do to make this more bearable."

There was nothing, of course. Both of them knew. Jabotinsky pondered the sentiment of the offer and deemed it inoffensive enough. "The only thing that helps a bit is distraction. Tell me something pleasant. Tell me about Devorah, the children. Will they be coming to New York soon?"

"No, I don't believe they will. Devorah's met someone else. A chemist. Some German refugee living in Haifa. Three years was apparently one too many. The neighbors began calling her the little widow."

"She'll come back to you, Shmuel. Of course she will. When the war is over."

He closed his eyes for a moment. Spiro moved toward the window and the breeze. On the sidewalk below a nurse pushed a woman in a wheelchair. They weren't going anywhere. Just being outside with the sun and the birds and the cars.

Another nurse entered Jabotinsky's room. She had the silent purposefulness of weather, not speaking to Jabotinsky as she rolled him to one side of the bed and the other, exchanging the old linens for new ones, then lifting his legs to run them over with a sponge, moving over their inert, mottled surface with an efficiency that was so expert it could be mistaken for care, scrubbing, scrubbing, thinking of who knows what, dinner or a balky radiator, reaching into his deeper spaces and treating them with the same force, places that, if Spiro wanted to, he could affix a kind of occult importance to, but instead he looked away as she continued about her business agriculturally, settling again for the window, the other nurse outside, the one with the wheelchair, now gone, now elsewhere, so Spiro just looked at the trees until he failed to realize Jabotinsky's nurse was finished.

"She's gone now," Jabotinsky said after the nurse had left.

The old man was by himself again. Unembarrassed. Spiro walked back, pulled a chair up close beside the bed.

"You've heard about the fire at Field's synagogue?"

"I read about it. A few months ago, wasn't it?"

"Yes. They seemed to have stopped looking for the cause. The investigation fizzled."

"Of course it did. What do the Americans care about one razed synagogue?"

"It wasn't just any synagogue. The rabbi, Field, has connections."

"Field is the one in charge here? The führer of America's Jews."

"Inasmuch as they have a leader, yes. To be honest, the concept of leadership seems somewhat foreign to them. As does discipline, sacrifice. What leads here? Plenty leads here. As it was meant to. Instead of

leaders they have banquet halls full of squabbling men. Field squabbles
the loudest. Or at least he did."

"Were you trying to give this Field and the rest of them something
else to think about? Something perhaps they had been ignoring?"

Jabotinsky read the strain in Spiro's jaw.

"And did you accomplish your objective?"

"I didn't know it was my objective until it was accomplished."

"That, Shmuel, is a grave failure in strategy."

"It is complicated. This woman. I don't know if . . . she was not
working on any given directive. She resists the usual limitations of the
universe. She thinks she can become anyone she wants to, that one's
identity can be taken on and off like a hat."

"She should be an actress not a Zionist."

"She is."

"A Zionist?" Jabotinsky sounded genuinely alarmed.

"An actress."

"Worse than the British, then. Have you had her?"

He snorted. "I envy her. Who wouldn't? Who wouldn't want to be
able to take the world so lightly? To her, even a burning synagogue is
no more than a set piece."

"But now?"

He waited. The bag of fluids dripped silently, steady as a clock.
"Now, I don't know. What she did has been very helpful for us. For
our cause. This fire, it's the first time that people here, any of them,
have experienced anything like that."

"The Americans."

"Yes, and Americans always want to do something when they feel
uneasy. They do, do, do. People who wouldn't return my calls—people who wouldn't acknowledge my existence—now they want to talk.
From Congress, from the papers. Now they feel like we have relevance.
There's interest, there's attention—"

"There's money."

"Loads of it. Of course. For most of these Americans that's what doing something means. Throwing money at it. Oh no, we're being attacked by the men from the moon. Quick, somebody make a donation. I never would have wanted something like this. For Field I feel dreadful. But to be on the other side of what was a moldering failure? I don't know."

"What about the actress?"

"We've removed her from the city. I have no idea what I'm going to do with her. I'll push her off a bridge, and if a boat happens to be going by below, so much the better. Some of the Committee feel like the whole thing is just going to go away quietly; others want to find a scapegoat. I've been told there's a gang of boys in the Bronx who got inspired by Coughlin and defaced some temples. But that's just one thought."

Jabotinsky held up his hands. He could still effect a change with the slightest gesture. "Shmuel," he said. "Do you remember that boy in the brigade, years ago, when we were crossing to the Port of Haifa. What was his name now? The gingy, Hungarian boy? The one who went mad in the desert and set fire to the Bedouin hut?"

"Jozef."

"Yes, that's right."

"I remember. There was a family inside."

"That boy Jozef was out of his mind. But do you remember what I told you? We do not have to apologize for anything. We are a people just like any other. All people want a home. All people need villains. We deserve them. Sometimes we deserve to be them. Don't drop this woman into the sea. A few rabbis in tuxedos shed tears. Let them weep. Let them weep while you reap the harvest in their cinders. This woman, who's to say she can't be useful? Have you forgotten all that I've taught you? Use what is useful. Use what is at hand. Bring this woman home. She helped you. She helped a cause, your cause. Ours, Shmuel. Protect what is yours." He let out a sigh. "This land is so strange."

It was. Strange beyond words. Fires blazed and no one noticed. Jews vanished and no one noticed. The rest of the planet was battering itself into continental graveyards and no one noticed. It made as much sense as a dog driving a car, the sun setting at dawn, a tent breathing black smoke in the unbreaking black of a desert night. A big place of nonsense.

And Jabotinsky was going to die here.

25.

ABE RETURNED TO the hotel late in the afternoon. The cold
had grown thicker now. An early scattering of wet, dying leaves
carpeted the pavement. He entered the lobby and felt a sudden stab
of imagined pleasure, a sensation he had denied himself until he was
inside.

"Miss Beidler, please," he said to the desk clerk.

"Would that be our foreign guest?"

Abe scowled but nodded.

"She checked out this morning. The foreign lady."

"My friend," he repeated.

"She paid up for the week, checked out a few hours ago. Seemed to
be in quite a hurry."

It took all his strength to smile. He nodded again, as though he'd
known about her leaving and somehow forgotten. "Did she leave anything? A note? A forwarding address?"

"Not with me. I could check with the evening clerk when he comes
in. A letter did come for her after she left. Do you think you'll see her?
Perhaps you could pass it along."

He tried to smile, to seem unfazed, held out his hand for the envelope.

The return address belonged to someone named Jacob Feinman
on 12th Street in Manhattan. He put the letter in his pocket, where it
nestled in the folds of her slip.

In an instant the world became drab again. Outside, the street smelled of the alley's garbage not yet picked up. The wind had grown stronger, the cold more bitter, yet he walked halfway home without buttoning his coat. The walk took longer than it should have; he could barely find his way, walked in the circles around town for the better part of an hour, kept losing focus, making wrong turns. The streets seemed unfamiliar. The clouds passed quickly overhead like a moving screen. As he walked, he thought back to the last time he saw her. The faint blue vein in her leg and mole on her lip were more real to him, more pressing and present than the ground beneath his feet. His whole soul willed him back into that room with her. A bitter cold blew through him, into his skin and bones. He laughed through the chill. Soon it would be winter. Winter in Utica. Another winter. Another war. How had he borne it all before without her?

A bristling of leaves startled him. He gazed up to see a flock of geese breaking through branches.

IV.
THE DEPARTURE

26.

STANDING AT 67TH Street and Central Park West, Ana Beidler thought the burning synagogue looked like an uneasy cat, rising, then lowering down, then rising again, unable to find any position of comfort. Or no, it looked like the surge of brightness she saw when stepping onto a lit stage: the familiar but unknowable insistence of light that obliterated the audience, left those who had come to see her as nothing but a presence, a pressure in the dark, registered by her other senses, stepping in for her light-stunned eyes. Briefly, horribly, it seemed to Ana that a curtain had risen, that the crowd around her had paid the price of admission, and she hadn't the slightest clue what the production was.

But they were there for the fire too. And it was no use playing with words. Fire was fire. Destruction carried no subtlety and was as poetic as a cough. She lit a cigarette, and somebody nearby gasped. Something in the burning synagogue, a window, a portion of the roof, burst, sending up a plume of cackling sparks.

"Lookatit!"

A little boy, five or six, watched from his father's shoulders. They had the same flax-colored hair and they both had jackets pulled over their pajamas. Ana wondered, of all the bodies around her, how many were just this side of naked? You don't always get to pick when and where the show goes up, do you?

"Lookatit!"

The boy's pajamas had police cars on them.

They wanted to see something, and Ana could hardly hold it against them. The question, as it was with every show she had ever done, wasn't whether or not people would show up. It was what they would say to each other when it was over.

After a while, she retreated through the crowd, walked ten blocks south. Here, the burning synagogue was no more than a dark patch above the trees, a clamoring in her head. She hailed a cab, rode most of the way across town with her eyes closed.

WHEN SHE ARRIVED at Jacob's apartment, the apartment she hadn't entered in four months, the door wasn't locked, and she found him sitting at his desk, typing. Jacob Feinman: director, playwright, possible redeemer-destroyer god, noticing and then ignoring her, the same as always.

Not much had changed in the apartment. Jacob's books in their piles. The spirals of papers and cards and ashtrays and clothing radiating out from his desk. The cracked dishes and the lonesome cupboards. The smell (moth and Lucky Strike smoke and the body of a man with irregular sleep habits). The lightbulb in the hallway was still out and hadn't been replaced. Her dressing gown was serving as a bathmat.

She looked around and suddenly felt tired. There was a clawing pain in her throat when she swallowed. She must have breathed in too much of the synagogue's smoke.

"*Gut morgn*," he said at last. He was thinner all over, but especially in the face, a sallowness to his cheeks that hadn't been there before. Ambition and failure had been working hard on him. He continued to type erratically. She wondered if he was only pressing on the keys to avoid speaking to her.

"Now then," he said when he finally looked up. "Where've you been?"

She didn't answer. She hadn't imagined that the sight of him would be so difficult. What had happened to her and Jacob now reminded her of the fire. A ceaseless ruining force.

"Well?"

"I've been watching a synagogue burn."

"Hell of a way to spend a winter."

"It was rather interesting, actually. It reminded me of the stage." She paused.

He thought about it for a moment. "What are you doing here, really?" He reached across his desk for a pack of Luckys, leaned back in his chair as he lit one. Then he raised his hand to her. "You know what? Don't tell me. Honestly, I think it's better that way."

"That's fine," she said. "However you want to view things is fine with me." She walked to the sofa, didn't so much sit as fall over the side of it, stretching her legs. "I only came because I'm going to be leaving soon. I wanted to say good-bye."

"Again?"

She shrugged.

"Where are you going this time?"

"I don't know yet. Someplace where I can be useful."

He started to suppress a laugh but gave up.

"There are a few things I need before I leave."

"Is sleep one of them? You look ragged."

He was right. She felt too weary to fight. The sofa was softer than she remembered. She had passed out here nights and awoken the following morning with a glass of scotch still in her hand. She shut her eyes. When she opened them he was beside her. Despite everything— there was a part of her that still felt for him, felt warmth, tenderness, little ripples of sympathy when she saw him slipping into a moth-eaten sweater or trying to change a lightbulb.

"Tell me where you're going," he said. "Odd as this may seem, I still find myself occasionally curious about your whereabouts."

She knew it to be true. She'd come a year before, straight from the refugee center with nothing but a suitcase. After not seeing her for fifteen years. He didn't stay angry or call her out on all she'd missed, but gave her food and shelter. He even found her a part in the new Pinsker production at Folksbiene. And what was his reward? The week before it opened, she vanished once again. It could hardly have surprised him. She hadn't changed in all the years.

Now she spoke without moving, without looking at him. "I'm sorry, Jacob. For everything. I've always done the best I can, which I realize isn't much. But if you're looking for recompense you'll have to get in line. It's a long one."

He seemed to soften then. "All right. Enough of that. Why don't you take it easy for once? Stick around for a while. Find some older gentleman to take us out to dinner. Like old times."

"I'm no good for that anymore. I haven't got the stamina. And Second Avenue is dying if it isn't already dead." She took a deep breath in and felt the remains of the smoke scratching her lungs. Then she sat up, looked at him directly. "Jacob," she said. "I'm being very sincere now. More sincere than I've ever been in my life. I'm going. I'm leaving this city forever."

She was fidgeting with her watch, and when she looked down at it, she realized it was the one Szymon had bought for her. Swiss. Gold. He'd bought it for her in a little shop in Vienna, kissed the inside of her wrist before he'd fastened the strap. She remembered that time as like being at the mouth of a vast river with no edge in sight. She freed the clasp and placed it on the coffee table. "You should have this," she said. "A gift for all you've done for me."

He picked it up, flipped it over his fingers. "They don't have time where you're going?"

She went to touch his arm but stopped herself. Something curdled in his expression then. "Go," he said. "Go for good this time, if that's what you want. But remember one thing: you weren't worth the dust on your shoes before you met me. You were a nobody, a nothing, a pretty *yidena* with nice tits. I got them pointed in the direction of the stage where it turned out you were liked. Remember that in Palestine or Mongolia or Shangri-La."

She felt no urge to defend herself. He had once loved her completely, fervently, and that sort of love always ended badly. She had hurt him and he wanted his hurt noted before their time was up. He wanted it counted among the consequences of her noble new life. And so she looked back at him and nodded.

"I'll remember," she said.

27.

A FTER SHE LEFT, Abe slept. In truth, it was a half-sleep, a kind of hovering above himself, his household, the business of putting his life back in order now that she was gone, trying to understand what had happened. From certain sturdy perches in his junkyard he might look out and survey what wreckage he had to peddle. Often, though, his eyes wound up on the city beyond his padlocked fence, at the scabby bungalows and warped A-frames sighing out past the highway and into the hills. From this somnolent perch all he saw was his own inert body, a pale and shapeless thing, like something that might have washed up on the shore of an ocean.

On the second day, in the middle of the night, his brother appeared to him again, a skulking shadow presence hovering near but also distant, impenetrable. Then, after days of hardly leaving his bedroom, claiming a flu, he opened his eyes to the sound of voices down below, Irene's voice and another woman's, pleasant but not familiar, not a neighbor or a friend. He pulled himself out of bed, pulled on his trousers, walked to the sink, splashed cold water on his face, and went downstairs. A schoolteacher. Someone from a relief agency. Her face carried a practiced kindness, a goodwill that came with the territory, not the spirit. That was his first thought. There was something familiar about the face as well. The unease in the eyes. The hapless mouth. She was sitting on the sofa where Ana used to sit, leaning over a cup of tea she held in both hands. Irene didn't look angry but perturbed, shaken. Perhaps she was here about Judith. Trouble at work. A relation of Sam's. "Can we help you?" Abe said from the stairs.

It was Irene and not the woman who answered.

"Abe," she said. "This is Elsie Greene. She is Max Hoffman's sister. She's come in from Chicago."

He came all the way down the steps. At the bottom, he saw the woman was crying, her eyes raw. The resemblance now became sickeningly clear. He had never seen Max cry and now considered himself grateful that he hadn't. Whatever had made him and his sister had not given them faces meant to withstand tears. She had no control over her own face, no grip on the movements, no hand on the sounds. Irene was crying as well, blotting her eyes with a crumpled tissue.

"What's happened?" Abe said.

"Oh, Abe," Irene said. "It's terrible news." The words caught in her throat.

Elsie looked squarely at him and Abe forced himself not to look away.

"He was found on a beach in Florida, a little ways south of Miami."

Abe could read his own expression of bafflement in the way the women looked at him.

"That's where he was, Abe," Irene said softly. "He'd gone to some kind of conference." She turned to Elsie. "About refugees."

She'd been called a few days earlier, his sister told them. The body was sent home by train and buried immediately. Home to Chicago.

"Some of the people at his conference noticed he was missing and the hotel phoned the police," Elsie said. "Somehow they pieced together the body that washed up and . . . " She stopped, not to cry but to contemplate something far off.

"I'm told one of the men at the conference identified him. He knew Max was from Chicago. The Miami police were able to contact my father," and she broke down again.

It was difficult for Abe, picturing Max someplace as *warm* as Miami, or the Miami that Abe imagined from the movies. That was the idea that he became snagged on. Max beneath a resplendent sun. It somehow made less sense than Max's wandering off. Max on the beach. Max in the ocean. Abe couldn't summon it. Not at all.

He hadn't known Max had a sister. Or maybe he knew without knowing. Like so much about his friend, the fact hadn't penetrated or added up to anything. Then again, had he ever asked? All his terseness and erudition and counsel aside, Max had been a person. A person with a sister and flesh and aches who dreamt in his sleep. Everything about his presence resisted these human traits but they were there, waiting for Abe to ask.

"He could hardly swim," Elsie said, as though Abe were broadcasting his thoughts. "Our father wanted him so desperately to learn. We grew up on the shores of one of the world's largest lakes. Max tried. It just didn't take with him."

With Irene supporting her, Elsie managed to compose herself a bit. She was larger than Max, pretty in a very unadorned way. In her worry there was grace and fullness of spirit, and Abe in a burst of understanding knew that she and Max had been very close.

"I wanted to let you know before the funeral," she said. "It seemed wrong, burying him before anyone in his hometown knew. But as you know we had to have the funeral as soon as we could. Still, I wanted to be here. To tell someone. To let them know." She remembered Max mentioning the Auers, dinners, card games, all mentioned fondly, all making the bedrock of his life in Utica.

"Has the *shiva* passed?" Abe said.

"Oh, the hell with all that," Elsie said, followed by a giggle within a sob. "Our father can sit in a dark house and not take a bath. I wanted to be in a place that mattered to Max, and I think this was it."

Abe sat down on the bottom step, taking himself out of the hushed conversation that continued between the women. He wanted words,

words to console himself, words that would allow him to comprehend, that would give course to the sadness that now moved through him in all directions; words to gather the facts and what he felt and pile them high like scrap so that he could climb and look out and see where he was. Words were the only thing that could help, but words failed Abe. Abe failed words.

His friend was gone and all he could muster, standing there at the foot of the stairs, was a simple, awful sentence. "Max is dead," he said.

ABE AND ELSIE drove to the house without speaking. Only when they pulled into the driveway did she begin to cry again and to talk, describing what had happened, the shock of it.

"It was only a month ago he was visiting. That's the part I can't make sense of. I keep seeing him sitting at our dinner table or on the porch beside me. He was upset. I tried to get him to open up to me. But Max was upset a lot of the time about one thing or another. I tried to ask him . . . I tried. You were a good friend, though, I know. He talked about you. Your family. You must have meant a lot to him. You see, Max never had very many friends, not even as a boy. He was the sweetest, kindest soul I've ever known, but there was something not quite . . . " The windows had fogged over. She pressed her finger to the glass, gazing at the streak it made while she spoke. "He was different was all. Sensitive. Boys didn't know how to be around him. They were cruel. And truth be told, our father was no better. I did the best I could to protect him, but there were times when I couldn't. He turned to his studies and his work for distraction." She shook her head, shook away some thought. It had begun to rain lightly. Small drops appeared against the gray windshield. He wanted desperately to be out of the car, to put space between himself and her grief.

He put his hand on her shoulder. She shivered slightly. "Let's get out," he told her.

He opened the door for her. He helped her out of the Buick. The sturdiness of her body seemed like an illusion now. She was weightless, frail; he couldn't imagine how she'd negotiated the train from Chicago by herself. In front of Max's house, a pair of branches, each about the size of a grown man, lay aslant across the walkway. Their ends were jagged, like the torn stalks of a vegetable. The tree they had fallen from was a drooping elm, halfway denuded of leaves. Its remaining branches were thin, mealy; they made Abe uneasy. The trunk showed scars of lightning strikes. The entire thing needed to come down. Abe tried to remind himself to remember.

"My brother. I knew him all his life. We lost our mother young and we were everything to each other. He was a good man but he was quiet. Reserved. When he was twenty-five, he got in his head that he'd go to Spain and join with the Republicans there and he never made it past France, ended up coming back after three months and enrolling in rabbinical school in New York. It wasn't a surprise. He wasn't meant to be a soldier. That just wasn't who he was. A man doesn't change overnight. I believe that—that we are who we are."

She paused for a moment, swallowed hard. Her hands were trembling again, her whole body. "A woman found him on the beach, a woman out for a walk. His body. My baby brother. I keep trying to imagine. We used to swim in Lake Michigan as little kids, the beach near 31st Street. Really, he'd just wade in up to his shins and then go back to the beach. He hated when he got sand in his face. I used to have him close his eyes and then I'd fill a bucket with lake water and rinse it off slowly. I can just see it now, the sand and sun on his skin. His poor body." She wiped her eyes roughly, smiled at Abe through her tears. He wanted to do something, to say something comforting. But what?

"And what is this tree trunk doing in the middle of his porch?" she said at last. He set Elsie against the car and hauled each of the branches out of the way, onto the lawn.

THE HOUSE WAS as it had been left. There were dishes drying on the counter. There was a sheet of paper in the typewriter on his desk. A book with a marker in it on the bedside table. It was a bachelor's home, tidy, but not homey. Bare walls. A bareness and coldness all around, no flowers or knickknacks or small touches.

In spite of her state, Elsie was brutally efficient with her brother's things. She went into the bedroom and within what seemed to Abe like a few minutes had all of his clothes sorted and began loading them into bags and suitcases. This was what she had prepared herself for, Abe thought. This act. This tangible and thought-free act. She could blast through it with little more reflection than she gave to the chores in her own house in Chicago. She moved with such swiftness, such delibera-tion, that Abe eventually removed himself from the room, fearing he was only in the way. Elsie did not seem to notice. He took a few plates and bowls out of the kitchen cabinets, stacked books from the shelves, but nothing he did felt as mechanically precise as Elsie's efforts. She worked as though she were alone in the flat. So he went and sat on the sofa. He had been over a few times, invited by Max for lunch once, occasions when a radiator or pipe needed fixing. In a sense he had felt as superfluous then as he did now. Max had no need for company—his world was outside, elsewhere, and that was where he could be joined— just as his sister had no need for help.

What sort of man makes something so lifeless his home? Warmth was needed, as were color, feeling; reminders that no one was going wanting. It was an instinct that probably dated back to caves but that never brooked any quarter with Max. No doubt there was something rabbinical about it.

While Elise kept up her work there was a knock at the door. It was the widow who lived upstairs. Abe ushered her outside, and then, remembering what Max had told him about her, her relation-ship with the Canadian naval man, the fatally somber nature of that pairing (Max giggling and turning red, telling Abe about the array of sounds they could produce together), led her down the street, before delivering the news. He did not want Elsie to hear her wailing. He would not let her offer her condolences in person. Tell me, Abe said, his hands gripping her trembling shoulders. Tell me and I will tell them to her.

AFTER THE PACKING there was the matter of selling the house, dealing with Max's accounts, something about a life insurance policy that the synagogue had taken out on Max and required Elsie's attention. She had booked herself into one of the murky hotels on the fringes of downtown but Max insisted she stay with them.

"It won't be an inconvenience," he said, and added without thinking, "we've just had a guest for some time so it won't be unusual for us at all."

It was dark when he pulled up, the light on in the kitchen. As he took off his coat and his boots in the foyer, he could hear Judith upstairs. Irene was cleaning up from the dinner he hadn't eaten, standing before the sink, her arms submerged in water. She didn't turn to face him when he approached.

"Irene, Elsie is going to stay with us while she finishes settling Max's affairs."

Irene turned and Abe noticed Elsie smiling sincerely for the first time all day. Any traces of the warmth Irene had shown that morning were gone.

"Of course," she said. "Will you carry her bags for her?"

They led her upstairs. Judith poked her head out of the room and then darted back in, like a kind of frightened animal. The guest room showed no signs of its previous inhabitant. It had reverted to its agreeably stale, deliberately homely natural state. The lingering commotion of Ana had faded. Her smells, her tenacious shadows, her breathy echoes, all gone. Elsie appraised the room with a relieved fatigue; without even removing her shoes she fell backward onto the bed.

"Forgive me," she said, looking at the ceiling light. "I've only now realized . . . "

"Say nothing, darling," Irene said. "No one has any more right to be run-down than you."

"Can we get you anything?" said Abe.

"If there is . . . perhaps I . . . I . . . "

Her thoughts were fraying. The day and its weight had finally brought her down, like one of Max's dead branches. The light in the room took on a very relaxed cast. For a moment, Abe felt like he was watching Judith as a baby falling asleep.

"Rest," said Irene. "We'll leave towels at the door. If you need anything—"

Elsie sat up suddenly. With an odd scowl she began patting the bed. She ran her hand over the blanket, looking for something. She reached under the sheets, just above the mattress. Abe watched with growing dread as she produced a vast, elaborate necklace of brass seed pods, a clanging lattice Elsie let hang from her finger.

"I'm sorry," Elsie said. "I felt it as soon as I lay down. Does it belong to your daughter? It's lovely."

"No," said Irene, accepting it delicately. "It must have been forgotten by our last guest." She smiled. "Rest now. We're here if you need us."

ELSIE STAYED THREE days, settling up whatever remained of Max's material life. With each closed transaction, another bit of Max seemed to be scoured away. Abe felt his friend's presence receding deeper and deeper from the world as he ferried Elsie across Utica, to a savings and thrift, a lawyer, the synagogue. Elsie had no time for rote sympathies or gentle negotiation. She dealt sternly with these men who were often used to grief as an unfortunate but unavoidable source of leverage: the benefit of a life insurance policy converted to an investment; the title to a car sold for far less than market value.

Some of them who knew Abe gave him looks imploring for help but he did nothing. Elsie disposed of each one and moved on to the next. "I apologize if I seem a little gruff," she said after one such meeting. "Our father is an attorney and a very harsh operator. I seem to have inherited more of him than I realized." Everything she did, everything she was, Abe saw through the lens of Max. It wasn't fair, not to Elsie, not to Max, whatever he was now. But he kept searching her for signs of her brother, overlaying her actions on memories of him. At times they fit, or matched; at moments he could not believe they were related. She wiped Max away until he was purely theoretical. Everything physical gone but for a name on a headstone somewhere in Chicago.

Irene accompanied Abe on their drive to the train station. "You've both been beyond kind," Elsie said. "I hope you'll come see us in Chicago someday. It would mean a great deal."

She cried for a moment, the first time she had done so since her arrival.

"We would be delighted," said Irene, putting a hand on Elsie's arm.

Abe stared down the length of the track, which vanished beneath a heavy, obliterating fog. The train would no doubt be delayed.

"We've always wanted to visit the Midwest. Haven't we, Abe?"

"Of course," he said, his gaze still focused on the opacity where the track wasn't.

And cities, he wanted to add. I have always enjoyed being in new cities.

THE NEW RABBI arrived the day of the first snow of the season, which began as drizzle, then turned to sleet, and finally, at nightfall, became the sharp, gritty powder that would rest on the city and everything around it for months to come. The rabbi was young, barely out of JTS, pudgy and aggressively jocular. He was either unaware of the circumstances leading to his appointment or was determined not to let them blot out his presence. His sermons were laced with jokes, puns, odd asides that he and only a few staunchly polite people laughed at.

"I don't mean to be choosy but I would prefer it if my wedding wasn't treated like a Porky Pig cartoon," said Judith, following a meeting about her impending wedding. The rabbi, who was just about Judith's age, cackled his way through the talk. It would be this new rabbi officiating, not Max.

"Be as choosy as you want," said Abe, "you're still stuck with him."

Judith's face had a harsh cast—the summer color all gone, her hair desiccated by the weather, the autumn shadows falling across her like streaks of black paint. She looked lovely all the same and Abe took her entreaty as an opportunity to admire her.

"Would you speak to him please? Would you try to impress upon him that I'd like my wedding to be taken seriously?"

He said he would. And he drove to the synagogue on several occasions. And each time could not bring himself to go inside. He stayed in the Buick, not letting go of the wheel. What could he say to this boy, for that's what he was, that wouldn't come across as a threat, as a condemnation of his ministering? What could he say that wasn't simply cursing the boy for not being Max?

THE WEDDING HUNG before them in the distance as the autumn deepened. Irene and Judith became more and more preoccupied with the details, leaving Abe out of their orbit, deliberately or no. He began feeling unexpected bursts of loneliness, regardless of whom he was with. It wasn't a feeling he was accustomed to, the sense of a space that followed him, cordoned him off from the rest of the world. He left the yard to watch movies: German troops marched through the streets of French cities and curses and boos rose up from the audience. A woman, roughly Irene's age, stood in the doorway to some business, watching the march, weeping. This giantess, this woman the size of a screen, a wife and mother, her head wrapped in a kerchief, bracketed by the entranceway to whatever the shop behind her was, a grocery or tailor, sobbing. He kept going back to the movies just to see her. When the newsreel changed, he stopped going. He felt hemmed, unseen. Especially at home. He kept an eye out for Shayke. His angry dead brother was better for company than no one.

Business was lively, as it often was when the weather turned. Certain needs became much more apparent to people who could ignore what they lacked in the warmer months. Abe turned no one away, gave no heed to the origin of what was lugged into his yard, paid pennies on the pound, kept a wad of bills handy for any cops who happened by.

"Tell me something," said one, an ancient Italian who'd never risen past a uniform and a squad car, settling into Abe's office for a chat after pocketing his fin. "You people have always been so good with business. How come you didn't just buy off Hitler?"

"I have no idea," said Abe.

Snow swirled outside. Canvas tarps shook violently in the wind.

"It's something you could have done. It's something I think you'll regret."

The cop spoke with genuine concern in his voice, sincere enough to penetrate the numbness that had taken hold of Abe.

THAT NIGHT, HE sat down at the kitchen table, sat heavily in the small chair and, for no reason, removed a single napkin from the napkin holder, spreading it out over his hand like a shroud. Irene was at the sink, scrubbing dishes. "I'm leaving. Tomorrow," he said. "There's something I have to do."

He was expecting questions, incomprehension, but instead she turned off the sink, wiped her hands on a dish towel. She turned to him and said in a voice as calm as any, "You're going to look for her?"

He didn't answer.

She turned back to the sink, as though to continue washing, but instead lowered her head, braced against the counter. "Good," she said softly.

"Irene . . . "

"It's fine, Abe. But you could do me the dignity of saying it out loud instead of skulking off. Say it."

Tears formed in his eyes, two large tears. They formed without his consent, rolled coldly down his cheeks onto the napkin. He looked down at the wet paper. More tears came, leaked down onto the yellowed linoleum. He shredded the napkin without using it to wipe his eyes. "Please," he said.

"Please what? Please beg you not to go?" She pulled up the plug, draining the basin, then turned to face him. "What do you want, exactly? You want me to pretend I don't know what happened, that I'm some sort of idiot and didn't see what was taking place?" She laughed. "Well, no thank you. I'm not a great actress like our houseguest. I couldn't pull it off. And honestly, at this point, it feels as though you've been gone for months. All summer you were gone. It's cold and you stalk around the city like a dumb ghost who doesn't know where to go. I talk to you and you don't hear. I touch you and you turn to stone. She's in your head. For months you've been gone. Even here with me, you're with her."

"Irene."

She looked around. "This kitchen," she said. "How many hours of my life have I . . . " The thought left her. The dregs of the water gurgled as it drained. She picked up a coffee cup, held it up, then let it drop to the floor where it shattered. She didn't throw it at him. It was a gesture of hopelessness, not anger. She simply opened her hands. The shards of porcelain spun and scattered wall to wall. She walked across them, toward him slowly, sitting on the floor beside his chair the way a child might.

"Listen to me now," she whispered. "Listen to what I'm about to tell you. I want you to go. At this point, it's a relief, and not only because of what happened. I don't want you to think that it's because of what happened." Then she stood again and shouted at him a single word. "Go!"

Before he could answer, she was hurrying out of the kitchen. He followed her up the stairs, down the hallway to their bedroom. He sat down on the foot of the bed and watched her, unable to move, unable to speak.

She pulled a suitcase out of his closet, pulled clothes out of his drawers and dropped them in as she said, "I am your wife and the mother of your child and I know that deep down you still love me, so show me the respect of accepting that I knew. I don't think I could bear it if you thought me such a fool not to know, not to notice. Believe me when I tell you that it's not because of what happened with you and her. I can't have you thinking it's because of that. It's because it hasn't helped."

"Helped? What are you saying?"

"For months, Abe, for months and months, I've lived with a corpse. Do you realize that? Do you not see it? Perhaps it's a corpse that gets up in the morning to go to work and comes home at a reasonable hour and sits at the dinner table and tolerates our daughter well enough, but it's a corpse nonetheless, and I can't do it anymore. Whatever's got ahold of you—I've stopped believing it can be cured. Not by me. When she came here, and you looked at her the way you looked at her, I thought, well, maybe it would help. I knew she wouldn't be here long and I thought maybe it would jolt some life into you. For a while, it did, but the moment she left, you crawled into this bed, went back to being a corpse. Well, I'm forty-two years old, Abe. I don't want to be married to a corpse. Not for the rest of my life. I don't want to sit around the dinner table in the evening and talk about synagogues being burned and children being shot and men and women gassed and all the other horrible, unspeakable, unimaginable cruelty taking place as we speak, things that make you not even want to be human, things that you can't do a damn thing about. That's enough. Now, I want to be happy. I want to think about my lucky, beautiful life. I want to think about how nice it is this time of year by Lake George, and how lovely the leaves are when they turn, and what Judith will look like in her wedding dress, and how precious her babies will be when she makes them. I want to think about the fact that my own baby is beautiful and healthy and safe. I want to play bridge. I want to take baths with you the way we used to and do crossword puzzles in my warm bed and make love and go to the movies. I don't want to go to bed at night thinking of corpses and mass graves and Nazis and murder and hate. I don't want a husband who's a corpse himself, consumed by dread. Maybe that makes me a small person, a bad person, but it's the person I am. So when you find the strength and will to leave this room, here's what I want you to do. Get dressed and take this suitcase and go find her. You think she can make you better, that she has the answer? Go. I wouldn't keep you from her if that's what you need. Judith and I will survive. We have family. We have the business, the house. Go and find her and be happy, or be miserable together which I guess is a way of being happy. But don't come back here until you can come back completely, a whole person. Not a walking corpse. Not a ghost."

She collapsed onto the bed beside where he sat, pressed her face into the blanket. He moved toward her slowly, lowered his head onto her hair. "I'm sorry," he whispered to her as she sobbed.

28.

AFTER THE CALL came from Harold Sacks of the Refugee Committee, informing him of Max's death, Spiro went into a homemade *shiva*. He had little idea of the actual rules but a general notion, memories rattling around in his head from Jaffa. He didn't eat or sleep or shower. He sat in his dim closet office for an entire day. He was supposed to rip his clothes but most of them were in poor enough shape already. Max.

Goddamn Max. Goddamn belief.

There was a general pain in his head, dulling sometimes and then piercing his consciousness. His only relief had been that he had been spared the body but once that thought entered his head an image came with it: Max's face, pale and bloated, the eyes terrified at the last, unseeing. He could file it away now with the image of the girl at the cafe. He could build his own menagerie of ghosts. You did this, he heard his father say. This was why Devorah had left him. He was careless. He was not in control of things as he pretended to be. History slipped away from him, spun out from his grasp.

His whole body hurt. He was sickened by his own odor, too, the staleness of his breath and his clothes. He went back to his apartment, showered, shaved. The next day he went into the office but couldn't bring himself to do more than sharpen pencils at his desk or read the Yiddish papers. The news out of Europe was worse than ever. But instead of buoying his resolve, it weighed him. Death, he realized, had its own inertia. There would come a point when there were too many bodies to break free of. Failure would beget failure until there was no use in trying.

Goddamn Max.

Goddamn Max in the goddamned ocean.

This was his state of mind when the letter arrived at the Committee headquarters, a letter from Stephen Field. It was addressed to Spiro personally. He turned the envelope over in his hands then tore it open. It was a check made out to the Committee for one hundred dollars. And behind the check was a small, handwritten note with two words printed in an old man's shaky script. *You win*, it said.

Spiro folded up the check, put it in his pocket, and tried not to think about it for the rest of the day. He had the two non-thoughts warring for his inattention: Max's death and Field's check. A drowned idealist and the minder of a ruined synagogue. Neither made sense. The oceans were calm, Sacks had said. Quiet as a mill pond. Maybe Max was too Northern, too much of cities to understand the ocean, its subsurface system of currents and forces. That was the best Spiro could explain that. Field's check. It was an object of pure mystery. He looked at it again. The handwriting showing the usual quakes of the aged. Drawn from the Chemical Bank. One hundred and xx/100. What do I win? he thought. Bodies. Ideas I cannot carry in my own head. That's what's my victory. Gestures that make no sense and any sense they might make, any possible reasoning that existed behind either action frightened or numbed or simply punished Spiro.

At six o'clock, he rode the subway north, faced his own reflection in the glass. The glare of the tunnel walls wavered then flashed to black as the lights went off and on. The subway rattled and groaned, giving up speed. He emerged on the east side of the park, an unfamiliar and disorienting sensation. The city's geography could impose rigidity to your thoughts, your perception. It was plotted with a definitiveness that was usually left to the Fates or other such unreal, hyper-powered beings. To bend against their strictures was to feel your own nature torquing, contorting. He stood contemplating the limestone facade of Field's building and was deeply uneasy. The doorman didn't ask him his business there. He stood pillar-stiff, waiting for Spiro to announce it.

"I've come to see Rabbi Field," he said.

"Is he expecting you?" the doorman asked.

"Not in the usual sense."

"I'll have to call up. Who should I say is here?"

"Say it's the leader of the Jewish army."

The man narrowed his eyes.

"Shmuel Spiro."

He called up, spoke softly into the phone. As he waited, Spiro became conscious of his own wet shoes, his wet pant legs, the plushness of the rug beneath his feet as he stood there dripping mud.

"You can go up," the doorman said, gesturing with his head toward the elevators.

The elevator man didn't bother to level the lift with the hallway, and Spiro tripped a little as he stepped out into the corridor. He made his way to 12F, but what he entered when he arrived there was not really an apartment but three apartments merged into a single home. The door was ajar. He knocked softly, then waited.

"You can come in, Mr. Spiro," a voice called from deeper inside.

He stepped into the foyer, stood there for a moment while he tried to get his bearings. A few feet from where he stood, the hallway went dim. Unlit sconces lined the walls, casting bird-sized shadows across the hardwood floor.

"This way, Mr. Spiro," the rabbi called. Spiro followed his voice. It was an old voice but not an unpleasant one.

He passed through a long hall, passed a library with the door flung open, books from floor to ceiling, rolling ladders and armchairs and a cart with crystal stemware, highballs and decanters filled with brandy. He passed a room with a billiard table, three closed doors he took to be other bedrooms, guest rooms. At the end of the hall he came to another room, an office. Only in America could he see what he was seeing, a Jew living like aristocracy, a Manhattan apartment dressed up like a country estate. Field was at the far end of the hallway, sitting beside a desk. Behind him, windows. Floor to ceiling windows framing a dark expanse Spiro knew was Central Park.

"Mr. Spiro," he said, looking up. "I've been wondering when you might come. My donation arrived?"

The rabbi wasn't what he'd expected. He'd seen him deliver a sermon two years earlier when Spiro felt lost and homesick and had been invited to the Free Synagogue for Yom Kippur. At the time, Field still appeared vital. Now, that vitality had left him, up into ashes with the rest of his temple. Spiro watched the way he carried himself as he stood, crossed to the liquor cart in the corner. He was a sliver of a man but he moved as though his limbs were led. His hands trembled as he poured the whiskey. He turned around and handed Spiro a glass then sipped from his own.

"Will you have a seat?" he asked, gesturing to a wide, upholstered chair beside the fireplace. Spiro walked to it, sank into the dark leather cushions. A few moments passed when neither man spoke. Spiro began to wonder if this was a mistake, if he simply should have cashed the check and been done with it. He was about to say as much when Field placed his glass on a marble coaster and said it for him.

He leaned forward, wishing suddenly that he had never sat down. "I came to thank you," he said simply.

A smile curled across the old man's lips. "To thank me," he repeated.

"For your donation. Also . . . my condolences. For your synagogue. It's past time I extended them."

The smile spread.

"I don't see what's so amusing."

"Your condolences. Don't insult us, Mr. Spiro. The time for that was months ago. You've come to gloat over the ashes. Nothing less and nothing more. You've come to show off your new position to the man you've dethroned."

"Is that what it's about to you? Who's in charge?"

"That's what our world is about. Why should you and I be any different?"

Spiro rose, placed his glass down on the windowsill. Then he took the check out of his pocket, held it between his fingers and tore it in half.

"It's not necessary for you to do that."

"Rabbi Field, there are fronts open now in Russia and in France and the Low Countries, across Indochina and North Africa. Do you know what the open front in this country is?"

Field leaned back in his chair. "Attention," he said.

Spiro threw down the torn check emphatically. "Eyes and minds and fingers that write checks and letters to officials. That's the battle in this country. We are engaging in rear guard actions against each other when we could be putting together a united front to help the people *who are being butchered*. A terrible thing happened to you, Rabbi, and as a result people are coming to us. That doesn't have to be your loss. You don't need to lose any more than you already have. Work with us. Help us. We will help you."

"What you've just described is the ideal blueprint for a fifth column. Those looking to hate us will have even more excuses to do so."

"What does it matter what people like that think? They'll hate us no matter what we do. Don't you know that?"

"I'll tell you what I know, Mr. Spiro. I know that an innocent old woman is dead, and that someone was willing to kill her to burn down my temple. I know that this person is still free, and that whoever he is, there are dozens more like him. I know that if it had been a church that had burned down, it would not be three FBI agents who came to see me about it but three dozen. I know that we're not as safe in this country as you think we are."

Spiro tried to interrupt, but Field shushed him, raised his voice even louder. "Listen to me," he said. "You and your comrades are so good at talking and talking and talking. Now I'm telling you to listen."

"I shouldn't have come," Spiro said. He was about to walk back into the hallway when Field stopped him.

"You and your people, you don't like us. You don't respect us."

"It's not a matter of respect. We don't understand. I don't understand how you can accuse me of behaving dangerously when across the ocean . . . "

"Yes, I know what's happening across the ocean. You don't have to tell me. But I know something about this country, too, which might not be so obvious. I know that the Jews of this country have accomplished something here that no other Jews in the history of the world have been able to accomplish. To live here in this republic, not only as Jews, but as citizens, citizens like everyone else. Tell me where else, at what other time in our long history, has that been accomplished? Not in Poland and not in France. Not across the steppes of Ukraine or the Russian Pale. Not in Spain nor Portugal. Not in South America or Shanghai. The Jews of Germany were very proud of their Germanness, but where did it get them? The reality is that nowhere, on no place on earth besides the place we now stand, have Jews ever achieved what we have achieved, to live as Jews, yes, but as Americans first. And you, you and your Committee, screaming across newspapers about your Jewish army and your Jewish state and your struggle to save and unite the Jews of the world, you want to take it all away."

"We don't. We don't want to take anything away. You give us far more credit than we deserve. We want to save people. We want to give Jews the dignity to defend themselves. Our people are being slaughtered, and we want to help them."

"You think I don't? You think I'm not haunted day and night by their letters, their desperate voices?"

"I think you are. I think you're a good man, a compassionate man, and that if, instead of opposing each other . . . " He moved closer, held out his hand. "Listen. We don't have the organization; you do. We don't have the history, the infrastructure, the support."

"You don't have the money."

"That too. That's exactly why we should merge your history and organization with our energy and momentum, then we could really make a difference . . . with rescue operations, with the army resolution before Congress, with everything."

"But why? Why would you want our help? You look at us, and you think we have so much power. Rich American Jews. You watch us at our fundraisers and galas and board meetings and luncheons, and you think, how trivial, how indulgent."

"Sometimes I think everything we do is indulgent, that just enjoying a nice meal or going for a walk or admiring a woman is indulgent. Sometimes I think we should be fighting all the time, that our lives should be nothing but fury."

"So you run your ads to make others furious."

"We run the ads because we think they might help. Because we think, how can we begin to stop what's happening if people don't even know what's happening."

The old man let out a slow, heavy sigh. "Your metaphorical fronts, Mr. Spiro, for attention. They may be real but, I hope you know, they are meaningless. They are a little boy with a pellet gun standing before a Panzer." It was late and Field appeared exhausted. "The only front that might mean anything for us and the people we are trying to save is a real one, here."

A terrible sadness came over Spiro then; it seemed to come over the entire room. The sadness he felt arose not from Field's stubbornness, but from the sense Spiro had that beneath the resentment and spite, there was a part of Field, a small part of him, that wanted to reach out. That was what the donation had been about—a jab, yes, but also a plea. He was trying to reach out and failing and trying despite the failure, despite the hopelessness. It reminded him of his own father, of the days when Spiro was still at university, and then in the militia, all the years he'd spent trying to convince him that building a Jewish nation would take more than faith and prayer, that it would take ideas buoyed by acts of strength. He would sit in his father's study and try to explain it to him and the old man would lean forward just as Field was doing now and, because he loved his son, he would try to understand, would try and fail to see what his son saw. There was an unbridgeable gulf between them, and it was terribly sad.

"I'll make you a deal," Field said, and for a moment, Spiro thought that he'd gotten through. "You and your friends on the Committee, the ones sending guns and dynamite to Palestine, you and these brave Jewish hoodlums, you take a few weeks away from your activities and help me find the monster who burned down my temple. You do things the way your friend Jabotinsky did them and string the killer up to the mast of one of your smuggled ships, and then we can work together. Then we can be friends."

An image: a ship, lazing across an unbroken sea. Ana tied to the mast, dead and laughing and naked and glowing, the rope around her neck red silk, the bullet hole in her temple cleaned and perfumed. The ship's hold filled with dead Jews stacked on one another, all of them clutching loaded rifles, their trigger fingers twitching, twitching. Bloat-faced dead Max Hoffman swimming beside them, waving, cheering, finally smiling. Spiro himself at the helm of the ship, desperate for land, any land, a port to call at and discharge this dismal cargo.

Spiro didn't speak. He didn't nod or make any gesture of understanding. Field turned his back on Spiro, toward the black pool of the park, which was just as well as Spiro himself turned and walked out, not even bothering to close the door to the apartment, moving down in the clattering elevator whose operator sang softly—*You're going to walk that lonesome valley, you've got to go there by yourself*—and past the doorman, just an angry Great Dane in a red overcoat, a pretend Cossack who put himself in Spiro's way because anyone who could come under such odd circumstances and leave so quickly was clearly up to no good, clearly deserved a well-timed shoulder that Spiro received dispassionately, regaining his step immediately and pirouetting out the door and into the first cab he saw. He gave the driver an address on the other side of the park, close to the Hudson. He still felt the reverberation of bone against bone while they crossed, wondered if Field might see the light of this cab darting beneath him, a tiny glowing bug scooting through the unforgiving night.

Tired. Very tired. Climbing the steps to his apartment (the elevator had been out of service since the Hoover administration), rubbing clanged shoulder, cursing the bolt of pain he felt reaching into his pocket for the key, cursing again when he saw the door wasn't even locked.

"I'm not going to remind you again, you have to lock the fucking door," he said in the darkened hallway of his apartment. "If I come home to an unlocked door again I'm changing the locks."

"You can't afford a locksmith," she said. "Don't come after me with hollow threats."

Spiro's was a railroad flat and Ana Beidler was in the kitchen, the last car on the train, seated at the table where he had left her that morning. He wasn't sure if the coffee cup in front of her was the same one she was drinking out of when he left.

"Went the day well?" she said. "Have we secured passage to bring all Jews to the moon?"

He rooted around the icebox for something to eat, found only a pair of eggs of questionable provenance that he tossed onto a frying pan anyway. He had no appetite but the eggs gave him something to look at that wasn't Ana.

"There was a death notice for Max Hoffman today. In the *Daily News*," she said.

"Please do not speak his name."

"Of all the people. Of all the—"

"Please."

He heard Ana slump in her chair. She had terrible posture when she wasn't in public. Her neck drooped, she faced the world with her shoulders. She was practically a cephalophore, one of the saints who carried around their own heads. But not a saint.

"Field knows," he said, flipping the eggs with a fork. "He knows we were involved with the fire."

He waited for Ana to respond.

"There was a federal investigation when it happened," he said to her silence. "A small one, more of a token. I assume he will now send them our way."

"And you'll serve me up to them without a second thought," she said.

He dumped the eggs onto a plate, added a heap of tomato ketchup. He sat across from her at the small table. She still slouched; her face was unmoved. The sight of her brought up something in him that was both repulsed and aroused.

"You'll have to go down through Mexico. We'll work things from Nicaragua or British Honduras. Shipping you straight to Ankara won't work anymore."

"Why bother with all of that?" she said, pushing herself forward. "Turn me in, say I was crazy, save your reputation, save your time."

"No," he said, taking a large bite of egg that he did not want. "I'm not doing that."

"Why? It makes perfect sense."

"Because you weren't crazy. Because we will be seen as synagogue-burners." He didn't raise his voice and continued to eat. He wanted her to disappear. He wanted some agent of God to descend and make her into dust, into a cloud. "Because we will be kaput."

She relaxed again and smiled. It was a victorious smile; she had gotten something out of him, not just a refusal to turn her in but something more.

"Stand quietly behind the curtain, Shmuel. Wait for the show to end. Wait for the applause."

It was all a show, wasn't it? Spiro had believed what they were doing was different, was played on a stage with no removal from everyday life. To Ana there was still a spotlight, still an audience, characters whose fates were instruments, a story that demanded an ending. She understood it and he had not. He had believed in an abiding chaos that one needed to wrestle to shape, to comprehend. But you couldn't impose order when it was already there. You couldn't claim to have any control over actions whose outcomes had been settled long before you arrived. The burning of Field's temple was a stage direction. Utica was a set. Max Hoffman was . . . Spiro stopped himself before he could reduce Hoffman to part of Ana's vision of the world. The dead were the dead were the dead and no license could be taken with that fact.

She sat across from him in his kitchen, arms folded, body limp, smiling.

"Somewhere in the Bronx right now, someone is looking up the phone number of the Committee and is going to call first thing in the morning. Because of what I did. Months ago."

And what, Spiro wondered, would that person in the Bronx do if the body of a star of the Yiddish stage turned Jewish army supporter were found tomorrow morning in the middle of Riverside Drive?

He finished his eggs, washed the dishes, found a bottle of whiskey at the back of a cupboard, took a long swig.

"I'll have some of that, thank you. You've forgotten your manners, Shmuel."

She took the bottle and drank. She was reckless like a man and she drank like a man, too, and not a Jewish one. The liquor didn't faze her. He stood and watched her as she crossed to his gramophone in the corner, and then there was Chopin. She drank some more. She was looking at him expectantly. "Talk to me," she said. He didn't want to talk anymore. He stood up and felt dizzy, reached for the chair. "I think I'll lie down on the floor for a while. Do you mind?" He got down on the ground. He wanted to be a body on the ground. Max. A useless body. Weightless.

"What are you doing?"

"Sometimes it feels good to lie on the floor. Chairs are so confining."

He liked talking to her from this position, talking and staring up at the gray ceiling, her voice disembodied, floating as she cleared the dishes.

The music whorled above him. He closed his eyes for a moment. When he opened them, she was sitting beside him, smoking.

"What time is it?" he asked.

She didn't answer. She had taken off her skirt, was sitting on the ground in her blouse and her black stockings, and without knowing why, he began to trace the silk line up the back of her leg. Stockings were fascinating to him, the illusion of shadow on flesh. He gazed up at her. Ana Beidler. Actress. Zionist. Expatriate. A lost child of the stage. A mad woman. Perhaps a genius. She had seen what needed doing and she had done it. She lacked inhibitions and remorse. This was a quality of monsters. But also, there was freedom in it. He envied her this freedom. He watched her through the haze of whiskey. He hated her, but also, found her enlivening. He was repelled and drawn to her all at once, had been from the moment he saw her. No matter what she said; he saw the truth. She lacked the capacity for true conviction or ideology. He saw through the artifice to her core, and there was no core to see. She was a projection of his own desires. She fed on chaos.

She was not made of flesh and blood but shadow and light. Now she leaned over him.

"Shall we make love?" she asked. "For old times' sake?" He didn't answer, but he didn't stop her, either. She lifted off her blouse and dropped it on the floor. Her breasts were small and perfect, perfectly smooth and dark with nipples like sea stones. She unbuttoned his shirt, his pants. His arms and legs felt heavy. His head was underwater. He tried to shake himself clear. He let her kiss him. She'd had him guessing from the beginning: who was she and what did she want? He supposed he was infatuated with her, but at the same time, he wished he'd never met her. He wanted to tame her, to subdue her, to take that volatility and passion that made her so remarkable, and temper it somehow, mold it. He was listening to the faint thumping of her heart beneath her breastbone when her voice broke through. "Shmuel," she said.

He closed his eyes and pictured Devorah lying in the small bedroom of their cottage. His old life was slipping, fading. The only clear thing was Ana's voice, the movement of her silhouette across the dark. He pushed her off of him, rose to standing.

"Good night," he said, walking back to his bedroom. She would have to pass through his room when she crossed the flat to the couch where she slept. He prayed she would wait until he was asleep, that she would move in silence.

29.

THE TRAIN WAS scheduled to leave Utica at 7:34 in the morning, but Abe arrived a little after six, stood there in the dim, predawn light, his suitcase beside him. At first it was only he and the vendor behind the newsstand. The man had spread out a napkin on his lap, was eating a grapefruit and a hard roll that crumbled in his hand. He smiled as he chewed. "You want your *Forward?*" he asked Abe as he approached.

"Not today," he said. "Today I want an American paper. I want good news today."

He put a section of grapefruit in his mouth, rubbed the white pulp on his fingertips onto his pants. When he'd finished eating he added, "Well good for you. Why not? We're in America after all. We should read like Americans."

Abe squinted at the sun.

"I didn't tell you. I finally heard from my family. Five letters came all at once. It was true what you said, the post doesn't work during war. I was expecting the worst but the news was good. Both of my brothers and their families escaped ahead of the Germans. They're in France now, safe."

"That's wonderful news. *Lomir hern nor gute bsures.*" May we hear only more good news.

They both looked out at the track. A bird landed on a crossbeam, hopped around in a circle, plucking. The old man took out a short, brown cigar and puffed into the sky. "You're here so early," he said. "The train doesn't come for another hour."

Abe shrugged. "I had nowhere else to be."

"You're going downstate on business? To visit family?" He pulled on the cigar and the tip contracted, red to orange.

"Yes," he said.

The fringes of the mountains were warming with morning light. There was a distant vibration of thunder. The old man smiled at no one, tapped his ashes to the ground.

"You think it'll rain?" Abe asked.

On this, he had no opinion. "The future," he said. "*Very veyst?*" Who can tell?

An hour later, Abe boarded the train. The car was nearly empty, as though it had been cleared for him, everything pushed aside to make way for this journey. He sat by a window and watched the sun rise higher over the still-slumbering city, a town that could fit in the palm of a hand. How charming it had seemed when he'd first arrived, straight out of the throngs and stench and sewer steam and hungry fevers of the Lower East Side. Now he had allowed all that charm to peel and chip away. What he saw now was not potential but the place itself: mud-crusted fields surrounding the city, then a string of paper mills and salt refineries, then nothing, just empty fields and windy highways. For this, he'd left all his childhood memories, his language, the town his family had lived in for two hundred years, the Europe of his youth. It had seemed a fair bargain at the time. Anything to escape the memory of Shayke, of what he'd done to his brother.

"TELL ME ABOUT your brother," Sonia said to Abe one afternoon under the bridge. She had a friend who was a member of Dror, the Socialist-Zionist youth movement. She'd gone to a meeting and seen him there, admired the way he spoke. "I want to meet him," she said to Abe. "Would you arrange it?"

"He wouldn't like you," Abe answered.

"No? Why not?" She sat back, pretended to be considering this while he pulled up his pants. She acted the same as always, cool, unbothered, but he could tell he'd hurt her.

"It's because he knows about us," he went on. "How I feel about you."

"And?" she said, rolling up her stockings. "What did he say? Was he scandalized? Or does he want me for himself?"

"Don't joke. I'd kill him if he touched you."

She laughed. "For me, you'd kill your own brother? You are a strange, strange boy. Don't you know brothers and sisters are supposed to love and be good to each other?"

"He hardly knows I exist. He's never had much time for me."

"Perhaps he'll change. No one's perfect, not even older brothers."

Except he was. That was the problem. Shayke had always been the good one, the perfect one. Taller, more clever, better at sports, better with girls. He got them so easily. They followed him around. He could have anyone, do anything, but all he wanted to do was to go to Palestine and work on a kibbutz and marry an ugly girl with wide hips so they could make a hundred babies to settle the land of Israel. But Abe didn't tell Sonia any of this. Instead, he simply said, "He told me I shouldn't see you anymore."

"He's probably right. . . . Give me one of those cigarettes, will you?" She brushed the dirt from her legs. "Look what you did to my slip." She stood up and stretched. Her body in the sunlight. Her skirt rising over her thighs as she yawned, arched her back. The sound of the river behind her. He loved her, even as he saw what was coming.

"He's not right about us," Abe told her.

"What does it matter? Some things are more important. I remember the day my little sister was born. My mother handed her to me. I couldn't believe how small her hands and feet were, and her little lips. I kissed her, and she puckered, and I loved her instantly but also felt this weight being strung around my neck."

"It's different with girls."

"Maybe," Sonia said, looking off toward the place where the river widened. A gnat landed on her thigh and she slapped it once, smeared the blood over her skin. "Still," she said, "You shouldn't kill him."

At first, Abe tried to forget Sonia's curiosity about his brother. He convinced himself that their missed rendezvous were unrelated. But then, a few weeks after their last meeting under the bridge, he spotted her walking across the town square on Shayke's arm, laughing, smiling, pressing herself close. And the worst part was that just as Abe had predicted, Shayke seemed embarrassed by her affection. Exactly like Shayke, he thought. Always too distracted by his own importance, the grandness of his cause, to see what was right next to him.

So that night, while Shayke was attending a rally in a nearby town, Abe did something he'd never done before. He crept into his brother's room while his parents read after dinner, and, as quietly as he could, rifled through Shayke's belongings, looking for what he had never seen but knew Shayke surely possessed, a pile of pamphlets and flyers promoting Zionism and workers' rights and Jewish self-defense. By modern standards, they were hardly shocking: There was decrying of the exploitation of peasant labor, a demand for international solidarity among workers, a call for demonstrations, labor strikes, and the like. It was the sort of agitation every line worker or college boy got earfuls of nowadays. But at that time it was forbidden; it was revolution, life-and-death danger right under his brother's bed.

He gathered up all the pamphlets and left them where his father would find them. That same night, he was awakened by his father's fury. "We have given you everything: a happy home, a loving family, food in your belly, clothes on your back, and you throw it in our faces, endangering us all."

Abe's sister came into his room, holding her hands over her ears. "What's wrong with him?" she asked.

Abe told her to go back to sleep, then got out of bed and walked to the doorway, pushed it open a crack, and watched his father pacing, his mother sitting in a chair by the stove, weeping, his brother leaning back in another chair, looking at neither of them, his face scowling.

"How did you find them?" he asked.

"How we found them is irrelevant," said Abe's father. "You should thank God we did, that it was us and not the police. You're a smart boy, Shayke. Do I have to tell you what they do to Jews keeping forbidden proclamations in their home—what they did to the Raveshelfsky boy down the street? Ten broken fingers before they even took him to the jail. Now he's in prison. Twelve years of solitary confinement. His mother's gone mad. I see her at the market talking to herself."

Abe's mother began to weep.

"Look at your mother. Look at her. She's given her life to you and your brother and sister. And how do you thank her? By putting us all in danger."

There was a loud crash. Shayke had gotten to his feet and thrown his chair across the room. "Danger!" he said. "You cannot hide from danger in this life."

Abe's father went to pick up the chair, and his mother tried to approach Shayke, but his brother recoiled, turned down the hallway toward his bedroom. A few minutes later, he came out carrying a small knapsack.

"Where are you going?" Abe's mother called to him. "Please, stop," she said. "Go back to your room. Go to sleep. Everything will make sense in the morning."

But he would not stop. He went to the pantry, put some potatoes and some carrots in his sack, scooped up the pamphlets on the table. Their mother was pleading now. "Please, please. Let us all go back to sleep."

When his bag was full, he walked up to his mother and embraced her. He kissed her on the cheek and looked around their home once more, and then he left.

AN HOUR OUTSIDE Utica, he bought a cup of coffee, willed himself to read the paper, first the *Dispatch-Observer* and then the *Times*, really just holding it up to keep his hands busy. A bit downstate, the car filled up. A young woman in a cloche hat sat beside him, peeled and ate an orange, wrote a letter on her lap, but she did not look at him. He could smell the orange bitters on her fingers mixed with her perfume. He closed his eyes and replayed the sensation of holding Ana's wrists, pressing his mouth against her cheeks, her hair. She had said things to him . . . words that made him feel like he mattered, like he could make his life mean something. Was that no longer real? Was it all pretend? The newspaper sat open and unread in his lap, these questions pushing away the print, until he looked down and saw the latest ad by the Committee. To 5,000,000 Jews in the Nazi Death-Trap the Bermuda Conference Was a "Cruel Mockery." When Will The United Nations Establish an Agency to Deal With the Problem of Hitler's War on a Whole People? He read it, closed the paper, closed his eyes.

Judith and Irene would be awake now, making coffee, dressing. He shook himself free from them, and then the rest of the trip passed quickly. Before long, everyone around him was standing. The train sped south. He tapped his pocket to make sure his wallet was inside, folded up his newspaper and clutched at the handle of his suitcase as he stood. Slowly, off-balance due to a sideways sway across the tracks and low, forward rumbling, he made his way down the aisle.

The guesthouse where he'd reserved a room was on Rivington and Ludlow, a six-story building of pale, painted brick, a strangely ornate building, windows capped in broken pediments. It was two blocks east of the Municipal Bath House where he remembered going his first week in America, yet nothing about the street or the neighborhood now seemed familiar. He checked in with an old man behind a marble counter, put his suitcase in the fourth-floor room, then came down through a common parlor where four men and a woman sat in corners, acknowledging no one. There was a dusty carpet, an old, wooden clock on the wall. The walls themselves were painted a pale yellow like custard left too long on the counter. A palace it was not, but the guests seemed content with these surroundings. The woman, knitting away at an orange afghan, tugged from an unseen spool of yarn hidden in some nook of her massive person. The men, plainly dressed but well groomed, read newspapers in such stillness it seemed as though the pages turned themselves.

The man behind the desk watched Abe watching. "First time visiting the city?" he said.

He turned, shook his head. "I used to live here . . . a long time ago."

"Lots of changes lately. You'll need a map." The man reached beneath the counter and produced one. Lean and white-haired and bespectacled, he wore a gray vest, a blue tie, a carefully tailored white shirt adorned with silver cufflinks. He spoke with no other accent than that of old New York, rounding his vowels and shortening his Rs. "You'll want to see the Empire State Building. Times Square. Radio City Music Hall."

"I'm not here to sightsee," he said. "I'm here to find someone."

"Where does this someone live? You need directions? You know where is the subway?"

He thinks I'm a greenhorn, thought Abe. There was no point in correcting him. He dropped his suitcase in the room, washed the grime of the train off his hands and face, then left the hotel, making his way west along Canal Street, taking in the avalanche of sound—the shrieks of children, their taunts and laughter, the calls of cart men, the rumbling of beer wagons, garbage carts, and coal trucks, all of it rising in volume and intensity as he left the hotelier's New York behind and descended into the heart of things.

Where the sweatshops had been when he first arrived in this country (one factory crammed into a four-floor building), five small businesses now operated. Gone were the hundreds of women lining up, shivering in filthy dresses and babushkas, crowding the alleys between the shirt factories. Where had they all gone? Brooklyn? Queens? Back to Europe? Upstate, like him? Up into ashes in factory fires they couldn't escape? Beaten down by drunken husbands, by poverty and disease, by hunger or hungry children? It had been real. He had seen it. He had been there with them. And now gone, gone. Everything passed.

He arrived at what, according to the return address on the envelope in his pocket, was the building where Jacob Feinman lived. He buzzed the bell and waited. No one answered. He buzzed again. A few minutes later a man and woman stopped in front of the building, and Abe slipped in behind them.

He had an idea about waiting in the stairwell, but instead he climbed the four flights of stairs and ventured down the hallway in the direction of apartment 4D. He went to knock but found the door unlatched. Voices, male and female, mingled within. He pushed the open door a few inches wider and found himself entering a few feet into the hallway. It was the female voice that drew him. He thought it might be Ana.

They were speaking loudly, arguing. As he inched further inside, he saw a third figure, a man seated and mostly out of view, whose legs but not face he could make out. He seemed to be sitting there very still while the other man shouted at the woman, a young woman with curly hair who sat in a hard-backed chair and now began to cry.

"Enough, enough, enough. Vivienne, enough!"

The girl dropped her hands from her eyes, and Abe saw that there were no tears in them. "What is it this time?" she said.

"Why are you crying?" the man on the sofa asked.

"Why am I crying?" she repeated. "I don't know how to answer that."

"It's a simple enough question, Vivienne. *Dlaczego placzesz? Pourquoi pleures-tu? Perche piangi?* Is there some other language you speak that I've neglected?"

"It says right here in the script . . . ?"

"I don't care what it says in the script. People don't go to see a play to find out what it says in the script."

Abe knocked loudly then walked forward. "Excuse me, I'm sorry to interrupt. I'm looking for . . . "

"Wait," said the man on the couch, hardly glancing up. "I'll be with you in a minute."

"There's no need for personal insults," said the other man. The woman, who now looked as though she might begin to cry in earnest, removed a cigarette case from her pocket and lit one with a trembling hand.

"Personal insults? How about professional insults? Artistic insults? Insults to my intelligence and my humanity, not to mention the audience." He turned to the woman. "You say you cry because the script tells you to cry. But the script has no power over you, me, or anyone. The script is horseshit, a ridiculous melodrama. There is no artistry in this script. It was written by some hack who is probably in Hollywood by now, which is exactly where I'd like to be so as to not have to deal with these orgies of mediocrity. You do not cry because the script tells you to any more than you laugh because someone tells you to laugh. You cry because this . . . " He stood and walked toward the girl then turned her around to face the other actor, holding her tightly by the backs of her shoulders. "You cry because this man, this man here, looking at you now, is the only man you have ever loved. And now he tells you that despite this love, he's going to marry the daughter of his father's business partner, not because he loves her but because it is 'the reasonable thing to do.' That is why you should be crying, Vivienne. That is why you, or more precisely, why Magda, cries. Not because the script says so."

The girl's cigarette had burned to its end. She took a delicate puff, and the ashes fell. The man beside her fetched an ashtray on the windowsill, took the smoldering butt from her.

"Now get out and spend the evening contemplating what I've told, if you are actually capable of contemplation."

The actress didn't move, just stood there trembling. "Screw you, Jacob," she said, quite softly.

"I'm sorry? What was that?"

"I said, 'screw you!'"

His eyebrows arched. The pen in his hand dropped. "Screw me? Truly? Did I truly hear correctly?"

"You heard all right."

"Ah, well, I see. In that case: You're fired. You are completely and profoundly fired. Get the fuck out of my apartment."

"Come on, Jacob," said the other actor.

"You want to be next?"

After they'd left, the man returned to his place on the sofa and resumed reading, staring down onto a pad of paper, squinting and making notes.

"What?" he said at last without glancing up. "If Grossman sent you to collect the rent, you tell the bastard it's coming. If these actors I cast can stop putzing around long enough to learn their lines, *The Pharaoh's Son* is going to be a huge hit. It's the dumbest show I've ever directed, which is a sure indication of box office success, so you tell the bastard to get off my back."

Abe cleared his throat, held up his hands. "I'm not from the theater. I'm not here for any rent."

"Who are you then?" He jotted another few notes then finally looked up. "Are you here to rob the place again? Well, go ahead. There's nothing left. A jar of pickles in the icebox. A couple mattresses and a miserable landlord on my ass every second of every day. Be my guest."

"I'm not here to rob you."

"What is it then?"

"You're Jacob Feinman?"

"Unfortunately."

"I'm looking for your sister."

He put down his pen, looked up. There was a moment when neither spoke, then he removed his glasses, began rubbing the lenses on his shirt. "My sister?" he repeated.

"Your sister."

"I don't have any sister."

"You're Jacob Feinman?"

"We seem to be going in circles."

"Look, I'm not here to cause her any trouble, if that's what you think. I'm a friend. I care about her very much."

"Mazel tov."

"She told me all about you. I've seen your letters. She was writing to you in Utica."

"Utica?"

"She was staying with my family there."

An expression of both pain and comprehension spread across his face, then a slow, deep sigh. "I think I'm beginning to understand."

"Listen. I'm sorry to show up like this. I wouldn't have done it if I wasn't desperate. But I have to find her. Can you help me? Do you know where she is?"

Jacob let the pad of paper he'd been holding fall to the floor. He removed his glasses again, this time rubbing his eyes with his thumb and forefinger. His mouth widened into a yawn but instead of air, out came something between a shout and a groan. "Ana Beidler," he said. "I need her bullshit like a hole in the head. As though I don't have enough to worry about, I have to deal with her, too. This is what I need with everything else going on? The union hounding me every second. Apparently, a man can no longer direct a show in this town without hiring every able-bodied Jew in New York. A low-budget art production and they want me to employ a minimum of nine stage-hands, ten musicians, fifteen ushers, five doormen, the doormen's cousins, five cashiers, a benefit manager, a general manager, a Yiddish publicity agent, a security man to keep the hordes from raiding the box office (when was the last time that happened?), superintendents, bill posters, scene painters, someone to pick the scene painters' noses and scratch the bill posters' asses. And, of course, they all must be paid fair wages. They all must be treated with respect. Would they like to eat my organs, too, while they're at it? Thanks but no thanks. The Yiddish theater is a dying animal, and the unions are picking over its carcass. I've known for years I needed to get out. This is my last show. I have to get to California if I have to sell every ounce of dignity to get there."

Abe shrugged. He was beginning to sense it would be easier to get what he wanted if he went along. "Why don't you then?"

"Good question. That's just the sort of question Ana would ask. I suppose it's a little thing called integrity. Sticking with a thing. Seeing a thing through even when times are tough. And now, on top of every-thing, I have to find a new actress for this schlock. Well, hey, if Ana's back in town, maybe I'll call her. Maybe she'll do it for me, if she's given up on her latest cause." He paused again then added, "You really came all the way from Utica to find her? Why would you do that?"

Abe hesitated. "You want the truth?"

"Probably not, but go ahead."

Abe took a deep breath, sat down on the chair where the actress had been crying, leaned forward.

The man stared at Abe. His own face was younger than his voice. His eyes, dark in hue to start with, were shadowed further by the over-hang of his brow. Not the worst nose but not the best, either. It jutted like a knob in his knobby face. He was tall, thin all over, a prominent Adam's apple and an understated mouth, and yet taken together these features did not make him appear ridiculous but brooding and severe.

It was an intelligent face, a face that would have looked at home poring over mathematical equations or a symphony's score, a face not intended for work out of doors.

Abe pulled a loose thread from the sleeve of his shirt.

"You're unraveling," said Jacob Feinman.

"Listen, I don't want to take up your whole day. I'll wait at my hotel and the next time you see her . . . "

He was waving it away. "Come on. Who am I to send away a friend of Ana's?"

"No, I can't impose."

"I insist. Of course, you don't want to sit around here. There's a club just down the street."

Abe stood there for a moment before answering. "Fine," he said. "Where is this place?"

Feinman led him toward the door, plucked his hat from a peg and put it on his head, slightly aslant. "On Second Avenue," he said. "Where else?"

DAYLIGHT FADED AS the two men walked north. Away from his apartment, Feinman seemed lighter and younger, infinitely at ease in his own skin. Abe, on the other hand, had never felt so out of place.

Only a few hundred miles from Utica, the air was entirely different, of a different season; it seemed warmer, heavier. A few pinpricks of stars shone palely in the gloaming sky, and the sky seemed broader, more expansive, than it did at home, even if much of it was blocked out by the tenement skyline. Feinman walked quickly. Abe was unsure whether to walk beside or slightly behind him. Either way, a trail of his cigarette smoke wafted toward his face.

It was still early evening when they arrived, but already a crowd was forming outside the cafe, or club, or playhouse, or whatever it was. Tall women and short men milled and smoked. The women wore elaborate dresses, ermine capelets, red satin turbans, full stage makeup, and costume jewels. The men wore blue suits, cashmere overcoats, white hats. A few wore white spats. "What is this place?" he asked Feinman, who was already cutting though the crowd.

"The cafe," he answered.

"What's it called?"

"I just told you. The cafe. That's all anyone calls it. It's not what it used to be, but it's still the center. Ten years ago, the maître d' here was considered the most powerful man on Second Avenue. He could get you a face-to-face with any producer in town. Now he just brings you to your table."

"You think Ana will come here?"

"Could be."

Inside, a small man, dressed in black, bowlegged, smelling of onions and hair grease, greeted Feinman with an embrace. "How goes it, my friend?"

"It goes."

He pointed toward the left side of the establishment where other patrons sat drinking, scribbling on notepads, talking closely in twos or loudly in groups. "Your table's ready, you and Mr. . . . . "

Feinman tried to answer but had already forgotten Abe's name.

"Auer," he said himself.

"For you and Mr. Auer. An investor for your new play?" the man asked in Yiddish.

"I should be so lucky. But, no. A friend of Ana's."

"How is Miss Beidler?" the waiter asked.

"I'm not the man to tell you," said Feinman. "You should ask him," he said, pointing to Abe.

"Trouble in paradise?"

"If she's in paradise, drive a horn into my head and send me to Hades."

"I'll get you a scotch instead."

"That'll do nicely."

The maître d' placed a hand on Feinman's back and led them deeper into the club's interior. There were at least a hundred people milling around them.

Abe sat down slowly, tried to get his bearings. The cafe seemed to be divided into sections. The cluster of tables where Feinman and Abe were being led was peopled by other men and women conservatively dressed, drinking martinis and manhattans and speaking in quiet tones. Behind this section, the tables got smaller and the patrons sloppier. They slouched in their seats, cradled instruments in their laps, nursed highballs of whiskey and ice, and smiled as long-legged women in dresses no more than slips drank and joked with them and, in a few cases, sat on their laps. Still farther behind the musicians, Abe could make out another room where there seemed to be no women at all, a separate space where men played pinochle and smoked cigars. At the next table over sat a short man with a trumpet in his hand and a blonde on his lap. She had slipped out of her shoes and was talking about her new stockings, pointing her toes and lifting her legs to show them off.

"Make yourself at home," Feinman said. "You drink scotch?"

The waiter brought them two. Abe took a sip, then another, wincing at the burn. A woman in a sequined gown and sequined headdress stepped onto a stage in the back and began a ballad. She was all starlight, a deep, honeyed light. Conversation softened for a moment and then resumed. He sank into his chair a little, took another sip. The scotch kept burning long after he swallowed. The smoke was dense and burned his eyes. Everything around him was cast in low lights and seemed to smolder. He scanned the space, hoping to see Ana, but she was nowhere. A waiter came over and set two plates of steaming beef and potatoes before them, and only when he smelled the steam did Abe realize he'd hardly eaten all day. Feinman looked at the food admiringly but didn't pick up his fork.

"Look at this beautiful meal," he said. "So beautiful it brings tears to the eyes. My cousins, my poor, persecuted cousins, were arrested in

Dresden two years ago. My uncle was a philosophy professor at the university. The last anyone heard from him, he was locked up someplace in Hinzert, some sort of collection point. He wrote that they were fed, but only one meal a day, cabbage soup and bread. This is a man with a voracious appetite for food, wine, women, conversation. According to family lore, he once devoured half a goose and a bottle of port for breakfast. Then forced to live on one bowl of cabbage soup. And months since his family's heard from him. God knows what he suffered, what he's become. And here I am before my roast beef, my beautiful roast beef, while my own uncle starves. What kind of man feasts while his relation starves? What kind of people? These are the questions Ana likes to ask of me. You know what I say? I look right at her and I say, 'Ana, if we fasted . . . if we all sealed our lips and went on a hunger strike, would it do any good?' This is a question I posed to her, trying to bring her back to the world of the sane. 'Would it really, truly, make a difference? Would the grumbling in my belly stop the rumbling of the German tanks? Would Herr Hitler or even Mr. Roosevelt duly note my wasting frame?' I think not. I think not. And for this conviction, she calls me an accomplice in the worst atrocity since the Inquisition. Well, I'm sorry," he said.

He sighed then downed his scotch, set the glass firmly on the table, then leaned into Abe and said, "Tell me. Are you political? Another one of that Jewish army man's disciples? Ana didn't have a chance with a man like that. Exactly the sort to make her knees go weak. Are you part of his . . . Committee, whatever it is? Those tough guys with their militias and their ads? It's not a trick question. I'm curious is all. Honestly curious. Has she convinced you to run away with her to . . . do what again? Fight the British? Fight the Germans?"

"Maybe help save people like your cousin. Try to do something for them. More than you're doing."

He raised his glass. "Touché," he said. "Well, good for you. And good luck to both of you. Of course, by the time you get there, Ana will mostly likely be on to something else."

Abe had begun to perspire. His stomach tightened and tensed. His pulse was pounding in his head. "You're not her brother, are you?"

Feinman raised his brow as he sipped his scotch. "No, sir. That, I am not. No, Ana and I are both only children in fact. She didn't tell you her whole autobiography up in Utica? I'd imagine without the usual distractions she'd do little else but talk about herself."

"She told me you were her brother."

"Well, I'm sure she had her reasons."

"Who, then? How do you know her?"

"Oh, me and Ana go way back. We were married for about five minutes, twelve, no, thirteen years ago."

Abe shook his head. "Her husband is trapped in Poland."

"Her second husband, you mean. At least, I assume he's the second. Not entirely a safe assumption. Who knows how many she picked up in intervening years with all her travels? I used to save her postcards, you know. Kept them in a coffee tin by the window. I got a kick out of these little glimpses into her itinerant life. Let's see if I can remember. First, she ran away to Vilna not long after the two of us split. She had her reasons, of course, her grand rationalizations. There was no authentic Yiddish theater left in New York. The city wasn't big enough for her to escape her mother's shadow. So off she went to join the Vilna troupe, to rehearse in an old circus building and tour the surrounding country. Ana, a glamorous, exotic American, was treated like a queen, which is how she prefers things. Vilna lasted for a decent stretch, two, three years. Then she moved on. Where was it next? Petersburg? It must have been Petersburg. Then Paris. Then back to London. Then Warsaw. I could be confusing the order. . . . What does it matter? You get the picture."

Abe pushed his plate away, looked over Feinman's shoulder, scanned the club.

"I see you're not impressed."

"Her past is not my concern."

"Sure it isn't. You care only about your shared future, your passion, and so on and so forth. Hey, you're not going to eat dinner? You don't like roast beef?"

"I'm not hungry."

"You can't let Ana's disappearing acts kill your appetite. A man would waste away."

The waiter appeared with more scotch, neat this time. Abe's limbs felt heavy, his tongue like lead. Across the club, a constellation of lights came on in the raftered ceiling. A man in a black suit sat down at a piano and began to play.

"Listen," Feinman said. "Don't take it personally. She worked her spell on you. It's obvious—something in the eyes."

"No she's not like that. She's . . . "

"I know, your houseguest. I heard you the first time. Ana brings that quality out in men, at first, anyway. She makes you want to be different and new, to be better than you've ever been, to want better things. She makes you disavow the person you were, to spit on your old life and values, curse them, and then she takes that new, noble part of you that she helped forge, and stomps all over it and runs off in some other direction so that all you want to do is to go back to being the putz you were before, only you can't, because you kissed it away, burned it up. She's a serial arsonist, Ana."

"You know what I think?" Abe said. "I think you don't know anything about her. Maybe you knew her once, a long time ago. Maybe you even loved her. But that was then. People change. The world changes. I think you talk too much to know anything about anyone."

"You want to insult me? Go ahead. I'm only telling you the truth."

"I don't believe you."

"Right. Because she's your great love. Because what passed between you two up in Utica was so special and magical and authentic. Well, maybe it was and maybe it wasn't. But I'll tell you what; the woman won't remember your name come spring, and do you know why?

Because happiness bores her. Love and friendship and goodness bore her. Even success, in the end, bores her. The woman is sustained only by want and ruin. In that way, I guess, anti-Semitism is the perfect cause for her. The perfect inextinguishable cause. It took me many years, but I finally figured it out."

Abe pushed his plate away, downed the remainder of his scotch. "And you're telling me all this out of the goodness of your heart?"

"I'm telling you because it's the truth. If you made her laugh, if you made her sigh or whisper sweet things in your ear, if you made her get that warm, faraway look in her eyes, you failed. You never had a chance. Take it for what it was and forget the rest. You two do a lot of screwing up in Utica? I suppose you did. It's something else she's good at. Take it for that."

Abe rose.

"Where are you going?"

He reached into his pocket and pulled out some bills, dropped them on the table. Feinman stood as well. "Come on," he said. "Don't blame the messenger. We're having a good time. The evening is young. The roast beef is delicious. The booze is flowing. What else is there in life? Believe me. You won't find her out there. There's nothing out there but scum and sad ambition."

"In here, too," Abe said.

"There you go. You're getting the hang of it now."

"Get out of my way."

"Why?"

"So I can find her, with or without your help. Now move."

"Or what? You going to call the maître d'? The cops?"

"No, I'm going to hit you."

"Come on," Feinman said. "You're sure you're not an actor?"

Abe looked around one last time, to see if anyone was looking. Then he hit him. Once. Not hard but straight on the nose. The man was smaller and lighter than Abe and stumbled back. It would have been a small stumble if it weren't for the step behind him, which brought him not only off his feet but also onto a neighboring table that toppled over as he fell to the ground. Conversations went quiet. Music stopped. Gazes turned. The maître d' came toward them.

"Jacob," he was saying. "Jacob, what's all the commotion? You know we can't have this here."

Abe got down on the floor and hovered over the man. He grabbed onto his jacket, pulled him forward by it. Blood ran from one nostril. It looked brown against his skin but red against his shirt.

"You hit me," he said. "I can't believe it. I'm trying to help you, and you hit me."

"And you want to know what else?" Abe said, leaning in close.

"What?"

"You tell me where I can find her, or I'm going to hit you again."

"You think I'm scared of you?"

Abe leaned closer. Feinman watched a pearl of sweat form at the edge of Abe's nose, twinkle resplendently for a second in the cafe's light, before falling and landing on his cheek, where it rested and burned.

FOR THREE MONTHS, Shayke's name was not spoken inside their home. "He is dead to us," Abe's father said. Abe's mother stopped sleeping. He'd hear her all through the night, pacing the length of the house, opening and closing cupboards, polishing silver, sweeping floors she'd swept clean that very day. Shayke was everywhere those months; they were never without him, even as his father insisted they banish him from their thoughts.

Then one night, Abe was woken by a barking dog. It was coming from a neighbor's yard. The barking grew louder, increasingly intense, then suddenly flattened into a whimper. There was a moment of silence. He heard his parents' voices down the hall. Cold air swept through the house. There was shouting and cursing outside, commotion in the courtyard, then the thud of rifle butts against the door. "Open up! A search!" Abe noticed the neighbors' lights turning on then off.

The police shoved their way inside, five, six of them, working together at first and then spreading out. Abe's mother yelled up for him and his sister to stay in their room. Abe led her into a corner, pulled her close. "Why are they doing that?" his sister cried, covering her ears. "Mama, mama, what are they doing?" Two men came into the bedroom where they were standing but did not acknowledge their presence, maybe because Abe was crouching beside his sister and so seemed more of a child than he was. They tore apart pallets and pillows and eiderdown. Feathers flew and drifted across the room. They pulled out the dressers' drawers, emptied the bookshelves, shaking books by their spines and then tossing them onto the ground. Abe's father appeared in the hallway. "Please, please. We have nothing here. We are a quiet family." They did not acknowledge him but continued with their search. They opened up the trunk where Abe's mother kept folded blankets, shook them out and tossed them on the ground. They cracked open the heads of Abe's sister's porcelain dolls, shook them over the carpet. Downstairs, one opened and then began to play the piano in the parlor. Abe's mother was beside them now, pressing his sister to her stomach.

When they were done, the house lay in shambles, the floors littered with pillow stuffing, shards of broken glass and china, trampled clothes. Every pamphlet they found stoked their search. Then, just when it seemed they were losing steam, one of the men grabbed Abe's father by the collar. "Where are they? Where are the weapons?"

His father held up his hands. "Please," he said, but his begging only enraged them more.

"Get the light," one of them called.

A match flickered in the dark. The blue flame of a kerosene lamp wavered in a doorway. Abe's father was trembling but trying to stand tall. His mother and sister were crying softly. Two of the policemen were laughing. All of them seemed drunk, smelled of vodka and sweat and horse hides.

One of the policemen held the kerosene in front of his face and another led the group toward the back door. They headed toward the outhouse. There was nothing the Auers could do but stand there and wait. He remembered taking his sister's hand.

How long passed before the men returned, he could not say. Ten minutes. Twenty. The door had been propped open and the house turned as cold as the street. A bitter wind blew through his pajamas. There was a loud noise inside the outhouse. The men's voices grew hushed then took on volume. A moment later they were shuffling back to the house, barging through the door. The one who had grabbed Abe's father by the shoulders was carrying a large box. "Look what we found in a hole in the ground," he said and tipped it forward, so Abe's father could see: Inside lay broken shotguns; old, rusty pistols and revolvers; knives; bayonets; a few sticks of dynamite. "Your son is quite a fixer, isn't he?" the detective said. "He must have been scrounging all around town to find these."

"Please," said Abe's father. "He is a good boy. Please, I'm begging you."

"Where is he?"

"I have no idea. We haven't seen him in months."

"An address? The names of his friends?"

"Even if I wanted to tell you, I couldn't."

The detective took a step back, seemed to be considering it all, and then his arm swung back and he struck Abe's father in the face.

A week later, they received a notice that Shayke had been arrested and was being held in the town jail. He was living in a cell the size of a horse's stall with a small window. He spent the rest of the winter there. In his letters, he described sleeping on a straw pallet on an iron cot, but all the other details of his suffering he omitted. He survived there for months mostly on the packages of food their mother sent or what was left of them after the guards picked off the best morsels. He stayed there until a brisk March morning when he and a dozen other political prisoners were transferred. Abe stood in a crowd of onlookers and watched his brother, half-starved and caked with filth, shackled and stooped, limp forward with a bent neck. He followed the other prisoners from the jail to the courtyard. A crowd stood by and watched this procession. Some wept. Some stood in silence. Some pleaded for their loved ones' release. Abe himself made no noise. He couldn't. He was too frightened, too sick with guilt. On every side, the prisoners were guarded by gendarmes on foot and Cossacks astride horses. The Cossacks herded them with whips toward a platform, forcing the prisoners into freight cars on groaning springs. The doors to the train cars opened, showing only darkness. The prisoners vanished into the darkness, one by one as a whistle blew. The doors were closed and chained. Steam hissed into the breaking dawn. The trains began to move. And like that, his only brother was gone, shipped to a work camp in the East.

After that, the Auer home became a graveyard. His mother never stopped mourning. His father retreated into himself, went days without speaking. His sister escaped as soon as she could through marriage, wedding a baker's son in a neighboring town who moved with her to Israel a few years later. And Abe, week by week, month by month, planned his own escape.

In addition to working as an apprentice in his father's shop, he took a second job sewing costumes for a Yiddish theater group. Entire weekends he passed sewing capes and robes and gowns and peasant frocks. Every ruble they gave him he stashed away, saving for a ticket.

In the meantime, he wrote to his uncle who'd been living in New York for nearly twenty years. He was so eager to meet his family in America, to see the world, but mostly, to work. If he should ever be so lucky as to find a place for himself across the sea, he'd work six days a week, dawn until dusk, anything to earn his keep.

After three or so of these letters, he finally received a reply.

Dearest Abraham,

Please know you are welcome here. We are a modest family, but there is always work to be done. We would be honored and humbled to have you.

Love,
Uncle Moshe

Two months later, he traveled by wagon to Lithuania, and there he boarded a Southampton-bound steamer. In Southampton, he boarded another ship, this one bound for New York.

The crossing took three and a half weeks, and during those weeks, in addition to thinking about the new life that awaited him, the new city, the new family, the almost infinite expanse of possibility and danger, he thought of Shayke. He lay alone at night, painfully alone and seasick but thankful for the third-class cabin he'd been able to afford, avoiding the infamous stench and throb of steerage. Alone on a sea voyage, he heard his thoughts with more clarity then ever before and he learned for the first time how to turn them off, how to turn away from his memory, toward the future. At last he could be away from his brother and his brother's absence. He could be away from his parents' constant gnawing fear and grief, away from the shadow of uncertainty that defined life for Jews under the czar. He could start over—he could pretend he was a different man.

HIS CONCEPTION OF New York's geography was faded enough that finding the address Feinman gave him proved a lengthy task that involved an overlong subway ride, several sets of contradictory directions from equally ornery looking businessman, and finally the merciful intervention of an Irish cop atop a black horse. He pointed Abe from Broadway down toward Riverside Avenue. The sun behind it was dipping into the New Jersey distance. Great craggy shadows fell from the Palisades. The Hudson was ablaze in the early arrival of the day. The building Abe found was narrow, far smaller than the ones that surrounded it. A humble brick construction between stuccoed behemoths. He approached quietly, climbed to the fourth floor. In the middle of the staircase his foot stumbled on something soft, likely a rodent. He kicked it away, climbed faster.

At the door, he knocked loudly. No one answered. He knocked again and this time called out her name. "Ana," he said. He waited another moment then pounded harder. Through the crack beneath, a light came on. Footsteps. He took a step backward, realized that, strangely, all the way there he'd been calm, determined but calm. Now his heart pounded.

He heard footsteps. The door opened slowly. It was not her, but a man, slight of stature, hesitant. "What is it?" he said in an accent Abe didn't recognize. He let the door open a few more inches. He had fair hair, a blond mustache.

"I'm sorry, I . . . Maybe I have the wrong address."

Abe began to walk away, but the man called out to him. "You're looking for Ana Beidler, aren't you? You're the gentleman from upstate?" There was resignation in his voice that made Abe very uncomfortable.

He turned back to the door, squinted into the dark. "Yes. Do you know where she is? I need to see her. Please." He recognized in his own voice his father's pleading.

The man didn't answer right away. "Why don't you come in for a moment?"

The man made tea for himself then urged Abe to have a seat in the apartment's only chair. There was an old dinner dish on the desk, a typewriter and an overfull ashtray. The apartment smelled faintly of aftershave and rotting fruit. The man introduced himself as Shmuel Spiro. He did not ask Abe his name. There was a newspaper on the floor with an ad for the Jewish army. Abe reached down and picked it up.

"How do you know Ana?" Abe said. "Does that mean she's here?"

Spiro did something terrible then. It seemed terrible to Abe. He smiled. Quickly. Faintly. More a fluttering than a full expression, and yet, everything Abe had hoped for vanished in it.

He knew by the smile, by the silence that followed, what the answer would be. All his hopes fled as the man smiled across the dim light.

"She's a colleague, in a manner of speaking," said Spiro.

"Is she here?" Abe said, urgently. His voice was the only weapon he had at his disposal against Spiro. Physically, he towered over the man, but he could tell Spiro feared neither threats nor fists. All he could do was impress his need—and that too seemed to carry little weight.

Spiro took a sip of tea and gestured down the hallway that ran as an artery through the flat.

"Search for her. You're welcome to."

"Can you tell me please where she is?" Abe's tone was now pleading. He did not want to sound desperate, but he did not know what other language to speak.

Spiro sat, drinking. "Do you want to know how I first met her?" Spiro asked. "The Committee was brand-new, so new it hardly existed. It was more a feeling in my gut than an actual organization. But the few supporters I had, the few people who wanted in, were all Americans. Some of them weren't even Jews! And the idea of this movement was that it would not be an American movement, but a Jewish one. The Committee for a Jewish Army of Stateless Jews. There was only one problem. We had no stateless Jews to speak of. The stateless Jews who might support us were strewn across Italy, Greece, Poland, France. But one day I read about a temporary center set up right here in New York for a few hundred refugees, recent arrivals from all across Europe. I had the idea that I'd go there, hand out some pamphlets, talk to people who would have more reason than any to be sympathetic to the cause. I had very high hopes for this venture, and as usually happens when such is the case, was deeply and immediately disappointed.

"The refugees I met there, the real refugees, had no interest in a Jewish army or any other kind. They were physically and emotionally exhausted, hungry, beaten down. Many were in mourning. They wanted to sleep and eat and heal. These were their concerns. That's where I found Ana Beidler."

"So you took advantage of her loneliness," Abe said. "You exploited it for your cause. You recruited her."

Spiro stood, paced. "Me? Exploit *her*? If there was any exploiting, it was the other way around."

Abe stood, crossed to the window. The heat emanating out from the radiator was unbearable. He tried to open the window but couldn't budge it. He leaned against the wall, tried to slow his breath. "You were lovers?" he asked.

"One evening, as we were closing down the office, I invited her to dinner, and after that to my apartment. We were lovers for a few weeks, but it became clear to me that she was more useful as a colleague, so I stopped inviting her to my apartment and she never seemed to mind. She kept coming to meetings, recruiting new blood. You see, she has a real talent for inflaming people."

Abe didn't move or speak for a long time. Instead of tea, Spiro lifted a bottle of gin from the corner of his desk, poured an inch of it into a fingerprinted glass. He raised it to Abe. "Here, this will help."

He took the glass and drank it down. When the burning faded he said, "Why us? Why Utica?"

"As a place to bide time it had many good qualities."

"She's gone?" Abe said, a question at first, and then a statement. "Gone."

"Keeping her here was no longer tenable. The movement found a location where she could be relocated permanently."

"The movement," Abe said. He thought of Irene folding old bed linens, stacking the even squares on top of the bedspread, how thin they'd be, the lint rough against her fingers. Everything real was thin and faded. There was no depth or luster left to life, no danger, no struggle, no joy.

The small man sipped from his tea. On the street below, another man was sweeping refuse into the gutter. Spiro was speaking. His voice felt far away. "A woman like Ana," he was saying.

Abe had no patience to hear what came next. What did Shmuel Spiro know about him, his story, or hers?

He closed his ears to him, listened to the sound like static inside his head, this emptiness. When Spiro's voice broke through, he was saying, "She did tell me about you. She told me to tell you that she'd never forget your nighttime walks, that she'd remember them always."

There was a wistfulness to his tone, the way *remember them always* seemed to drift upward like smoke. Abe realized this was how Ana spoke. It was her inflection. Had Spiro rubbed off on her or had she changed him? What did it matter: they were liars, all of them, an army of liars. He looked down at the newspaper on the ground. Another ad. It was one he hadn't seen before. KEEP THREE MILLION JEWS FROM BECOMING GHOSTS. Shayke appeared behind him briefly, a flickering, anguished presence. He read over his shoulder, then skulked back into the nothingness from which he'd come.

BY THE TIME Abe returned to the guesthouse and retrieved the key to his room from the ancient doorman, it was late morning. He spent a few hours sleeping on top of the covers, his eyes dry and throat soar. The window faced a brick wall, so there was no sun to wake him, just the ticking of a small clock on a nightstand beside the bed.

The whole next day he wandered the streets of the Lower East Side without any strategy or plan, stepping inside old theaters, cafes, tobacco shops, shoe stores, and luncheonettes. He sat in a tea house for two hours, moving a cube of sugar around on his plate. He was sitting there when an idea occurred to him, an idea so exquisitely painful that he had to laugh it away. The idea was this: She was nothing. No one. Nobody special. She was the same as everyone. Just a woman trying to figure out how to live, what to do, what to want. A person like him, like Max, like Irene.

Irene. Judith and Irene. The weight of their names pushed down on him, pressed against his chest, his breath. How could he ever go home to them after what he'd done? He was sitting on a leather chair in the lobby of his hotel when the door swung open and an old man called out to the clerk behind the counter, to Abe and the woman by the window and everyone who could hear. "Turn on the radio. Turn it on."

No one moved at first. No one understood. They were all silent, leaning forward in their chairs. Then the clerk walked to the radio. Outside, too, there was a change in volume, crowding along the sidewalk.

"What's happened?" the clerk asked softly, turning the knob through the static.

Abe felt he knew before the man had spoken.

"They've done it," he said.

"Who has done what?" the woman by the window asked. "The Germans are coming?"

"The Japanese. They've bombed us. Early this morning. It's happening. It's happening here."

AFTER SHAYKE WAS sent away to a prison camp in the East, before Abe left for America, he met with Sonia one last time in their usual place beneath the bridge. She seemed different then. She'd bought a new shirt dress, combed and parted her hair. No makeup now. No careless runs in her stockings. She was going to Palestine as Shayke would have wanted. She was going to start her life again. A new life.

"I won't be needing these," she told him. She removed the strand of pearls from her purse, his mother's pearls. Abe took them from her, felt the smooth weight of them in his hands. He could not look at her. The pearls were cool against his fingers, pretty, useless things. He flung them into the river. It was so quiet before the plink. Peaceful. Then again after. He listened to her walk away without a good-bye.

"Please," he said, once she had gone. "Come back." But really, what did it matter? What else could she give him? All that was around him, the river and the land and the town and the sky, seemed awash in pain and shame. Shayke was gone. He was here and Shayke was gone and there was no reason for this state of being, no fairness, no reason. He covered his face with his hands. He wanted so badly to go after her, to say more. He wanted to go on and on and un-remember, to make it right. But it was already too late; he'd lost the thread.

30.

IRENE WAS SITTING at the kitchen table when Abe arrived home from the city. He walked up the steps as though it were any afternoon. The house was the same; it was he who was changed, his feet heavy, his legs slow. He left his suitcase below the coat rack, stood there waiting. Music played in Judith's room. A schoolgirl's ballad. A trail of slush on the foyer grout. The smell of cinnamon, warm apples. In the kitchen, the table was covered in white lilacs. Irene sat before them, staring off, a scissors in her hands. "It's like you died," she said. "The flowers. They just keep coming." She was snipping the stems. There was a vase in the middle of the table. A simple glass vase, half-filled. The tender green pieces fell into her lap, onto the floor. She didn't look up at him, not even as he approached, just kept snipping, dropping each blossom into the drink. There was a hum of static in the living room. The radio was on. A soft, electric drone. The late afternoon sun poured in through the window, as though it were still summer, shattering over her arms, her face. "I've already boxed up all your clothes, if that's what you've come for. If you don't want them, you could do me the kindness of giving them away."

It was true, he thought. He could give them all away, everything that was his, everything that had made him feel safe, loved. But what good would it do? He would still be where he was, inside himself. Wherever he looked now, the world would seem dull, devoid of light and life. He approached Irene slowly. He walked to where she was sitting, kneeled down, taking her hands. "I don't know anything," he told her. He squeezed her hands because he wanted to remember how it had been before. She didn't squeeze back but she didn't withdraw. "Can you help me remember?" he asked.

"Remember what, Abe?"

"How to forget."

She sighed. She had no time for such requests. "You didn't find what you were looking for in New York?" A small smile played across her mouth. How absurd he would seem to her, to any reasonable person. He wanted to hide from her, from everyone. At the same time, he wanted to say something loving, something beautiful and impossibly kind. He longed to tell her she was everything, that he would try to be better, to be new. He would have liked to beg her forgiveness, to claim that he'd been lured from his senses by . . . he didn't even know what it was. He wanted to make some sort of speech, the kind Jacob Feinman might make, but he couldn't manage it. Whatever poetry was in him, Ana had taken it, snuffed it out. "Can you ever forgive me?" he asked. It was all he could summon.

She laughed out loud. She laughed as she had laughed standing before the wedding altar, after their most ecstatic couplings, and also the small, close minutes after Judith was born. That was Irene. She laughed when others were solemn or quiet. He remembered now; it was something he'd loved about her.

"Ever," she repeated. "How can I think about ever when I don't know what I'm making for dinner, or what tomorrow will bring, or tonight, or one minute from now? The future is a mystery. Don't you know that, Abe?"

He lowered himself to the floor. Her skirt was cotton, cool against his face. He gathered it up in his hands. He kissed her through the fabric, kissed her knees, one and then the other, again and again.

Not long after, she told him that no, she wouldn't forgive him, but she would try to move forward, if he thought he could do the same. First, though, she needed to shower. She needed to put away the laundry and peel the potatoes for dinner. She needed to address invitations for the wedding and drop off Abe's coat at the tailor because he'd been catching it in the car door again. Reconciliation would come later if it came at all. Now was Judith's time. The boy she loved would surely join up, the Army, maybe the Navy. So now perhaps their sweet girl, always so lucky and protected, wouldn't be so lucky anymore.

Irene went upstairs. He listened to the hiss of the pipes as she showered. Later, he turned on the radio and learned of other horrors: bullets raining down on sinking ships in the Pacific, an island of fire, charred corpses floating like driftwood across a blackened sea, a crippled fleet that would not go unavenged. He stood there and listened to the news without letting it in. Then he did something he'd never done before. He turned it off.

31.

A FTER THE ATTACK on Pearl Harbor, the city was browned out, its usual glittering muted to the hue of old embers. Ana overheard the rumors, businessmen huddled around newsstands, women in line at the grocer. Here were some of the things she overheard: the Germans had developed long-range aircraft or high-speed submarines. They had devised a plan to do to New York what they were doing to London. Pearl Harbor was first. No one knew what might come next, if the Eastern seaboard was such a great leap. It would be hard to imagine this if anything were still hard to imagine. Because everything now seemed possible, people moved more quickly, crouched in and out of cabs with greater haste, fleeing not only the brittle January days but also the uncertainty of open spaces. Doors were held but not for long. Commuters huddled inside their coats as they scurried to work, to home. The whole city was wound tight as a watch and waiting, a general holding of breaths, the usual brightness and exuberance of people's lives dimmed down as noticeably as the browned-out skyline. Ana recognized it more than most, coming from where she'd been. She could see the aura of fear that hung over them. She could hear the tightening in their voices when they talked, and in Abe's, too, that night he came to find her when she'd sat crouched in the bathroom of Shmuel's apartment, listening, wanting to go to him but unable. It was better to hold back, to be ruthless and unsentimental in such matters.

Sitting on the floor, trying both to make out his words and not to hear them, not to let them penetrate, a thought occurred to her. Before she saw it coming, it had her by the throat. The idea was that all these men who fell in love with her throughout her life, knocking into each other like dominoes and landing at her feet, all these men claiming desire and devotion, didn't really love her at all. Not even a bit. Not the way Abe loved his wife, or Shmuel his army, or Jacob his art. What they thought they loved was nothing more than the way she saw them, or pretended to see them, for a few years, a few months, a few breathless moments. The thing they loved was not her, not Ana, but this gift she gave them that was also a curse—the ability to make believe in the luster and substance of their own small lives. She gave them this gift and then she took it away. She could hear it leaving Abe as he listened to Shmuel. She could hear it in the hollowness of his voice.

"He's gone now," Shmuel called to her at last. "You can come out."

After he left, there was another day of indecision. Ships in general weren't easy to come by. But then the news came in from Hawaii, and all at once it occurred to her that now she didn't have to do anything. She could go anywhere she wanted or nowhere at all. She was safe now, no longer in need of hiding or protection. No one was worrying about a synagogue fire now that they had a war to fight. No one was looking for her—or at her. The one thing she couldn't bear.

AT NIGHT, SHE went for long walks up and down Second Avenue, just as she'd done as a woman of twenty with Jacob by her side. One evening she found herself strolling later than usual. It was cold, even for December. A light snow was falling. It dampened her hair, her lips, but not the street or the steps of the old theaters. A Monday night, nothing was playing, and yet the avenue still felt alive to Ana. It sang to her as she walked north. She felt carried by it through the cold. At the corner of 29th Street, she came upon the Orpheum, or what had been the Orpheum. It was something else now, a movie house, but from the outside, all the old trappings remained. She pushed through the heavy doors. Inside, the noise of the traffic softened. A movie was playing, its noise also muffled. The carpet beneath her feet was rich red, an oriental maze of golden swirls and waves, walls chiseled plaster, the corners adorned with electric lanterns dimmed to look like old gas lamps, bulbs encased in pleated, translucent fabric. Across the lobby rose a winding staircase with a brass railing. The stairs widened at the bottom like the skirt of an evening gown, and, in the crevices between the bottom step and the floor, discarded tickets and kernels of stale popcorn, some dampened, some pristine, littered the carpet. Still, if she closed her eyes, it was the same place she'd known as a child.

SHE TUCKED HER hat under her arm and unwound her scarf. How wonderfully warm it was inside, how welcoming. She moved further into the interior, down a long hallway, toward the theater itself. The voices from the screen grew louder. She tried not to hear. Just before the entrance, there was a narrow corridor, a dark space where it was possible to stand without seeing the show itself or being seen by those watching. This was where she stood. She wanted to stand inside the theater, of whatever was left of it, one last time. She wanted to curl up inside the quiet, lovely darkness, close her eyes, and see in her mind the stage as it had been. The stage. A floating raft, a still cloud pierced by a spotlight in the shape of a moon. This was how she had imagined it as a girl, sitting in the front row. This was what she had thought, watching her mother sing and faint and whisper to her lovers inside the glow. How beautiful she was, the great Celia Epstein. How lovely to behold. And yet her light carried neither warmth nor love. It was a dead light—an illusion. Still, Ana had loved to watch her, had longed for her to become the person she was when she stood inside that light. Sitting out in the audience as a girl, she'd thought how wonderful it would be if only the show would never end, if only the spotlight would never dim and the curtain never rise. As a girl, she had believed if she wanted it badly enough, she could make it happen. Her longing had felt strong enough to bend and shape the world around her. She supposed it still did.

A FEW DAYS after Christmas, she packed a single suitcase. The one advantage to the itinerant life was that there were never many loose ends to tie up. She went alone to the station, purchased a one-way ticket on the Twentieth Century Limited to California. It didn't leave until six, but at five o'clock exactly a sturdy-shouldered porter rolled out a red carpet from the front of the terminal to the platform of track 34, a gesture no one would have appreciated as much as Ana's mother. She pushed through the crowds of boys on their way to training, the tearful good-byes with girlfriends and mothers. The Limited was full but not crowded. Another porter offered her a hand as she stepped up, then a small bouquet of violets to sweeten the journey. A beautiful train, even more beautiful than the Orient Express she and Szymon had always dreamed of riding to Shanghai.

She slipped inside the tube of fluted steel, fumbled with her purse and bag, breathed easy only when she'd settled into her seat and could gaze out at the other trains, gleaming, blue-gray creatures waiting side-by-side. They reminded her of chorus girls before a show.

All the details tended to. Nothing to do but wait. It was a relief to her when the wheels released because then she was beyond second guessing. The engine sighed. There was that unsettling instant when it wasn't clear whether her train or the one on the opposite track was moving. But a moment later, she watched the station glide away. The train rushed past the high-rises and tenements, then came the gravel lots and wooded plots of land surrounding the city. Then wider open spaces. They slipped past her window. They slipped into her past. The past vanished so quickly behind her. Not for the first time in her life, she experienced time not simply as a thing to be hurried through and endured but as a solid substance, something less like a line and more like a sea. She was at sea in it, skimming the surface. Her past, her family's past, and her people's was deep and unreachable beneath her, invisible yet buoying her up. The future was like the sky, also inaccessible but easier to see.

There was a man across the aisle, a handsome man in a tan fedora reading the *Times*. A little older. No wedding ring. Nice smile. He wore silver-rimmed glasses. His hair flopped a little over one lens. He peered at her over the corner of his paper, faint creases around his eyes. An hour into the journey, she put a cigarette in her mouth and pretended to look for a lighter. He was quick on the draw. He was from California, going back home. She knew this even before he told her. It was in his voice, his easy way of talking, his eager, open face. She moved to the seat next to him. It occurred to her he might be useful down the line, so she didn't turn away, even when the boredom hit. She gave him a mysterious, sideways smile and found herself unconsciously putting on an accent, not European now but something else. She's a Southern belle—a Jewish Southern belle. She's from Atlanta. Not far outside Atlanta, she hears herself saying. They exchanged the usual pleasantries. No, he's never been down that way himself. He's a city boy at heart. Eventually he turns back to his paper, she to her magazine. Still, she notices him noticing her, peeking up now and then as the train carries them west, away from Second Avenue, away from her mother's world, the fire, the war.

She speeds along, alone again, and the future seems, as it did before, both empty and full of promise. In her mind, she can shape it, mold it around her longings and dreams. Only the present moment, thin as the pages of the magazine she holds in her hands, is real. She turns the pages without reading them. The train carries her slowly at first, and then more quickly, gaining speed as it moves west. In the beginning, she watches the icy fields and rotting barns go by, as well as the darkly shifting shadows across New Jersey. Later, as the train chugs through the beautiful and desolate landscape of Appalachia, she closes her eyes, lets herself feel carried. She finds it is no longer the scenery that interests her, but the way it disappears.

epilogue

THE STATION

THE PLACE WHERE Max found himself was both familiar and strange, a halfway place. It was not what he had expected, and yet he felt at home there.

In this other place, the trains pulled in every hour, on the hour, from sunrise to sunset, and Max's job was to greet them. He waited on a sunny bench by the station, only it wasn't really a station. There was no building, no ticket counter, no platform and no stairs. There wasn't even a track. There was just a wide field of prairie grass and sunflower stalks as high as his chest and eucalyptus trees that turned blue-green in morning and purple in the evening sky, and the bench on which he sat.

The trains seemed out of place among the natural beauty, black, groaning hunks of steel, doors nailed shut, seeping gas and soot. They opened up, and the human cargo tumbled out, a tangle of gray flesh and twisted limbs, human figures so deformed by the journey they looked less human than the gnarled trunks of the trees in the distance. Max and the other receivers pulled them from the wreckage one by one and began the process of repatriation. Their clothes, which were no more than sodden rags, were stripped or cut from their bodies. They were led, and those who couldn't walk were carried, to the shallows of a wide sea where they were lain out on palm leaves and scrubbed with pumice until their skin shone pink again and their hair and nails glistened, until they were clean and pure as babies, even the old ones who were not old here but ageless. After that, the receivers took them to a dining hall where they sat at long tables and ate bread hot from the hearth, and wine bursting with the flavor of not just grapes but every plant and every herb, of the earth itself, and savory soups and custards, and meat and fish and milk and honey, buckets of it, as much as they could get. After that they were taken to the village and taught how to sing again and work and laugh. In the village, they first seemed familiar to him, their faces so similar to the ones he had known in his life, the faces of the people he had wanted to help and save. But over time, others came, and they were no longer familiar to him. They were every size and every color. They spoke every language, those that could speak. Some slept for months in a sunny bed before they could make a sound. It was an awful journey. Some couldn't make it to the village themselves, and Max or the other greeters would carry them.

There was one man, both old and ageless, who was carried across a vast poppy field, carried in Max's arms like he was his own child, like he weighed nothing, like he was made only of light.

It was good work. And Max was happy to do it, but sometimes, still, beneath this happiness, there was a tinge of something bittersweet, some unmet, unmeetable longing.

Maybe he would see Hirschler here, he thought. Maybe he would see his sister or his mother. It didn't seem likely, but it didn't seem impossible, either, in this place that was neither real nor imagined. He looked for their faces among the others, among the men coming in on the trains and those in the village. He was vigilant in his look-ing, always on guard. Sometimes, he thought he recognized a likeness in someone's face, but then the expression changed, and the likeness vanished, and he felt foolish and dejected.

Another receiver caught him staring off toward the distance one morning, staring off at the mountains that were blue-gray under the rising sun. He must have noticed the yearning in his expression. "You're still looking for someone?" he asked, smiling.

Max didn't say yes, and he didn't say no.

"You won't find them here," he said.

"I know."

"We can never meet again those we loved. It's the one condition."

"I know that, too."

In the distance, a black mark appeared on the horizon, another train. There were so many of them.

"It seems like they'll never stop," Max said. And they never did.

author's note

W HILE *THE HOUSEGUEST* is a work of fiction, I relied heavily on the following works for historical background and insight: *The Abandonment of the Jews: America and the Holocaust, 1941–1945*, by David S. Wyman; *A Race Against Death: Peter Bergson, America, and the Holocaust*, by David S. Wyman and Rafael Medoff; *Millions of Jews to Rescue: A Bergson Group Leader's Account of the Campaign to Save Jews from the Holocaust*, by Samuel Merlin; *Stardust Lost: The Triumph, Tragedy, and Meshugas of the Yiddish Theater in America*, by Stefan Kanfer; *A Life on the Stage*, by Jacob Adler; *Vagabond Stars: A World History of Yiddish Theater*, by Nahma Sandrow; and *Der Payatz: Around the World With Yiddish Theater*, by Herman Yablokoff. While certain real individuals (Ze'ev Jabotinsky, for instance) or events (the *St. Louis*, to name one) appear here, a degree of creative license has been taken, especially with regard to chronology.

acknowledgements

I 'D LIKE TO extend my gratitude to the Iowa Writers' Workshop, the Posen Foundation, the Michener-Copernicus Foundation, the Yaddo Corporation, the Virginia Center for the Creative Arts, and the Ragdale Foundation for their support and for their vote of confidence in my work.

I feel lucky to have found such passionate advocates for this book in Ellen Levine and in my phenomenal editor, Dan Smetanka, as well as Megan Fishmann, Kathy Daneman, and all the folks at Counterpoint. I'd also like to thank the following people for their guidance, support, friendship, and encouragement: Ken, Maddy, and Sari Brooks, Ann Campbell, Ethan Canin, Kevin Clouther, Abby Geni, Gwynne Johnson, Dorian Karchmar, Maria Massie, Dan Pope, Kiki Petrosino, Beth Remis, The Segall family, Susan Burmeister-Brown and Linda Swanson-Davies, Elena Vassallo Crossman, Sunny Yudkoff, and Jason Zech. Finally, and most emphatically, I'd like to thank Pete Segall, Roscoe, and Iris for making this book, and all good things in my life, possible.